About the

C000278744

A New York Times and *USA* Today bestselling author
Christine Rimmer has written more than a hundred
contemporary romances for Mills & Boon. She consistently
writes love stories that are sweet, sexy, humorous, and
heartfelt. She lives in Oregon with her family. Visit
Christine at christinerimmer.com

Cara Colter shares ten acres in British Columbia with
her real-life hero Rob, ten horses, a dog, and a cat. She
has three grown children and a grandson. Cara is a
recipient of the Career Achievement Award in the Love
and Laughter category from the *RT*. Cara invites you to
visit her on Facebook!

Amy Andrews is a multi-award winning, *USA Today*
bestselling author who has written over forty contemporary
romances for several Mills & Boon series. She's an Aussie
who loves good books, fab food, great wine and frequent
travel – preferably all four together. She lives by the ocean
with her husband of twenty-nine years. To keep up with
her latest releases and giveaways, visit Amy's website to
sign up for her newsletter at amyandrews.com.au

About the Authors

...TODAY bestselling author,
...written more than a hundred...

Cold Christmas Nights

CHRISTINE RIMMER

CARA COLTER

AMY ANDREWS

MILLS & BOON

All rights reserved including the right of reproduction in whole or in part in any form. This edition is published by arrangement with Harlequin Enterprises ULC.

This is a work of fiction. Names, characters, places, locations and incidents are purely fictional and bear no relationship to any real life individuals, living or dead, or to any actual places, business establishments, locations, events or incidents. Any resemblance is entirely coincidental.

This book is sold subject to the condition that it shall not, by way of trade or otherwise, be lent, resold, hired out or otherwise circulated without the prior consent of the publisher in any form of binding or cover other than that in which it is published and without a similar condition including this condition being imposed on the subsequent purchaser.

® and TM are trademarks owned and used by the trademark owner and/or its licensee. Trademarks marked with ® are registered with the United Kingdom Patent Office and/or the Office for Harmonisation in the Internal Market and in other countries.

First Published in Great Britain 2023
By Mills & Boon, an imprint of HarperCollins*Publishers* Ltd,
1 London Bridge Street, London, SE1 9GF

www.harpercollins.co.uk

HarperCollins*Publishers*
Macken House, 39/40 Mayor Street Upper,
Dublin 1, D01 C9W8, Ireland

Cold Christmas Nights © 2023 Harlequin Enterprises ULC.

Same Time, Next Christmas © 2018 Christine Rimmer
Cinderella's Prince Under the Mistletoe © 2019 Harlequin Enterprises ULC
Swept Away by the Seductive Stranger © 2016 Amy Andrews

Special thanks and acknowledgement are given to Cara Colter for her contribution to the *A Crown by Christmas* series.

ISBN: 978-0-263-32116-6

This book is produced from independently certified FSC™ paper to ensure responsible forest management.

For more information visit: www.harpercollins.co.uk/green

Printed and Bound in the UK using 100% Renewable Electricity at CPI Group (UK) Ltd, Croydon, CR0 4YY

SAME TIME, NEXT CHRISTMAS

CHRISTINE RIMMER

For MSR, always.

Chapter One

December 23, four years ago...

Even with the rain coming down so hard he could barely make out the twisting gravel road ahead of him, Matthias Bravo spotted the light shining through the trees.

The Jeep lurched around another twist in the road. For a few seconds before the trees obscured his view, Matt could see his getaway cabin in the clearing up ahead. Yep. The light was coming from the two windows that flanked the front door.

Some idiot had broken in.

Swearing under his breath, Matt steered his Jeep to the almost nonexistent side of the road and switched off the engine and lights.

The rain poured down harder, pounding the roof,

roaring so loud he couldn't hear himself think. Out the windshield, the trees with their moss-covered trunks were a blur through the rippling curtain made of water.

Should he have just stayed home in Valentine Bay for Christmas?

Probably. His injured leg throbbed and he was increasingly certain he'd caught that weird bug his brothers had warned him about. He had a mother of a headache and even though he'd turned the heater off several miles back, he was sweating.

"Buck up, buddy." He slapped his own cheek just to remind himself that torrential rain, a sliced-up leg, a headache and a fever were not the worst things he'd ever lived through.

And at the moment, he had a mission. The SOB in his cabin needed taking down—or at the very least, roughing up a tad and kicking out on his ass.

Matt kept his rifle in a hidden safe at the back of the Jeep. Unfortunately, the safe was accessed through the rear door.

"No time like the present to do what needs doing."

Yeah. He was talking to himself. Kind of a bad sign.

Was he having a resurgence of the PTSD he'd been managing so well for over a year now?

No. Uh-uh. Zero symptoms of a recurrence. No more guilt than usual. He wasn't drunk and hadn't been in a long time. No sleep problems, depression or increased anxiety.

Simply a break-in he needed to handle.

And going in without a weapon? How stupid would that be?

He put on his field jacket, pulled up the hood, shoved open his door and jumped out, biting back a groan when his hurt leg took his weight.

The good news: it wasn't that far to the rear door. In no time, he was back inside the vehicle, sweating profusely, dripping rain all over the seat, with the rifle in one hand and a box of shells in the other.

Two minutes later, rifle loaded and ready for action, he was limping through the downpour toward the cabin. Keeping to the cover of the trees, he worked his way around the clearing, doing a full three-sixty, checking for vehicles and anyone lurking outside, finding nothing that shouldn't be there.

Recon accomplished, he approached the building from the side. Dropping to the wet ground, he crawled to the steps, staying low as he climbed them. His leg hurt like hell, shards of pain stabbing him with every move he made. It was bleeding again right through the thick makeshift bandage he'd tied on the wound.

Too bad. For now, he needed to block the pain and focus.

As he rolled up onto the covered porch, he swiped back his dripping hood and crawled over beneath the front window.

With slow care, he eased up just enough to peer over the sill.

He got an eyeful.

A good-looking brunette—midtwenties, he would guess—sat on the hearth, warming herself at a blazing fire. She wore only a bra and panties. Articles of clothing lay spread out around her, steaming as they dried.

Was she alone? He didn't see anyone else in there. The cabin was essentially one big room, with bath and sleeping loft. From his crouch at the window, he could see the bathroom, its door wide open. Nobody in there. And he had a straight visual shot right through to the back door. Nada. Just the pretty, half-naked brunette.

She looked totally harmless.

Still, he should check the situation out from every possible angle before making his move.

Was he maybe being a little bit paranoid? Yeah, possibly.

But better safe than sorry.

He dragged himself over beneath the other front window. The view from there was pretty much the same. The woman looked so innocent, leaning back on her hands now, long, smooth legs stretched out and crossed at the ankles. She raised a slim hand and forked her fingers through her thick, dark hair.

Grimly, he pulled up his hood and crawled down the steps into the deluge again. Circling the cabin once more, close-in this time, he ducked to peer into each window as he passed.

Every view revealed the leggy brunette, alone, drying off by the fire.

By the time he limped back to the front of the building and crept up onto the porch again, he was all but certain the woman was on her own.

Still, she could be dangerous. Maybe. And dangerous or not, she *had* broken in and helped herself to his firewood. Not to mention he still couldn't completely discount the possibility that there was someone upstairs.

He'd just have to get the jump on her, hope she really was alone and that no damn fool hid in the loft, ready to make trouble.

Sliding to the side, Matt came upright flush against the front door. Slowly and silently, he turned the knob. The knob had no lock, but he needed to see if the dead bolt was still engaged. It was. He took the keys from his pocket. At the speed of a lazy snail, in order not to alert the trespasser within, he unlocked the dead bolt.

That accomplished, he put the keys away and turned the knob with agonizing slowness until the door was open barely a crack. Stepping back, he kicked the door wide. It slammed against the inside wall as he leveled the barrel of his rifle on the saucer-eyed girl.

"Freeze!" he shouted. "Do it now!"

Sabra Bond gaped at the armed man who filled the wide-open doorway.

He was a very big guy, dressed for action in camo pants, heavy boots and a hooded canvas coat. And she wore nothing but old cotton panties and a sports bra.

No doubt about it. Her life was a mess—and getting worse by the second.

Sheepishly, she put her hands up.

The man glared down the barrel of that rifle at her. "What do you think you're doing in my cabin?"

"I, um, I was on my way back to Portland from my father's farm," she babbled. "I parked at the fish hatchery and started hiking along the creek toward the falls. The rain came. It got so bad that I—"

"Stop." He swung the business end of his rifle upward toward the loft. "Anyone upstairs? Do not lie to me."

"No one." He leveled the weapon on her again. "Just me!" she squeaked. "I swear it." She waited for him to lower the gun. No such luck. The barrel remained pointed right at her. And, for some incomprehensible reason, she couldn't quit explaining herself. "I was hiking and thinking, you know? The time got away from me. I'd gone miles before the rain started. It kept getting worse, which led me to the unpleasant discovery that my waterproof jacket is only water resistant. Then I found your cabin…"

"And you broke in," he snarled.

Had she ever felt more naked? Highly unlikely. "I was just going to stand on the porch and wait for the rain to stop. But it only came down harder and I kept getting colder."

"So you broke in," he accused again, one side of his full mouth curling in a sneer.

Okay, he had a point. She *had* broken in. "I jimmied a window and climbed through," she admitted with a heavy sigh.

Still drawing a bead on her, water dripping from his coat, he stepped beyond the threshold and kicked the door shut. Then he pointed the gun at her pack. "Empty that. Just turn it over and dump everything out."

Eager to prove how totally unthreatening she was, Sabra grabbed the pack, unzipped it, took it by the bottom seam and gave it a good shake. A first-aid kit, an empty water bottle, a UC Santa Cruz Slugs hat and sweatshirt, and a bottle of sunscreen dropped out.

"Pockets and compartments, too," he commanded.

She unhooked the front flap and shook it some more. Her phone, a tube of lip balm, a comb and a couple of hair elastics tumbled to the floor. "That's it." She dropped the empty pack. "That's all of it." When he continued to glare at her, she added, "Dude. It was only a day hike."

"No gun." He paced from one side of the cabin to the other. She realized he was scoping out the upstairs, getting a good look at whatever might be up there.

Apparently satisfied at last that she really was alone, he pointed the gun her way all over again and squinted at her as though trying to peer into her brain and see what mayhem she might be contemplating.

Hands still raised, she shook her head. "I'm alone. No gun, no knives, no nothing. Just me in my underwear and a bunch of soggy clothes—and listen. I'm sorry I broke in. It was a bad choice on my part." *And not the only one I've made lately.* "How 'bout if I just get dressed and go?"

He studied her some more, all squinty-eyed and suspicious. Then, at last, he seemed to accept the fact that she was harmless. He lowered the rifle. "Sorry," he grumbled. "I'm overcautious sometimes."

"Apology accepted," she replied without a single trace of the anger and outrage the big man deserved— because no longer having to stare down the dark barrel of that gun?

Just about the greatest thing that had ever happened to her.

As she experienced the beautiful sensation of pure relief, he emptied the shells from his rifle, stuffed them in a pocket and turned to hang the weapon on the rack above the door. The moment he turned his back to her, she grabbed her Slugs sweatshirt and yanked it on over her head.

When he faced her again, he demanded, "You got anyone you can call to come get you?" She was flipping her still-damp hair out from under the neck of the sweatshirt as he added, "Someone with four-wheel drive. They'll probably need chains or snow tires, too." When she just stared in disbelief, he said, "That frog strangler out there? Supposed to turn to snow. Soon."

A snowstorm? Seriously? "It is?"

He gave a snort of pure derision. "Oughtta check the weather report before you go wandering off into the woods."

Okay, not cool. First, he points a gun at her and then he insults her common sense. The guy was really beginning to annoy her. Sabra had lived not fifteen miles from this cabin of his for most of her life. Sometimes you couldn't count on the weather report and he ought to know that. "I did check the weather. This morning, before I left on my way to Portland. Light rain possible, it said."

"It's Oregon. The weather can change."

His condescending response didn't call for an answer, so she didn't give him one. Instead, she grabbed her still-soggy pants and put them on, too, wishing she'd had sense enough to keep driving right past the sign for the fish hatchery. A hike along the creek to the falls had seemed like a good idea at the time, a way to lift her spirits a little, to clear her troubled mind before going on back to Portland to face finding a new apartment during the remaining two weeks and two days of her vacation from work—a vacation that was supposed to have been her honeymoon.

The big guy grunted. "And you didn't answer my question. Got anyone you can call?"

"Well, let me see…" Her mom had been dead for six years now. Her dad was three hours away in Eugene until New Year's. Five days ago, on the day before she was supposed to have gotten married, she and her ex-fiancé had called it quits for reasons too upsetting to even think about at the moment. And she just wasn't ready to ask any of her Portland friends to drive eighty miles through a blizzard on the day before Christmas Eve to save her from a stranger with a bad attitude in an isolated cabin in the middle of the forest. "No. I don't have anyone to call."

The big guy did some swearing. Finally, he muttered, "Let me get my tree in here and I'll drive you wherever you need to go."

Get outta town. Mr. Grouchy Pants had a *tree*? She was almost as surprised as when he'd kicked open the door. "Uh, you mean *you* have a Christmas tree?"

His scowl deepened. "It's Christmas, isn't it?"

She put up both hands again. "It's just, well, you don't seem like the Christmas-tree type."

"I like Christmas." He narrowed his blue eyes at her. "I like it *alone*."

"Gotcha. And thank you—for the offer of a ride, I mean. If you can get me to my car at the fish hatchery, I can take it from there just fine. As for the tree, I'll help you bring it in."

"You stay here. I don't need you."

"Good to know." She tugged on her socks and boots and not-quite-waterproof jacket as he pulled a tree stand out from under the sink, filled it with water and put it down near the door—and now that she wasn't terrified half out of her wits, she noticed that he was limping.

His right pants leg was torn up, hanging in tatters to the knee. Beneath the tatters, she could see a bit of bloody bandage—a very bloody bandage, actually, bright red and wet. It looked like he was bleeding into his boot.

He straightened from positioning the tree stand and took the three steps to the door.

She got up. "Do you know that you're bleeding?" He didn't bother to answer. She followed him outside. "Listen. Slow down. Let me help you."

"Stay on the porch." He growled the command as he flipped up the hood of his jacket and stepped out into the driving rain again. "I'll bring my Jeep to the steps."

She waited—because, hey. If he didn't want her help, he wasn't going to get it. Still, she felt marginally guilty for just standing there with a porch roof over her head as she watched him limp off into the downpour.

He vanished around the first turn in the road. It was getting dark. She wrapped her arms across her middle and refused to worry about that bloody bandage on his leg and the way he walked with a limp— not to mention he'd looked kind of flushed, hadn't he? Like maybe he had a fever in addition to whatever was going on with that leg...

Faintly, she heard a vehicle start up. A moment later, a camo-green Jeep Rubicon rolled into sight. It eased to a stop a few feet from the steps and the big guy got out. She pulled up her hood and ran down to join him as he began untying the tree lashed to the rack on the roof.

He didn't argue when she took the top end. "I'll lead," was all he said.

Oh, no kidding—and not only because he was so damn bossy. It was a thick noble fir with a wide circle of bottom branches that wouldn't make it through the door any other way.

He assumed the forward position and she trotted after him, back up the steps and into the warmth of the cabin. At the tree stand, he got hold of the trunk in the middle, raising it to an upright position.

She crouched down to guide it into place and tighten the screws, sitting back on her heels when the job was done. "Okay. You can let it go." He eyed her warily from above, his giant arm engulfed by the thick branches as he gripped the trunk. His face was still flushed and there were beads of moisture at his hairline—sweat, not rain, she would take a bet on that. "It's in and it's stable, I promise you," she said.

With a shrug, he let go.

The tree stood tall. It was glorious, blue-green and well shaped, the branches emerging in perfectly balanced tiers, just right for displaying strings of lights and a treasure trove of ornaments. Best of all, it smelled of her sweetest memories, of Christmases past, when her mom was still alive. Ruth Bond had loved Christmas. Every December, she would fill their house at Berry Bog Farm with all the best Christmas smells—evergreen, peppermint, cinnamon, vanilla…

"Not bad," he muttered.

She put away her memories. They only made her sad, anyway. "It's a beauty, all right."

He aimed another scowl at her. "Good, then. Get your gear and let's go." Was he swaying on his feet?

She rose to her height. "I don't know what's wrong

with your leg, but you don't look well. You'd better sit down and let me see what I can do for you."

"I'm fine."

"Get real. You are not fine and you are getting worse."

He only grew more mulish. "We're leaving."

"I'm not getting in that Jeep with you behind the wheel." She braced her hands on her hips. He just went on glaring, swaying gently on his feet like a giant tree in a high wind. She quelled her aggravation at his pigheadedness and got busy convincing him he should trust her to handle whatever was wrong with him. "I was raised on a farm not far from here. My mom was a nurse. She taught me how to treat any number of nasty injuries. Just let me take a look at your leg."

"I'll deal with that later."

"You are wobbling on your feet and your face is red. You're sweating. I believe you have a fever."

"Did I ask for your opinion?"

"It's not safe for you to be—"

"I'm fine."

"You're not."

"Just get your stuff, okay?"

"No. Not okay." She made a show of taking off her jacket and hanging it by the door. "I'm not leaving this cabin until we've dealt with whatever's going on with your leg."

There was a long string of silent seconds—a battle of wills. He swayed and scowled. She did nothing except stand there and wait for the big lug to give in and be reasonable.

In the end, reason won. "All right," he said. He shrugged out of his coat and hung it up next to hers.

And then, at last, he limped to the Navajo-print sofa in the center of the room and sat down. He bent to his injured leg—and paused to glance up at her. "When I take off this dressing, it's probably going to be messy. We'll need towels. There's a stack of old ones in the bathroom, upper left in the wooden cabinet."

She went in there and got them.

When she handed them over, he said, "And a first-aid backpack, same cabinet, lower right." He set the stack of towels on the sofa beside him.

"I've got a first-aid kit." It was still on the floor by the hearth where she'd dumped it when he'd ordered her to shake out her pack. She started for it.

"I saw your kit," he said. She paused to glance back at him as he bent to rip his pants leg wider, revealing an impressively muscular, bloodstained, hairy leg. "Mine's bigger."

She almost laughed as she turned for the bathroom again. "Well, of course it is."

His kit had everything in it but an operating table.

She brought it into the main room and set it down on the plank floor at the end of the sofa. He'd already pushed the pine coffee table to the side, spread towels on the floor in front of him and rolled his tattered pants leg to midthigh, tying the torn ends together to keep them out of the way.

She watched as he unlaced his boot. A bead of sweat dripped down his face and plopped to his thigh. "Here." She knelt. "I'll ease it off for you."

"I've got it." With a grunt, he removed the boot. A few drops of blood fell to the towels. His sock was soggy with it, the blood soaking into the terrycloth when he put his foot back down.

"Interesting field dressing." She indicated the article of clothing tied around his lower leg.

One thick shoulder lifted in a half shrug. "Another T-shirt bites the dust."

"Is it stuck to the wound?"

"Naw. Wound's too wet." He untied the knots that held the T-shirt in place.

When he took the bloody rag away, she got a good look at the job ahead of her. The wound was an eight-inch crescent-shaped gash on the outside of his calf. It was deep. With the makeshift bandage gone, the flap of sliced flesh flopped down. At least it didn't appear to go all the way through to the bone. Blood dripped from it sluggishly.

"Let me see…" Cautiously, so as not to spook him, she placed her index and middle fingers on his knee and gave a gentle push. He accepted her guidance, dipping the knee inward so she could get a closer look at the injury. "Butterfly bandages won't hold that together," she said. "Neither will glue. It's going to need stitches."

For the first time since he'd kicked open the door, one side of his mouth hitched up in a hint of a smile. "I had a feeling you were going to say that." His blue eyes held hers. "You sure you're up for this?"

"Absolutely."

"You really know what to do?"

"Yes. I've sewn up a number of injured farm animals and once my dad got gored by a mean bull when my mom wasn't home. I stitched him right up."

He studied her face for a good five seconds. Then he offered a hand. "Matthias Bravo."

She took it. "Sabra Bond."

Chapter Two

Sabra washed up at the kitchen-area sink, turning and leaning against the counter as she dried her hands. "Got a plastic tub?"

"Under the sink." He seemed so calm now, so accepting. "Look. I'm sorry if I scared you, okay?" His eyes were different, kinder.

She nodded. "I broke in."

"I overreacted."

She gazed at him steadily. "We're good."

A slow breath escaped him. "Thanks."

For an odd, extended moment, they simply stared at each other. "Okay, then," she said finally. "Let's get this over with."

Grabbing the tub from under the sink, she filled it with warm water and carried it over to him. As he washed his blood-caked foot and lower leg, she laid out the tools and supplies she would need. His first-aid pack really did have everything, including inject-able lidocaine.

"Lucky man," she said. "You get to be numb for this."

"Life is good," he answered lazily, leaning against the cushions, letting his big head fall back and staring kind of vacantly at the crisscrossing beams overhead.

Wearing nitrile gloves from his fancy kit, she mopped up blood from around the injury and then injected the painkiller. Next, she irrigated the wound just the way her mom had taught her to do.

As she worked, he took his own temperature. "Hundred and two," he muttered unhappily.

She tipped her head at the acetaminophen and the tall glass of water she'd set out for him. "Take the pills and drink the water."

He obeyed. When he set the empty glass back down, he admitted, "This bug's been going around. Two of my brothers had it. Laid them out pretty good. At least it didn't last long. I was feeling punk this morning. I told myself it was nothing to worry about…"

"Focus on the good news," she advised.

"Right." He gave her a wry look. "I'm sick, but if I'm lucky, I won't be sick for long."

She carried the tub to the bathroom, dumped it, rinsed it and left it there. When she returned to him, she repositioned the coffee table, sat on the end of it and covered her thighs with a towel. "Let's see that leg." She tapped her knees with her palms, and he stretched the injured leg across them.

"Can you turn your leg so the wound is up and keep it in that position?"

"No problem." He rolled his foot inward, turning his outer calf up.

She put on a fresh pair of gloves and got to work.

It took a lot of stitches to do the job. He seemed content to just sprawl there, staring at the ceiling as she sewed him up.

But, now she had him at her mercy, there were a few questions she wanted to ask. "Did somebody come after you with an ax?" He lifted his head and mustered a steely stare. She grinned in response. It was so strange. Not long ago, he'd scared the crap out of her. Yet now he didn't frighten her in the least. She actually felt completely comfortable kidding him a little. "Do not make me hurt you."

He snorted. "It's embarrassing."

"I'll never tell a soul."

"It was raining when I cut down that tree. I forgot to bring gloves and my hands were soaking wet. Plus, I was feeling pretty bad from this damn bug I seem to have caught."

She tied off a stitch. "So then, what you're telling me is you almost chopped off your own leg?"

He let his head fall back again. "I come from a long line of woodsmen on my mother's side," he said wearily. "No self-respecting member of my family ever got hurt while cutting down an eight-foot tree."

"Until you."

"Go ahead, Sabra Bond, rub it in."

"Where'd you get that tree?" She tied off another stitch. "I didn't see a tag on it. Have you been poaching, Matthias?"

"You can call me Matt." He said it in a lovely, low rumble that made her think of a purring cat—a very large one. The kind that could easily turn dangerous. "Everyone calls me Matt."

"I kind of like Matthias."

"Suit yourself."

"I'll ask again. Did you steal that gorgeous tree from the people of Oregon?"

He grunted. "I'll have you know I'm a game warden, a Fish and Wildlife state trooper. I *catch* the poachers—so no, I didn't steal that tree. I took it from property that belongs to my family."

"Ah. All right, then. I guess I won't have to turn you in."

"You can't imagine my relief."

"I have another question."

"Why am I not surprised?"

"Didn't it occur to you to head for a hospital or an urgent care after you took that ax to your leg?"

He didn't answer immediately. She was considering how much to goad him when he muttered, "Pride and denial are powerful things."

By the time she'd smoothed antibiotic ointment over the stitched-up wound and covered it with a bandage, he was sweating more heavily than ever. She helped him off with his other boot. "Come on," she coaxed. "Stretch out on the sofa, why don't you?"

"Just for a few minutes," he mumbled, but remained sitting up. He started emptying his pockets, dragging out his phone, keys and wallet, dropping them next to the lamp on the little table at the end of the sofa. From another pocket, he took the shells from his rifle. He put them on the little table, too, and then leaned back against the cushions again.

She asked, "Do you have another sock to keep that bare foot warm?"

"You don't have to—"

"Just tell me where it is."

He swiped sweat from his brow. "In the dresser upstairs, top drawer, left."

Sabra ran up there and came down with a pillow from the bed and a clean pair of socks. She propped the pillow against one arm of the sofa and knelt to put on the socks for him. By then, he wasn't even bothering to argue that she didn't need to help him. He looked exhausted, his skin a little gray beneath the flush of fever.

She plumped the pillow she'd taken from the bed upstairs. "Lie down, Matthias." He gave in and stretched out, so tall that his feet hung off the end. "Here you go." She settled an afghan over him and tucked it in around him. "Okay, I'll be right back." And she hustled over to the sink to run cold water on a cloth.

"Feels good," he said, when she gently rubbed the wet cloth across his forehead and over his cheeks. "So nice and cool. Thank you…" Under the blanket, his injured leg jerked. He winced and stifled a groan. The lidocaine was probably wearing off. But the acetaminophen should be cutting the pain a little— and lowering his fever.

"Just rest," she said softly.

"All right. For few minutes, maybe. Not long. I'll be fine and I'll take you where you need to go."

She made a sound of agreement low in her throat, though she knew he wasn't going anywhere for at least a day or two.

Within ten minutes, he was asleep.

Quietly, so as not to wake him, she cleaned up after the impromptu medical procedure. She even rinsed out his bloody boot and put it near the hearth to dry.

Two hours later, at a little after eight in the evening, Matthias was still on the couch. He kept fading in and out of a fevered sleep. There wasn't much Sabra could do for him but bathe his sweaty face to cool him off a little and retuck the blanket around him whenever he kicked it off.

She put another log on the fire and went through the cupboards and the small fridge in the kitchen area. He had plenty of food, the nonperishable kind. Beans. Rice. Flour. Pasta. Cans of condensed milk, of vegetables and fruit. She opened some chili and ate it straight from the can, washing it down with a glass of cold water.

Matthias slept on, stirring fitfully, muttering to himself. Now and then he called out the names of men, "Mark, no!" and "Nelson, don't do it!" and "Finn, where are you?" as if in warning or despair. He also muttered a woman's name, "Christy," more than once and vowed in a low, ragged rumble, "Never again."

He woke around nine. "Sabra?" he asked, his voice dry. Hoarse.

"Right here."

"Water?"

She brought him a tall glassful. "Don't get up. Let me help." She slipped her free hand under his big, sweaty head and held the glass to his mouth as he drained it.

With a whispered "Thank you" and a weary sigh, he settled against the pillow again.

She moistened another cloth in the icy water from the sink and bathed his face for him. "You know what, Matthias?"

"Ungh?"

"I'm going to go ahead and unload your Jeep for you."

He made another low sound in his throat. She decided to take that sound for agreement.

"Well, great." She patted his shoulder. "I'll just get after that, then. Go back to sleep." Scooping his keys off the side table, she put on her jacket and quietly tiptoed out to the porch.

The gorgeous sight that greeted her stole her breath and stopped her in her tracks.

Just as Matthias had predicted, the rain had turned to snow. She gazed at a world gone glittering white.

In the golden light that spilled out the cabin windows, the fat flakes fell thick and heavy. They'd piled up on the ground and decorated the branches of the western hemlock and Sitka spruce trees. There was a good three inches already.

"So beautiful," she whispered aloud and all of her worries just fell away, both at the mess that currently added up to her life and the challenges she'd faced in the past few hours.

How could she be anything but happy in this moment? Christmas was falling from the sky.

She knew what was coming. She would be staying in this cabin for at least a few days with the man who'd introduced himself by pointing his rifle at her. Should she be more upset about that?

Probably.

But after they'd gotten past those terrifying first

minutes when she'd feared he might shoot her, things had definitely started looking up. He was a good patient, and he seemed kindhearted beneath that gruff exterior.

And this situation? It felt less like an ordeal and more like an adventure. As if she'd fallen out of her own thoroughly depressing life—and into a weird and wonderful Christmassy escapade.

Stuck in a one-room cabin with a big, buff injured stranger for Christmas?

She'd take that over her real life any day of the week.

As it turned out, she didn't need the car key. Matthias had left the Jeep unlocked.

And there were treasures in there—three large boxes of groceries. Fresh stuff, greens and tomatoes. Apples. Bananas. Eggs, milk and cheese. A gorgeous rib roast, a fat chicken and some really pretty pork chops.

It was a good thing she'd decided to bring it all in, too. By morning everything would have been frozen.

She carried the food in first, then his laptop, a box of brightly wrapped Christmas gifts probably from his family and another boxful of books, as well.

After the boxes, she brought in three duffel bags containing men's clothes and fresh linens. Detouring to the bathroom, she stacked the linens in the cabinet. She carried the bags of clothes up to the loft, leaving them near the top of the stairs for him to deal with when he felt better.

Her sick, surly stranger definitely needed some chicken soup. She hacked up the chicken. She put the pieces on to simmer in a pot of water with onions and garlic, a little celery and some spices from the cute little spice rack mounted on the side of a cabinet.

The night wore on. She fished the cooked chicken from the pot. Once it was cool enough to handle, she got rid of the bones, chopped the meat and returned it to the pot, along with some potatoes and carrots.

On the sofa, Matthias tossed and turned, sometimes muttering to the guys named Nelson and Mark, even crying out once or twice. She soothed him when he startled awake and stroked his sweaty face with a cold cloth.

When the soup was ready, she fed it to him. He ate a whole bowlful, looking up at her through only slightly dazed blue eyes as she spooned it into his mouth. Once he'd taken the last spoonful, he said, "I've changed my mind. You can stay."

"Good. Because no one's leaving this cabin for at least a couple of days. It's seriously snowing."

"Didn't I warn you?"

"Yes, you did. And it's piling up fast, too. You're gonna be stuck with me through Christmas, anyway."

"It's all right. I can deal with you." He sat up suddenly. Before she could order him to lie back down, he said, "I really need to take a whiz—get me the cane from that basket by the door, would you?"

"You need more than a cane right now. You can lean on me."

His expression turned mulish. "You're amazing and I'm really glad you broke into my cabin. But as for staggering to the head, I can do it on my own. Get me the damn cane."

"If you tear any of your stitches falling on your ass—"

"I won't. The cane."

She gave in. *He* wasn't going to. The cane was handmade of some hard, dark wood, with a rough-hewn bear head carved into the handle. She carried it back to him. "Still here and happy to help," she suggested.

"I can manage." He winced as he swung his feet to the floor and then he looked up at her, waiting.

She got the message loud and clear. Pausing only to push the coffee table well out of his way, she stepped aside.

He braced one hand on the cane and the other on the sofa arm and dragged himself upright. It took him a while and he leaned heavily on the cane, but he made it to the bathroom and back on his own.

Once he was prone on the couch again, he allowed her to tuck the afghan in around him. She gave him more painkillers. Fifteen minutes later, he was sound asleep.

By then, it was past three in the morning. She checked her phone and found text messages—from her dad and also from Iris and Peyton, her best friends in Portland. They all three knew that it had ended with her fiancé, James. She hadn't shared the gory details with her dad, but she'd told her BFFs everything. The texts asked how she was doing, if she was managing all right?

They—her friends and her dad—believed she was spending the holiday on her own at the farm. However, with no one there but her, the farmhouse had seemed to echo with loneliness, so she'd told Nils and Marjorie Wilson, who worked and lived on the property, that she was leaving. She'd thrown her stuff in her Subaru and headed back to Portland, stopping off at the fish hatchery on the spur of the moment.

And ending up stranded in a cabin in the woods with a stranger named Matthias.

Really, it was all too much to get into via text. She was safe and warm with plenty of food—and having a much better time than she'd had alone at the farmhouse. There was nothing anyone could do for her right now. They would only freak out if she tried to explain where she was and how she'd gotten there.

Sabra wished them each a merry Christmas. She mentioned that it was snowing heavily and implied to her girlfriends that she was still at the farm and might be out of touch for a few days due to the storm. To her dad, she wrote that she'd gone back to Portland—it wasn't a lie, exactly. She *had* gone. She just hadn't gotten there yet.

Though cell service in the forest was spotty at best, a minor miracle occurred and all three texts went through instantly—after which she second-guessed herself. Because she probably ought to tell someone that she was alone with a stranger in the middle of the woods.

But who? And to what real purpose? What would she even say?

Okay, I'm not exactly where I said I was. I'm actually snowed in at an isolated cabin surrounded by the Clatsop State Forest with some guy named Matthias Bravo, who's passed out on the sofa due to illness and injury...

No. Uh-uh. She'd made the right decision in the

first place. Why worry them when there was nothing they could do?

She powered off the phone to save the battery and wandered upstairs, where she turned on the lamps on either side of the bed and went looking for the Christmas decorations Matthias had to have somewhere.

Score! There were several plastic tubs of them stuck in a nook under the eaves. She carried them downstairs and stacked them next to that gorgeous tree.

By then, she was yawning. All of a sudden, the energy had drained right out of her. She went back to the loft and fell across the bed fully clothed.

Sabra woke to gray daylight coming in the one tiny window over the bed—and to the heavenly smell of fresh coffee.

With a grunt, she pushed herself to her feet and followed her nose down to the main floor and the coffee maker on the counter. A clean mug waited beside it. Matthias must have set it out for her, which almost made her smile.

And Sabra Bond never smiled before at least one cup of morning coffee.

Once the mug was full, she turned and leaned against the counter to enjoy that first, all-important sip.

Matthias was sitting up on the sofa, his bad leg stretched out across the cushions, holding a mug of his own, watching her. "Rough night, huh?"

She gave him her sternest frown. "You should not have been up and you are not allowed to speak to me until I finish at least one full cup of coffee."

He shrugged. But she could tell that he was trying not to grin.

She took another big gulp. "Your face is still flushed. That means you still have a fever."

He sipped his coffee and did not say a word. Which was good. Great. Exactly what she'd asked for.

She knocked back another mouthful. "At least you're not sweating anymore. Have you taken more acetaminophen since last night?"

He regarded her with mock gravity and slowly shook his head in the negative.

She set down her mug, grabbed a glass, filled it with water and carried it over to him. "There you go. Take your pills. I'll need to check your bandage and then I'll cook us some breakfast."

He tipped his golden head down and looked at her from under thick, burnished eyebrows. His mouth kept twitching. Apparently, he was finding her extremely amusing.

"What?" she demanded.

He only shook his head again.

She marched back to the counter, leaned against it once more and enjoyed the rest of her coffee in blessed silence.

"You don't happen to have an extra toothbrush, by any chance?" she asked once she'd drained the last drop from the mug. He just gave her more silent smirking. "Oh, stop it. You may speak."

"You're such a charmer in the morning."

She grunted. "Toothbrush?"

"Under the bathroom sink. Small plastic tub. There should be a couple of them still in the wrappers and some of those sample-sized tubes of toothpaste."

"Thank you—need more coffee before I go in there? Because I am completely serious. For today at least, you're not getting up unless you really need to."

He set his mug on the coffee table and reached for the bottle of painkillers. "No more coffee right now. I'll have another cup with breakfast."

The fire was all but out. She added a little kindling and another log. As soon as the flames licked up, she faced him. "Do not get up from that couch while I'm in there."

He was stretched out on his back again, adjusting the afghan, but he dropped it to make a show of putting his hands up in surrender. "I will not move from this spot until you give me permission."

She grabbed her pack. "That's what I wanted to hear."

In the bathroom, she didn't even glance at the mirror. Not at first. The coffee had gone right to her bladder, so she took care of that. It wasn't until she stood at the sink to wash her hands that she saw what Matthias had been trying not to laugh about.

She had three deep sleep wrinkles on the left side of her face and her hair was smashed flat on that side, with another ratty-looking section of it standing straight up from the top of her head.

A little grooming was definitely in order. She took off her clothes and gave herself a quick sponge bath, after which she brushed her teeth, put her clothes back on and combed her hair, weaving it into a single braid down her back.

By then, she almost looked human.

Snow had piled up on the sill outside the tiny bathroom window. She went on tiptoe to peer through the clear part of the glass.

A blanket of unbroken white extended, smooth and sparkly, to the tree line. The trees themselves were more white than green. And it was still coming down.

Everything out that window looked brand-new. And she felt…gleeful.

She had someone to spend her Christmas with. And a gorgeous tree to decorate.

So what if that someone was a stranger and the tree wasn't hers? This totally unexpected interlude in the forest was just fine with her. She felt energized, very close to happy. And ready for anything.

For the first time in a long time, she looked forward with real anticipation to whatever was going to happen next.

Chapter Three

Matt was feeling almost human again. Yeah, his leg ached a little. But he'd taken his temperature before he made the coffee. It was down two degrees. His headache was gone.

Sabra came out of the bathroom looking a lot more pulled together than when she'd gone in. Though really, she'd been damn cute with her hair sticking up every which way, giving him the evil eye, ordering him to keep his mouth shut until she'd had her coffee.

"How about some oatmeal?" she asked as she refilled his coffee mug. "Think you could keep that down?"

He had zero desire to eat mush. "Did I dream it or did you haul everything in from the Jeep last night?"

"No dream. I brought the food and your other things inside."

"And you made soup."

"Yes, I did."

"It was delicious. I can't tell you how much I appreciate everything you've done and I would like eggs, bacon and toast. Please."

She handed him the mug and then stood above him, holding the coffee carafe, her head tipped to the side as she studied him. "I'm not going to be happy with you if it all comes right back up." She put on her don't-mess-with-me look, just to let him know who was boss.

Damn. The woman had attitude. And she took care of business. She was tough and resourceful and pretty much unflappable—with a dry sense of humor.

Not to mention she looked amazing in panties and a sports bra.

Matt liked her. A lot. He was a little blown away at how much. As a rule, he was cautious around new people. But for her, he would definitely make an exception. He said what he was thinking. "I could have done a lot worse than to get snowed in with you."

For that, he got a small nod and a hint of a smile. "I'm glad you're feeling better. I just want you to be careful not to overdo it."

"Eggs," he said longingly. "Toast. Bacon."

She made a disapproving face, but then she cooked him the breakfast he asked for. He did his part and kept the food down. After the meal, she changed his bandage. His leg wasn't pretty, but there was no sign of infection.

Once she'd changed the dressing, she got him some sweats and clean underwear from the duffel bags she'd brought in from the car. She even allowed him to hobble into the bathroom on his own steam.

He brushed his teeth, cleaned himself up a little and changed into the stuff she'd brought downstairs for him. When he emerged into the main room, she said he looked a little green and ordered him to lie down.

"I have a request," she said as she tucked the old afghan in around him.

"My Jeep? My bank account number? The deed to this cabin? Whatever you want from me, it's yours."

She laughed. The sound was low and a little bit husky. Every time she bent close, he could smell her. She'd used the Ivory soap in the bathroom, yeah, but beneath that, her body itself smelled clean and sweet, like fresh-baked bread or maybe sugar cookies. Sugar cookies and woman.

A knockout combination.

Really, she had it all going on. He'd never realized before that he might have a type. *Hi, I'm Matt Bravo and I like my women hot, smart, competent and bossy.* As soon as he was capable of washing up in the bathroom without needing a nap afterward, it was going to get really difficult not to put a move on her.

Now, though? He was weak as a baby and fading fast, making her one-hundred-percent safe from his bad intentions.

"Keep your bank account," she said with a grin. "It's your tree I'm after."

He imagined reaching up, running a finger down the velvety skin of her neck, maybe tugging on that thick braid down her back—and what was this he was feeling? Like he had a crush on her or something.

Matt didn't do crushes. He'd been in love once and

it had all gone to hell like everything else in his life at that time. Nowadays, he went out occasionally with women who wanted the same thing he did—satisfying sex. And no sleeping over.

Although, in all honesty, if he was going to crush on a woman, it would have to be this one.

"Matthias? You okay?"

He picked up the conversation where he'd dropped it. "I noticed you found the decorations and brought them down."

She grinned. "It's Christmas Eve. You're in no condition to decorate that tree and it's not going to decorate itself. Is it all right with you if I do it?"

She was way too much fun to tease. "You sure you don't want the Jeep? It's a Rubicon. Super fancy. You can go off-road in it, take a seventy-degree downhill grade on rugged terrain without even stopping to consider the risks—because there are none."

A sound escaped her, a snappy little "Ffft." She gave him a light slap on the shoulder with the back of her hand. "Stop messing with me. Say yes."

He stared up into those beautiful brown eyes. "Yes."

"Well, all right." She retucked a bit of his blanket. "That wasn't so hard, was it?"

He reached back and punched his pillow a little, all for show. "Have fun."

"I will."

"And try to keep the noise down. I need my sleep." He turned his head toward the back of the sofa and closed his eyes.

But not two minutes later, he rolled his head back the other way so he could watch her work.

Methodical and exacting, that was her tree-decorating style. She found the lights, plugging in each string first, replacing the few bulbs that had gone out. There weren't many bad bulbs because Matt took care of his gear. Also, the lights weren't that old.

This was his third Christmas at the cabin. His great-uncle Percy Valentine had given the place to him when Matt was discharged from the service. *A few wooded acres and a one-room cabin, Matthias,* Uncle Percy had said. *I'm thinking it will be a quiet place just for you, a place where you can find yourself again.*

Matt wasn't all that sure he'd found himself yet, but he liked having his own place not far from home to go when he needed it. He had a large family and they kept after him to start showing up for Christmas, which had always been a big deal for all of them.

His mom had loved Christmas and she used to do it up right. She and his dad had died when Matt was sixteen, but his older brother Daniel had stepped up, taken custody of all of them and continued all the family Christmas traditions.

He loved them, every one of them. He would do just about anything for them. But for Christmas, he liked the cabin better. He liked going off into a world of his own now and then, needed it even. Especially for the holidays. There was something about this time of the year that made the ghosts of his past most likely to haunt him.

Through half-closed eyes, he watched as Sabra strung the lights. She tucked them in among the thick branches just so, making sure there were no bare spaces, the same way he would have done. When she neared the top, she found the folding footstool in the closet under the stairs and used it to string those lights all the way up.

She had the lights on and was starting to hang ornaments when his eyes got too heavy to keep open even partway. Feeling peaceful and damn close to happy, he drifted off to sleep.

When he woke again, Sabra was curled in a ball in the old brown armchair across from the sofa, asleep. She'd found a book, no doubt from the bookcase on the side wall. It lay open across her drawn-up thighs, her dark head drooping over it.

The tree was finished. She'd done a great job of it. He just lay there on the sofa and admired it for a few minutes, tall and proud, shining so bright. She'd even put his presents from the family under it.

But he was thirsty and his water glass was empty. He sat up and reached for the cane that he'd propped at the end of the sofa.

That small movement woke her. "Wha…?" She blinked at him owlishly. "Hey. You're awake." She rubbed the back of her neck.

He pushed back the afghan and brought his legs to the floor. "The tree is gorgeous."

She smiled, a secret, pleased little smile. "Thanks. How're you feeling?"

"Better." He pushed himself upright and she didn't even try to stop him.

"You look better. Your color's good. Want some soup?"

"If I can sit at the table to eat it."

"You think you're up for that?"

"I know I am."

* * *

Matthias *was* better. Lots better.

So much better that, after dinner that night, when he wanted to go out on the porch, she agreed without even a word of protest.

"You'll need a warmer coat," he said, and sent her upstairs to get one of his.

The coat dwarfed her smaller frame. On her, it came to midthigh and the arms covered her hands. She loved it. It would keep her toasty warm even out in the frozen night air—and it smelled like him, of cedar and something kind of minty.

On the porch, there were two rustic-looking log chairs. Sabra pushed the chairs closer together and they sat down.

The snow had finally stopped. They'd gotten several feet of the stuff, which meant they would definitely be stuck here for at least the next few days.

Sabra didn't mind. She felt far away from her real life, off in this silent, frozen world with a man who'd been a stranger to her only the day before.

He said, "My mom used to love the snow. It doesn't snow that often in Valentine Bay, but when it did she would get us all out into the yard to make snowmen. There was never that much of it, so our snowmen were wimpy ones. They melted fast."

"You're from Valentine Bay, then?" Valentine Bay was on the coast, a little south of Warrenton, which was at the mouth of the Columbia River.

He turned to look at her, brow furrowing. "Didn't I tell you I'm from Valentine Bay?"

"You've told me now—and you said your mom *used* to love the snow?"

"That's right. She died eleven years ago. My dad, too. In a tsunami in Thailand, of all the crazy ways to go."

"You've lost both of them? That had to be hard." She wanted to reach out and hug him. But that would be weird, wouldn't it? She felt like she knew him. But she didn't, not really. She needed to try to remember to respect the guy's space.

"It was a long time ago. My oldest brother Daniel took over and raised us the rest of the way. He and his wife Lillie just continued right on, everything essentially the way it used be, including the usual Christmas traditions. Even now, they all spend Christmas day at the house where we grew up. They open their presents together, share breakfast and cook a big Christmas dinner."

"But you want to spend your Christmas alone."

"That's right."

A minute ago, she'd been warning herself to respect the man's space. Too bad. Right now, she couldn't resist trying to find out more. "Last night, you were talking in your sleep."

He gave her a long look. It wasn't an encouraging one. "Notice the way I'm not asking what I said?"

"Don't want to talk about Mark and Nelson and Finn?"

He didn't. And he made that perfectly clear—by changing the subject. "You said you grew up on a farm?"

"Yes, I did."

"Near here, you said?"

"Yeah. Near Svensen."

"That's in Astoria."

"Yeah, pretty much."

"But you were headed for Portland when you suddenly decided on a hike to the falls?"

"I live in Portland now. I manage the front of the house at a restaurant in the Pearl." The Pearl District was the right place to open an upscale, farm-to-table restaurant. Delia Mae's was one of those.

"Got tired of farming?" His breath came out as fog.

She gathered his giant coat a little closer around her against the cold. "Not really. I'm a farmer by birth, vocation and education. I've got a bachelor's degree in environmental studies with an emphasis in agro-ecology."

"From UC Santa Cruz, am I right?"

"The Slugs hat and sweatshirt?"

"Dead giveaway." He smiled, slow and sexy, his white, even teeth gleaming in the porch light's glow. She stared at him, thinking that he really was a hot-looking guy, with those killer blue eyes, a shadow of beard scruff on his sculpted jaw and that thick, unruly dark blond hair.

And what were they talking about?

Farming. Right. "Our farm has been in the Bond family for generations. My dad and mom were a true love match, mutually dedicated to each other, the farm and to me, their only child. All my growing-up years, the plan was for me to work right along with them, and to take the reins when the time came. But then, when I was nineteen and in my first year at Santa Cruz, my mom died while driving home from a quick shopping trip into downtown Astoria on a gray day in February. Her pickup lost traction on the icy road. The truck spun out and crashed into the guardrail."

Matthias didn't even hesitate. He reached out between their two chairs, clasped her shoulder with his large, strong hand and gave a nice, firm squeeze. They shared a glance, a long one that made her feel completely understood.

His reassuring touch made it all the easier to confess, "I have a hard time now, at the farm. It's been six years since my mom died, but my dad has never really recovered from the loss. I guess, to be honest, neither have I. After college, I just wanted something completely different."

"And now you run a restaurant."

"The chef would disagree. But yeah. I manage the waitstaff, the hiring, supervising and scheduling, all that."

He shifted in the hard chair, wincing a little.

"Your leg is bothering you," she said. "We should go in."

"I like it out here." He seemed to be studying her face.

"What?"

"I like *you*, Sabra." From the snow-covered trees, an owl hooted. "I like you very much, as a matter of fact."

A little thrill shivered through her. She relished it. And then she thought about James. She'd almost married him less than a week ago. It was turning out to be much too easy to forget him.

"What'd I say?" Matthias looked worried.

"Something nice. Too bad I'm not looking for anything remotely resembling romance."

"It's not a problem," he said in that matter-of-fact way of his. "Neither am I."

She felt a flash of disappointment, and quickly banished it. "Excellent. No romance. No…fooling around. None of that. We have a deal."

He nodded. "Agreed. And I sense a story here. You should tell it to me."

"Though you won't tell me yours?"

"I'm sure yours is more interesting than mine." Again, he shifted. His leg hurt. He just refused to admit it.

"I'm braver than you, Matthias."

He didn't even try to argue the point. "I have no doubt that you are."

"I'll put it right out there, tell you all about my failures in love."

He looked at her sideways. "You're after something. What?"

She laughed. "I'm not telling you anything until you come back inside."

In the cabin, they hung their coats by the door. Matt took off his boots and settled on the sofa with his bad leg stretched out.

"You want some hot chocolate or something?" she offered.

Was she stalling? He wanted that story. He gestured at the armchair. "Sit. Start talking."

She laughed that husky laugh of hers. The sound made a lightness inside him. She was something special, all right. And this was suddenly turning out to be his favorite Christmas ever.

She took off her own boots, filled his water glass for him and put another log on the fire.

Finally, she dropped into the brown chair across the coffee table from him. "Okay. It's like this. I've been engaged twice. The first time was at Santa Cruz. I fell hard for a bass-playing philosophy major named Stan."

"I already hate him."

"Why?"

"Was he your first lover?" As soon as he asked, he wished he hadn't. A question like that could be considered to be crossing a certain line.

But she didn't seem turned off by it. "How did you know?"

"Just a guess—and I'm not sure yet why I hate him. Because I like *you*, I think, and I know it didn't last with him. I'm guessing that was all his fault."

"I don't want to be unfair to Stan."

Matt laughed. It came out sounding rusty. He wasn't a big laugher, as a rule. "Go ahead. Be unfair to Stan. There's only you and me here. And I'm on *your* side."

"All right, fine." She gave a single, definitive nod. "Please feel free to hate him. He claimed to love me madly. He asked me to marry him."

"Let me guess. You said yes."

"Hey. I was twenty-one. Even though losing my mom had rocked the foundations of my world, I still had hopes and dreams back then."

"Did you move in together?"

"We did. We had this cute apartment not far from the ocean and we were planning an earthcentric wedding on a mountaintop."

"But the wedding never happened."

"No, it did not. Because one morning, I woke up alone. Stan had left me a note."

"Don't tell me the note was on his pillow."

Stifling a giggle, she nodded.

"Okay, Sabra. Hit me with it. What did the note say?"

"That he couldn't do it, couldn't marry me. Marriage was just too bougie, he wrote."

"*Bougie?* He wrote that exact word?" At her nod, he said, "And you wondered why I hate Stan."

"He also wrote that I was a good person, but I didn't really crank his chain. He had to follow his bliss to Austin and become a rock star."

"What a complete douchebasket."

"Yeah, I guess he was, kind of."

"*Kind* of? People shouldn't make promises they don't mean to keep."

Sabra sat forward in the big brown armchair.

Was he speaking from painful experience? She really wanted to know. But he didn't want to talk about himself—not as of now, anyway. And those deep blue eyes had turned wary, as though he guessed she was tempted to ask him a question he wouldn't answer.

"Keep talking," he commanded. "What happened after Stan?"

"After Stan, I decided that my judgment about men was out of whack and I swore to myself I wouldn't get serious with a guy until I was at least thirty."

Now he was looking at her sideways, a skeptical sort of look. "Thirty, huh?"

"That's right."

"And as of today, you are…?"

"Twenty-five," she gave out grudgingly.

"And why am I thinking you've broken your own rule and gotten serious since Stan?"

"Don't gloat, Matthias. It's not attractive—and you know, I kind of can't believe I'm telling you all this. I think I've said enough."

"No. Uh-uh. You have to tell me the rest."

"Why?"

"Uh." His wide brow wrinkled up. "Because I'm an invalid and you are helping me through this difficult time."

She couldn't hold back a snort of laughter. "I really think you're going to survive whether I tell you about James or not."

"So. The next guy's name is James?"

She groaned. "The *next* guy? Like there've been a hundred of them?"

He sat very still. She could practically see the wheels turning inside his big head. "Wait. I think that came out wrong."

"No, it didn't. Not at all. I'm just messing with you."

"You're probably thinking I'm a jerk just like Stan." He looked so worried about that. She wanted to grab him and hug him and tell him everything was fine—and that was at least the second time tonight she'd considered putting her hands on him for other than purely medical reasons.

It had to stop.

"No," she said. "I honestly don't think you're a jerk—and look, Matthias, I've been meaning to ask you…"

* * *

Matthias *felt* like a jerk, whether or not Sabra considered him one. He'd been having a great time with her, like they'd known each other forever.

Until he went and put his foot in it. As a rule, he was careful around women. He wasn't ready for anything serious, so he watched himself, made sure he didn't give off the wrong signals.

But Sabra. Well, already she was kind of getting under his skin. There was so damn much to admire about her—*and* she was fun. And hot.

But they'd agreed that the man/woman thing wasn't happening. He was friend-zoned and he could live with that. Anything more, well…

It would be too easy to fall for her. And he didn't want to fall for anyone. Not yet. Maybe never. The last year or so, he'd finally started to feel like his life was back on track. True, getting something going with a woman could turn out to be the best thing that ever happened to him.

But it might send him spinning off the rails.

He just wasn't ready to find out which.

"Do you maybe have some sweats I could wear?" she asked. "Something soft to sleep in would be great…"

She was going to bed now? It wasn't much past nine.

No doubt about it. He'd definitely screwed up.

"Uh, sure," he said, and tried not to let his disappointment show. "Take anything you want from whatever's upstairs."

"I was thinking I might even have a bath, if that's all right with you?"

"Now?"

"Well, I mean, no time like the present, right?"

"Absolutely. Go ahead."

She got up. "Can I get you anything before I—?"

"No. Really. I'm good."

She took off up the stairs. Not five minutes later, she came running back down with an armful of his clothes and disappeared into the bathroom.

He sat there and stared at the tree and tried not to imagine what she was doing behind that shut door. Really, he must be getting better fast—he had the erection to prove it.

Friend-zoned, you idiot. And that's how you want it.

He needed to take his mind off his exceptionally clear mental image of Sabra, naked in the tub, her almost-black hair piled up on her head, random strands curling in the steam rising from the water, clinging to the silky skin of her neck as she raised one of those gorgeous long legs of hers and braced her foot on the side of the tub.

Lazily, humming a holiday tune under her breath, she would begin to work up a lather. Soap bubbles would dribble slowly along her inner thigh...

Matt swore, a graphic string of bad words.

And then he grabbed his cane and shot to his feet, only swaying a little as his bad leg took his weight—yeah, he'd promised her he would stay on the sofa unless he had a good reason to get up.

Well, clearing his mind of certain way-too-tempting images was a good enough reason for him.

He limped over to the bookcase. She'd set the box

of books he'd brought from home right there in the corner on the floor.

Might as well shelve them. He got to work, his leg complaining a little when he bent down to grab the next volume. But it wasn't that painful and it kept his mind from wandering to places it had no business going.

He was three-quarters of the way through the box when the bathroom door opened.

"Matthias. What the—? You promised you'd stay off your feet."

Yep. He could already smell the steaminess from across the room—soap and wet and heat and woman.

"Matthias?"

Slowly, so as not to make a fool of himself lurching on his bad leg and proving how right she was that he shouldn't be on his feet, he turned to her.

Cutest damn thing he ever saw.

She was covered head to toe, dwarfed by his Clatsop Community College sweatshirt and a pair of his sweatpants she must have rolled at the waist, his red-toed work socks like clown shoes on her narrow feet.

Damn it to hell, she looked amazing, all rosy and soft, swimming in his clothes—and she'd washed her hair, too. It was still wet, curling sweetly on her shoulders.

His throat felt like it had a log stuck in it. He gave a quick cough to clear it. "I, um, just thought I might as well get these books out of the box."

She simply looked at him, shaking her head.

"C'mon," he coaxed. "I'm doing fine. It's not that big a deal."

She pressed her soft lips together—hiding a smile

or holding back more scolding words? He couldn't tell which. But then she said, "I washed out my things. They're hanging over the tub and the shower bar. Hope that's okay."

"You don't even need to ask."

"All right, then."

A silence. Not an awkward one, surprisingly. She regarded him almost fondly—or was that pure wishful thinking on his part?

She spoke first. "Thought I would grab a book or two, read myself to sleep."

He wanted to beg, *Stay. Talk to me some more.* But all he said was, "Help yourself."

Big socks flapping, she crossed the room to him and made her choices as he just stood there between the box and the bookcase, breathing in the steamy scent of her, wishing she would move closer so he could smell her better.

She chose a thriller and a love story set in the Second World War that had won a bunch of literary awards a few years ago. "Okay, then," she said finally. "Anything else I can do before I go? Shall I unplug the tree?"

"Nope. I'm almost done here. Then I'll lie down, I promise."

"Fair enough." Both books tucked under one arm, she turned for the stairs.

He bent to grab another volume, shelved it, bent to grab the next.

"Matthias?" He straightened and turned. She'd made it to the top. "Merry Christmas."

He stared up at her, aching for something he didn't

want to name, feeling equal parts longing and gladness—longing for what he knew he wouldn't have.

Gladness just to be here in his cabin in the forest, stranded. With her.

"Merry Christmas, Sabra."

She granted him a smile, a slow one. And then she turned and vanished from his sight.

Chapter Four

Christmas day, Sabra woke to morning light streaming in the loft window. She could smell coffee, which meant that Matthias had been on his feet again.

She went downstairs scowling. But that was more her natural precoffee face than disapproval. The tree was lit up, looking fabulous. He was sitting on the sofa, his laptop across his stretched-out legs, apparently not in pain, his color excellent.

He'd left a mug waiting for her by the coffee maker, same as yesterday. She filled it and drank it just the way she liked it, without a word spoken.

Once it was empty, she set the mug on the counter. "Did you happen to take your temperature?"

He ran his thumb over the touch pad. "Normal."

"You have internet on that laptop?"

He tipped his head toward his phone on the coffee

table. "Not using it now—but yeah, when I need it. Mobile data through my cell. It's a little spotty here in the middle of nowhere, but it works well enough." He looked up and smiled at her. Bam! The gray winter morning just got a whole lot brighter. "I also have a speaker. We can have Christmas music."

"How wonderful is that?" She wandered over to see what game he was playing. "Solitaire?"

"It's mindless. I find it calming." He won a game and the cards flew around and settled to start over.

She went on into the bathroom, where her clothes weren't quite dry yet and her hair looked almost as bad as it had the morning before.

After breakfast, Matthias said he wanted a real bath. She went into the bathroom first, gathered up her things and took them upstairs, after which she found a roll of plastic wrap and waterproofed his bandaged lower leg.

He hobbled into the bathroom and didn't come out for an hour. When he finally emerged smelling of toothpaste and shampoo, she checked his stitches. There was no swelling and less redness than the day before.

"Lookin' good," she said.

"Great. I'm putting on the tunes." He used a cable to hook up his speaker to his phone. Christmas music filled the cabin.

She insisted that he open his presents. "Just sit there," she said, "nice and comfy on the couch. I'll bring them to you."

"That doesn't seem fair."

"If I'm happy doing it, it's fair enough."

His presents were the stuff guys get from their families at Christmas. Shirts and socks and a nice heavy jacket. A humorous coffee mug. Gift cards. More books.

Sabra enjoyed the process. For the first time since her mom died, she was loving every minute of Christmas. Sitting out on the porch in the freezing cold, coming downstairs in the morning to the coffee Matthias had already made though she'd ordered him not to—everything, all of it, seemed sparkly and fresh, entertaining and baggage-free.

When the last gift card had been stripped of its shiny wrapper and pretty ribbons, he said, "There's one more under there somewhere."

"You sure? I think that's all."

"I'll find it." He reached for his bear-headed cane.

"Nope. Sit." She got down on hands and knees and peered through the thick tiers of branches. "I see it." It was tucked in close to the trunk. Pulling it free, she sat back on her heels. The snowman wrapping paper was wrinkled and the bow was made of household twine. "I don't remember this one."

"I had to make do with what I found in the kitchen drawers."

"It's for me?" Her throat kind of clutched. Maybe. A little.

"Yeah—and don't make a big deal of it or start in on how I shouldn't have been on my feet."

She slanted him a sideways look. "Lotta rules you got when it comes to giving someone a present, Matthias."

"It's Christmas. I wanted you to have *something*, okay?"

"Um. Okay." She gazed at him steadily, thinking what a great guy he was under the gruffness and self-protective, macho-man bluster.

"It's nothing," he mumbled. "Just open it."

Oh, she definitely was tempted to dish out a little lecture about how a guy should never call any gift "nothing." But then he would consider that making a "big deal." Better not to even get started. She untied the twine bow and tore off the wrinkled paper.

Inside was a See's Candy box and inside that, a folded piece of paper bag and a small, roughly carved wooden animal. "It's so cute." She held it up. "A hedgehog?"

"Close. A porcupine. I made it last night, sitting out on the porch after you went to bed."

She started to chide him for not going to sleep early as he'd promised—but then pressed her lips together before any words escaped. His gift touched her heart and being out on the porch for a while didn't seem to have hurt him any.

He said, "Me and my Swiss Army knife, we have a great time together."

She turned the little carving in her hands, admiring his work. "I love it. Truly. Thank you."

He gave a one-shouldered shrug. "I thought you might want a souvenir, something to remind you of all that can happen if you go wandering into the woods at Christmastime. You could end up facing down a crazy man with a gun and then having to perform emergency surgery." He grinned.

She felt an answering smile lift the corners of her mouth. "Why a porcupine?"

"No reason, really. I got out my knife and a nice bit of wood that was just the right shape to become a porcupine."

"Great choice. I'm a porcupine sort of girl—kinda prickly."

"But cute."

Was she blushing? God. Probably. "Did you make your cane?" She tipped her head toward where it leaned against the end of the sofa.

"Yes, I did."

She had that urge again—to jump up and hug him. Again, she resisted it. But her defenses were weakening. The more time she spent with him, the more she wanted to touch him, to have him touch her.

Shifting her legs out from under her, she sat cross-legged on the floor, set the sweet little porcupine beside her and unfolded the paper-bag note.

Merry Christmas, Sabra,

I'll make your coffee whether you allow me to or not. And I'll shut up while you drink it. Feel free to break into my cabin anytime.

Matthias

She glanced up to find him watching her. "You realize you just gave me an open invitation to invade your forest retreat whenever the mood strikes."

He gazed at her so steadily. "Anytime. I mean that."

Did she believe him? Not really. But still, it pleased her no end that he seemed to like having her around.

* * *

It was a great Christmas, Matt thought, easy and lazy. No tension, zero drama.

They roasted the prime rib he'd brought and sat down to dinner in the early afternoon. There was time on the porch to enjoy the snowy clearing and the tall white-mantled trees. He had board games and they played them. She won at Scrabble. He kicked her pretty butt at Risk.

Not long after dark, as they were considering a game of cribbage, the power went out. She got the footstool from under the stairs and handed him down the two boxes of candles he kept ready and waiting on top of the kitchen cabinets. They lit the candles, set them around the room and ended up abandoning the cribbage board, gravitating to their usual places instead—Matt on the sofa, Sabra curled up in the brown easy chair.

He felt comfortable enough with her to bring up the awkwardness the night before. "I really didn't mean to insult you last night—you know, what I said about you and that guy named James…"

She gave him a look he was already coming to recognize, sort of patient. And tender. "I told you that I wasn't insulted."

"But then you jumped to your feet and ran and hid in the bathroom."

"Did not," she said sharply. "I took a *bath*." She huffed out a breath. "Please."

He said nothing. He was getting to know her well enough to have a general idea of when to keep his mouth shut around her, let her come to the truth at her own speed.

And she did, first shifting in the chair, drawing her legs up the other way, wrapping her slim arms around them. "I thought maybe I was getting too personal, I guess."

"You weren't. If you want to tell it, I'm listening."

Her sleek eyebrows drew together as she thought it over. "It *is* helpful, to have someone to talk to. You're a good listener and this is just the right situation, you know? You and me alone in this cabin, away from the rest of the world. I think it shocked me last night, how easy it was to say hard stuff to you. You're the stranger I'll probably never see again once the roads are clear and we can go our separate ways." She swiped a hand down her shining dark hair and flicked her braid back over her shoulder.

He could sit here forever, just looking at her.

She had it right, though—yeah, he ached to kiss her. To touch her. To see where this attraction he felt for her might go.

But at the same time, he'd been careful not to tell her too much about himself, about his life. He'd come a long way in the past few years. But not far enough. He still wasn't ready to jump off into the deep end with a woman again.

And Sabra Bond? She was the kind a guy should be ready to go deep with.

Sabra hugged her knees a little closer, thinking how the man across the coffee table from her reminded her of her dad a little—her dad the way he used to be, back in the old days, before they'd lost her mom. Like her father, Matthias was self-contained. He really listened. He took her seriously but he knew how to kid around, too. He also seemed the sort of man who would tell the truth even when it hurt.

"So, where was I?" she asked.

He tipped his dark gold head to the side, considering, for several long seconds before replying. "You told me about Stan, who left in the middle of the night to move to Austin and become a rock star, the lousy bastard. What about James?"

"James. Right. After Stan, I swore off men."

"How'd that work out?"

"For a while, I had no romantic relationships of any kind. Then, in my last year at Santa Cruz, I met James Wise. James is from a wealthy Monterey family and he was studying computer game design—not really seriously, though, as it turned out."

"Right. Because...trust fund?"

"A giant one. He was fooling around with game design and his parents were constantly pressuring him to join the family real estate development firm."

"So you two were a thing, you and James?"

She nodded. "We were. He was fun and he didn't seem to take things too seriously. I was so proud of myself for finally having a no-strings sexual relationship."

"But then...?"

"After we dated for a month or two, James started pushing for marriage."

Matthias made a low, knowing sort of sound. "And you explained that you planned to be single for years yet."

"I did, yes. We split up at graduation. I moved to Portland."

"A fresh start."

"That's right. I got my own place and a job at that restaurant I told you about, where I met Iris and Peyton, who became my best friends. I kept promising my friends I would enjoy my freedom, get out and experience a few hot and sexy nights with men I never intended to spend forever with. Somehow, that never happened. And then James showed up in Portland."

"Because he couldn't live without you."

"That is exactly what he said." She turned sideways and hung her legs over the chair arm, using the other arm as a backrest, shoving a throw pillow behind her for extra support. "And how'd you know that?"

"Lucky guess. Continue."

"Well, I really had missed him. Yeah, I knew he was a little…irresponsible, maybe. But he was so romantic and sweet—and lighthearted, you know? Since my mom's death, a little lightheartedness means a lot. He kind of swept me off my feet. We got a place together and he kept pushing for marriage…"

"And you finally said yes."

"Nailed it."

"But what about those no-strings flings you promised your girlfriends you'd be having?"

"Never got around to them. And I know, the plan was I would wait till I was thirty to even get serious. Yet, somehow, there I was, saying yes to James—also, full disclosure? I'd never actually met his family or taken him to meet my dad."

"Uh-oh."

"Tell me about it." She groaned. "I ask you, could there have *been* more red flags?"

"Don't beat yourself up. It's all in the past, right?"

A little shudder went through her. "Right. The very

recent past, unfortunately—but anyhow, we agreed we'd skip the fancy wedding. I'd never wanted one of those and he could not have cared less either way. We set a date for a quickie Vegas ceremony, which was to have taken place exactly six days ago today. Then after the wedding, the plan was that James would sweep me off for a Christmas vacation-slash-honeymoon in the Seychelles."

"Christmas in the tropics. That does sound romantic. Ten points for James."

"I thought so, too. And I did insist he had to at least meet my dad first, so we went to the farm for Thanksgiving."

"Did you have a nice visit?"

She narrowed her eyes at him. "Go ahead, Matthias. Pour on the irony."

"Sorry." He didn't look the least regretful.

"You're enjoying this far too much."

"I'm only teasing you—you know, being *light-hearted*?"

She pulled the pillow out from behind her back and threw it at him.

He caught it. "Whoa. Just missed the candle."

"Watch out. I'll do worse than knock over a candle."

He put the pillow under his injured leg. "So? The visit to the farm…?"

"It was bad. My dad was polite to James, but two days in, Dad got me alone and asked me if I was really sure about marrying the guy."

"Ouch. That's tough."

"And I reacted with anger. I said some mean things about how, since we'd lost Mom, he didn't care about anything—but now, all of a sudden, he's got a negative opinion he just has to share concerning my choice of a life mate."

"Admit it," Matthias interjected in that rough, matter-of-fact tone she already knew so well. "You were worried that your dad might be right."

She decided his remark didn't require a response. "After the awfulness with my dad, James and I went back to Portland."

"Your dad was right, though—am I right?"

She wished she had another pillow to throw at him. "Seven days ago, the day before we were supposed to head for Vegas, James's parents arrived out of nowhere at our apartment."

"Not good?"

"Horrible. They'd come to collect their errant son before he made the biggest mistake of his life— marrying some nobody farmer's daughter when the woman he grew up with, a woman from an excellent family, a woman who loved him with all her heart, was waiting for him in Monterey—with their little boy who needed his daddy."

"What the—? James had a kid?"

She nodded. "One he'd never said a word to me about."

"Okay, now I want to kick his snotty little rich-guy ass."

"Thank you. Anyway, James asks his parents to leave. They go. At this point, I'm reeling. I demand an explanation—and James just blurts out the truth he never bothered to share with me before. He says yes, there's a little boy. That in the year between graduation and when he showed up in Portland, he'd gotten back with his childhood sweetheart and she'd had his baby. He says he hates that maybe his parents are right. Monica—his baby mama—really does need him and so does his son. He says he's sorry, but he can't marry me and he's leaving for Monterey right away."

"Sabra."

She glared across the coffee table at him to keep from getting weepy over her terrible life choices. "What?"

"This all happened a week ago?"

"James went back to Monterey exactly one week ago today, yes."

Matthias took the pillow out from under his leg, plopped it on the coffee table and scooted around so he could rest his leg on it again. Then he patted the space beside him. "Come here."

"Why?"

He only patted the empty cushion some more.

"Fine." She got up and sat next to him.

And he hooked his giant arm around her and pulled her close. "Lean on me. It's not going to kill you."

She let her head drop to his enormous shoulder, breathed in his minty, manly evergreen scent—and felt comforted. "Thanks."

His breath brushed the crown of her head. He might even have pressed a kiss there, though she couldn't be sure. "Continue."

"What else is there to say? I gave him back his ring and he packed a suitcase and left. I told myself to look on the bright side. I had three weeks off work for the honeymoon that wasn't happening, time off from the daily grind to pull it together, find a new place and sublet the apartment I can't afford to keep by myself."

"Plus, you'd dodged a major bullet not marrying a cheating, dumb-ass rich kid from Monterey."

"Yay, me." It felt good to be held by him. She snuggled in a little closer. When she tipped her head back to glance up at him, he bent close and touched his nose to hers, causing a sweet little shiver to radiate out from that small point of contact.

"You okay?" he asked, blue eyes narrowed with concern.

"I am," she replied, resting her head on his shoulder. "I threw some clothes in a bag and went to the farm, where my dad was still wandering around like a ghost of himself. But at least he hugged me and said he loved me and he was glad I hadn't married the wrong man. He wanted me to come with him for Christmas with my mom's side of the family, but I wasn't up for it. After Dad left, it got really lonely at the farm, so I started back to Portland—and the rest, you know."

"Luckily for me, you ended up here in time to save my sorry ass from my own hopeless pigheadedness."

"You're welcome." She eased free of his hold to bring a knee up on the sofa cushion and turn toward him. "And at least I've learned something from the disaster that was James."

"What's that?"

"For the next five years, minimum, the only relationships I'm having are the casual kind."

He scratched his chin, pretending to think deeply about what she'd just said. "I don't know, Sabra. Isn't that what you promised yourself after things went south with Stan? You seem to be kind of a sucker for a marriage proposal."

She was tempted to fake outrage. But really, why

bother? He was absolutely right on both counts. "Yeah, I do have that teensy problem of being monogamous to the core." A sad little laugh escaped her. "It's bred in the bone with me, I guess."

"Why's that?"

"My parents fell in love when they were kids—and their dedication to each other? Absolute. I just want what they had, but so far it's not happening." Matthias was watching her with a kind of musing expression. And she felt...bold. And maybe a little bit giddy. She took it further. "I'm probably never trying love again. And I'm incapable of having casual sex with men I don't know. That means I'm doomed to spend my life only having sex with myself—and I know, I know. TMI in a big way." Matthias chuckled. It was a rough sound, that chuckle. And very attractive. She felt strangely proud every time she made him laugh. "And now that I've totally overshared the story of my pitiful love life, you sure you don't want to do a little sharing, too?"

He grunted. "Do I look like the sharing type to you?"

She didn't back down. "Yeah. You do. Talk to me about the things you said in your sleep the other night."

He went straight to tough-guy denial. "No idea what you're talking about."

"The name Nelson doesn't even ring a bell?"

"Who?" he sneered—but in a teasing kind of way that seemed to give her permission to keep pushing.

Sabra pushed. "So...you don't want to talk about Mark or Finn, either, or the woman you mentioned. Christy, I think her name was..."

He squinted at her, as though he was trying to see inside her head. "You really want to hear this crap?"

"I'm sure it's *not* crap. And yes, I really do."

"All right, then." And just like that, he gave it up. "Christy was my high school sweetheart. We were still together after a couple of years of community college. I was messing up all over the place back then, drinking, exploring the effects of a number of recreational drugs and playing video games instead of taking care of business. My issues had issues, I guess you could say. But at least I knew Christy was the love of my life."

"That's sweet."

He snorted derisively. "Wait for the rest of it. At twenty, after squeaking through my sophomore year with a C-minus average, my older brother Daniel gave me a good talking-to—a few blows were thrown. But he did get through to me. I decided to enlist, to serve my country and get my act together.

"Before I left for boot camp, I proposed and Christy said yes. We agreed to a two-year engagement so that she could finish college before the wedding. A year later, while I was overseas, she Dear Johned me via email and then married the guy she'd been cheating on me with."

"Oh, dear God, Matthias. That's bad."

"What happened with Christy was by no means the worst of it." His eyes were flat now, far away.

She felt terrible for him and almost let him off the hook. But he fascinated her. She wanted to know his story, to understand what had shaped the man he was now.

"Nelson and Mark were good men," he continued

in a monotone. "We served together in the Middle East. They didn't make it home. I got discharged due to injury. I was a mess. There were surgeries and lots of therapy—both kinds, physical and for my screwed-up head. Finn was my brother."

"Was?" she asked in a small voice, stunned by this litany of tragedy.

"It's possible he's still alive. He disappeared when he was only eight. That was my fault. I was six years older and I was supposed to be watching him. We still have investigators looking for him."

"I'm so sorry," she said, aching for him and for those he'd lost. "I really don't know what to say…"

"Don't worry about it. Can we talk about something else now, you think?"

"Absolutely."

And just like that, he shook it off and teased her, "I guess, with you being incapable of casual sex, I don't have to wonder if you took advantage of me that first night when I was at my weakest."

She followed his lead and teased him right back. "Don't look so hopeful."

"Damn. It was only a dream, then?"

"All right, I admit it." She fluttered her eyelashes madly. "For you, I have made a monogamy exception. You loved it—actually, it was good for both of us."

"I kind of figured it would be." He said that with way more sincerity than the joking moment called for.

And all of a sudden, the warm, candlelit cabin was charged with a whole new kind of heat.

Okay, yeah. The guy was super hot in his big, buff, ex-military kind of way. Plus, they'd forged a sort of instant intimacy, two strangers alone in the middle of the woods.

But getting into anything *really* intimate with him would be a bad idea. After all, she'd just gotten messed over by her second fiancé.

Having sex with Matthias would only be asking for trouble.

Wouldn't it?

Or would it be wonderful? Passionate and sweet and magical. And right.

Chemistry-wise, he really did it for her—at least, as far as she could tell without even having kissed him yet.

Why should she run from that, from the possibility of that? Maybe they could have something beautiful.

Something for right now. Just between the two of them.

Maybe, for the first time, she, Sabra Bond, could actually have a fling. That would be progress for someone like her.

They stared at each other in the flickering candlelight.

Was he just possibly thinking the same thing she was?

Sex.

Matt was definitely thinking about sex. About how much he wanted it. With the woman sitting next to him. "Sabra."

Her big eyes got bigger. "Um, yeah?"

"Whatever I say now is just going to sound like so much bull—"

She whipped up a hand. "No. No, it's not. I get you,

Matthias. I do. I think, you and me, we're on the same page about this whole relationship thing. It hasn't even been a full week since I almost married a man who'd failed to tell me he had a child. I'm not ready for anything serious, not in the least. I need about a decade to figure myself out first."

"Yeah. I get that." He gave it to her straight out. "I'm not ready, either."

"But I, well, I *have* been thinking about it," she confessed. "About the two of us, here, alone. Like strangers. And yet somehow, at the same time, not strangers at all."

Were they moving too far, too fast? Yeah, probably.

He tried to lighten things up a little. "It's all the excitement and glamour, right? I mean, I know we're having a wild old time here, playing board games, sitting out on the porch watching the snow melt."

She laughed. He really liked her laugh, all husky and musical at once. But then she answered with complete sincerity. "I'm having the best time. I really am."

And what could he do but reply honestly, in kind? "Me, too." He wanted to kiss her. What man wouldn't? And as their hours together drifted by, it kept getting harder to remember why kissing her wouldn't be wise.

She got up and went back to her chair. He wanted to reach out, catch her hand, beg her to stay there on the sofa beside him. But he had no right to do any such thing.

She settled in across the coffee table, gathering her knees up against her chest, resting her pretty chin on them. "I have a proposition for you."

His heart rate picked up. "Hit me with it."

"What if we both agreed that this, right now, in this

cabin at Christmas, just you and me—this is it? This is all. When it's over and we go our separate ways, that's the last we'll ever see of each other."

He felt regret, that it was going nowhere between the two of them—regret and relief in equal measure. A man needed to be realistic about what he was capable of. And what he wasn't. As for Sabra, well, she'd just gotten free of one romantic mess. A new one was the last thing she needed. "You're saying we won't be exchanging numbers?"

"That's right. No details about how to get in touch later. And no looking each other up on social media, no trying to track each other down."

"We say goodbye and walk away."

"Yes." She sat a little straighter in the chair. "What do you think?"

He stuck out his hand across the coffee table. She shifted, tucking her legs to the side, leaning forward in the chair and then reaching out to meet him.

"Deal," he said as he wrapped his fingers around hers.

Chapter Five

The second Matt released her hand, the power popped back on.

The lights flickered, and then steadied. The tree came alive, blazing bright.

"You think it'll go out again?" she asked in a whisper.

"Hell if I know." He shifted his bad leg back onto the sofa, stretching it out as before.

They sat there, waiting, for a good count of twenty. When the lights stayed on, she bent forward to blow out the candle between them.

"Leave it for a little while, just in case," he suggested.

"Sure." She gazed across the coffee table at him—and started backing off the plan. "I, well, I just realized…" Her cheeks were bright red. She was absolutely adorable.

"Realized what?" he asked, keeping his expression serious, though inside he was grinning. Yeah, he wanted to do her ten ways to Sunday.

But if it never happened, he would still have so much—the memory of her smile, the clever bite of her sharp words. The way she only got calmer when things got scary. And how, even after he'd introduced himself by threatening her with a rifle, she'd stepped right up to do what needed doing, not only patching him up, but also taking good care of him while he was out of it.

No matter how it all turned out, this was a Christmas he wouldn't forget. Even if he never so much as kissed her, he felt a definite connection to her and he was one of those guys who didn't make connections easily.

She did some throat clearing. "It just occurred to me…"

"Yeah?"

"I don't have condoms. I'm going to take a wild guess and say you don't, either."

Wrong. Last summer he'd let Jerry Davidson, a lifelong friend, fellow game warden and self-styled player, use the cabin as a romantic getaway. Jerry had left a box of them upstairs.

"Are you getting cold feet?" he asked gently.

She scowled. "Matthias, just tell me. Do you have condoms or not?"

"I do, yeah. Upstairs in the dresser, top drawer on the right."

She blinked. "Oh. Well, okay, then—and what about your leg?"

He gave a shrug. "It could cramp my style a little, I have to admit."

"Do you want, um, to back out, then?"

He grinned. She did that to him, made him grin. Made him see the world as a better place. Made him feel comfortable in his own skin, somehow. "Not a chance."

She answered his grin with one of her own. "Then you're only saying that we should be careful, take it slow?"

"Yeah. Slow. Slow is good." He gestured at his stretched-out leg. "Slow also happens to be just about all I can manage at this point."

She leaned in a little closer. "You think you could make it up the stairs?"

"Baby, I know I could."

Her grin turned to a soft little smile. "Slowly, right?"

"That's right."

All of a sudden, she was a ball of nervous energy. She shot out of the chair. "How about some hot chocolate?"

"Sounds good." He started to get up.

"No. You stay right there. I'll get it." And she bolted for the kitchen area, where she began rattling pans. He considered following her over there for no other reason than that he liked being near her—plus, he wanted to be sure she wasn't suddenly freaking out over the plans they'd just made.

But maybe she needed a few minutes to herself. Maybe she was going to tell him that, on second thought, getting into bed with him was a bad idea.

Well, if she'd changed her mind, she would say so.

No need to go looking for disappointment. If it was coming, it would find him soon enough.

He picked up his phone and got the music started again, choosing slower songs this time, Christmas ballads and easy-listening jazz.

When she returned with two mugs, she set one in front of her chair and then edged around the coffee table to put his down where he could reach it comfortably. "Here you go."

"Thanks." Before she could retreat to the other side of the table, he caught her arm in an easily breakable grip.

Her eyes widened and her mouth looked so soft and full. He couldn't wait to kiss her. "I gave you marshmallows," she said softly, like it was their secret that no one else could know.

"I love marshmallows."

"Excellent," she replied in a breathless whisper.

He exerted a gentle pressure on her arm, pulling her down a little closer, so he could smell the clean sweetness of her skin, feel the warmth of her, imagine the beauty hidden under his baggy sweatshirt and track pants.

She didn't resist him, though she gulped hard and her breathing had grown erratic. Another quivery little smile pulled at the corners of her mouth.

One more tug was all it took. Those soft lips touched his. She sighed. The sound flowed through him. It was a happy sort of sound, warm.

Welcoming, even.

He smiled against her lips, letting go of her arm as he claimed her mouth, being careful to give her every opportunity to pull away or call a halt.

She did neither.

And he went on kissing her, keeping it light and tentative at first, brushing his lips across hers. He caught her pillowy lower lip between his teeth, biting down just enough to make her give him a little moan as he eased his fingers up over the slim curve of her shoulder.

Taking hold of her thick braid, he wrapped it around his hand, a rope of silk. She hummed into his mouth, her lips softening, giving to him, letting him in to explore the smooth, wet surfaces beyond her parted lips.

"Sabra," he whispered.

She murmured his name, "Matthias," in return.

He liked that, the way she always used his full name. Other people rarely did.

Slowly, he let the wrapped braid uncoil. That freed his hand to slip under it and clasp her nape. Her skin was warm satin, so smooth against his roughened palm. He ran his thumb and forefinger down the sides of her neck, relishing the feel of her. The fine hairs at her nape brushed at him, tickling a little in a way that both aroused him and made him smile.

He needed her closer.

Exerting gentle pressure with his hand on her nape, he guided her down to sit across his thighs.

She broke the kiss to ask, "Your leg?"

"It's fine." He caught her mouth again. She opened with a yearning little moan.

The kiss continued as he clasped her braid once more and ran his hand slowly down it. He tugged the elastic free, tossed it in the general direction of the coffee table, and then set about working his fingers through the long strands until they fell loose down her back and across her shoulders. The dark waves felt good between his fingers. They clung to his hand as he continued to kiss her slowly and thoroughly.

Letting her know that there was no rush.

That it was just the two of them, alone, together, for at least the next couple of days.

Plenty of time to explore each other, *know* each other in the best sort of way.

She pulled back, the black fans of her eyelashes lifting slowly. Her pupils had widened. She looked dazed. He probably did, too.

He leaned in to take her mouth again, a quick, hard kiss. "I can't wait to get my clothes off you."

She laughed—and then whispered, "We get to *unwrap* each other."

"Exactly."

"We are each other's Christmas present."

He pressed his forehead to hers as he ran the backs of his fingers up and down the side of her throat. "Best. Present. Ever."

She caught his jaw and held his gaze. "I love your eyes. They are the deepest, truest blue—kiss me again."

He did. She opened for him instantly and he took what she offered him, tasting her deeply, running his hands up and down her slim back, gathering her closer, so he could feel her breasts, their softness pressing against his chest.

That time, when she lifted her mouth from his, she got up. He didn't try to stop her. The whole point was not to rush.

She went and sat across the coffee table. "Drink your cocoa while it's still hot."

* * *

An hour later, the lights were still on.

He turned off the music. She blew out the candles and unplugged the tree. He grabbed the pillow she'd brought down for him that first night and followed her up the stairs.

Halfway up, she paused and glanced back at him over her shoulder. "You doing all right?"

His leg? He'd forgotten all about it. He had more important things on his mind. "Yeah. I'm good."

She gave him a little nod and they continued on up into the loft. Through the single window, the full moon was visible, a ghostly silver disc obscured by a thin curtain of clouds.

At the bed, she flipped on one of the lamps. He passed her his pillow. She set it next to hers and turned back the blankets. He went to the dresser for the box of condoms, taking out a few, carrying them back to the far side of the bed, setting them on the nightstand.

Though she'd teased him about unwrapping each other, they didn't linger over getting their clothes off, but got right after it, tossing track pants and sweat-shirts in a pile on a chair.

She was so damn pretty, slim and tight and strong, her dark hair in loose, messy curls on her shoulders.

He reached for her. She came into his arms and she fit there just right, her skin so smooth, her eyes wide and hopeful, fluttering shut as he lowered his mouth to hers.

She tasted of hope—the kind of hope he rarely allowed himself anymore, hope for a future that included more than himself, alone, getting by. She made him feel close to her, intimate in the deepest way.

Even if it was only for right now.

Those quick, clever hands of hers caressed him, gliding up his chest, exploring, her fingers pausing to stroke their way out along his shoulders and then back in to link around his neck. "So good to kiss you," she whispered against his mouth.

"The best," he agreed. He wanted to taste every inch of her and now was his chance.

Working his way downward, he dropped nipping kisses in a trail along the side of her neck, and then in a looping pattern across her upper chest.

She murmured encouragements, her hands first cradling his face and then slipping up into his hair.

Her breasts were so beautiful, small and high, full on the underside, the nipples already hard. He tasted them, drawing them in deep as she grasped his hair tighter, holding him there, at her heart.

But there was so much more woman he needed to kiss. He kept moving, kissing on downward, dropping to his knees, not giving a damn if he split a stitch or two.

"You okay?" she asked, her head bent down to him, her hair brushing the side of his face.

"Never better." He kissed her smooth, pretty belly and then dropped more kisses around to the side of her, where he nipped at the sweetly curved bones beneath the silky flesh, feeling lost in the best kind of way—lost to the taste and smell of her.

She must have been lost, as well. Dropping her head back, she moaned at the shadowed rafters above.

"So pretty." He blew a teasing breath into the neatly trimmed sable hair at her mound, bringing his hands up to pet her a little.

"Oh!" she said. "Oh, my!" And she giggled, reaching for him, cradling his face again. She was swaying on her feet.

He caught her by the side of her hip to steady her. She felt so good, he couldn't resist sliding his hand around her, getting a big handful of her smooth round backside.

She looked down at him then, her eyes deep and dark, beckoning him. Their gazes locked. "Kiss me," she whispered. "Right there."

And he did, using his tongue, his teeth, everything, then bringing his eager hands back to the center of her, parting her for his mouth.

Already, she was slick and wet. He made her more so, darting his tongue in, licking her, then holding her still, spreading her wider with his fingers, so he could get in close and tight.

By then, she was whimpering, muttering excited encouragements. "Yes!" and "Please!" and "That! More. Oh, that…"

He gave her what she asked for, staying with her all the way, using his fingers to stroke into her. Using his tongue, too, until she went over with a low, keening cry.

He could have stayed right there on his knees forever, touching her, kissing her, petting her, whispering dark promises of all he would do to her.

But then, with a happy sigh, she dropped back away from him onto the bed, her slim arms spread wide.

"I think I just died." She lifted her head and watched him as he braced his hands on either side of her fine thighs. "Your stitches!" she cried, that mouth he couldn't wait to kiss again forming a worried frown as he pushed himself upright.

"My stitches are just fine," he promised. "It's my knees that are shaking."

She reached up slim arms as he rose above her. "Come down here. Please. I need you close."

He went down, falling across the bed with her, catching himself on his forearms in order not to crush her completely. "I'm right here."

"And I am so glad." She touched him, learning him, her palms smoothing over his back, his shoulders, along his arms. Her fingers lingered on the ridges of scar tissue that marred his chest, neck and arms. She didn't remark on them, though.

He appreciated that.

There was nothing to say about them. He was one of the lucky ones. He'd come back from the Middle East damaged, battered—but all in one piece, after all.

He dipped close to capture her mouth again as her quick hand eased between them and encircled his hardness. When she did that, he couldn't hold back a groan.

Tightening her grip on him, she gave a little tug, bringing another rough sound from him as she pushed him onto his back and rose above him. Curving down over him, she claimed him with her mouth.

Lightning flashed along his nerve endings and the blood pumped hot and fast through his veins. She drove him just to the edge and then slacked off to tease and flick him with her tongue as she continued to work him over with those talented hands—both hands, together.

Somehow, he lasted for several minutes of that glorious torture.

But there did come a point where he had to stop her. Catching hold of her wrist, tipping up her chin with the other hand, he warned in a growl, "I'm about to go over."

She grinned, a saucy little grin. "Please do."

"Not till I'm inside you."

"But I like it. I want you to—"

"Come up here." He took her under the arms and pulled her up on top of him, so they were face-to-face, her long legs folded on either side of his body. "You are so beautiful." And then he speared his fingers into her hair, pulling it maybe a little harder than he should have. But she didn't complain.

Not Sabra. She only gave a sweet little moan and opened for his kiss.

Those idiots who'd left her?

What the hell was the matter with those two?

If she was his, he would keep her forever, keep her happy, keep her satisfied. He would never be the chump who let her go.

But she *wasn't* his.

And he needed to remember that.

Remember that neither of them was ready for anything life changing, and that was all right.

They had tonight, the next day, maybe a few days after that. They had this Christmastime with just the two of them, Sabra and Matthias, alone in his cabin in the forest.

He went on kissing her, deep and hard and endlessly, reaching out a hand for the night table and a condom. With a groan, she broke their kiss and gazed down at him through wide, wondering eyes as she lifted her slim body away from him enough for him to deal with the business of protection.

"I'll stay on top." She bent close again and scraped his scruffy jaw with her teeth. He breathed in the scent of her, so sweet, musky now. "Okay?" she asked.

"Best offer I've had in years." He groaned as she wrapped her hand around him and guided him into place. "Look at me," he whispered, as he slipped an inch inside.

She met his eyes, held them, and lowered slowly down. "Yes. Oh, yes..."

It hurt so good, her body all around him, wet and hot and so damn tight. "Sabra."

"Yes..."

She let out a sharp, pleasured cry as she took him all the way.

There was a moment of complete stillness between them. They waited, breath held. And then she moaned. She curved her body over him, her hair falling forward to caress his cheek and rub against his neck.

Then they were moving together. He pushed up into her, matching her rhythm as she picked up speed.

The way she rode him? Nothing like it. Sweet and slow and long.

Hard and fast and mercilessly. He could go forever, be with her forever, lost inside her sweetness.

Held.

Known.

Cherished.

He wanted it to last and last. Was that really so much to ask?

She seemed to understand his wish, to want it, too.

For a while, they played with each other, slowing when one of them got too close to the edge, then getting swept up in the hungry glory of it all over again, going frantic and fast. She rode him so hard. He would never get enough of her, of being inside her.

Too bad they really couldn't hold out indefinitely.

He felt her climax take her, the walls of her sex clutching around him. He gritted his teeth, clasping the fine, firm curves of her hips, holding on more tightly than he should have, trying to outlast her.

By some miracle he managed it, lived through the wonder of her pulsing hard and fast around him.

When she collapsed on his chest with a sigh of happy surrender, he let go, let his finish roll through him—burning, breathtaking, overpowering. He gave himself up to it with a triumphant shout.

The snow started to melt the next day.

Sabra wished it would freeze again and stay that way. She fantasized about being stuck in the cabin forever, just her and Matthias in a world all their own.

But the snow kept melting. By the twenty-eighth, there was nothing left of it beyond a few dirty patches dotting the clearing and the dirt road leading out. Matthias drove her to the fish hatchery, where she got in her little blue Subaru Outback and followed him back to the cabin.

They stayed on.

To sit on the porch as the night fell, to wander into the forest hand in hand, laughing together under the tall trees, sharing stories of their families, of their lives up till now.

They spent a lot of time naked upstairs in the bed

under the eaves. And downstairs, on the couch, in the big brown chair, wherever and whenever the mood struck—which was often.

And every time was better than the time before.

On New Year's Eve, they didn't bother to get dressed the whole day. They made love and napped all wrapped up together and toasted in the New Year with whiskey from a dusty bottle Matthias pulled from the back of a cupboard.

And then, all of a sudden, totally out of nowhere, it was New Year's Day.

She didn't want to go.

But that was the thing. She *had* to go. She had her life to cobble back together. She had her promise to herself, to *get* a life, a full and happy life, on her own.

And they had a deal. It was a good deal. Christmas together.

And nothing more.

He helped her carry her stuff to her Outback. It only took one trip. And then he held her in his arms and kissed her, a kiss so right and so consuming, she had no idea how she was going to make herself get in the car and drive away.

He cradled her face in those big, wonderful hands and his blue eyes held hers. "God. I don't want to say goodbye."

Her eyes burned with tears she wouldn't let fall. "Me neither." It came out in a ragged whisper because her throat had clutched with sadness and yearning for what would never be. She lifted up and brushed her lips to his once more, breathing in the evergreen scent of him. *I will never forget*, she promised in her heart. Overhead, a bird cried, a long, keening sound. "Goodbye, Matthias."

"Wait." He pulled something from his jacket pocket. "Give me your hand."

She held it out. He took it, turned it palm up and set a key there, then gently folded her fingers over the cool metal. She looked up at him, confused, searching his face that she'd already come to love—just a little. "What's this?"

"A key to the cabin."

"But—"

He stopped her with a finger against her lips. "So here's my offer. I work flexible hours, fill in for everyone else all year long. Except at Christmas, when they give me first crack at the schedule. I'll be right here, same time, next year, from the twenty-third till New Year's Day. Alone. If you maybe find that you wouldn't mind spending another Christmas with me, just the two of us, just for Christmastime, well then, you have the key."

"Matthias, I—"

"Uh-uh." He brushed his thumb across her mouth. She felt that slight touch all the way down to the core of her. His eyes were oceans she wanted to drown in, an endless sky in which she longed to take flight. "Don't decide now. A lot can happen in a year."

She threw her arms around him and buried her face against his shoulder. "I miss you already."

He said her name, low. Rough. They held each other hard and tight.

And then, by silent mutual agreement, they both let go and staggered back from each other. She stuck the key in her pocket to join the wooden porcupine he'd given her.

He pulled open her door for her and shut it once she was behind the wheel, tapping the door in a final salute.

She watched him turn and go up the steps.

That was as much as she could take of him walking away. She started the engine, put it in Drive and headed for Portland.

Chapter Six

Matt, the following June...

It was Friday night at Beach Street Brews in Valentine Bay. The music was too loud and the acoustics were terrible. The barnlike brew pub was wall-to-wall bodies, everybody laughing, shouting, meeting up, partying down.

Matt nursed a beer and wished he hadn't come.

Jerry Davidson, his friend since first grade, pulled out the chair next to him and dropped into it. "C'mon!" Jerry shouted in Matt's ear. "I met a girl. She's at the bar. And she's got a good-looking friend."

Matt raised his mug and took another sip. "Have fun."

The band crashed through the final bars of Kongos' "Come with Me Now." The applause was thunderous. "We'll be back," growled the front man into the mic.

When the clapping faded down, Matt enjoyed the relative silence.

Until Jerry leaned close and started talking again. "It's that girl, isn't it? The one from the cabin? You're thinking about her, aren't you?"

He was, yeah. But no way was he getting into that with Jerry. He never should have told his friend about Sabra. Sabra was *his*. A perfect memory to treasure. He didn't have a whole hell of a lot of those and Jerry needed to quit telling him to move on.

"Leave it alone," Matt said. "I told you. It's not going anywhere. It was great and now it's over." *Unless she shows up again at Christmas.*

God. He hoped she would.

But too much could happen in the space of a year. Sabra was hot and smart, kind and funny and easy to talk to. In spite of her vow to stay single for years, by Christmas, some lucky bastard would coax her into giving love another try. Matt hated that guy with a pure, cold fury. Whoever the hell he might turn out to be.

At least once a week he almost convinced himself it would be okay to look her up online. He never did it, though. And he *wouldn't* do it. They had an agreement and he would keep the promise he'd made to her.

Jerry clapped him on the shoulder. "You need to relax and have a good time."

"Jer. How many years you been giving me that advice?"

"Hmm." Jerry stroked his short, thick ginger beard. "Several."

"Do I ever listen?"

"Before last Christmas, you used to. Now and then."

"I'm not in the mood." Matt tipped his head toward the bar. "And a pretty woman is waiting on you."

Jerry glanced up to give his latest conquest a quick wave. "You're insane not to come with me."

"Go."

Jerry gave it up and headed back to the bar.

Matt nursed his beer and wished it was Christmas.

Sabra, that September...

"More wine?" Iris held up the excellent bottle of Oregon pinot noir. At Sabra's nod, her friend refilled her glass.

It was girl's night in at Iris and Peyton's apartment in downtown Portland—just the three of them. Sabra could safely afford to indulge in the wine. Back in January, she'd rented a one-bedroom in this same building, so home was two flights of stairs or a very short elevator ride away.

Peyton, her caramel-colored hair piled in a messy bun on the top of her head, turned from the stir-fry she was cooking and asked Sabra, "So can I tell him to give you a call?"

"He's a hottie." Iris did a little cha-cha-cha with her shoulders, her hair, which she wore in natural corkscrew curls, bouncing in time with the movement. "And no drama, which we all love."

He was Jack Kellan, the new sous chef at Delia Mae's, where they all worked.

"Jack is a great guy," Sabra said, thinking of Matthias as she did every time her friends got after her to get out and mix it up—and no, she hadn't told anyone about what had happened at Christmas. It was her secret pleasure, having known him, everything they'd shared. Often, she found herself wondering where he was and what he might be doing right now.

But no, she wasn't getting attached, wasn't pining for her Christmas lover. Uh-uh. No way.

Iris scoffed. "Could you *be* any less enthusiastic?" Iris had that Tyra-Banks-meets-Wendy-Williams thing going on. All power, smarts and sass. Nobody messed with Iris. "This swearing-off-men thing? Sabra, honey, it's not a good look on you."

Totally out of nowhere, emotion made her eyes burn and her throat clutch. "I'm just not ready yet, you know?"

Iris set down the bottle of pinot and peered at her more closely across the kitchen island. "Something's really got you bothered. What?"

"Come on, now." Peyton turned off the heat under the stir-fry and she and Iris converged on either side of Sabra. "You'll feel better if you talk about it."

"Is it your dad?" Iris ventured gently.

Sabra drooped on her stool as her friends shared a knowing look.

"It's her dad," confirmed Peyton.

Sabra had been up to the farm a few days before. As usual, she'd come home earlier than planned. "He's just worse every time I see him. He's thinner, more withdrawn than ever. I want to be there for him, but he won't talk about it, about Mom. It's like there's a brick wall between him and the rest of the world. Nobody gets in, not even me."

"Oh, honey…" Iris grabbed her in a hug and Peyton wrapped her arms around both of them.

Sabra leaned her head on Iris's shoulder. "I keep telling myself he'll get better. But the years keep going by and he only seems sadder and further away, like he's slowly fading down to nothing. It scares me, it does. And I don't know what to do about it."

Her friends rubbed her back and hugged her some more. They offered a number of suggestions and Sabra thanked them and promised to try to get her dad to maybe join a men's group or see a therapist. They all agreed that Adam Bond had been a prisoner of his grief for much too long.

There was more wine and Peyton's delicious stir-fry. Iris talked about the guy she'd just broken up with and Peyton was all dewy-eyed over the new man in her life. By midnight, Sabra was feeling the wine. She looked from one dear friend's face to the other—and she just couldn't hold back any longer.

"Ahem. There is something else I keep meaning to tell you guys…"

"Hmm," said Peyton thoughtfully. She and Iris exchanged yet another speaking glance.

Iris nodded. "We knew it."

"Spill," commanded Peyton.

Sabra set down her empty glass. "It's like this. Last Christmas, when I was supposedly snowed in at the farm?"

"Supposedly?" Iris scowled. "Meaning you weren't?"

Sabra busted to it. "I wasn't at the farm and I wasn't alone."

"A man," said Peyton. It wasn't a question.

"That's right. I stopped off on the way back here to Portland for a hike—you know, trying to get out of my own head a little. I started walking and it started raining. I took shelter at this empty cabin. And then the owner arrived..."

They listened without interrupting as she told them about Matthias, about her Christmas at the cabin, about pretty much all of it, including how he'd given her a key as she was leaving, just in case she might want to spend another Christmas with him.

Iris screeched in delight and Peyton declared, "Now, that's what I'm talking about. James the jerk? He couldn't keep you down. He goes back to the baby mama he'd forgotten to mention and what do you do? Head out for some hot, sexy times with a hermit in the forest."

Sabra whacked her friend lightly with the back of her hand. "Matthias is not a hermit. He has a real job and a big family in Valentine Bay."

"He just hides out alone in an isolated cabin for Christmas," teased her friend.

"Not last Christmas, he didn't," Sabra said smugly. Her friends high-fived her for that and she added more seriously, "He's had some rough times in his life and he likes to get off by himself now and then, that's all."

Peyton scolded, "You took way too long to tell us, you know. It's been months and months. It's almost the holidays all over again."

"Yeah, well. Sorry. But I wasn't going to tell *any-one*, ever. Overall, it was a beautiful time, the *best* time. And after I got back to Portland, well, I kind of thought of it as our secret, Matthias's and mine."

"We get it," said Iris.

"But we're still glad you finally told us," Peyton chimed in.

Iris nodded. "It's a yummy story, you and the cabin guy."

Peyton was watching Sabra a little too closely. "Look at me," she commanded. When Sabra met her gaze, Peyton shook her head. "I knew it. You're in love with him, aren't you?"

No way. "Nope. Not a chance. I'm immune to love now, not going there again."

"Of course you will go there again," argued Iris.

"Well, if I do, it won't be for years. And anyway, how could I possibly be in love with him? I knew him for ten days."

"You should just call him," Iris advised.

"I told you. I don't have his number and I'm not tracking him down online because getting in touch wasn't part of the deal—and yeah, I still have the key to the cabin. But that doesn't mean I'll be meeting him in December."

Her friends didn't argue with her, but she saw the speaking glance that passed between them.

Matt, December 1...

The three-legged Siberian husky Matt had named Zoya followed him into his bedroom.

He'd found her hobbling along the highway on his way home from Warrenton, four months ago now. No collar, no tags. He'd coaxed her to come to him and, after some hesitation, she did, so he'd driven her to the shelter here in Valentine Bay. They'd checked for an ID chip. She didn't have one.

Two weeks later, he stopped by the shelter to see if her former owner had come for her.

Hadn't happened. No one had adopted her, either.

The vet who helped out at the shelter said the husky was just full-grown, two or three years old and in excellent health. Her left front leg had been amputated, probably while she was still a puppy. She was well trained, happy natured and responded to all the basic commands.

Matt had done some research and then had a long talk with the vet about caring for a tripod dog. By then, he was pretty much all in on Zoya.

He brought her home. It was a little like having a kid, a well-behaved kid who wanted to please. He took her to doggy day care every workday, where she got lots of attention and pack time with other dogs.

Him. With a dog.

Matt wasn't sure what exactly had gotten into him to take her. But when she looked at him with those unearthly blue eyes, well, he could relate, that was all. She needed a human of her own. And he'd been available. Plus, it was time he stepped up, made a commitment to another creature even if he wasn't ready to give love with a woman any kind of a chance.

His four sisters all adored her. He'd taken her to a couple of family gatherings. The first time he showed up with Zoya, the oldest of his sisters, Aislinn, had pulled him aside...

"I have to ask." Aislinn gazed at him piercingly. "A *Siberian* husky?"

He understood her implication. "Yeah, well. I probably would have adopted her anyway, but it seemed more than right, you know? I only have to hear the word *Siberian* and I think of Finn. It's good to be reminded, to never forget."

Ais's dark eyes welled with moisture. "Nobody blames you."

"I know. But I do blame myself because I am culpable. If I'd behaved differently that day, Finn might be here with us now."

"Mom blamed *herself*."

"Yeah, well, there's plenty of blame to go around."

"Matt. Mom gave you permission to go off on your own—and then she told Finn that it was fine if he went with you."

"It is what it is, that's all. Now, stop looking so sad and let's hug it out."

With a cry, Ais threw herself at him. He wrapped his arms around her and held on tight, feeling grateful.

For his family, who had never given up on him no matter how messed up he got. For Zoya, who seemed more than happy to have him as her human.

And also for Sabra Bond, who had managed to show him in the short ten days he'd spent with her that maybe someday he might be capable of making a good life with the right woman, of starting a family of his own.

"How 'bout a walk, girl?"

Zoya gave an eager little whine and dropped to her haunches.

Matt crouched to give her a good scratch around the ruff. "All right, then. Let me get changed and we're on it."

He took off his uniform, pausing when he stepped

out of his pants for a look at the crescent-shaped scar from that little run-in with his own ax last Christmas. It was no more than a thin, curved line now. Sabra had patched him up good as new. The older scar on his other leg was much worse, with explosions of white scar tissue and a trench-like indentation in the flesh along the inside of his shin. There were pins and bolts in there holding everything together. He'd almost lost that leg below the knee.

But almost only counts in horseshoes. And now, that leg worked fine, except for some occasional stiffness and intermittent pain, especially in cold weather when it could ache like a sonofagun.

In his socks and boxer briefs, he grabbed a red Sharpie from a cup on the dresser and went to the closet. Sticking the Sharpie between his teeth to free both hands, he hung up his uniform. Once that was done, he shoved everything to the side, the hangers rattling as they slid along the rod.

The calendar was waiting, tacked to the wall. It was a large, themed calendar he'd found at Freddy's—Wild and Scenic Oregon. He'd bought it for what could only be called sentimental reasons. Bought it because he couldn't stop thinking of Sabra.

Sappy or not, marking off the days till Christmas had made him feel closer to a woman he hadn't seen in months, a woman he'd actually known for one week and three days.

For November, the calendar offered a spectacular photo of the Three Sisters, a trio of volcanic peaks in Oregon's section of the Cascade Range. Below the Three Sisters, he'd x-ed out each of November's days in red.

Lifting the calendar off the tack, he turned it to December and a picture of Fort Clatsop in the snow. He hooked it back in place and pulled the top off the Sharpie. With a lot more satisfaction than the simple action should have inspired, he x-ed off December 1.

Already, there was a big red circle around the ten days from December 23 to New Year's.

Satisfaction turned to real excitement.

Only twenty-one days to go.

December 23, three years ago...

It was late afternoon when Matt turned onto the dirt road that would take him to the cabin.

He had a fine-looking tree roped to the roof rack and the back seat packed with food, Christmas presents, and the usual duffel bags of clothes and gear. The weather was milder this year, real Western Oregon weather—cloudy with a constant threat of rain, no snow in the forecast.

Zoya, in her crate, had the rear of the vehicle. He would have loved having her in the passenger seat next to him, but with only one front leg, a sudden lurch or a fast stop could too easily send her pitching to the floor.

He was nervous, crazy nervous—nervous enough to be embarrassed at himself. The eager drumming of his pulse only got more so as he neared the clearing. He came around the second-to-last turn where he'd seen the lights in the windows the year before, hope rising...

Nothing.

Maybe she was waiting on the front porch.

He took the final turn.

Nobody there.

The nervous jitters fled. Now his whole body felt heavy, weighed down at the center with disappointment, as he pulled to a stop in front of the porch.

She hadn't come—not yet, anyway.

And he really had no right to expect that she would. He'd offered. It was her move.

And maybe she'd simply decided that one Christmas alone with him had been plenty. She was smart and beautiful and so much fun to be with. She'd probably found someone else.

He had to face the likelihood that she wouldn't show.

That she'd moved on.

That he would never see her face again.

He could accept that. He would *have* to accept it, his own crazy longing and the carefully marked calendar in his bedroom closet aside.

Reality was a bitch sometimes and that wasn't news.

He got out, opened the hatch in back, let Zoya out of her crate and helped her down to the ground. "Come on, girl. Let's get everything inside."

An hour later, he had the fire going, the Jeep unpacked, the groceries put away, and Zoya all set with food and water by her open crate. The tree stood proud in the stand by the window, not far from the front door. It was bigger and thicker than last year, filling the cabin with its Christmassy evergreen scent. A box of presents waited beside it. He'd even carried all his gear upstairs.

The disappointment?

Worse by the minute.

But he wasn't going to let it get him down. "Okay, sweetheart," he said to his dog. "I'm going to bring down the decorations and we'll get this party started."

Zoya made a happy sound, followed by a wide yawn. She rolled over and offered her belly to scratch, her pink tongue lolling out the side of her mouth, making her look adorably eager and also slightly demented.

"Goofy girl." He crouched to give her some attention. But before he got all the way down, she rolled back over and sat up, ears perking.

And then he heard the sound he'd been yearning for: tires crunching gravel.

His heart suddenly booming like it would beat its way right out of his chest, he straightened. Out the front windows, he watched as the familiar blue Subaru Outback pulled to a stop.

Chapter Seven

By a supreme effort of will, Matt managed not to race out there, throw open her car door, drag her into his arms, toss her over his shoulder and carry her straight up the stairs.

His tread measured, with Zoya at his heels, he crossed the cabin floor, opened the door and stepped out into the cold, gray afternoon. The dog whined, a worried sort of sound. She liked people, but new ones made her nervous—at first, anyway.

"Sit."

Zoya dropped to her haunches on the porch, still whining, tail twitching.

Sabra. Just the sight of her filled him with more powerful emotions than he knew how to name.

She got out of the car.

Hot damn, she looked amazing in tight jeans, lace-up boots and a big sweater printed with Christmas trees.

"You cut your hair." It came to just below her chin now.

Standing there by her car, looking shy and so damn pretty, she reached up and fiddled with her bangs. Her gorgeous face was flushed, her deep brown eyes even bigger than he remembered. "I don't know. I just wanted a change."

"It looks good on you."

A secret smile flashed across those lips he couldn't wait to taste again. She gave a tiny nod in acknowledgment of the compliment, her gaze shifting to Zoya. "You have a dog?"

Zoya knew when someone was talking about her. She quivered harder and whined hopefully. "More like she has me. I found her on the highway, dropped her off at the animal shelter—and then couldn't stop thinking about her."

Sabra laughed. God, what a beautiful sound. "Can't resist a pretty stray, huh? Such gorgeous blue eyes she's got. What's her name?"

"Zoya."

"I like it. Is it Polish, or…?"

"Russian." He gave a shrug. "She's a Siberian husky. It seemed to fit."

"Is it okay if I introduce myself?"

"Sure."

She clicked her tongue and called the dog.

When Zoya hesitated, he encouraged her. "It's all right, girl. Go." And she went, tail wagging, hopping down the steps to greet the woman Matt couldn't wait to kiss.

He followed the husky down to the ground and gave the woman and the dog a minute to get to know each other. By the time Sabra rose from giving Zoya the attention she craved, he couldn't wait any longer.

He caught her arm, heat zapping through him just to have his hand on her, even with the thick sweater keeping him from getting skin to skin. "Hey."

"Hey."

"I'm really glad to see you." It came out in a low growl.

She giggled, the cutest, happiest little sound. "Prove it."

"Excellent suggestion." He pulled her in close, wrapping both arms around her. And then he kissed her.

Zap. Like an electric charge flashing from her lips to his. Her mouth tasted better than he remembered, which couldn't be possible. Could it? He framed her face with his two hands and kissed her some more.

It wasn't enough. He needed her inside, up the stairs, out of her clothes...

She let out a little cry as he broke the kiss—but only to get one arm beneath her knees. With the other at her back, he scooped her high against his chest.

"I'm taking you inside," he announced.

"Yes," she replied, right before he crashed his mouth down on hers again.

He groaned in pure happiness, breathing in the scent of her, so fresh, with a hint of oranges, probably from her shampoo. Whatever. She smelled amazing. She smelled like everything he'd been longing for, everything he'd feared he would never touch or smell or taste again.

Kissing her as he went, he strode up the steps, across the porch and on inside, pausing only to wait for Zoya to come in after them before kicking the door shut with his foot.

Sabra broke the kiss to look around, her hands clasped behind his neck, fingers stroking his nape like she couldn't get enough of the feel of his skin. "The tree looks so good, even better than last year. And it smells like heaven." She pressed her nose against his throat. "It smells like you…"

"We'll decorate it," he said gruffly when she tipped her head away enough to meet his eyes again. "Later." He nuzzled her cool, velvety cheek, brushed a couple of quick kisses across her lips.

"You're so handsome. So big. So…" She laughed, a carefree sort of sound. "I am *so* glad to see you."

"Likewise, only double that—wait. Make that quintuple."

She stroked a hand at his temple, combing her fingers back into his hair. "I have stuff to bring in."

"Later." Zoya stood on her three legs looking up at them, tipping her head from side to side, not quite sure what the hell was going on. "Stay," he commanded, as he headed for the stairs.

"Your leg seems better."

"Good as new."

"I can walk, you know," she chided.

"Yeah. But I don't know if I can let go of you." He took her mouth again. Desire sparked and sizzled through his veins. Already, he was so hard it hurt.

"I've missed you, too," she whispered into the kiss.

"Not as much as I've missed you." He took the stairs two at a time and carried her straight to the bed, setting her down on it, grabbing the hem of her big sweater. "I like this sweater."

"Thanks."

"Let's get it off you." He pulled it up.

She raised her arms and he took it away, tossing it in the general direction of a nearby chair. She dropped back on her hands. He drank in the sight of her, in her skinny jeans and a lacy red bra, the kind a woman wears when a man might be likely to see it, to take it off her.

"So pretty." He eased his index finger between one silky strap and her skin and rubbed it up and down, from the slight swell of her breast to her shoulder and back again. Happiness filled him, bright and hot, to go with the pleasure-pain of his powerful desire. He bent closer, right over her, planting both fists on the mattress to either side of her. "I have an idea."

Her eyes went wide. "Yeah?"

"Let's get *everything* off you. Let's do that now."

A slow smile was her answer.

He dropped to his knees at her feet and untied her boots, pulling them off and her snowflake-patterned socks right after them. She shoved down her jeans. He dragged them free and tossed them aside.

In her red bra and a lacy little thong to match, she reached for him, pulling him up beside her—and then slipping over the edge of the bed to kneel and get to work on *his* boots.

He helped her, bending down and untying one as she untied the other. They paused only long enough to share a quick, rough kiss and in no time, he was out of his boots and socks. The rest of his clothes followed quickly. He ripped them off as she climbed back on the bed and sat on folded knees.

Resting her long-fingered hands on her smooth thighs, breathing fast, she stared at him through eyes gone black with longing. Reaching behind her, she started to unclasp her bra.

"No." He bent across the bed to still her arms. "Let me do that." *Or not.* He allowed himself a slow smile. "And on second thought, this bra and that thong might be too pretty to take off."

She caught the corner of her mouth with her teeth, her eyes promising him everything as she brought her hands to rest on her thighs again.

He took her by the wrists and tugged. She knelt up. Scooping an arm around her, he hauled her to the edge of the bed and tight against him. "It's been too long," he muttered, dipping his head to kiss that sweet spot where her neck met her shoulder.

The scent of her filled him—oranges, flowers, that beautiful sweetness, the essence of her, going musky now with her arousal.

He kissed her, another deep one, running his tongue over hers, gliding it against the ridges of her pretty teeth.

So many perfect places to put his mouth.

He got to work on that, leaving her lips with some reluctance, but consoling himself with the taste of her skin, licking the clean, gorgeous line of her jaw, moving on down to bite the tight flesh over her collarbone. She moaned when he did that and tried to pull him closer. He resisted. He had plans of his own.

Slowly, he lowered her bra straps with his teeth, using a finger to ease the lacy cups of the bra under her breasts so he could kiss those pretty, puckered nipples. She looked so amazing, with her face flushed, her eyes enormous, pure black, hazy with need, and her breasts overflowing the cups of that red bra.

He backed up again. When she moaned in protest and grabbed for him, he commanded, "Stretch out your legs."

She scooted back to the middle of the bed and stuck her feet out in front of her. "Like this?"

"Just like that." He grabbed her ankles and pulled. With a surprised laugh, she braced her hands behind her as he hauled her to the edge of the bed again.

"Lie back," he instructed as he went to his knees, pushing her smooth thighs apart to get in close and tight.

As he kissed her through the lace of that teeny-tiny thong, she moaned and fisted her fingers in his hair. "Matthias, please!" He glanced up at her sharp cry. "It's been a year. Come up here, right now. Come here to me."

He couldn't argue—didn't want to argue. He needed to be joined with her. He needed that right now.

And the gorgeous, soaking-wet thong? In the way.

He hooked his fingers in at both sides of it, pulled it down and tossed it halfway across the room. She undid the pretty bra and dropped it to the floor as he rose to yank open the bedside drawer. He had the condom out and on in record time.

"Come down here." She grabbed hold of his arm and pulled him on top of her, opening for him, wrapping those strong legs around him. Holding him hard and tight with one arm, she wriggled the other between them, took him in hand and guided him right to where they both wanted him.

"At last," she whispered, pushing her beautiful body up hard against him, wrapping her legs around him even tighter than before.

He was wild for her, too. With a surge of his hips, he was deep inside.

She cried out as he filled her.

"Too fast?" He groaned the words. "Did I hurt you?"

"No way." She grabbed on with both hands, yanking him in even tighter. "Oh, I have missed you."

"Missed you, too," he echoed. "So much…"

And he lost himself in her. There was only Sabra, the feel of her beautiful body around him, taking him deep.

They rolled and she was above him. That was so right, just what he needed—until they were rolling again, sharing a laugh that turned into rough moans as they arrived on their sides, facing each other, her leg thrown across him, pulling him so close. She urged him on with her eager cries.

He didn't want it to end. She pulled him on top again. Somehow, he held out through her first climax, gritting his teeth a little, groaning at the splendid agony of it as she pulsed around him. It was like nothing else, ever—to feel her giving way, giving it up, losing herself in his arms.

When she went limp beneath him, he sank into her, kissing her, stroking her tangled hair, waiting for the moment when she began to move again.

He didn't have to wait long.

Hooking her legs around him once more, she

surged up against him. With a deep groan, he joined her in the rhythm she set as she chased her second finish all the way to the top and over into free fall.

That time, he gave it up, too, driving deep within her as the pleasure rolled through him, rocketing down his spine, opening him up and sending him soaring.

Leaving him breathless, stunned—and deeply happy in a way he couldn't remember ever being before.

By the time Matthias let her out of bed an hour later, Sabra was starving.

Luckily, she'd brought fresh sourdough bread and a variety of sandwich fixings. They carried the food in from the Subaru and she made sandwiches while he unloaded the rest of her things.

Once they'd filled their growling bellies, he put on the Christmas tunes and they decorated the tree—working together this year, which meant the whole process was a whole lot more fun and took half the time it had the year before.

She'd brought ornaments. "You need at least one new ornament every year," she explained.

"I do?" He got that look guys get when women tell them how it ought to be, that *Huh*? kind of look that said women's logic really didn't compute.

"I brought three." She grabbed her pack from its hook on the far side of the door and pulled them out, each in its own small box. "Open them."

He obeyed, taking them from the boxes and hanging them on the tree. They included a porcupine carved from a pinecone, a crystal snowflake—and a blown glass pickle.

"Each has an important sentimental meaning…" She let the words trail off significantly.

He was up for the game. "Let me guess. The porcupine because I gave you one last year. And the snowflake to remind me that being snowed in can be the best time a guy ever had—he just needs to be snowed in with you."

She nodded approvingly. "What about the pickle?"

He turned to study the ornament in question, which he'd hung on a high branch. It was nubby and dark green, dusted with glitter, twinkling in the light. "It's a very handsome pickle, I have to say."

"You're stalling."

"Hmm." He pretended to be deep in thought over the possible significance of a pickle.

She scoffed at him. "You haven't got a clue."

"Wait." He put up a hand. "It's all coming back to me now."

"Yeah, right."

"Didn't I read somewhere that you hide a pickle ornament on the tree and the kid who finds it gets something special? Also, I think I remember hearing that pickle ornaments bring good luck."

"You're actually smirking," she accused.

"Me? No way. I never smirk."

"You knew all along."

He caught her hand and pulled her in close. "Do you think I'll get lucky?" He kissed her. "Never mind. I already have."

"Oh, yeah," she answered softly. "Pickle or no pickle, from now until New Year's, I'm your sure thing."

* * *

Later, they had hot chocolate on the front porch, with Zoya stretched out at their feet and gnawing enthusiastically on a rawhide bone.

Sabra had barely emptied her mug and set it down on the porch beside her chair when Matthias held out his hand to her.

The second she laid her fingers in his, he was pulling her up and out of the chair, over onto his lap.

Things got steamy fast. In no time, she was topless, with her pants undone.

She loved every minute of it, out there in the cold December night, with the hottest man she'd ever met to keep her toasty warm.

The next morning, he snuck down the stairs while she was still drowsing. When she followed the smell of fresh coffee down to the main floor, he didn't say a word until she'd savored that first cup.

"I have a Christmas Eve request," she said over breakfast.

He rose from his chair to bend close and kiss her, a kiss that tasted of coffee and cinnamon rolls and the promise of more kisses to come. "Anything. Name it."

"I want to finish the hike to the falls that I started last year."

He sank back to his chair. "It's rough going. Lots of brush and then several stretches over heavily logged country, where it's nothing but dirt and giant tree stumps, most of them out of the ground, gnarly with huge roots."

She gave him her sweetest smile. "You said 'anything.' And I still want to go."

They set out half an hour later.

Matthias kept Zoya on a leash most of the way. They wound through barren stretches of rough, logged terrain, eventually entering the forest again, where the trail was so completely overgrown, it grew difficult to make out the path.

They bushwhacked their way through it. At one point, Sabra turned to look back for no particular reason—and saw snowcapped Mt. Rainier in the distance. She got out her phone and snapped a picture of it.

They went on to the top of the falls. It wasn't much to look at. The trees grew close and bushy, obscuring the view. They drank from their water bottles and he poured some into a collapsible bowl for Zoya.

"It's beautiful from below." He pointed into the steep canyon. "I mean, if you're up for beating your way down through the bushes."

"Yes!" She said it with feeling, to bolster her own flagging enthusiasm for the task. The overcast sky seemed to be getting darker. "No rain in the forecast, right?"

He gave her his smug look. "Or so all the weather services have predicted."

"We should get back, huh?"

He pretended to consider her question. "I thought you wanted to get a good view of the falls."

She leaned his way and bumped him with her shoulder. "That sounds like a challenge."

He gave a lazy shrug. "It's no problem if you think it's too much for you."

She popped the plug back into her water bottle. "That does it. We are going down."

And down they went.

Zoya was amazing, effortlessly balanced on only three legs. She bounced along through the underbrush, never flagging. Sabra and Matthias had a little more difficulty, but they kept after it—and were rewarded at the bottom by the gorgeous sight of the tumbling white water from down below.

"Worth it?" he asked.

"Definitely." She got a bunch of pictures on her phone.

"Come here." He hooked his giant arm around her waist and hauled her close, claiming her lips in a long, deliciously dizzying kiss. She got lost in that kiss—lost in *him*, in Matthias, in the miracle of this thing between them that was still so compelling after a whole year apart.

Twice in her life, she'd almost said *I do*, but she'd never felt anything like this before. She loved just being with him, making love for hours, laughing together, sharing the most basic, simple pleasures, the two of them and Zoya, in a one-room cabin.

Or out in the wild at the foot of a waterfall.

A drop of rain plopped on her forehead. Then another, then a whole bunch of them.

It was like someone up there had turned on a faucet. The sky just opened wide and the water poured down.

They both tipped their faces up to it, laughing.

"Why am I not the least bit surprised?" she asked.

He kissed her again, quick and hard, as the water ran down her face and trickled between their fused lips.

"Come on." He pulled up her hood and snapped

the closure at her throat. "Let's find shelter. We can wait out the worst of it."

"What shelter?" She scoffed at him. "I haven't seen any shelter."

"Follow me." He pulled up his own hood. "Zoya, heel." He set off, the dog looping immediately into position on his left side. "Good girl." He pulled a treat from his pocket. Zoya took it from his hand as he started back up the hillside. Sabra fell in behind them.

When they got to the trail, it was still coming down, every bit as thick and hard as the day they'd met. They set off back the way they'd come. She had waterproof gear this time, so most of her stayed dry. It could have been worse.

About a mile or so later, Matthias veered from the path they'd taken originally. The brush grew denser and the rain came down harder, if that was even possible.

"Did you say there would be shelter?" she asked hopefully from behind him.

Just as the question escaped her lips, a shelflike rock formation came into view ahead. She spotted the darkened space between the stones. He ducked into the shadows, Zoya right behind him.

Sabra followed. It was a shallow depression in the rock, not quite a cave, but deep enough to get them out of the deluge.

"Get comfortable." He slid off his pack and sat with his back to the inner wall. Zoya shook herself, sending muddy water flying, and then flopped down beside him as Sabra set her pack with his. "It could be a while." He reached up a hand to her.

She took it, dropping to his other side, pulling on

his hand so that she could settle his arm across her shoulders. "Cozy."

"Ignore the muddy dog smell."

She pushed back her hood and sniffed the air. "Heaven." And it kind of was, just to be with him. A world apart, only the two of them and Zoya and the roar of the rain outside their rocky shelter. She asked, "What's your deepest fear?"

"Getting serious, are we?" He pressed his cold lips to the wet hair at her temple.

"Too grim? Don't answer."

"No, it's good. I can go there. A desk job would be pretty terrifying."

"You're right." She leaned her head on his shoulder. "All that sitting. Very scary."

"I like to keep moving."

"Me, too."

"What are *you* afraid of?" he asked.

She didn't even need to think about it. "That I'll never be able to make myself go back and live at our farm."

He waited until she looked up into his waiting eyes. "It's that bad?"

"Yeah. Because it was so good once. I have too many beautiful memories there, you know? The farm was always my future, always what I wanted to do with my life. And now it's just a sad place to me. I go for a visit, and all I want is to leave again."

He tipped up her chin with the back of his hand. "How's your dad doing?"

She gazed up into those deep blue eyes and felt *seen*, somehow. Cherished. Protected. Completely accepted. "He's thin, my dad. It's like he's slowly disappearing. I need to spend more time with him. But I can't bear to be there. Still, I *need* to be there. I told him at Thanksgiving that I would move home, work the farm with him, the way we always planned. I said I wanted to spend more time with him."

"You sound doubtful."

"I guess he noticed that, too. He said that he was doing fine and he knew that coming home wasn't going to work for me. He said that I had my own life and I should do what *I* wanted."

"He's a good guy, huh?"

"My dad? The best—just, you know, sad. The lights are on but he's not really home." She laid her head on his shoulder again. They watched the rain together.

She must have dozed off, because she suddenly became aware that the rain had subsided to a light drizzle. Zoya's tags jingled as she gave herself a scratch.

And suddenly, Sabra wanted to get up, move on. "Let's hit the trail, huh?"

"Sure."

They shouldered their packs and set out again.

Matt really wouldn't have minded at all if this holiday season never came to an end. It was so easy and natural with Sabra. They could talk or not talk. Tell each other painful truths, or hike for an hour without a word spoken. Didn't matter. It was all good.

Back at the cabin, they gave Zoya a bath.

Then they rinsed the mud out of the tub and took a long bath together. That led to some good times on the sofa and then later upstairs.

They came down to eat and to play Scrabble naked.

She beat the pants off him—or she would've, if he'd had pants on.

By midnight, she was yawning. She went on upstairs alone. He put his clothes back on. Then he and Zoya, some nice blocks of basswood and his Swiss Army knife spent a couple of quality hours out on the porch.

He climbed the stairs to the loft smiling.

When he slid under the covers with her, she shivered and complained that his feet were freezing. But when he pulled her close and wrapped himself around her, she gave a happy sigh and went right back to sleep.

Christmas morning zipped past in a haze of holiday tunes, kisses and laughter.

Matt had left the gifts from his family at home to open later and they gave each other simple things, silly things. He'd carved her another porcupine, a bigger one, for a doorstop. She had two gifts for him: a giant coffee mug with the woodsman's coat of arms, which included crossed axes and a sustainable forestry slogan; and a grenade-size wilderness survival kit that contained everything from safety pins to fish hooks and lines, water bags, candles and a knife.

The afternoon was clear and they went for another hike.

On the twenty-sixth, they drove down the coast to the pretty town of Manzanita and had dinner at a great seafood place there. He'd almost suggested they try a restaurant he liked in Astoria, but then decided against it. They had an agreement, after all, to keep their real lives separate. She'd told him last year that her farm was near Svensen, which was technically in Astoria. He kind of thought it might be pushing things, to take her too close to home.

And he *wasn't* pushing, he kept reminding himself. She'd said she wasn't ready for anything more than the great time they were having. And he wasn't ready for a relationship, either.

Or he hadn't been.

Until a certain fine brunette broke into his cabin and made him start thinking impossible things. Like how well they fit together.

Like how maybe he *was* ready to talk about trying again with a woman—with *her*.

He kept a damn calendar in his closet, didn't he? A paper one. Who even used paper calendars anymore?

Just lovesick guys like him, schmaltzy guys who had to literally count the days, mark them off with big red x'es, until he could finally see her again.

But how to have the taking-it-to-the-next-level conversation?

He felt like he could say anything to her—except for the thing he most wanted to say.

Sabra, I want more with you. More than Christmas and New Year's. I want the rest of the winter.

And the spring and the summer. And the fall?

I want that, too.

I want it all, Sabra. I want it all with you.

But the days zipped by and he said nothing.

And then the more he thought about it, well, maybe he really wasn't ready. If he was ready, he would open his mouth and say so, now wouldn't he?

* * *

The only problem with this Christmastime as far as Sabra was concerned?

It was all flying by too fast.

Phone numbers, she kept thinking.

Maybe they could just do that, exchange phone numbers. Really, they were so close now, a deep sort of closeness, sometimes easy. Sometimes deliciously intense.

She couldn't bear to just drive away and not see him until next year—or maybe never, if he found someone else while they were apart. If he...

Well, who knew what might happen in the space of twelve months? They hadn't even talked about whether or not they would meet up again next year.

She needed his phone number. She needed to be able to call him and text him and send him pictures. Of her. In a pink lace bra and an itty-bitty thong.

Seriously, the great sex aside, it was going to be tough for her, when she left him this year. She felt so close to him. It would be like ripping off a body part to say goodbye.

But then, that was her problem, wasn't it?

She got so attached. There was no in-between with her. She fell for a guy and started picking out the china patterns.

This, with Matthias, was supposed to be different. It was supposed to be a way to have it all with this amazing man, but in a Christmas-sized package. With a date-certain goodbye.

Exchanging numbers was a slippery slope and she was not going down it. She was enjoying every minute with him.

And then, on the first of January, she was letting go.

* * *

All of a sudden, it was New Year's Eve.

Matt and Sabra stayed in bed, as they had the year before, only getting up for food and bathroom breaks and to take a shower together—and twice, to take Zoya out for a little exercise.

Matt willed the hours to pass slowly—which only made them whiz by all the faster.

Sabra dropped off to sleep at a little after midnight. He lay there beside her, watching her beautiful face, wanting to wake her up just to have her big eyes to look into, just to whisper with her, have her touch him, have her truly *with* him for every moment he could steal.

Man, he was gone on her.

It was powerful, what he felt for her. Too powerful, maybe.

Dangerous to him, even. To his hard-earned equilibrium.

He'd lived through a boatload of loss and guilt. The guilt over Finn had almost destroyed him before he was even old enough to legally order a beer.

Sometimes he still dreamed about it, about that moment when he turned around in the snowy, silent Siberian wilderness, and his annoying eight-year-old brother wasn't there.

He'd been angry that day—for the whole, endless trip up till then—angry at his parents, at the crap that they put him through, with their damn love of traveling, of seeing the world. That year, it was Russia. They saw Moscow and Saint Petersburg—and of course, they had to visit the Siberian wilderness.

Daniel, the oldest, had somehow gotten out of that

trip. That made Matt the main babysitter of his seven younger siblings.

It had happened on a day trip from Irkutsk. They'd stopped for lunch somewhere snowy and endless; off in the distance, a stand of tall, bare-looking trees. Matt just had to get away. He decided on a walk across the flat snow-covered land, out into the tall trees. He told his parents he was going.

"Alone," he said, scowling.

His mom had waved a hand. "Don't be such a grouch, Matt. Have your walk. We'll keep the other kids here."

He set out.

And Finn, always adventurous, never one to do what he was told to do, had tagged along behind him.

Matt ordered him to go back to the others.

Finn just insisted, *Mom said I could come with you*, and kept following. And then he started chattering, about how he thought the huskies that pulled their sled were so cool, with their weird, bright blue eyes, how he wanted a husky, and he was going to ask Mom for one.

Matt still remembered turning on him, glaring. *"Just shut up, will you, Finnegan? Just. Please. Stop. Talking."*

Finn had stared up at him, wide-eyed. Hurt. Proud. And now silent.

He never said another word.

Five minutes later, Matt turned around again and Finn was gone.

That really was his fault, losing Finn. The guilt that ate at him from the inside was guilt he had earned with his own harsh words, with the ensuing silence that he'd let go on too long.

His parents died two years later, on the first trip they'd taken since Finn disappeared. That trip was just the two of them, Marie and George Bravo, a little getaway to Thailand, to try to recapture the magic they found in traveling after the tragic loss of their youngest son. They'd checked in to the resort just in time for the arrival of the tsunami that killed them.

To Matt, the Thailand getaway had seemed a direct result of his losing Finn in Russia. He'd been sure in his guilty heart that his parents would never have been in Thailand if not for him.

After his parents died, Matt was constantly in trouble. And if you could drink it, snort it or smoke it, Matt was up for it in high school and during those two years at CCC. The only good thing in his life then had been Christy, his girl.

He told Christy everything, all of his many sins. She loved him and forgave him and made him feel better. Until she grew tired of waiting for him to come home from the other side of the world, dumped him and married someone else.

As for Mark and Nelson, well, at least he didn't actively blame himself for their deaths in Iraq. All he'd done in that case was to survive—which had brought its own kind of guilt.

Survivor guilt, he'd learned through living it, was just as bad as the guilt you felt for losing your own brother. It had taken a whole lot of counseling to get on with his life after Iraq.

But he *had* gotten on with it. He was doing all

right now, with a good life and work that he loved. He'd even taken a big step and gotten himself a dog.

And now there was Sabra. And he couldn't help wanting more than Christmas with her.

Just ask for her number. How dangerous can that be?

Damn dangerous, you long-gone fool.

When a man finally finds a certain equilibrium in his life, he's reluctant to rock the boat—even for a chance to take things further with someone like Sabra.

Morning came way too soon. He made her coffee and she drank it in the usual shared silence.

Then he dragged her upstairs again, where they made love once more.

They came down and had breakfast, went outside and sat out on the porch for a while.

And then, around noon, Sabra said she had to get going.

Matt helped her load her stuff into the Subaru. It took no time at all, the minutes zipping by when all he wanted was to grab onto them, make them stand still.

Too soon, they were saying their goodbyes, just like last year, but with Zoya beside them.

Sabra knelt to give his dog a last hug.

When she rose again, she said, "I don't have the words." She gazed up at him through those deep brown eyes that he knew he'd be seeing in his dreams all year long. "It's been pretty much perfect and I hate to go."

Don't, then. Stay. "I hate to *see* you go."

She eased her hand into a pocket and came out with the key.

No way. He caught her wrist and wrapped her fingers tight around it. "Next year. Same time. I'll be here. I hope you will, too."

"Matthias." Those big eyes were even brighter with the shine of barely held-back tears. "Oh, I will miss you…"

Stay.

But he didn't say it. Instead, he reached out and took her by the shoulders, pulling her in close, burying his nose against her hair, which smelled of sunshine and oranges. She wrapped her arms around him, too. He never wanted to let her go.

But it had to be done.

Slowly, she lifted her head. He watched a tear get away from her. It gleamed as it slid down her cheek. Bending close, he pressed his mouth to the salty wetness.

She turned her head just enough so their lips could meet. He gathered her even tighter in his arms, claiming her mouth, tasting her deeply.

The kiss went on for a very long time. He wished it might last forever, that some miracle might happen to make it so she wouldn't go.

But she hadn't said a word about taking it further—and neither had he.

Her arms loosened around him. He made himself take his hands off her and reached for the door handle, pulling it wide.

She got in and he shut it.

With a last wave through the glass of the window, she started the engine.

He stepped back. Zoya gave a whine.

"Sit," he commanded.

The husky dropped to her haunches beside him. He watched Sabra go, not turning for the porch steps until the blue Subaru disappeared around the first bend in the twisting dirt road.

Chapter Eight

The following May...

Sabra stood by the empty hospital bed her father didn't need anymore. She held a plastic bag full of clothes and other personal belongings that Adam Bond wouldn't ever wear again.

Really, there was nothing more to do here at Peaceful Rest Hospice Care. She should go.

But still, she just stood there, her dad's last words to her whispering through her head. *Don't cry, sweetheart. I love you and I hate to leave you, but I'm ready to go. You see, it's not really cancer. It's just my broken heart...*

"There you are." Peyton stood in the open door to the hallway.

Iris, who stood behind her, asked, "Have you got everything?"

Words had somehow deserted her. Sabra hard-swallowed a pointless sob and held up the bag of useless clothing.

"Oh, honey," said Peyton, and came for her, Iris right behind her.

They put their arms around her, Iris on one side and Peyton on the other. She let herself lean on them and felt a deep gratitude that they were there with her.

"Come on," whispered Iris, giving her shoulders a comforting squeeze. "It's time to go."

That June...

At Berry Bog Farm, the office was the large extra room at the rear of the house, between the kitchen and the laundry room, just off the narrow hallway that opened onto a screened-in porch.

Sabra sat at the old oak desk that had been her father's and his father's before him. She scrolled through the spreadsheet showing income and expenses as she waited for Nils Wilson, her father's longtime friend and top farmhand.

The back door to the screen porch gave a little screech as it opened.

She called out, "In the office, Nils!" and listened to the sound of his footfalls on the wide-plank floor as he approached.

He appeared in the doorway to the back hall, tall and skinny as ever, with a long face to match the rest of him. Deep grooves had etched themselves on either side of his mouth and across his high, narrow forehead. "Hey, pumpkin." He'd always called her pumpkin, for as long as she could remember.

She got up and went to him for a hug. He enfolded her in his long arms. She breathed in the smell of cut grass and dirt that always seemed to cling to him, a scent she found infinitely comforting, a scent to soothe her troubled soul. She asked after his wife of thirty-two years. "How's Marjorie?"

"About the same." Twenty-four years ago, when Sabra was still toddling around in diapers, Nils and Marjorie had put up a manufactured home across the front yard from the farmhouse. Marjorie worked wherever she was needed. She raised goats and chickens and she ran the farm's fresh flower business. She sold gorgeous bunches of them at local markets and also to several florist shops in the area. "She runs me ragged." Nils put on a long-suffering look.

Sabra smiled at that. "And you wouldn't have it any other way."

"Humph," said Nils, meaning yes. He liked to play it grumpy sometimes, but everyone knew how much he loved his wife.

"I missed her this morning when I drove in." Sabra gestured toward the two guest chairs opposite the desk. Nils followed her over there and they sat down.

"You know how she is," said Nils. "Up with the roosters, ready to work."

"I know. I'll catch her this evening."

"Come for dinner?"

"I'll be there."

He reached across the short distance between them to put his wrinkled, work-roughened hand over hers. "How're you holdin' up?"

Her throat ached, suddenly, the ache of tears. She gulped them down. "All right."

He shook his head. "Pumpkin, you were his shining light."

She sniffed and sat up straighter. "No. Mom was that. But he was a good dad. The best." *And I should have been here for him.*

Nils gave her hand a squeeze before pulling back. "So. We're gonna talk business now, is that it?"

"Yes, we are."

"Good. When are you coming home to stay?"

That lump in her throat? It was bigger than ever. "Well, I, um…"

Nils got the message. "You're not coming home." He said it flatly, his disappointment clear.

"I just, well, I hope you and Marjorie will stay on."

"Of course we will."

"We'll change our arrangement. I will drive up every couple of weeks, to keep on top of things. But you'll be running the place. Both you and Marjorie will be getting more money."

"Pumpkin, I got no doubt you will be fair with us. That's not the question. It's about you."

"Nils, I—"

"No. Now, you hear me out. You are a Bond, a farmer to the core. You were born to run Berry Bog Farm. I just want you to think on it. You belong here with us. Won't you come home at last?"

"I'm just, well, I'm not ready to do that and I don't know when I will be ready."

What she didn't tell him was that she was considering putting the farm up for sale. She *would* tell him, of course, as soon as she'd made up her mind.

Right now, though?

She felt she ought to sell, that she would never be able to come back and live here, that just showing up every few weeks to go over the books and handle any necessary business was almost more than she could bear. There were far too many memories here, from happy through bittersweet all the way to devastating.

So yeah. She ought to sell. If she did, she would see to it that Nils and Marjorie were provided for. But no matter how much she settled on them, they wouldn't be happy if she sold the place. The farm was their home.

And really, she couldn't stand the thought of that, either, of letting the land that was her heritage go.

Which left her in a bleak limbo of grief and indecision.

Later, in the evening, after dinner with the Wilsons, she trudged upstairs to her dad's room and tackled packing up his things. As she cleaned out his closet, her thoughts turned to Matthias. She missed him. She ached to have a long talk with him, to feel his muscled arms around her. Life would be so much more bearable if she could have him near.

She paused, her head in the closet, one of her dad's plaid jackets in her hands—a Pendleton, red and black. Adam Bond had always been a sucker for a nice Pendleton. Shirts, jackets, coats, you name it. He had a lot of them. They were excellent quality. People knew he liked them and gave them to him for Christmas and his birthday.

A sob stuck in her throat because he would never wear his Pendletons again.

Backing out of the closet with the jacket in her

hand, she sank to the edge of the bed, putting her palm down flat on the wedding ring quilt her mom had made before Sabra was even a twinkle in her dad's eye.

Idly, she traced the circular stitching in the quilt, thinking of Matthias—his blue, blue eyes, his beautiful, reluctant smile. The way he held her, sometimes hard and tight, like he wanted to absorb her body into his. And sometimes so tenderly, with a deep, true sort of care.

Really, it wouldn't be difficult at all to track him down. He worked for the Department of Fish and Wildlife locally and he had a big family in Valentine Bay.

Would he be angry with her for breaking their rules?

Or would he hold out his arms to her and gather her close? Would he say how happy he was that she'd come to find him? Would he promise her that eventually this grayness would pass, that things would get better and life would make sense again?

She laughed out loud to the empty room, a hard, unhappy sound.

Because she was being sloppy and sentimental. She wasn't going to contact him. She and Matthias had what they had. It was tenuous and magical and only for Christmas.

No way would she ruin it by trying to make it more.

That July...

Matt had two remaining relatives on his mother's side of the family—Great-Uncle Percy Valentine, who'd given him the cabin, and Percy's sister, Great-Aunt Daffodil Valentine.

In their eighties, the never-married brother and sister lived at Valentine House on the edge of Valentine City Park. Matt found his great-aunt and uncle charming and eccentric, sharp-witted and no-nonsense. Daffy and Percy came to all the big family gatherings. But Matt made it a point to drop by and see them at home now and then, too.

He always brought takeout when he came. This time, Daffy had requested "Bacon cheeseburgers with the works, young man."

Matt knew how to take an order and arrived bearing grease-spotted white bags from a Valentine Bay landmark, Raeleen's Roadside Grill. He'd brought the cheeseburgers, fries, onion rings and milkshakes—chocolate for him and Daffy, vanilla for Uncle Percy.

Letha March, who'd been cooking and cleaning at Valentine House for as long as Matt could remember, answered the door and ushered him and Zoya into the formal parlor, which contained too much antique furniture, an ugly floral-pattered rug, and his great-aunt and uncle.

"You got Raeleen's!" Daffy clapped her wrinkled hands in delight. "You always were my favorite great-nephew."

"Aunt Daffy, I know you say that to all of us."

Daffy patted his cheek and smiled up at him fondly as Percy bent to greet Zoya. Letha got out the TV trays so they could chow down right there in the parlor the way they always did.

As they ate, Uncle Percy reported on his progress with the search for Finn. Percy, who often referred to himself as "the family sleuth," had been in charge of the search from the beginning. He worked with private investigators, a series of them. Each PI would find out what he or she could and turn in a report. And then Percy would hire someone else to try again. Each investigator got the benefit of the information his predecessors had uncovered. For all the years of searching, they hadn't found much.

But Percy would never give up. And he and Matt had agreed that when, for whatever reason, Percy could no longer run the search, Matt would step up.

"So there you have it," Percy concluded. "As usual, it's not a lot."

Matt thanked him and they made encouraging noises at each other in order not to get too discouraged. No matter how hopeless it seemed sometimes, the worst thing would be to give up and stop looking.

Daffy slipped Zoya a French fry. "Now tell us what is happening in your life, Matthias." She and Percy always called him by his full name.

Same as Sabra did.

Sabra.

He'd been thinking of her constantly. He wanted more time with her, wanted to take it beyond the cabin, make it real between them. They could go slow. She was in Portland, after all. They would have to make some effort to be together.

But he was willing. He wanted to be with her. Whatever it took.

"What is that faraway look in your eye?" asked Uncle Percy.

Matt shocked the hell out of himself by telling them the truth. "I've met someone. Her name is Sabra Bond.

Born and raised on a farm near Astoria. Now she manages a restaurant in Portland. She has dark hair and big brown eyes and she's smart and funny and tough and beautiful. I'm crazy about her."

He told them how and when he'd met her and about the two Christmases they'd spent together at the cabin. He even explained about the agreement—just the two of them, just for Christmas, no contact otherwise.

"But you want more," said Aunt Daffy.

"I do, yeah."

"It does my old heart good," said Uncle Percy, "to see you coming back from all you've been through."

Daffy gave a slow nod. "You are truly healing, Matthias, and that is a beautiful thing to see."

Uncle Percy reached over and clapped a hand on his arm. "Finding yourself, that's what you're doing. Didn't I tell you that you would?"

"Yes, you did."

"We're so happy for you," cried Daffy.

"I just… I'm not sure how to try for more with her, not sure how to ask her, not sure what to say."

"Just speak from your heart," advised Daffy. "The specific words will come to you, as long as you show your true self and tell her clearly what you want."

Percy added, "Be honest and forthright and it will all work out."

Later that night, at home, Matt considered taking Percy's advice to heart immediately. How hard could it be to find her, really? Online searches aside, there were only so many farms on the outskirts of Astoria.

But then, well, no.

Stalking the woman wasn't part of their deal.

Being patient wouldn't kill him. He would wait for Christmas and pray she showed up this year, too.

Matt marked another X on his calendar, bringing him one day closer to seeing her again.

That September...

"Come on, man." Jerry tipped his head toward the dark-haired woman three tables over. "She's a knockout and she likes you. What are you saving it for, I'd just like to know?" It was yet another Friday night at Beach Street Brews and as always, Jerry was after him to hook up with someone.

Matt wondered why he'd come. "Cut it out, Jer. Let me enjoy my beer." Matt needed that beer. He also needed not to be hassled while drinking it.

A week before, his brother Daniel's wife Lillie had given birth to twins, Jake and Frannie. The twins were fine, but two days after the birth, Lillie had died from complications mostly due to lupus. It was a tough time in the Bravo family.

And the last thing Matt needed right now was a night with a stranger.

Jerry poured himself another glass from the pitcher on the table between them. "This is getting ridiculous. I've gotta meet your holiday hookup, see what's so special you're willing to go all year without—"

"Drop it, Jerry." Matt turned and looked his aggravating friend squarely in the eye. "Just let it go."

"I don't get it. That's all I'm sayin'."

"Yeah, well. You've said it. Repeatedly. I heard you. Stop."

"It's not healthy to—"

"That does it." Matt shoved back his chair. "I'm outta here."

"Aw, c'mon, man. Don't get mad."

"You have fun, Jerry." Matt threw some bills on the table.

Jerry looked kind of crestfallen. "Listen. I'm sorry. I've got a big mouth, I know. I should try to keep a lid on it."

"Yeah, you should—and you're forgiven."

"Great. C'mon, stay."

He clapped his friend on the shoulder. "Gotta go."

"So…maybe *I* should make a move on her?" Jerry gave the dark-haired woman a wave.

Matt just shook his head and made for the door.

Three months left until Christmas at the cabin. Losing Lillie really had him thinking that life flew by way too fast, that everything could change when you least expected it and a man needed to grab what he wanted and hold on tight.

This year, if Sabra showed up, he was not letting her go without asking for more.

December 23, two years ago…

She was already there!

Matt saw the lights gleaming from the cabin windows at the same turn where he'd spotted them two years before. His heart seemed to leap upward in his chest and lodge squarely in his throat. His pulse raced, gladness burning along every nerve in his body as he rounded the next turn and the turn after that.

The front door swung open as he rolled into the yard and pulled to a stop behind the Subaru.

Sabra emerged dressed in a long black sweater and leggings printed with reindeer and snowflakes, knee-high boots on her feet. Her hair was longer this time, the dark curls loose on her shoulders. He couldn't wait to get his hands in them.

Shoving the car into Park, he turned off the engine, threw the door wide and jumped out to catch her as she hurled herself into his outstretched arms.

"At last," they whispered in unison.

And then he was kissing her, breathing in her sweet, incomparable scent, going deep, hard and hungry. She laughed as he angled his mouth the other way and she jumped up, lifting those fine legs and wrapping them good and tight around him, her arms twined behind his neck.

He was halfway up the steps, devouring her mouth as he went, before she broke their lip-lock and started to speak. "I'm so—"

"Get back here." He cradled her head, holding her still so he could claim those beautiful lips again.

Before he crashed into her that time, she got a single word out. "Zoya?"

He groaned, gentled his hold and pressed his forehead to hers. "See what you do to me? I almost forgot my own dog."

She took his face between her hands and offered eagerly, "One more kiss?"

He gave it to her, long and deep, turning as he kissed her, heading back down the steps. She dropped her feet to the ground at the back of the vehicle. He let her go reluctantly and opened the hatch. Zoya rose in her crate, stretching and yawning. "Sorry, girl," he muttered. Behind him, he heard Sabra chuckle.

"C'mon out." He opened the crate and helped the husky down to the ground.

"Zoya! It's so good to see you." Sabra knelt to greet her, scratching her ruff, giving her long strokes down her back as Zoya whined and wriggled with happiness. "I've missed you so much…"

Matt waited impatiently for her to finish her reunion with his dog. When she finally rose, he reached for her again.

She danced away, laughing, her gaze on the tree tied to the roof rack. "I swear, you found a thicker tree than last year. So gorgeous…"

"Just beautiful," he agreed. He wasn't referring to the tree. Catching her elbow, he pulled her close again. "So then. Where were we?"

Those dark eyes held a teasing light. "We should bring it in, put it in water and—"

With a growl, he covered her sweet mouth with his, taking her by the waist and then lifting her. She got the hint, surrendering her mouth to him as she wrapped her legs and arms around him again.

He carried her up the steps and in the door without stopping that time, counting on Zoya to stick close behind. As soon as they cleared the threshold, Sabra stuck out a hand and shoved the door shut.

Reluctantly, he lifted his mouth from hers, noting that not only had she gotten the fire going, she'd set out water for Zoya. The dog was already lapping it up.

"Oh, I cannot believe you're actually here." Her smile could light up the darkest corner of the blackest night.

"It's been too long," he grumbled.

"Oh, yes it has." She caught his lower lip between

her pretty teeth and bit down lightly, sending heat and need flaring even higher within him.

"That does it," he muttered. "We're going upstairs."

"Yes," she replied, suddenly earnest. "*Now*, Matthias. Please."

He told Zoya to stay and started walking, carrying her up there, kissing her the whole way.

At the bed, she clung to him. He started undressing her anyway, pulling her long sweater up and away, not even pausing to give her lacy purple bra the attention it deserved, just unhooking it, ripping the straps down and whipping it off her, revealing those beautiful high pink-tipped breasts. "Everything. Off," he commanded, peeling her legs from around him, setting her down on the mattress.

She didn't argue. He stripped and she stripped. In a short chain of heated seconds, they were both naked. He went down to the bed with her, grabbing for her, gathering her close.

This was no time to play.

It had been way too long and he couldn't wait. Lucky for him, she seemed to feel the same.

"Hurry," she egged him on. "I have missed you so much..."

He touched the heart of her: soaking wet, so ready.

"Yes," she begged him. "Please. I want you now."

With a groan, he stuck out a hand for the bedside drawer.

She curled her fingers tightly around him, bringing a rough moan of pure need from him as she held his aching length in place. He rolled the condom halfway on and she took over, snugging it all the way down.

That did it. He was not waiting for one second longer.

Taking her by the shoulders, he rolled her under him, easing his thigh between hers and coming into her with a single deep thrust.

She moaned his name and wrapped her legs and arms around him, pulling him in so tight against her, as though she couldn't bear to leave an inch of empty space between her body and his.

They moved together, hard and fast. There was nothing but the feel of her, the taste of her mouth, the scent of her silky hair tangling around him, the heat of her claiming him, taking him down.

He gave himself up to it—to her, to this magic between them, to the longing that never left him in the whole year without her.

"Yes!" she cried, and then crooned his name, "Matthias, missed you. Missed you so much…"

Just barely, he held himself back from the brink, waiting for her, drawing it out into sweet, endless agony.

And then, at last, she cried out and he felt her pulsing around him. Through a monumental effort of will, he stayed with her as she came apart in his arms. Finally, with a shout of pure triumph, he gave in and let his finish take him down.

So tightly, he held her, never wanting to let go.

But when he finally loosened his hold on her, she gave a gentle push to his shoulders. He took the hint and braced up on his arms to grin down at her.

But his grin didn't last.

She met his gaze, her eyes haunted looking in her

flushed face. Her soft mouth trembled. "Oh, Matthias."

"What? Sabra, what's the matter?"

Her face crumpled and she burst into tears.

Chapter Nine

"Sabra—sweetheart, talk to me. Come on, what is it?" Matthias was staring down at her, golden eyebrows drawn together, clearly stunned at this out-of-nowhere crying jag.

The tears poured from her, blurring her vision. "Sorry. So sorry. I can't… I don't…" Apparently, complete sentences were not available to her right now. She sniffled loudly and swiped at her nose.

"Stay right there," he instructed, easing his body off hers. She squinted through her blurry eyes, trying to contain her sobs as he removed the condom and tied it off. The tears wouldn't stop falling.

Miserable, she turned away from him. Curling herself in a ball, she tried to get control of herself, but for some reason, that only made the tears come faster.

The bed shifted as he rose.

A minute later, he touched her shoulder, the gentlest, kindest sort of touch. "Hey. Here you go…"

With a watery little sob, she rolled back to face him. "Just ignore me. That's what you should do. Just go on downstairs and—"

"I'm going nowhere. Here. Take these." He handed her a couple of tissues.

"Oh, Matthias." She swiped at her nose and her cheeks. "This, um, isn't about you. I hope you know that. I'm so glad to see you. So glad to be with you. But this…" She gestured with the tissues at the whole of herself. "I don't know why I'm doing this. I don't know…what's the matter with me, to be such a big crybaby right now." She sniffled and stared up at him, *willing* him to understand, though she'd said nothing coherent so far, nothing to help him figure out what was bothering her. "I don't know what I'm saying, even. Because, what *am* I saying? I have no idea."

"It's okay."

"No, it is not."

"Well, I can see that. But I mean, between me and you, everything is okay. I'm right here and whatever you need, I'll do whatever it takes to make sure you get it." He got back on the bed with her. "Now, come here." He took her shoulders gently. She scrambled into his lap like an overgrown child and buried her face against his broad, warm chest. "You're safe," he soothed. "I'm right here." He stroked her hair, petted her shoulder, rubbed his big hand up and down her back.

She huddled against him, relishing the comfort he offered, matching her breaths to his in order to calm herself, endlessly grateful to have his steady strength to cling to.

For several minutes, neither of them spoke. He held her and she was held by him. Finally, she looked up to find his eyes waiting.

"What is it?" he asked. "Talk to me."

She sniffled and wiped more tears away. "My dad died."

His forehead scrunched up. "Oh, Sabra." He ran his hand down her hair, brushed a kiss against her still-wet cheek. "When?"

"In the spring. He, um, it was cancer, non-Hodgkin's lymphoma. He didn't get treatment. Not for years, I found out later. And by the time he did, it was too late. He, well, he wanted to die. He told me so, right there at the end—not that he *had* to tell me. I knew. He never got over my mom's death. He just, well, he didn't want to be in this world without her."

Matthias pulled her close again. She felt his warm breath brush the crown of her head. "I'm so sorry…"

She wiped her nose with the wadded-up tissues. "I should feel better about it. I mean, he got what he wanted, right?"

He kissed her temple. "That doesn't mean you can't miss him and want him back with you."

"He was ready. He said so."

"But *you* weren't ready to lose him."

She tipped her face up to meet his clear blue eyes again. "You're right. I wasn't ready. I also wasn't *there* when he needed me. He would always say he was fine and he understood that I needed to get out, make my own way, move to Portland, all that." Another hard sob escaped her. She dabbed her eyes and shook her head. "I should have tried harder, should have kept after him, gotten him to a doctor sooner. When he said he was all right, I just accepted it, took his word for it. And now, well, he's gone and I've got more regrets than I can name. I can't bear to sell the farm, but I couldn't stand to live there, either. It's like I'm being torn in different directions and I can't make up my mind, can't decide which way to go."

"So don't decide."

She blinked at him, surprised. "*Don't* decide?"

"Do you have someone you trust taking care of the farm?"

"Yeah, but—"

"If you don't *have* to decide right now, don't. Wait."

"Wait for…?"

"Until you're ready."

"But I'm a mess. How am I supposed to know when I'm ready?"

He looked at her so tenderly, not smiling, very serious. But there was a smile lurking in his eyes, a smile that reassured her, that seemed to promise everything would somehow work out right in the end. "The question is, do you think you're ready to decide about the farm right now?"

"God, no."

"Well, there you go. Take it from someone who's had a whole hell of a lot of therapy. When you're grieving, it's not a good time to have to make big choices. Sometimes life doesn't cooperate and a choice *has* to be made anyway. Then you do the best you can and hope it all works out. But you just said you don't have to decide right this minute. So don't. Procrastination isn't always a bad thing."

She turned the idea over in her mind. "Don't decide…"

"Not until you either *have* to decide, or you're sure of what you want."

What he said made a lot of sense. "Okay then. I will seriously consider procrastination." She giggled at the absurdity of it—and realized she felt better. She really did. Sometimes a girl just needed a long, ugly cry and some excellent advice.

She snuggled in close, enjoying his body heat. For a little while, they simply sat there in the middle of the rumpled bed, holding each other.

"What about you?" she asked softly. "Any big changes in your life since last Christmas?"

He told her of his sister-in-law, who'd died in early September after giving birth to twins. "Her name was Lillie. She was only a year older than me, but still, she was kind of a second mother to all of us after our parents died, so losing her is a little like losing our mom all over again."

She lifted up enough to kiss his cheek. "That's so sad."

"Yeah. We all miss her. And my brother Daniel, her husband, has always been one of those too-serious kind of guys. Since Lillie died, I don't think anyone has seen Daniel crack a smile."

"Give him time."

"Hey. What else can we do?"

"Life is just so *hard* sometimes…" She tucked her head beneath his chin and he idly stroked her hair.

Downstairs, she heard Zoya's claws tapping the wood floor. The husky gave a hopeful little whine.

Sabra stirred. "We should get moving. Your dog is lonely and your Jeep is not going to unload itself."

The next day, Christmas Eve, they decorated the tree and Matt took her out to dinner at that seafood place in Manzanita. When they got back to the cabin, they sat out on the porch until after midnight, laughing together, holding hands between their separate chairs until he coaxed her over onto his lap. It started snowing.

"It's beautiful," she said as they watched the delicate flakes drifting down.

"And the best kind, too," he agreed.

She chuckled and leaned her head against his shoulder. "Yeah. The kind that doesn't stick."

By Christmas morning, the snow had turned to rain.

All Christmas day and the day after, Matt tried to find the right moment to talk about the future. That moment hadn't come yet, though. But he was waiting for it, certain he would know when the time was right.

It was a bittersweet sort of Christmas. Sabra had lost her dad and Lillie was gone from the Bravo family much too soon. Still, Matt was hopeful. He felt close to Sabra—closer than ever, really.

Every hour with her was a gift, fleeting, gone too soon. But exactly what he needed, nonetheless. She was everything he wanted, everything he'd almost given up hope of having in his life.

Like last year, they went hiking together. He loved that she enjoyed a good, sweaty hike, that she didn't mind slogging through the rain on rough, overgrown terrain for the simple satisfaction of doing it, of catching sight of a hawk high in the sky or a misty waterfall from deep in some forgotten ravine.

He wanted her, *all* of her. He wanted her exclusively and forever. They were meant to be together. He just knew it was time for them to make it *more*.

Too bad that the right moment to ask for her phone number never quite seemed to come.

And the days? They were going by much too fast.

Five days after Christmas, they got up nice and early. Matt made the coffee and was silent while Sabra had her first cup. They ate breakfast and took Zoya for a walk.

Back in the cabin, Sabra grabbed his hand and led him upstairs. They peeled off their clothes and climbed into bed. The lovemaking was slow and lazy and so good. It only got really intense toward the end.

They'd just fallen away from each other, laughing and panting, when Zoya started whining downstairs.

Sabra sat up, listening. "Is that a car outside?"

Zoya barked then, three warning barks in succession.

By then, Matt was out of the bed and pulling on his jeans. "I'll see what's up." He zipped up his pants and ran down the stairs barefoot, buttoning up his flannel shirt as he went.

The knock on the door came just as he reached the main floor. From the foot of the stairs, he could see out the front windows.

Parked behind his Jeep and Sabra's Outback was a

Silverado 4x4 with the Oregon State Police logo on the door and State Trooper printed over the front wheel.

Matt instructed Zoya to sit and opened the door. "Jerry," he said wearily.

Jerry grinned. "Hey, buddy. Hope I didn't interrupt anything. I was in the area and I thought, why not stop in and say hi?"

As if he didn't know what his old friend was up to. "You should call first."

Jerry got that busted look. "Yeah, well I…" He swiped off his hat and leaned around him. "Hey!"

"Hello," Sabra said as she came up beside him wearing the sweater and jeans he'd taken off her a half hour before.

Matt introduced them.

Sabra seemed okay with Jerry dropping in. Matt had mentioned his friend to her in passing more than once. She was aware that Jerry and Matt had known each other most of their lives.

Really, it shouldn't be a big deal, but it pissed Matt off that Jerry had dropped in without checking first, mostly because of what Jer had said that night in September, about how he *had* to meet Sabra, had to see what was so special about her.

"You want some coffee?" Matt asked grudgingly, causing Sabra to shoot him a questioning frown. She'd guessed from his tone that he wasn't happy.

Jerry gave a forced laugh. He knew he was out of bounds. "Coffee would be great."

They had coffee and some Christmas cookies Sabra had brought. They made casual conversation. Jerry said the tree was beautiful and too bad the snow hadn't stuck at least through Christmas day and blah-

blah-blah. At least he was charming and friendly with Sabra.

"I'll walk you out," Matt said when Jerry got up to go.

"Uh, sure." Jerry said how great it was to have met Sabra and she made the same noises back at him.

"I'll be right back," Matt promised.

She gave him a nod, and he followed Jerry out to his patrol truck.

"Okay, what?" mumbled Jerry when they reached the driver's door. "Just say it."

"You got a phone. I got a phone. Why didn't you call first?"

Jerry put his hat back on. "I wanted to meet her, okay? I was afraid you'd say no." Matt just looked at him, dead-on. Jerry stuck his hands in his pockets. "All right, yeah. I should have called. And I'm sorry." He looked kind of sad.

And why was it always damn-near impossible to stay pissed off at Jerry? "I told you the situation. As of now, friends and family don't enter into what I have with her."

"I get it. My bad."

"Don't pull anything like that again."

"Never." Jerry looked appropriately chastised—but then he slanted Matt a hopeful glance. "She's hot and I like her—and you said 'as of now'? You're planning to take it to the next level, then? Because really, man, I only want you to get whatever makes you happy."

Matt kind of wanted to grab his friend and hug him. But he needed to be sure that Jerry got the message. "Stay out of it, Jer."

"Yeah. I hear you, man. Loud and clear." He climbed in behind the wheel. "Happy New Year, buddy."

"Happy New Year."

"I liked your friend," Sabra said when Matt got back inside the cabin.

"Everybody likes Jer. He told me he thinks you're hot."

One side of her gorgeous mouth quirked up in a reluctant smile. "I'm flattered—I think." She caught the corner of her lip between her teeth, hesitating.

"Go ahead and say it."

"Well, is everything okay with you and him? You seemed kind of annoyed with him."

His heart rate accelerated and his skin felt too hot. He wanted to tell her, right then, how he felt, what he longed for with her.

Was this it, the right time, finally? He stared at her unforgettable face that he missed the whole year long and ached to go for it, this very minute, to finally ask her to consider giving him more than the holidays.

Staring at her, though? It never was enough. He reached out and slipped his hand under the silky fall of her hair. Curling his rough fingers around her smooth nape, he pulled her nice and close. She tipped up her chin and he claimed a kiss.

And when he lifted his head, somehow the moment to ask the big question had passed.

"Well?" she prompted.

"I wasn't happy that he just dropped in without calling, that's all."

"Isn't that kind of what friends do?"

"Sure, mostly. But Jerry *knows*."

"About us, you mean?"

He nodded. "I told him that I'm crazy about you."

She smiled then, a full-out smile. "You did?"

He wished she would smile at him like that every day. Every day, all year round. "Absolutely. Jerry knows we just have Christmastime, that it's just you and me, away from our real lives."

"So, if he'd asked first, you would have told him to stay away?"

"I don't know. I would've asked you. Found out how you felt about his coming by. We would have decided together." And now he *had* to know. "How *do* you feel about it?"

She was biting the corner of her lip again. "I guess you're right. It's supposed to be just us, just for the holidays. Inviting our friends in isn't part of the deal."

Ouch. That wasn't at all what he'd hoped she might say.

Tell her. Ask her. Do it now.

But he hesitated a moment too long.

And she asked, "When you went out to the truck with him, did you make it up with him?"

He let the main issue go to answer her question. "I did. I can never stay mad at Jerry."

"Well, good." She stepped in close again, put her slim hands on his chest and slid them up to link around his neck. "What do you say we take Zoya for a nice long walk?" At their feet, the husky whined her approval of that suggestion. "The weather's just right for it."

He grunted. "Yeah, cloudy with a chance of rain."

"Welcome to Oregon." She kissed him, after which they put on their boots and took the dog outside.

* * *

The rest of that day was gone in an instant and the night that followed raced by even faster.

All of a sudden, it was New Year's Eve. Time for naked Scrabble and naked Clue—naked everything, really. Matt and Sabra only got dressed to take the dog outside.

At midnight, they toasted in the New Year with a nice a bottle of champagne courtesy of Sabra. Upstairs, they made love again. And again after that.

She drifted off to sleep around two in the morning.

Matt stayed awake, planning what he would say before she left tomorrow, trying to think of just the right words that would make her agree they were ready for more than the holidays together.

By noon New Year's Day, he still hadn't said anything. Apparently, he was a complete wimp when it came to asking for what he wanted the most.

At a little after one in the afternoon, she said she had to get her stuff together and get on the road. He helped her load up the Outback, as he had the year before and the year before that.

And then, way too soon, long before he was ready, they were standing by her driver's door and she was saying goodbye. She knelt and made a fuss over Zoya, and then she rose and moved in close, sliding her hands up over his chest slowly, the way she loved to do, hooking them at the back of his neck.

"I hate to leave." She kissed him, a quick brush of those soft lips across his.

He stared down at her, aching inside. She was getting away from him and if she left now without him opening his damn mouth and saying what he needed to say, he would have to break their agreement and track her down in Portland. Either that, or he wouldn't set eyes on her for another damn year—maybe never if something happened and one of them didn't show up next December.

He'd been waiting for the right moment, the right moment that somehow never came. And now here they were and she was going and it was *this* moment.

Or never.

"Matthias?" Her sleek eyebrows drew together in concern. "What's the matter? What's happened?"

He clasped her shoulders—too hard, enough that she winced. "Sorry." He forced himself to loosen his grip. "I…" The words tried to stick in his throat. He pushed them out. "Sabra, I want more."

She stared up at him, her eyes growing wider. "Um, you want…?" He waited. But that was it. That was all she got out.

He tried again. "*This*, you and me for Christmas. It's beautiful. Perfect. Except that it's not enough for me, not anymore. I want to be with you, spend time with you when it's not Christmas. I want to see you in February, in June and in the fall. I want, well, I was thinking we could just start with phone numbers, maybe? Just exchange numbers and then try getting together soon, see how it goes."

She only stared up at him, eyes enormous in her suddenly pale face.

Was this going all wrong?

He kind of thought it might be.

Should he back off?

Probably.

But he'd been such a damn coward for the last ten days. He needed to go for it. Now that he'd finally opened his mouth and said what he wanted, he needed to take it all the way. "Sabra, I—"

She silenced him by putting up her hand between them, pressing her fingers to his lips. "Oh, I just, well, I thought we understood each other, we agreed that we—"

"Stop." He caught her wrist. "Let me finish."

With a shaky sigh, she nodded, carefully pulling free of his grip, stepping back from him—one step. Two.

He got on with it, because no way could he wait another year to tell her what was in his heart. "I'm in love with you, Sabra." A tiny cry escaped her, but she caught herself, pressing her hand to her mouth, swallowing down whatever she might have said next. He barreled on. "I want the rest of my life with you. But I know I'm never going to get it if I don't tell you how much I want you, want *us*, you and me, together. In the real world. I want to meet your friends and introduce you to my family. I want to show you my hometown and get the tour of your farm. I don't want to push you, I—"

"That's not fair." She spoke in an angry whisper.

He blinked down at her. "Excuse me?"

"You *are* pushing me, Matthias. You're asking me for things that I don't know how to give."

Okay, now. That kind of bugged him. That made him mad. He said, way too quietly, "How am I going to have a prayer of getting more from you if I don't ask for it?"

"Well, it's just that we have an agreement. And yet, all of a sudden, you're all about forever."

"Sabra, it's been two years—two years and three Christmases. That is hardly 'all of a sudden.'"

Her soft mouth twisted. "You know what I mean."

"Uh, no. I guess I don't."

"Well, um, last year, for instance?"

"What about it?"

"Last year, I was kind of thinking the same thing."

Hope exploded in his chest. "You were? Because so was I. I wanted to ask you then, for more time, for a chance, but I didn't know where to start."

"Yes, well, it was the same for me." She didn't look happy. Shouldn't she look happy, now they'd both confessed that they wanted the same thing?

He didn't get it. "Well, then?" he prodded. "Sabra, what is the problem? You want more, you just said so. You want more and so do I." He dared a step closer.

She jerked back, whipping up a hand. "You don't understand. That was last year. Everything's different now."

"Why? I don't get it. We're still the same people."

"No. No, we're not." She shook her head wildly. "Everything's changed for me, since my dad died."

"Sabra…"

"No. Wait. Listen, please. I see things so differently. I understand now that I've been kidding myself, thinking someday I would find love and happiness with someone, with *you*."

"But you have it. You have me. I love you."

"Oh, please," she scoffed. "Love and happiness? They just end, Matthias. They end and they leave you alone, with nothing. They leave you a shell of who you were, leave you just getting through the endless days, waiting for the time when it doesn't hurt anymore. And I, well, I can't. I just can't."

"But you said—"

"This." She talked right over him, lifting both hands out to her sides in an encompassing gesture, one that seemed to include him and the cabin, the clearing, the forest, the whole of the small world they shared over Christmas. *"This* is all I have in me. This is all it will ever be. I can never give you anything more and if you need something more, well, then you need to go out and get it."

Sabra glared at Matthias. And he just stared at her—a hurt look, and angry, too.

Well, fine. Let him stare. Let him be angry, as angry as she was—that he'd done this, that he'd sprung this on her. She couldn't take this. She didn't know how to deal.

At the same time, deep within her, a small voice chided that she was way overreacting, that her emotions were knocked all out of whack by her grief over her dad.

She felt so much for the man standing in front of her, felt desire and affection, felt *love.* Yeah. She did. She felt love, deep and strong. She didn't want to lose him.

But she *was* losing him. She *would* lose him. That was how life was—shining moments of joy and beauty, followed by a loneliness that killed.

Considering a future with him right now? It was like trying to decide what to do about the farm. She couldn't go back there and she couldn't let go of it.

It was all mixed up together—the farm, Matthias, her dad.

Her dad, who was gone now. She missed him so much and she despised herself for that, for daring to miss him, when she hadn't been there for him during the last, lonely years of his life.

She'd left him to waste away on his own when he needed her most.

And this, with Matthias, well, what more was there to say? "I really do have to go."

Matt got the message. He got it loud and clear.

She'd cut him off at the knees, wrecked him but good. She had to go?

Terrific. He wanted her out of there, wanted *not* to be looking into those big, wounded eyes.

He reached out and pulled open the door to the Subaru. "Drive safe, Sabra." The words tasted like sawdust in his mouth. Still, he did wish her well. "You take care of yourself."

She stared at him, her eyes bigger than ever, her face much too pale. And then, slowly, she nodded. "You, too." She got in behind the wheel.

This is how it ends, he thought. No goodbye kiss, no hope that there ever might be more.

Not so much as a mention of next year.

There probably wouldn't be a next year—not for the two of them, together. Somehow, he was going to have to learn to accept that.

After this, well, what was there to come back for?

He wanted more and she didn't. Really, where did they go from here?

He shut the door, called to his dog and went up the steps to the cabin without once looking back.

Chapter Ten

Sabra, the following March...

She didn't know what had come over her, really.

A...lightening. A strange sense of promise where for months there had been nothing but despair.

On the spur of the moment, she took four days off work in the middle of the month and drove up to the farm. Nils and Marjorie were at their house when she pulled into the yard. They ran out to greet her, grabbing her in tight hugs, saying what a nice surprise it was to see her. Meaning it, too.

Marjorie took her out to see the lambs. She also met with Nils for a couple of hours. They went over the books, discussed the upcoming market season. Soon, they would be planting blueberries, raspberries, blackberries and strawberries. They talked about the huge number of turkey orders for Thanksgiving—so many, in fact, that they'd already had to stop taking them. Next year, Nils planned to raise more birds.

Sabra joined Marjorie and Nils for dinner. Later, alone in the main house, she wandered the rooms. A cleaning team came in every three weeks to keep things tidy, so the place was in okay shape. But the greenhouse window in the kitchen needed someone to put a few potted plants in there and then take care of them.

And really, when you came right down to it, a kitchen remodel wouldn't hurt, either. In time. And a paint job, definitely. The old homestead could do with a general freshening-up if she ever intended to live here again.

Live here again?

Where had that idea come from?

She shook her head and put the thought from her mind.

That night, she slept in her old room, a dreamless, peaceful sort of sleep—or mostly dreamless, anyway.

Just before dawn she woke and realized she'd been dreaming of Matthias, a simple dream. They were here, in the farmhouse, together. In her dream, they went out to the front porch and sat in the twin rockers her dad had found years ago at a yard sale and refinished himself. Zoya snoozed at their feet.

Sabra sat up in bed, stretched, yawned and looked out the window where the pink fingers of morning light inched across the horizon. Shoving back the covers, she ran over there, pushed the window up and breathed in the cool morning smell of new grass and damp earth.

Spring was here. Already. And leaning on the sill she felt…close. To her mother and her father, to all the generations of Bonds before her.

The idea dawned like the new morning.

She didn't want to sell the farm.

She wanted to move home to stay.

Sabra, that July…

"So just track him down," insisted Iris. "You blew it and you need to reach out, tell him you messed up, that your head was all turned around over your dad dying. You need to beg him for another chance."

"I can't." Sabra dropped a stack of folded clothes into an open box.

"Can't?" Iris scoffed. "Won't. That's what you really mean."

"It wouldn't be right to him," said Sabra.

"Oh, yeah, it would. It's the rightest thing in the world, telling a man who loves you that you love him, too, and want to be with him."

They were at Sabra's apartment—Sabra, Iris and Peyton, too. Sabra was moving home to the farm and her friends were pitching in, helping her pack up to go.

She tried to make Iris understand. "It wasn't our deal to go looking for each other, to go butting into each other's regular lives. If I want to change the agreement, I need to do it when I see him, at Christmas."

"Who says you'll see him at Christmas?"

"Well, what I mean is that next Christmas would be the time to try again, if that's even possible anymore."

Iris shook her head. "Uh-uh. Not buying. You're just making excuses not to step up right now and get straight with the man you love."

Peyton emerged from the closet, her arms full of clothes. "Honey, I'm with Iris on this one." She dropped the clothes on the bed for Sabra to box up. "You screwed up. You need to fix it."

"And I will. At Christmas. I still have the key. I'll show up, as always, and I'll pray that he does, too."

Iris put both hands to her head and made an exploding gesture. "Wrong. Bad. You need to act now. He could find someone else in the next five months."

"He could have found someone else already," Sabra said, something inside of her dying a little at the very thought. "I *told* him to find someone else. I can't go breaking our rules and chasing after him now. If he's found someone new, I've got no right to try to get in the middle of that. I've got no right and I *won't*."

Iris opened her mouth to argue some more, but Peyton caught her eye and shook her head. "It's your call," Iris conceded at last. "But just for the record, I think you're making a big mistake."

Matt, early August...

Friday night at Beach Street Brews was as crowded and loud as ever. Matt was glad to be out, though. Sometimes a guy needed a beer, a bar full of people, and some mediocre rock and roll played at earsplitting levels.

The noise and party atmosphere distracted him, kept him from brooding over Sabra. It had been seven months since she'd made it painfully clear that they were going nowhere. Not ever. He needed to get over her, to get over *himself.*

It was past time for him to stop being an emo idiot and move the hell on. Life was too damn short to spend it longing for a woman who would never give him more than a holiday hookup. He was ready, after all these years, for a real relationship.

And damn it, he was through letting the important things pass him by.

Jerry, across the table from him, leaned in. "Someone's been asking to meet you." Jerry tipped his red head at two pretty women, a blonde and a brunette, as they approached their booth. "The blonde," said Jerry. "Mary's her name…"

The two women reached the booth. Jerry scooted over and patted the empty space next to him. The brunette sat down.

The blonde smiled shyly at Matt. "Matt Bravo," he said.

Her smile got brighter. "Mary Westbrook."

He moved over toward the wall and Mary slid in beside him.

They started talking, Matt and Mary. She'd gone to Valentine Bay High, graduated the same year as his sister Aislinn. Now Mary worked as a physical therapist at a local clinic. She had sky-blue eyes, a great laugh and an easy, friendly way about her.

No, she wasn't Sabra.

But Matt liked her. He liked her a lot.

Early November...

Matt sat on the sofa in his brother Daniel's study at the Bravo family house on Rhinehart Hill. Across the room, beyond his brother's big desk, the window that looked out over the front porch framed a portrait in fall colors, the maples deep red, the oaks gone to gold. Daniel's fourteen-month-old twins, Jake and Frannie, were upstairs with their latest nanny. Sometimes it was hard to believe how big those kids were now, and that it had been over a year since they lost Lillie.

A glass of scotch in each hand, Daniel came and sat in the armchair across the low table from Matt. He handed Matt a glass and offered a toast. "To you, Matt. And to the new woman in your life."

"Thanks." Matt touched his glass to his brother's and sipped. The scotch was excellent, smoky and hot going down.

Daniel took a slow sip, too. "I've been instructed to inform you that we all expect to be meeting Mary at Thanksgiving."

Matt chuckled. "Instructed, huh?"

Daniel didn't crack a smile. But then, he rarely did. "We have four sisters, in case you've forgotten."

"Sisters," Matt kidded back. "Right. I vaguely remember them, yeah."

"They're all pleased to learn you've met someone special. They want to get to know her. Connor and Liam do, too." Connor and Liam were third- and fourth-born in the family, respectively. "And so do I."

"Well, Aislinn has already been after me to bring Mary." The truth was, he'd hesitated over inviting

Mary. "I was kind of thinking it was too soon, you know?"

Daniel said, "It's never too soon if you really like someone."

An image took shape in his mind. It wasn't of Mary and he ordered it gone. "Well, good. I did invite her. She said yes. Mary's looking forward to meeting the family."

"I'm glad. And I'm happy for you…"

Two days later…

Unbuttoning his uniform shirt as he went, Matt led the way into his bedroom, Zoya hopping along behind. She stretched out on the rug by the bed and panted up at him contentedly as he finished getting out of his work clothes and stuffed them in the hamper.

That night, he was taking Mary out to eat and then to a stand-up comedy show at the Valentine Bay Theatre. He grabbed a pair of jeans from a drawer, tossed them across the bed and went to the closet for a shirt to wear under his jacket.

When he grabbed the blue button-down off the rod, he caught sight of a corner of this year's Wild and Scenic Oregon calendar still tacked to the wall. The hangers clattered loudly along the rod as he shoved them back, hard.

Why had he even bought the damn thing this year—and not only bought it, but for several months, continued crossing off the days?

Apparently, for some men, being told to forget it was just never enough.

The calendar was turned to October, with a view

of the Deschutes National Forest in fall. Below the beautiful picture of trees in autumn, the calendar page itself showed not a single red X. He'd stopped marking the days the month before.

And why was he keeping it? The calendar was of zero use or interest to him now.

He yanked it off the wall. The tack went flying. He heard it bounce on the closet floor, somewhere he'd probably step on it in bare feet one day soon.

Too bad. He didn't have time to crawl around looking for it now. Carrying the shirt in one hand and the calendar in the other, he ducked out of the closet. Marching straight to the dresser, he tossed the calendar in the wastebasket there. Then he dropped the shirt on the bed with his jeans and turned for the bathroom to grab a quick shower.

Sabra, early December...

In downtown Astoria, the shop windows and the streets were all decked out for Christmas. Acres of lighted garland bedecked with shiny ornaments and bells looped between the streetlights. Live trees in pots lined the sidewalk, each one lit up and hung with bright decorations.

At the corner, a lone musician played "White Christmas" on a xylophone. Sabra paused with a few other bundled-up shoppers to listen to the tune. When the song came to an end, she tossed a dollar in the open case at the musician's feet. Pulling her heavy jacket a little closer against the winter chill, she crossed the street and continued on to midway along the next block.

The store she sought was called Sugar and Spice. Like every other shop on the street, it had Christmas displays in the front windows, scenes of festively dressed mannequins, ones that were definitely more spicy than sweet. One mannequin wore a sexy elf costume and another, a red thong sewn with tiny, winking party lights. One had her hands bound behind her back with handcuffs, a Santa hat slipping sexily over one eye while a male mannequin in a leather jockstrap and policeman's hat tickled her with a giant green feather.

Inside, the girl behind the counter wore a skimpy Mrs. Santa Claus costume and a gray wig topped by a crown of Christmas tree lights. "Hey. What can I help you with?"

"Just looking…" Sabra headed for the racks of revealing lingerie.

Sexy Mrs. Claus followed her over there. "Are you wanting anything in particular?"

Help from an expert?

Really, what could it hurt? "It's like this," Sabra said as she checked through the bra-and-panty sets. "I'm in—or at least, I've *been* in—this wonderful relationship. But we aren't together all the time. We meet up for several days, once a year."

Mrs. Claus looked confused. "What's the kink?"

Sabra laughed. "It's just once a year, over Christmas, no contact otherwise. Is that a kink?"

Mrs. Claus let that question go. "Let me try again. So…there's a problem in this relationship?"

"Well, the thing is, last year it ended badly and it was all my fault."

Mrs. Claus made a soft, sympathetic sound. "Oh, no."

"Yeah. And, see, I don't want to break our rules.

I'm not going to stalk the guy. But this year, I'll be there at the usual place and time in case he does show. I'm going to knock myself out to make things right, make it..."

"More?" suggested Mrs. Claus.

Sabra paused in her impatient flicking from one panty set to the next. "More. Yes. That's it. I want more with him. Last year, he was already there in the *more* department. He wanted to take the biggest chance of all with me. But I wasn't ready. I said some things that I wish I hadn't. It's very likely he took what I said to mean it was over between us. And now, I only want a prayer that he might be willing to give me another shot. I don't need handcuffs or a latex suit. I just want to feel confident. If he shows up and I get lucky enough to make it as far as taking off my clothes..."

"You want him wowed." Mrs. Claus had that look, the one a sales professional gets when she finally understands exactly what her customer is shopping for. "You don't want to role-play or try something new. You just want to be you, the sexiest possible you."

Sabra grabbed an itty-bitty black satin number, held it up and joked, "You don't happen to have this in camo?"

Mrs. Claus's smile was slow and also triumphant. "As a matter of fact, we do."

Sabra bought the sexy camo undies and several other seductive bits of lace and satin. She knew that cute underwear wasn't the answer to anything, really. If Matthias was through with her, a see-through bra wouldn't change his mind.

And yet, she felt hopeful and excited.

She was ready to go all in with him, at last. All he had to do was show up this year and she would pull out all the stops to get just one more chance with him.

December 23, last year...

Sabra's heart just about detonated in her chest when she turned the last corner and rolled into the clearing. Matthias, in a uniform that looked identical to the one his friend Jerry had been wearing when he stopped by the year before, leaned back against the tailgate of a state trooper patrol truck.

He's here! He came!

For a few glorious, too-brief seconds, she knew she was getting the second chance she'd longed for, that this year, she was going to make everything come out right.

She pulled her car to a stop several feet back from the man and the truck.

About then, in the silence that followed turning off the engine, she started putting it together.

This was all wrong.

No lights in the cabin, Matthias in his uniform, with a mud-splattered state police vehicle behind him. No Zoya. No gorgeous Christmas tree tied to a rack on the roof.

And he hadn't moved yet. He remained at the tailgate, big arms across his chest, his hat shading his eyes.

Her hands shook and her stomach pitched and rolled. She sat there in the driver's seat, her heart hurling itself madly against the wall of her chest, unable to move for a good count of ten.

But this was her show, now wasn't it? She could already see that he wasn't planning a tender reunion. If she didn't want to talk to him, she ought to start the engine again and drive away.

That seemed the less painful option in the short run—and also the one that would always leave her wondering, leave her hanging. Leave her wishing she'd asked him straight out for another chance.

If he said no, well, *Goodbye* was an actual word. And she needed to hear him say it out loud.

First step: get out of the damn car.

But still she didn't move. Her mind sparked wildly, impulses firing madly, going off like bottle rockets in her brain, shooting along the endless network of nerves in her body, leading her exactly nowhere.

Grabbing the latch with shaking fingers, she gave it a yank.

The door opened and she swung her legs out, rising without pausing to steady herself. Surprisingly, she didn't go pitching over facedown in the dirt.

She was on her feet and moving toward him. A couple of yards away from him, she stopped. He swiped off his hat. The pain in her chest was damn near unbearable.

His blue eyes told her nothing. They *gave* her nothing.

The sun was out, of all things. It brought out the silvery threads in his dark blond hair. He was so beautiful, all square-jawed and uncompromising, with that broad chest and those big arms she wanted wrapped good and hard around her.

Not mine. The two words ripped through her brain

like a buzz saw. Whatever they'd had, it was gone now. He was not hers and he never would be.

She'd had her chance and she hadn't been ready. It was no one's fault, really. Timing did matter and hers had been seriously bad. "I take it you're not staying."

Matt had dreaded this moment.

He'd known that whatever happened—if she showed, if she didn't—it was going to be bad.

But this—the very sight of her, the stricken look on her face—it was worse than he'd ever imagined it could be.

"I didn't really expect you to show," he said. The words felt cruel as they fell from his lips. He'd driven out here feeling angry and wronged, self-righteous. Ready to lay it on her that he'd taken her advice and found someone new, willing her to be here so he could have the final say.

But now, having simply watched her get out of her car and walk over to him, having looked her square in her beautiful face, all that sanctimonious fury had drained out of him. He had no anger left to sustain him.

"I'm on duty," he said.

"Uh, yeah. I kind of figured that."

"But I came by just in case you showed up, so you wouldn't wonder—I mean, you know. Be left hanging."

"Thank you." The skin was too pale around her soft lips. He needed to reach for her, hold her, soothe her.

He wrapped both arms across his chest good and tight, the hat dangling from between the fingers of his right hand. It was the only way to keep himself from grabbing her close.

Spit it out, you SOB. Just say it. "I've met someone."

"Ah." The sound was so soft. Full of pain. And understanding. Two bright spots of color flamed high on her cheeks. He was hurting her, hurting her so bad.

What she'd done to him last year? It was nothing compared to what he was putting her through now.

He needed to explain himself, he realized, needed to say something *real* to her, something true, from his heart. "Sabra, I swear to you, I never would have moved on."

She swallowed convulsively and gave him a sharp nod. "Yeah." It came out a ragged little whisper. "I know that. I do."

"You were so insistent. So sure."

"Yes. You're right. I was."

"You *told* me to find someone else."

"And you did." She smiled. It seemed to take a lot of effort. "I'm, um, glad for you. I want you to be happy, Matthias, I honestly do."

"You have meant so much to me," he said, striving for the right words, the true words, from his heart. "More than I seem to know how to say."

Kind, Sabra thought. *He's trying so hard to be kind.*

So why did it feel like he was ripping her heart out?

Worst of all, she got it. She saw it so clearly. What he was doing to her now was essentially what she'd done to him a year ago.

She'd hurt him, told him outright he would never have what he longed for from her. He'd done what he had to do to get over her. She knew she had no one to blame but herself.

Now she just needed to hold it together, get through this with some small shred of dignity intact.

She was about to open her mouth and wish him well with his new love—and the words got clogged in her throat.

Because she just couldn't.

If another woman loved him now and did it well and fully, well, all right then. He should be with that woman.

But to completely give up, right here and now?

She just wasn't that good of a person. "I have a request."

"Name it."

"I have the key and I'll give it to you if that's how you want it. But I'm asking you to let me keep it for one more year. Let me keep it and I will be here, same time as always, next year. If you're still with your new love, just stay away till the sun is down. If you don't show by dark, that will be all I need to know. I'll lock up and push the key under the door. You'll never see me again."

There was more. So much more she needed to say, including the most important words...

I love you, Matthias. I love you and I should have said so last year.

But she hadn't. Instead, she'd told him to find someone else. And now they were here, in the cold December sunlight, saying goodbye. And she had no right at all to speak her love out loud.

She shut her mouth and waited, certain he would

say that he wanted his key back and he wanted it right now.

But he only stood there, holding his hat, arms folded hard against her, his expression blank, those beautiful eyes of his so guarded.

Time stretched out on a razor's edge of loss and misery. She tried to reassure herself.

He wasn't asking for the key back, was he? That was a good sign.

Wasn't it?

She almost let herself feel the faintest glimmer of hope.

But then he broke the awful silence. "Goodbye, Sabra."

And with that, he put his hat back on and turned on his heel, heading for the driver's side of the pickup. She just stood there, afraid to move for fear she would shatter.

He got in, turned the engine on, circled the cabin and disappeared down the twisting dirt road.

She held it together, barely, until the sound of his engine faded away in the distance.

Then her knees stopped working. With a strangled cry, she sank to a crouch. "Get up," she muttered, disgusted with herself.

But it was no good. Her heart was aching so bad and there was really no alternative but to give herself up to the pain.

At least he was gone. He wouldn't have to see this.

It was just her and her broken heart, the bitter taste of regret on her tongue.

Wrapping her arms around herself, Sabra gave in

completely. Slowly, she toppled onto her side. Curling up into herself on the cold winter ground, she let her tears fall.

Chapter Eleven

Sabra, the following March...

"This kitchen is gorgeous," Peyton declared from her favorite spot at Sabra's new chef-quality stove. "You did it all. The farm sink, these quartz counters. Clean white cabinets with all the storage options and inner drawers. I'm so jealous."

Sabra, sitting at the island next to Iris, sipped her wine. "You saw it before. A bad memory from the early '80s. Uh-uh. It was crying out for an update and we've been doing better than ever since I finally moved home and started tackling my job here, day-to-day. I've hooked us up with two new restaurants, big accounts. It all helps—and you, my dear Peyton, are invited to make your magic in my new kitchen anytime." The wonderful smell of Peyton's special pasta sauce graced the air. "You, too." Sabra elbowed Iris playfully and then raised her wineglass. "Just bring more of this wine with you when you come."

An hour later, they sat on the long benches at the harvest table her great-grandfather had built and shared the meal Peyton had cooked for them. It wasn't until they'd taken their coffee into the living room that Sabra's friends started in on her about the "cabin guy" and how she needed to get over him.

Iris insisted, "You can't spend the whole year just sitting around waiting on a guy who's with someone else and only showed up last year to say goodbye."

Pain, fresh and sharp, stabbed through her at the thought of that too-bright December day. "Who says I'm just sitting around? I've got a farm to run."

"Please, girlfriend. We're not talking about work and you know we're not. We're talking about your social life, which is essentially nonexistent."

"Wait a minute. I have *you* guys. I have other friends, too, longtime friends I grew up with. We've reconnected since I moved home and we get together now and then, meet up for a show or lunch, or whatever."

"You do hear yourself," Peyton chimed in. "*Friends*, you said."

"We are talking *men*," said Iris. "And not men *friends*. Uh-uh. You owe yourself at least a few hot nights, some seriously sexy times."

"That's not going to happen. It's not who I am and I'm fine with that."

"Just download a few dating apps," Peyton pleaded.

"FarmersOnly.com, for crying out loud," moaned Iris.

"But I—"

"No." Iris shook a finger at her. "No excuses. Even if everything goes the way you hope it will next Christmas, even if it's over with the other woman, if he drops to his knees and begs for one more chance with you—that changes nothing. You *owe* that man nothing. From now until then is a long time. You owe it to *yourself* to make good use of that time."

"Make *use* of it?" Sabra scoffed. "What does that even mean?"

"It means that you went from Stan the Swine to James the Jerk to once a year with the cabin guy. It's not going to kill you to step out of your comfort zone and see what's out there. You need to mix it up a little. You just might find a man who's as ready for you as you are for him."

"But I *told* you. Matthias *was* ready. *I* messed it up."

"Don't you dare blame yourself." Iris was nothing if not loyal. "You'd lost your *dad*. That man you're pining for now could have been a *little* more understanding."

"And you've already boxed yourself in," Peyton chided. "You won't contact the guy before Christmas."

"I told you, that's our agreement and—"

"Understood." Peyton cut her off, but in a gentle tone. "My point is, there's nothing more you can do for now in terms of Matthias."

"So?"

"So, it's a lot of months until December. Make those months count, that's all we're saying."

"It's a numbers game," declared Iris. "You've got

to get out there and kiss a lot of toads before you're ever going to meet the right guy for you."

"I've already met the right guy," Sabra said quietly, knowing in her deepest heart that it was true. "I've met the right guy—and he's with someone else now."

Her friends shook their heads.

They sipped their coffee in silence for a few seconds.

"Just try," Peyton urged softly at last. "A few dates, that's all. Give some other guy a shot."

Sabra wasn't exactly sure how they'd done it. But Peyton and Iris had prevailed. She had three dating apps on her phone now.

And she made an effort. She truly did. She filled out her profile information in detail, honestly. And she asked Marjorie, who had a certain aptitude with a digital camera, to take some good pictures of her which she posted with her profiles.

And then she started interacting, reaching out to guys whose profiles and pictures looked interesting, responding when someone reached out to her. She went with her instincts. If a guy seemed creepy or catfishy, she let him know she wasn't interested and moved on.

Truth to tell, none of them *really* interested her. Because she wanted Matthias and she just plain *wasn't* interested.

When she'd failed to so much as meet a guy for coffee by the end of April, Iris gave her a pep talk about not trying hard enough, about the need to get out there, in real life.

Sabra knew her friend had a point. There was trying—and there was *really* trying. Yeah, she'd put up the profiles and interacted a little online, but nothing more.

And that made her kind of an internet dating jerk, now didn't it? She wasn't benching or breadcrumbing anyone. She was simply wasting the time of the men she right-swiped. She needed to do better, make a real effort, if only to prove to herself that there wasn't some unknown guy waiting out there who was just right for her, a guy who could have her asking, *Matthias Bravo, who?*

Could that ever actually happen?

No. Uh-uh. She knew with absolute certainty that it couldn't.

However, more than once in her life she'd been totally wrong. Romantically speaking, at this point in time, she was 0 for 3. What did she know, really, about any of this?

Sabra kept at it.

No, she wasn't ready to get up close and in person with these guys she was making contact with online. But at least by mid-May, she'd stepped up her game from mere messaging to Skype and FaceTime. It was so much easier to eliminate a guy once she'd seen him in action, heard his voice while his mouth was moving—and there she went again, thinking in terms of eliminating a man rather than trying really hard to meet someone new.

Finally, in June, she did it, took a giant step forward.

She agreed to meet a nice guy named Dave at the Astoria Farmer's Market. Dave seemed every bit as nice in person as he had during their messaging phase and on FaceTime. Too bad there was zero spark. None. A complete and utter lack of chemistry.

Worse, she felt like she was cheating on Matthias.

As they reached the last booth, Dave asked her out to dinner that night.

She turned him down. Dave got the message. She never heard from him again. Which was all for the best.

She did coffee dates after that. Several of them. During each one, she nursed a latte and wished she was anywhere but there.

She went out with a podiatrist who talked really fast and all about himself through a very expensive dinner. Then later, on the sidewalk outside the restaurant, he grabbed her and tried to choke her with his tongue down her throat. Somehow, she resisted the urge to smack his self-absorbed face and simply told him never to try anything like that again with her.

He called her a tease and a few other uglier names. And then, of all things, he grabbed her hand, kissed it and apologized profusely.

She said, "Apology accepted. Just please, never contact me again."

After the podiatrist, she took a break from dating. She figured she needed it. Deserved it, even.

Then, in late September, on CompatibleMate.com, she met a lawyer named Ted.

They went out to a concert and she had a good time. When he kissed her at her door, it was…pleasant.

And pleasant was pretty awful. A man's kiss should be much more than *pleasant*, or what was the point?

Still, that's what Ted's kiss was. Pleasant.

She experienced none of the goodness the right

kiss always brings—no shivers racing up and down her spine, no galloping heart, no fireworks whatsoever. In fact, what she felt was a deep sadness, a longing for Matthias.

But Ted really did seem like a great guy. She liked him.

He asked her out again two weeks later and she said yes to dinner and a show. That time, when he kissed her as they were saying goodnight, she knew beyond any doubt that she never wanted to kiss him again.

And when he called her a few nights later to ask her out for Friday night, she knew she should turn him down, tell him how much she liked him, explain somehow that merely liking him wasn't enough, that she was wasting his time and that wasn't right.

But there was nothing *wrong* with him—other than the simple fact that he wasn't Matthias. In no way was that Ted's fault.

She opened her mouth to express her regrets—and a yes fell out.

They went to dinner again. Ted seemed happy. Buoyant, even. He talked about his firm and how well he was doing there. He asked about the farm and he actually seemed interested when she proudly described the orchard of sapling fruit trees they'd put in that spring.

Over dessert, Ted leaned across the table, his dark eyes gleaming, a happy grin on his handsome face. "I have to tell you. I never thought this would work for me. But Sabra, now I've found you, I'm changing my mind about meeting someone online. I know we haven't really taken it to the next level, so to speak. But still. This is special, what's happening between us. Don't you feel it? Here we are on date three and I'm honestly thinking we're going somewhere."

Going somewhere?

No way.

Sabra kind of hated herself at that moment. She knew she had to stop this, that she had no right to go one second longer without getting real with the guy. "I'm sorry, Ted."

He sat back. "Sorry?"

"The truth is, you and I are never reaching the next level. We're going nowhere. I'm in love with someone else and I can't do this anymore."

Ted's eyes were no longer gleaming. "Tell me something, Sabra," he said, cool and flat. "If you're in love with someone else, why the hell aren't you with him—and you know what?" He shoved back his chair and plunked his napkin on the table. "Don't answer that because I don't even care."

Muttering invectives against online dating in general and, more specifically, crazy women who mess with a guy's mind, he headed for the door.

With a sigh, Sabra signaled for the check.

Late October...

"I'm done, you guys," Sabra said. "Finished. Not going there—online or otherwise. Because you know what? Ted was right. It's wrong to use one guy to try to forget another. And I'm never doing that again."

Her friends regarded her solemnly from the other side of her harvest table. "We do get it," admitted Peyton.

Iris, as always, asked the hardest question. "What will you do if he doesn't show in December?"

Her heart broke all over again at the very thought. But she drew herself up straight. "Die a little. Suffer a lot—and please don't look so worried. I love Matthias. I want him. No one else but him. I have to go all the way with that first. If he's not there on December twenty-third, *that's* when I'll have to figure out what comes next." She looked from one dear face to the other. "I know. I get it. I mean, who does what he and I have done? What two sane people make an agreement to have each other just for the holidays—and then keep that agreement for years? I know that sounds batcrap crazy, I do. But it worked for us. It was what we both needed. Our agreement created the space we both required, the time and patience to learn to love again. I truly believe that if my dad hadn't died, Matthias and I would be married by now. But he did die and that threw everything into chaos for me. Matthias asked me for more and I answered no, unequivocally. I told him never. I said if he wanted more, he needed to go and find someone else. Which brought us here."

"Matthias should have waited," grumbled Iris, swiping a tear from her cheek. "He should have given you more space."

"Space? I had *years* of space. And he did wait. I knew it. I felt it, the year before I lost my dad. I knew he wanted more that year and *I* wanted more, too. But neither of us stepped up and said so. Still, when we parted that year, I knew that the next year, we would be taking it further. That didn't happen because the next year, I was a mess. But he *had* waited. He'd waited out that whole year."

Peyton said sheepishly, "Honey, we just want you to be prepared, you know? Just in case he, well, I mean…" Her voice trailed off.

Sabra put it right out there. "You honestly don't think he's going to be there, do you?" Both of her friends remained silent. But the truth was in their eyes. Peyton glanced away. And Iris gave a sad little shrug. Sabra said firmly, "There is no preparing for that. If he doesn't show, for me it's going to be as bad as it was last Christmas."

"But…" Peyton swallowed hard. "I mean, you *will* get through it, right? You'll be okay?"

Sabra did understand the deeper implications of the question. And she loved her friends all the more for venturing into this difficult territory. "I adored my dad. I miss him every day and I wish I'd done more to help him live without my mom. In many ways, I'm like him. A total romantic, devoted until death. But I'm like my mom, too. And my mom was stronger than my dad was, strong *and* practical." Sabra reached across the rough wood surface of the old table.

Her friends were there to meet her. Peyton's hand settled on hers and then Iris's hand covered Peyton's.

"You'll make it through, one way or another," said Iris. "That's what you're telling us, right?"

"One way or another, yes. If he doesn't show, I may curl up in a fetal position and cry my eyes out just like I did last year. I may spend a lot of time being depressed and self-indulgent. I may be miserable for months. It's possible that, after being with him, knowing him, *loving* him, there's just no one else for me, that he's it for me, the one. Whatever happens, though, however it ends up with him this year, I promise you both that I will make it through."

December 23, this year...

An emotional wreck.

That described Sabra's condition exactly as she drove toward the cabin. An emotional wreck who almost ended up an *actual* wreck. Twice.

She kept spacing off, praying he would be there, then *certain* he would be there. And then *knowing* absolutely that she was deluding herself completely. He wasn't going to be there and how would she bear it?

It was during one of those spaced-out moments that a deer bolted out into the road and then stopped stock-still and stared at her through her windshield, as if to say, *Whoa. A car. Where'd that come from?*

She slammed on the brakes and skidded to a stop just in time. The deer—a nice buck, a six pointer—stared at her for a good ten seconds more before leaping off into the brush again.

She took her foot off the brake and carefully steered to the shoulder of the road, where she dropped her forehead to the steering wheel and waited for her heart to stop trying to punch its way out of her chest.

When her mouth no longer tasted like old pennies and her hands had stopped shaking, she set out again.

The second almost-wreck happened after she'd turned off the highway into the woods, onto the series of unimproved roads that would finally take her to the cabin and her own personal moment of truth. Really, she didn't know what happened that second time. She was looking at the road, both hands on the wheel.

But her mind? Her heart? Her whole being?

Elsewhere, far away, lost in memories of Christmases past. Of nights on the porch in a world buried in snow, of his hands—so big and yet deft and quick, whittling a small piece of wood into a porcupine, just for her, touching her naked body, showing her all the ways he could make her moan.

The giant tree seemed to rise up in front of her out of nowhere. With a shriek, she slammed the brakes again, sliding on the dirt road, her heartbeat so loud in her ears it sounded like drums, her whole body gone strangely tingly and numb with the sheer unreality of what was happening.

By some miracle, she eased the wheel to the right with the slide of gravel beneath her tires. The Subaru cleared the tree by mere inches. She came to a stop with the tree looming in her side window.

After that near-death experience, she turned off the engine, slumped back in her seat, shut her eyes and reminded herself that she'd promised Iris and Peyton she would get through this, one way or another. It would be so wrong for her to end up a statistic—especially if she finished herself off before even getting to the cabin and finding out that, just maybe, the man she hoped to meet there had shown up ready to try again, exactly as she dreamed he might.

He could be there right this minute, waiting to take her in his arms and swear that from this day forward, she was his only one.

Oh, if only that could really happen.

She was on fire to be the one for him, to claim him as hers. She yearned for this to be it, *their* year, the year they finally built something more than a beautiful Christmas together.

But none of that was even possible if she didn't keep her eyes on the road and get her ass to the cabin.

She started up the car again and put it in gear.

Five minutes later, her spirits hit a new low. The suspense was unbearable. And she really should face reality.

Her friends were right. Matthias had found someone else and she needed to accept that. She needed to stop this idiocy and find a way to move on as she'd once told him to do.

She should give up this foolishness, she kept thinking, give it up and go home. There was no point. She was only driving toward more heartbreak.

But she didn't turn around.

When she reached the last stretch of dirt road leading up to the cabin, her heart was hammering so hard and so fast, she worried it might just explode from her body. They would find her days from now, the front end of the Outback crunched against a tree, her lifeless form slumped in the seat, a gaping, empty hole in the middle of her chest.

She rounded the last curve and the cabin came into view.

Her nearly-exploded heart stopped dead—and then began beating again faster than ever as she pulled to a stop behind the muddy Jeep.

The gray world had come alive again. With anticipation. With promise. With her love that filled her up and overflowed, bringing the woods and the clearing, the rustic cabin, even the car in which she sat, into sharper focus, everything so vivid, in living color.

She heard a gleeful laugh. It was her own. "Yes!" she cried aloud. "Yes, yes, yes!"

Oh, it was perfect. The best moment ever. Her seemingly hopeless dream, finally, at last, coming true.

Golden light shone from the windows and smoke curled lazily from the stone chimney, drifting upward toward the gray sky. She managed to turn off the engine.

And then she just sat there, barely breathing, unable to move, still marginally terrified that she was reading this all wrong, that the man inside the cabin wasn't really waiting there for her.

Until the front door swung open.

And at last, after so long—*too* long, forever and a day—she saw him.

So tall and broad, in camo pants, boots and a mud-colored shirt, his dirty-blond hair a little longer than last year, every inch of him powerful, strong, muscular. Cut.

Joy burst like a blinding light inside her as her gaze met his. She saw it all then. In the blue fire of his eyes, in his slow, welcoming smile.

Mine, she thought. *All mine. As I am his. At last.*

Chapter Twelve

He came for her, moving fast down the porch steps, boots eating up the distance between them, eyes promising everything.

Love. Heat. Wonder. The kind of bond that weathers the worst storms. Joy and laughter and the two of them, together, forever and ever, building a family, making a rich and meaningful life.

She threw open her door just as he reached her. Popping the seat belt latch, she flung herself toward him.

He caught her, those strong arms going around her. She landed on her feet against his broad, hard chest.

"Oh, thank God..." They breathed the prayerful words in unison. And then his beautiful mouth crashed down on hers.

The clean, man-and-cedar scent of him was all

around her, encompassing her, exciting her even more. The kiss grew deeper, and his hold on her got tighter.

One minute, she had her two feet on the ground and the next, he swept her up against his chest, still kissing her, still holding her the way she'd dreamed he might again someday.

Like she was his and he was hers and he would never, ever let her go. He turned for the house, kissing her as he went.

Up the steps he took her, through the open door.

The scent of evergreen intensified as he kicked the door shut. He'd already brought the tree in and propped it up in the stand. Zoya lay by the fire, panting a little. She rolled over inviting a belly scratch and let out a whine of greeting. Sabra saw the tree and the dog in fleeting glimpses, keeping her mouth locked to his, worshipping him with that kiss.

Matthias kept walking, carrying her across the rough boards of the floor, to the stairs and up them.

The kiss never broke.

Until he threw her on the bed. She bounced twice, laughing.

"Take everything off." His eyes made a million very sexy promises. "Do it fast."

Not a problem. Not in the least. They stripped in unison, clothes flying everywhere. She'd worn one of those sexy bra-and-panty sets she'd bought the year before, but she gave him no time to appreciate them. She tore them off and tossed them aside.

And he?

Oh, he was everything she remembered, all she longed for—honed and deep-chested, with those sculpted arms that took her breath away. Such a big man.

Everywhere.

She held up her arms to him and he came down to her, grabbing her close again, slamming his mouth on hers.

It was frantic and hungry, not smooth in the least. Needful and desperate, necessary as air. They rolled, their hands everywhere, relearning each other, every muscle, every secret curve. There were more kisses, deep ones that turned her heart inside out. His fingers found the core of her, so wet, so ready.

They needed more.

They needed everything, to be joined, each to the other.

He produced a condom seemingly from thin air.

"Planned ahead, did you?" she asked, trying to tease him, ending up sounding breathless and needy.

His eyes burned into hers. "I want this, Sabra. Us. I want it forever."

"Yes," she said, before he'd even finished asking. "Forever. You and me."

"Don't leave me. Don't do that again. Don't drive me away." He stroked her cheek.

"I won't. I swear it. I'm ready now, Matthias. Ready for the rest of our lives, you and me. I love you. You're the only one, and you always will be."

"Sabra…" He kissed her again, wildly, his fingers tunneling in her hair, his mouth demanding every-thing, all of her. "My love," he whispered against her parted lips. "I love you, always. I was such a fool."

"It's not as if you were the only fool." She broke away enough to plead, "Let me…" And she took the condom from him, removed the wrapper and carefully slid it on.

Once she had it in place, he lifted her as though she weighed nothing. Stretching out on his back, he set her down on top of him.

She was so ready. Beyond ready. Rising to her knees, she lined him up with her heat and took him inside—all the way, to the hilt.

He groaned and she bent to him, claiming his mouth with hers, rocking her hips on him in long, needful strokes. He clasped her bottom with those strong hands, one palm on each cheek, and moved with her, surging up into her, sending her reeling.

She came with a gleeful cry.

And then he was rolling them, taking the top position. Rising up over her, he pushed in deep and true.

That time, when her second finish shattered through her, he joined her. They cried out in unison, going over as one, holding each other, Matthias and Sabra.

Together.

At last.

An hour or two later, they went downstairs naked. She greeted Zoya and admired the tree.

He didn't let her linger in the main room long, though. Pulling her into the bathroom, he filled the tub, added bath salts, climbed in and crooked a finger at her to join him.

She did, eagerly, settling in between his legs, leaning back on him. He really did make the firmest, most supportive sort of pillow. For a while, they floated in the hot water that smelled of lemons and mint.

He told her that he had a missing sister.

"What? You're kidding me."

He nuzzled her hair. "Nope. This past year, we found out that the oldest of my sisters, Aislinn, was switched at birth."

"So then, Aislinn isn't your sister by blood?"

"No. If she hadn't been switched, her name would be Madison Delaney."

"Wait." Sabra sat up, sending water sloshing. "Not *the* Madison Delaney, America's darling, the movie star?"

"Yes." Gently, Matthias pulled her back to rest against his chest. "We have a long-lost sister, and she is a movie star."

"Wow."

"Exactly. We've been trying to reach out to her. So far, our attempts have been rebuffed—either by her or by the people who protect her, we're not sure which."

"But you're not giving up." It wasn't a question.

He replied as she knew he would. "One way or another, we'll find a way to get through to her. As we will find Finn. Someday. Somehow…"

"I know you will," she whispered, and they were silent for a time.

But then, he bent his head to her and pressed his rough cheek to her smooth one. "Forever," he said gruffly. "I mean it. You still on for that?"

"Always." She lifted her arm from the water and reached back to slide her wet hand around the nape of his neck, tipping her head up to him for a quick kiss.

But one kiss from him? Never enough.

Already she could feel him, growing hard and ready, wanting her as she wanted him—again.

* * *

Sometime later, she told him that she'd moved back to the farm.

"When was that?" he asked.

"It's been a long time now. I moved in July, a year and a half ago."

He nuzzled her hair, which she'd piled on her head to keep it from getting too wet. "So then, you were already living there last Christmas, when I showed up just long enough to tell you it was over."

"Yeah."

He muttered something bleak. She couldn't make out the exact words, and she decided not to ask. Instead, she took his hand from the side of the tub and pulled it down into the water, across her stomach, so his arm was wrapped around her.

"Are you happy there, at your family's farm?" He bit the shell of her ear, so lightly, causing a thrilled little shiver to slide through her.

"Very." She slithered around, splashing water everywhere, until she was face-to-face with him. "I'm hoping to stay there."

"Hoping?"

"Well, I want to be with you. And maybe you want to stay in Valentine Bay." He kissed the end of her nose and she backpedaled, "If I'm moving too fast for you—?"

"No way. There is no 'too fast' when it comes to you and me, not anymore. We've wasted too much time already." He took her slippery shoulders and pulled her up so he could claim her mouth in a lazy, thorough kiss. When he finally allowed her to sink back into the cooling water, he said, "Yes. I'll move to your farm with you."

She reached up, pressed her hand to his bristly cheek. "You haven't even seen the place yet."

"I don't need to see it. You've moved home and that makes you happy. I love you and for me, home is where you are. You've mentioned that your farm is in Astoria, which means my field office is nearby. Getting to work won't be an issue—and do you realize you've never told me the name of this farm of yours?"

"Berry Bog Farm."

"Perfect."

"What's perfect?"

"Everything." He traced her eyebrows, one and then the other. "I'm going to need your phone number as soon as we get out of this tub."

"You got it."

"I'm serious, Sabra. I won't let you leave this cabin, not even to sit on the porch, until your number is safe in my phone."

"I'll get right on that."

"You'd better," he warned, but when she started to climb from the tub, he held her there. "Not yet. In a little while."

With a sigh, she kissed his square chin. "This is kind of nice, you and me, naked in the tub together…"

"*Kind of nice* doesn't even come close." He pressed his wet hand to her cheek, then made a cradle of his index finger and lifted her chin so their eyes met. "The thing with Mary…?"

Her heart felt caged, suddenly, hurting in her too-small chest. "That's her name? Mary?"

He nodded. And then he pressed his forehead to

hers and whispered, "I never should have started it with her. I was so hurt and mad at you."

She whispered her own confession. "I was so screwed up over my dad, screwed up and afraid, of you and me, of how powerful and good it was between us, of trusting what we have together—and then of someday losing you, like my dad lost my mom. So I told you to go out and look for what you needed. No way can I blame you for taking me at my word. I just hope... Oh, I don't know. I feel bad for her. For you. For all of it."

"It's been over with her for a year," he said. "A year, as of today."

She stared at him, confused. "You broke up with her on the twenty-third of *last* December?"

"That's right."

"The same day you drove up here to tell me you were with her?"

"That's the one."

"But I don't, I mean, how...?"

He pulled on a damp curl of her hair and then guided it tenderly behind her ear. "I knew it wouldn't work with her the minute I saw your face last year. I was just too damn stubborn to admit it right then. But as soon as I left you standing there alone, I knew what I had to do. I drove back to Valentine Bay feeling like a first-class jerk, wondering how I was going to break it to Mary that I couldn't be with her, that it was all wrong."

"Oh, Matt. And at the holidays, no less. What a mess I made. I'm so sorry."

But he gave her that wonderful, wry smile she loved so much. "It could have been worse. As it turned out, I didn't have to play the jerk, after all. Mary broke up with *me*."

She gasped. "No."

"Oh, yeah. We had a date to see a Christmas play that night. I went to pick her up and she asked me to come in for a minute. I stepped over the threshold— and then we just stood there by the door and she said how she'd been thinking, that it just wasn't working for her with me, that it wasn't love and she didn't feel it ever could be, that she and I needed to face the truth and move on. She really meant it," he said, his wry smile in evidence again. "We ended it right then, simple as that."

Sabra cradled his beard-scruffy cheek. "I do want to apologize sincerely, for hurting you, for sending you off to find someone else. I really messed that up. I could have lost you forever."

Matthias frowned. "I pushed too hard at the wrong time. You were all turned around over losing your dad. I wasn't patient and I should have been. As for losing me, you never could, not really. Somehow, I would always find my way back to you."

"And I. To you." They did that thing lovers do, having sex with their eyes. Then, with a happy sigh, she floated to her back once more and rested against him. "I have to ask…"

His warm breath stirred her hair as he pressed a kiss to the crown of her head. "Anything."

"All that time, from last Christmas to now. Did you know you would come to meet me today?"

"I did. No question, as sure as I knew I would draw my next breath. I also spent too many sleepless nights positive that you would give up on me, find someone else, change your mind. I could think of a million ways it was not going to work out, picture myself waiting here for hour after hour, alone."

"There's no one else, I promise," she said fervently.

He bent and pressed a kiss into that tender spot where her neck met her shoulder. "Baby, something in your voice says there's a story you're not telling me."

She blew out a hard breath and admitted, "My friends said I really had to try seeing other guys…"

He was suddenly too quiet behind her. Was he even breathing? "And did you?" he asked.

"I did, yes."

"And…?"

She winced. "You really want to hear this?"

"Damn straight I do."

She told him everything, all about her adventures in online dating, starting with the online chats and the coffee dates, moving on to the Farmer's Market day with Dave, the awful evening with the grabby podiatrist and the three dates with Ted.

When she first started putting it all out there, Matthias remained still as a statue behind her. But he slowly relaxed. He said he would like to go a few rounds with that foot doctor. And he made a sound of approval when she got to how she told Ted that she was in love with someone else and added, "Meaning you," just in case he had a single doubt by now who owned her heart.

Once she'd told him everything, she asked, "How come you didn't just come looking for me sooner? You could have saved me from all those bad dates, saved yourself from worrying that I wouldn't show up here for Christmas. I don't think I would have been that hard to find."

His hand stroked slowly along her arm, fingers brushing up and down. "That wasn't our agreement."

She slithered around again, getting front to front. "I can't believe you know that, that you understand that."

He looked vaguely puzzled. "*Should* I have tracked you down?"

"I have no idea." Sending water splashing, she rose up to kiss him and then settled back down against his broad chest. "What I do know," she said, "is that I've always felt that trying to find you between Christmases would be wrong. I felt it was important that we both respected the agreement we'd made together, that if the terms were going to change, they had to change at Christmastime."

He caught her face between his wet hands and pulled her up so her parted lips were only an inch from his. "Everything is changed, as of now. We're agreed on that, right?"

She bobbed her head up and down in his hold. "Yes, we are. I'm in. You're in. Both of us. A hundred percent."

"We're together now. We're taking this thing we have public and we're doing that before New Year's."

"Yes. You and me, in front of the whole world—have you got vacation time this year?"

His lips brushed hers again. "I'm off until January second."

"Good. We'll visit your family in Valentine Bay. I'm taking you to the farm—and we have to go to Portland. I need you to meet my best friends, Peyton and Iris."

He smiled against her mouth. "So then, we have a plan."

"Oh, yes we do."

"Make no mistake." He kissed her, hard and quick. "Marriage. We're doing it, the whole thing. The ring. The white dress. The vows—and what about kids? You do want kids?"

"Oh, Matthias. Yes. Definitely. All of the above. I can't wait to marry you."

"I think we've both waited more than long enough." But then he frowned. "Have I blown this? I should be on my knees now, shouldn't I?"

That time, *she* kissed *him*. "Naked in the bathtub is working just fine."

"All right, then." He pulled her closer and sprinkled kisses in a line along her cheek. When he reached her ear, he whispered, "We're not just each other's Christmas present anymore. What we have is for the whole year round."

"For the rest of our lives," she vowed.

And they sealed their promise of forever with a long, sweet kiss.

Epilogue

They stayed at the cabin for Christmas, enjoying all the traditions they'd created together in the years before.

On Christmas morning, he handed her a small package wrapped in shiny red paper and tied with a white satin bow. She opened it carefully, feeling strangely expectant, full of nerves and happiness.

Inside was a ring-sized box with a porcupine carved in the top. "You made this."

"Guilty," he said in that gruff, low voice that she loved more than anything—well, except for everything else about him. She loved all that, too.

She glanced up at him. He was kind of blurry. But that happens when a girl's eyes are filled with sudden tears. "Matthias. I love you."

He reached out a hand and eased his warm, rough

fingers under her hair. Clasping her nape, he pulled her in close. "Don't cry." He kissed her forehead. "It's a present. Presents shouldn't make you cry."

"Of course they should." She sniffled. "But only if they're really good ones." A couple of tears got away from her and trickled down her cheeks.

He kissed those tears, first on one cheek and then the other. Then he went for her lips. That kiss lasted a while. They were always doing that, kissing and forgetting about everything else.

Finally, Zoya gave a hopeful whine. They both glanced down to see the dog sitting at their feet, her vivid blue eyes tracking—Matthias to Sabra and back to Matthias again.

"Aww. Zoya needs love, too." With a chuckle, Sabra dropped to a crouch to give the dog a quick hug.

When she got up again, she held up the box and admired his workmanship. "It's beautiful." It even had two tiny brass hinges to keep the lid attached.

He gazed at her so steadily, a bemused expression on that face she knew she would never tire of looking at. From the speaker on the kitchen table, Mariah Carey sang "All I Want for Christmas Is You." Happiness crowded out every other emotion. She glanced away and swiped at more joyful tears.

"Sabra."

She met his eyes again. "Hmm?"

"Are you ever going to open it?"

A lovely, warm shiver went through her as she lifted the carved lid.

Inside, on a bed of dark blue velvet, a single pear-shaped diamond glittered at her from a platinum band.

"Oh, you gorgeous thing," she said, the words more breath than sound.

"It's okay?" he asked, adorably anxious.

"It is exactly right. Just beyond beautiful, Matthias. Thank you." She went up on tiptoe for another quick kiss. And then she passed the open box to him. "Put it on for me?"

He did as she asked, bending to set the box on the coffee table and then sinking lower, all the way to one knee. "Sabra Bond." He reached for her left hand.

She gave it, loving the feel of his fingers closing around hers, protective. Arousing. Companionable, too.

"I never expected you." His eyes gleamed up at her, teasing her, loving her. "You broke into my cabin and ran off with my heart." She gave a little squeak of delight at his words and brought her right hand to her own heart. "It hasn't been easy for us," he said. "We've both been messed up and messed over. And it's taken way too long for each of us to be ready at the same time. But now, here we are, four years from that first year. Finally making it work. And it all feels just right, somehow." He slipped the ring onto her finger. It did feel right, a perfect fit. "There is no one but you, Sabra. You are in my dreams at night and the one I want to find beside me when I wake up in the morning. I love you," he said. "Will you marry me?"

Those pesky, joyful tears were blurring her vision again. She blinked them away. "Oh, yes, I will marry you, Matthias Bravo—and didn't I say that two days ago, in the tub?"

He looked at her like he might eat her right up. "No man ever gets tired of hearing the word *yes*."

* * *

The next morning, as they were packing for their round-trip tour of farm, friends and family, Matt heard a vehicle drive into the yard.

He looked out the front window. "Terrific," he muttered, meaning it wasn't.

Sabra, descending the stairs with her suitcase in hand, laughed. "Oh, come on. It can't be that bad."

"It's Jerry," he grumbled. "He's here to check on us." Outside, his lifelong friend got out of his patrol pickup and hitched up his belt.

Sabra set the suitcase down at the base of the stairs. "Invite him in. We'll have coffee."

Jerry, mounting the porch steps, spotted Matt in the window and grinned. Matt scowled back at him.

Did a dirty look slow Jerry down? Not a chance. He kept coming, straight to the door.

Matt pulled it open. "What a surprise," he said flatly, because it wasn't. Jerry showing up with no warning was just par for the course. "Got a problem with your phone again?"

Jerry took off his hat. "You could have dropped me a text, man." He looked hurt. "Let me know that everything was working out. I kinda got worried. I just wanted to check in, make sure that you're all right."

Now Matt felt like the thoughtless one. Probably because Jerry had a valid point. "Okay. I apologize for not keeping you in the loop."

Jerry brightened instantly. "Thanks. And Merry Christmas."

Sabra, busy at the coffee maker, called, "Hi, Jerry. Coffee?"

That big, toothy smile took over Jerry's handsome face. "Sabra. Good to see you again. Coffee would be great."

Matt stepped aside and his friend came in.

Sabra served the coffee and offered some cranberry-orange bread to go with it. They sat at the table.

Jerry saw the ring and got up, grabbed Matt in a bear hug and clapped him on the back. "You lucky sonofagun. Finally, huh?" He turned to Sabra as he hitched a thumb in Matt's direction. "This guy. He's been waiting years for you."

Sabra just smiled her sweetest smile. "We've both waited. It's felt like forever. But now, at last, it's all worked out."

Jerry dropped back into his chair, ate a hunk of cranberry bread, and glanced around the cabin at the boxes on the counter and the suitcase by the stairs. "Where're you guys going?"

"All the places we didn't go in other years," Matt replied, knowing he was being needlessly mysterious—but doing it anyway because sometimes he enjoyed giving his friend a little grief.

Sabra sent him a reproachful glance and laid out their itinerary. "I have a farm in Astoria. We're going there for a couple of days, then down to Portland so I can introduce my hunky fiancé to my closest friends. And then on to Valentine Bay where I get to meet the Bravos."

"We would have been in touch when we got to town," said Matt. "I'm figuring we'll be having some kind of get-together, probably at Daniel and Keely's."

Back at the end of July, Daniel had married Lillie's cousin, Keely Ostergard, who had made the perennially grouchy Daniel the happiest guy alive—scratch that. *Second* happiest.

Now that he and Sabra were finally together and staying that way, Matt knew *he* was the happiest.

Jerry asked hopefully, "So are you saying I'm included for the party at Daniel's?"

"It's a promise," said Matt.

"What a great house," Matthias said when Sabra led him and Zoya up the front steps of the farmhouse.

"My great-great-grandfather built it," she informed him with pride.

She took him inside and showed him the rooms. He admired her new kitchen and agreed to start moving in right away, as soon as they were done with their holiday travels.

They left Zoya downstairs and Sabra took him up to see the second floor. She pulled him from one room to the next, saving the master suite for last.

She'd repainted it a soft blue-gray and changed out all the furniture. The new bed was king-size.

Of course, they had to try it out.

Matthias said it was a great bed. "But it could be a fold-up cot, as long as it has you in it."

An hour or so later, they put their clothes back on and went downstairs. Matthias got Zoya's leash and the three of them went out for a tour of Berry Bog Farm.

That night, Marjorie had them over for dinner. The Wilsons were so sweet, both of them beaming from ear to ear to learn that Sabra was engaged to her "young man," as they called Matthias. They were so pleased to learn that Matthias would be moving in with her at the farm.

In Portland, Sabra's friend Peyton welcomed Matt warmly. But he didn't miss the narrow-eyed looks Iris kept sending him.

They stayed in Iris's extra bedroom, which had become vacant when Peyton moved in with her long-time boyfriend a few months before. The plan was for two nights in Portland and then on to Valentine Bay.

The first night went well, Matt thought. They all got together at Peyton's. Matt liked her boyfriend, Nick. Peyton was a really good cook, so the food was terrific. They stayed late, till almost two.

In the morning, when he woke up in Iris's spare room, Sabra was still sleeping. He lay there beside her, watching her breathe, thinking that he'd never been this happy, loving the way her hair was all matted on one side of her head and admiring the thick, inky shine to her eyelashes, fanned out so prettily against the velvety curve of her cheek.

About then, as he was getting really hopelessly sappy and sentimental over this amazing woman who had actually said yes to forever with him, Zoya, over on the thick rug by the window, sat up with a whine.

She needed to go out.

He managed to get dressed, get his coat and the leash, and usher the dog out of the room without disturbing the sleeping woman in the bed.

At the door to the outer hall, he grabbed the key

that Iris kept in a bowl on the entry table. Outside, it was snowing, a light, wet snow, the kind that doesn't stick. He walked the dog to the little park down the street, where they had a big playset for kids and a tube mounted on a pole containing plastic bags for dog owners who hadn't thought to bring their own.

Zoya took care of business. He cleaned up after her and then walked her through the gently falling snow. They circled the block, pausing at every tree and rock and hydrant that happened to catch the husky's eye.

Back at the apartment, he let himself in, took Zoya off her leash and followed her to the kitchen where his nose told him there was coffee.

Iris was already up, sitting at the table sipping from a mug with Me? Sarcastic? Never. printed on the side. She didn't waste any time. "We need to talk. Before Sabra gets up. It won't take long."

Iris allowed him to get out of his coat, wash his hands and pour himself some coffee. When he slid into the chair across from her, she said, "This better be for real for you, that's all I'm saying."

The thing was, he understood her concern. Not because he was ever backing out on what he finally had with Sabra, but because of how long it had taken them to get here—and also the thing with Mary. That never should have happened. He would always feel like crap about that.

"I don't know how to say it, Iris. I love her. She's the happiness I never thought I'd find. I screwed up last year. I know that. But that was because of…" Anything he said was just going to sound like an excuse—worse. It would *be* an excuse. For his failure of belief when everything seemed hopeless, his failure to hold steady against all the odds.

Iris scoffed, "You got nothin'. Am I right?"

What could he say? "You *are* right. I should have done better. I took her at her word when she told me there was no future for us."

Iris glanced away. When she faced him again, she took a big gulp of coffee and set the cup down, wrapping her lean, dark hands around it, holding on tight.

He tried again, "The thing is, it *worked* for us, you know? The way it's all turned out, it was…right. It was what we both needed. Every step was important to find our way to this life we're going to make together from now on."

"You know that you sound just like her, right?"

"If I do, it's because she and I understand each other. You think *I* was happy when she told me that you and Peyton insisted she go out with other guys—and that she *did*?"

"She told you about that?"

"Yeah. She told me and, no, I don't like any other guy even having a prayer with her. But I get it. I get why you pushed her to do it. And I accept that it turned out to be something she *needed* to do."

Iris rose, refilled her mug and topped his off.

When she sat back down, neither of them said anything for several minutes. They sipped coffee as Zoya crunched kibble from the bowl Iris had put at the end of the counter for her.

Finally, Iris looked directly at him. "Okay, here's the deal, Matthias. I really didn't want to like you. But I kind of think I do."

* * *

In Valentine Bay, they stayed at Matthias's small house, which was perched on a hill overlooking his hometown. Now that he was moving to the farm, he would be subletting the place until the lease ran out.

Sabra liked his little house. It had two bedrooms and a small yard. In his room, he led her to his closet and shoved back a rod full of clothes to point out the calendar hanging there, every day marked with a big red X through the twenty-second of December.

"Note the large red circle around the twenty-third to the thirty-first," he said.

She grabbed him and kissed him, a long kiss full of love and wonder, just because he was hers.

When she finally let go of him, he explained, "I kept one every year from our first year—except last year," he admitted. "Last year, I bought the calendar, but then, well…"

"Come here." She pulled him close again. "I get it and there is no need to explain."

That called for another kiss, which called for another after that…

The house Matthias had been raised in wasn't far from his place. His brother Daniel and his family lived there now and also his youngest sister, Grace.

On December thirtieth, Sabra and Grace were together in the kitchen making sandwiches for lunch.

Grace mentioned Mary. Matthias's sister said that he'd brought Mary to the family Thanksgiving the year before.

"Mary's a nice woman," Grace said. "But we all knew she wasn't the one." She spread mustard on a slice of rye. "You, on the other hand…" She pointed the table knife at Sabra and fake threatened, "Don't you ever leave him."

Sabra had a one-word reply for that. "Never."

"Good answer." Grace dipped the knife in the mustard jar again and grabbed a second slice of bread. "So, have you set a date yet?"

"Not yet, but the sooner the better as far as I'm concerned."

"You want a big wedding?"

"No. Small. And simple. Just close friends and family."

"How about New Year's Day?" Grace slid her a sideways glance.

"*This* New Year's? The day after tomorrow?"

"Hey. It was just a thought…" Grace stuck the knife back in the mustard jar.

Sabra unwrapped a block of Tillamook cheddar. "I do like the way you think."

"Why, thank you." Grace held up a hand across the kitchen island and Sabra high-fived it.

"I would need to check with Matthias…"

Grace gave a goofy snort accompanied by an eye roll. "As if we don't already know what his answer's gonna be."

"…and then I would have to get on it immediately, see if my friends in Portland and at the farm might be able to swing it. And then, if they can, head for the courthouse in Astoria to get the license right away— and what about a waiting period? Isn't there one of those?"

"As a rule it's three days, but you can get the waiting period waived for a fee. I know because Aislinn got married this past year. She and her husband Jaxon went straight from the marriage license bureau to the church."

"Perfect—and what about a dress? Omigod. I need the dress!"

"Well, then, what are you waiting for? Get with Matt and then get on the phone."

They stared at each other over the half-made sandwiches. Sabra broke the silence. "I believe I will do that."

Grace let out a shout of pure glee and grabbed her in a hug.

On New Year's Day, Matt married the only woman for him. The ceremony took place in the family room right there at the house where he'd grown up.

Iris and Peyton served as maids of honor. Nils Wilson gave Sabra away. Jerry stood up as Matt's best man. Daniel's two-year-old daughter, Frannie, was the flower girl and Jake, Frannie's twin, the ring bearer. Both Zoya and Daniel's basset hound Maisey Fae had festive collars decorated with red velvet poinsettias. Matt wore his best suit. Sabra looked more beautiful than ever in a day-length, cream-colored silk dress with a short veil.

They said their vows before the big window that looked out on the wide front porch, a cozy fire in the giant fireplace. The family Christmas tree, resplendent with a thousand twinkling lights, loomed majestic across the room as snow drifted down outside.

"Always," he promised.

"Forever," she vowed.

Matt pulled her into his arms and kissed her—that special kiss, the kiss like no other, the one that marked the beginning of their new life together as husband and wife.

* * * * *

CINDERELLA'S PRINCE UNDER THE MISTLETOE

CARA COLTER

To the entire *A Crown by Christmas* team, editors and
writers, who made the magic happen.

CHAPTER ONE

IMOGEN ALBRIGHT GAVE the perfectly made bed one more completely unnecessary swipe with her hand. The Egyptian cotton sheets, with their one thousand thread count, were soft beneath her fingertips, and a light, deliciously clean fragrance tickled her nostrils.

A little nervously, Imogen tucked a honey-blond strand of her shoulder-length hair behind her ear and glanced around the room. As were all the rooms at the Crystal Lake Lodge, a boutique hotel high in the Canadian Rockies, this room was subtly luxurious and faintly mountain themed with its beautifully hand-hewn wooden furniture and the river rock fireplace at one end of the room.

But was it good enough for a prince?

Ever since she was a little girl and the hotel was managed by her parents, Crystal Lake Lodge, with its promise of luxury in the heart of true wilderness, had attracted an elite clientele. Imogen had grown up with a fuss being made over her and her two sisters, by famous actors, heads of state and sports figures. Some came every year, and a few remained as friends to the family. When they were teenagers, Imogen and her sisters had been the envy of all their friends with their autographed collections of celebrity photos.

But to her knowledge, Crystal Lake Lodge had never hosted royalty before.

One thing about rubbing shoulders with the rich and famous all her life? Imogen knew, better than most, that the fabulously wealthy and well-known were just people. With few exceptions, especially when they came here, they wanted the barriers to come down, to be treated as normal and to be liked for themselves.

Prince Antonio Valenti might have an entirely different attitude, though, if the thick protocol book that had been delivered just yesterday was any indication! There was something so intimidating about that heavy binder that she had not yet opened it.

Was the delivery of the protocol book the reason she felt so nervous? She never felt nervous before guests arrived.

But there was some mystery shrouding this arrival.

For one thing, the Prince was not arriving with an entourage. He was coming by himself with a single bodyguard. For another, the booking had been made with hardly any advance notice.

And for yet another, it was the shoulder season. Imogen wandered to the window and looked out. Even though she had lived here all her life, she felt her breath catch in her throat.

The Lodge was perched high on a mountainside. The views were stunning: from this distance, the town in the narrow valley below looked like one of those Christmas miniature villages that people collected.

The community had been built around the shores of Crystal Lake, which was tranquil and turquoise, reflecting the blaze of fall colors around it. The valley walls were carpeted with emerald green forests that gave way to craggy rock faces. The mountains soared upward to dance with bright blue sky, their pyramid-shaped peaks crowned in brilliant white mounds of snow.

It was October and so the thick stands of pine and fir and balsam were interspersed with larch, the needles spun to stunning gold, lit from within by the late-afternoon autumn sun. Imogen knew if she opened the window, the scents of fall would envelop her: clean and crisp, with the faintest overtones of wood smoke.

Still, as gorgeous as it all was, the question remained: Why would the Prince come now? The summer season— that lake dotted with kayaks and canoes, the air full of the screams of children brave enough to try the mountain waters—was over.

And the ski season was at least a month from beginning.

The mountain trails in this area were world famous for hikers and recreational mountain climbers. When the Lodge had clientele at this time of year, that was who they usually were—outdoor enthusiasts.

And yet when this booking came in and she had asked the reason for the visit, she had been rebuffed as if she had overstepped a line by asking. Then, they had requested she book the whole hotel, though there were only two of them arriving—the Prince and his security man. Thank goodness it *was* the shoulder season, or she would not have been able to accommodate that request.

"Gabi," she said, backing out of the room, giving it one last glance, and then closing the door. "Where are you when I need you?"

"Did you say something?"

One of the local girls, Rachel, who helped at the hotel, popped her head out of the room they were preparing for the security man. Newly married, her baby bump was becoming quite pronounced.

Why did it seem baby season was hitting Crystal Lake in such a big way?

Everywhere Imogen looked there were babies on the way, or people toting brand-new infants. And every single time, she felt that pang of loss and regret.

"Sorry, no, I was talking to myself," Imogen explained.

"I heard you say something about Gabi."

"I was just wondering where she was, that's all."

"Well, everyone is wondering what is up with Gabi, so let me know when you figure it out."

Imogen smiled at the pregnant girl. This was what was lovely—and occasionally aggravating—about small towns. No one could ever have a secret. *Did* Gabi have a secret?

Instead of promising to share gossip, Imogen said, "Rachel, you be careful. No lifting!"

"Ha. My mother was chopping wood when she started having labor with me."

Imogen knew that, despite this assertion, Rachel's pregnancy had not been without complications. She had been going to the city to see a specialist, and the delivery was planned for a hospital there.

Imogen had actually asked the young woman to stop working, but Rachel had brushed off the suggestion with the claim that she was from sturdier stock than that. Imogen was fairly certain Rachel kept working because her young family needed the money, and so she had put her on light duty and told her absolutely no chemicals were to be used for cleaning.

Imogen moved away from Rachel and her thoughts returned to Gabi. Gabriella Ross ran the bookstore in Crystal Lake. They were lifelong friends. They had always been there for each other, but their friendship had deepened even more when Imogen's sisters had accepted jobs overseas and her parents had moved to a warmer climate. When Gabriella's aunt and uncle had passed away, they had become each other's family. They knew each other's secrets and heartbreaks and dreams in the way only closest friends do.

Until recently, that was. Imogen frowned as she went down the wide, curved staircase and headed down a back hallway to the kitchen. Gabi had seemed stressed and preoccupied lately. Normally, she would have been helping Imogen get ready for the arrival of a crown prince. Normally, her friend would have been over the moon with excitement.

Gabi was very bookish, and by now, usually Imogen could have counted on her to have researched all there was to know about the island kingdom of Casavalle. Gabi would have read that protocol book, beginning to end, in about an hour and provided Imogen with a short synopsis of its contents.

"Including what they like to eat," Imogen said, swinging open the door to the huge, stainless steel, industrial fridge in the Lodge kitchen.

But instead of having her nose buried in a book, discerning everything there was to know about the royal family of Casavalle, Gabi had disappeared, with only the vaguest of explanations.

Gabriella *did* have a secret.

Secrecy between the two women was unsettling. It was Gabi who had helped Imogen through the end of her engagement, and it was Gabi who knew, to this day, that tears shone very close to that bright smile Imogen displayed when someone mentioned Kevin to her. Or when she glanced at the engagement picture of the two of them that she could not bring herself to delete as the screen saver on her cell phone.

She felt her heart squeeze, as it always did when she thought of him. He had wanted children so desperately. This was the other thing Gabi knew about her: that Imogen would never have babies.

She had suspected for a number of years, since a serious ski injury, that there might be problems. But after she and Kevin had been dating three years, he had taken her to her favorite Chinese food restaurant, and when she had broken open her fortune cookie, a small diamond ring had winked at her.

"I want you to be my wife. I want us to have babies together."

Of course she had said yes. That picture on her cell phone had been taken by a thrilled waitress seconds after Imogen had put on the ring. But was it the fact that he had included the baby part in his proposal that had made her, finally, investigate further?

Imogen remembered the day she had told Kevin the results of her tests, the distress on his face. He had stammered that of course, it didn't matter, but she had known it had. And she had been right: when she had set him free, he had lost no time in finding a new love. Though he and Imogen had been together for three years and had only just begun to discuss marriage, he had married someone else with appalling speed. They already had a baby on the way. And try as she might to be happy about it…

"Stop it!" Imogen ordered herself, when she felt her throat closing with emotion. She would not ponder endlessly the unfairness of life. She would not! She sorted through a few items in the fridge. They were not what they normally stocked. Instead, tiny individual Cornish game hens, strange sausages, unrecognizable vegetables, tropical fruits and exotic condiment bottles filled the shelves.

Thankfully, she did not have to figure out how to prepare anything. These exotic items had arrived at the request of a retired world-class chef who would be here tomorrow morning in advance of the arrival of Prince Antonio.

Imogen closed the fridge door and cocked her head. The sound of a helicopter—spotting for fires, conducting tourist trips and ferrying heli-skiers—was not uncommon in Crystal Lake. But it was more unusual at this quiet time of year.

She went to the kitchen door and opened it, craning her neck at the skies. Despite the bright sunshine of the day, the air was shockingly cold. She glanced toward Mount Crystal, and sure enough she could see a dark cloud coming to a slow boil over the peak. From long experience with changeable mountain climates, she knew what this meant.

Snow's coming, she thought, just as a small helicopter broke the tree line and then hovered over the Lodge, trees swaying in its backwash, red and orange fall leaves scattering. It tilted, lifted gracefully over the roof, and then the noise intensified.

Imogen went out the back door and quickly followed a stone pathway that wound around the Lodge. She arrived at the front just in time to see the helicopter slowly lowering over the sweeping lawn. Her hair went every which way as the helicopter rocked its way slowly to the ground, until the struts were solidly situated. The noise was deafening for a moment.

It might have only been a two-seater, but the helicopter was silver and sleek, with a dark windshield. It was like something out of a James Bond movie. The roar suddenly went silent as the engines were cut and the rotors drifted to a halt. She saw a crown insignia, gold against silver on the tailpiece of the helicopter.

Her mouth fell open. They were not expecting their royal visitor until tomorrow! They were not expecting an arrival by helicopter.

And, most importantly, she had planned on giving that protocol book a thorough going-over tonight. *Now what?*

As she watched, the pilot got out and held the door. Though he wore no uniform, everything about him, from his bearing to his closely cropped hair, said he was military. He scanned the grounds to the edges of the trees with narrowed eyes. His gaze fell on her, and he squinted long and hard before letting his eyes move on, taking in the building, his watchful gaze resting on doors and windows.

The set of his shoulders relaxed slightly, and he stepped away from the door of the helicopter, holding it open.

Another man stepped out, and the man holding the door bowed slightly and said something to him. She couldn't hear exactly what he said, but she was certain he called the other man Luca.

She might have contemplated the name a bit more— they were expecting a prince named Antonio, after all— but Imogen felt the breath sucked from her body and the autumn mountain glory all around her fade into oblivion.

The man who had been addressed as Luca was astounding. Neat, luxuriously thick hair, as dark as fresh-brewed coffee, touched his brow. His eyes were also the deep brown of coffee, his skin ever so faintly golden, the fullness of his bottom lip and the cleft in his chin absolutely sinful. He was perhaps an inch over six feet, his shoulders broad under a beautifully cut suit jacket. His legs were long under tapered pants pressed to knife-blade sharpness.

He exuded an air of power and self-containment, such as Imogen was not sure she had ever experienced before.

She was also struck by a sense of having seen him before, but of course, in today's world, all royal family members were celebrities. That must be why she felt a tickle of recognition: she had probably seen his face on the front page of a gossip rag. It was, after all, exactly the kind of face that would entice people—especially female people—to buy a copy.

What now? Obviously, even though the temptation was great, she could not run back into the Lodge, as she had a desire to do. She was fairly certain, even without having read the protocol book, that she was probably expected to execute some kind of curtsy. She had planned to practice one. Really, she had!

In fact, she had pictured her and Gabriella, giggling insanely and curtsying to each other.

Apparently nothing about this particular visit was going to go according to plan.

Imogen ran a hand through her scattered hair and lifted her chin. She took a deep breath and stepped forward. No matter what the protocol book said, she wasn't going to go up to the Prince in her work jeans and blue plaid flannel shirt and try to curtsy!

CHAPTER TWO

IMOGEN APPROACHED THE two men. Both swung around to look at her. Both were frowning. This was not the usual reaction of vacationers arriving to the pristine beauty of the mountainside lodge! A bit flustered, she managed to paste a smile on her face.

"Prince Luca?" she said. "I'm sorry, we were expecting Prince Antonio."

Both men looked at her as if it wasn't up to her to tell them who she was expecting.

"Welcome to the Crystal Lake Lodge," she stammered, resisting an impulse to touch her hand to her forehead and bow away!

She extended her hand. Too late, she thought maybe she was not supposed to extend her hand. The soldier type looked at her, dismayed, and as if he might block her from touching the Prince with his own body.

But the Prince stopped him with a barely discernible motion of his head. He took her proffered hand.

His touch was warm and dry and exquisitely strong, subtly but unarguably sensual. His eyes, so dark and deliciously brown, met hers squarely.

Something about his eyes increased that thought that tickled the back of her brain: *I know him.*

But of course she did not know him. And for someone

who had met dozens of celebrities, her next reaction was startling. Ridiculously, she felt like a starstruck teen who had gotten way too close to her rock idol. With all the grace she could muster, she extracted her hand from his grip before she fell under some kind of enchantment. She reminded herself, sternly, that enchantments were over for her.

As if a prince would ever look to a woman like her to be a partner in his enchantment, anyway. Life was not a fairy tale! Fairy tales ended with happily-ever-after. And beyond the final line of the story—beyond the "the end"—was the unwritten expectation of babies. She guessed this was probably even truer for royal families. Weren't they highly focused on heirs? On the continuation of their line?

"Prince Luca," she managed to say. "Or Prince Antonio?"

Neither men offered to clarify who he was, so regaining her composure as quickly as possible, she said, "I'm Imogen Albright. I'm the Lodge manager."

"My pleasure, Miss Albright," he said. "It is Miss?"

The words were said with the deep composure of a man who was very used to meeting people in a variety of circumstances.

There was no need to feel as if his voice—deep, faintly accented, husky—was a caress on the back of her neck.

"Yes, it is," she said, blushing as though it were a failure of some sort. She turned quickly and offered her hand to the other man.

"Cristiano," he said briefly, taking her hand and bowing slightly.

She didn't feel any jolt of electricity from his hand!

For a moment there was silence, and she rushed to fill it. "Obviously, you wouldn't have flown from Casavalle in it, so how does one customize a helicopter with an insignia in such a short time?"

The Prince lifted a shoulder, but Cristiano answered.

"It was on order, anyway, from a North American company. We asked the delivery date be pushed up and changed the city of delivery."

It made her very aware of the kind of power and wealth the Prince casually wielded—no wish too great to be granted—and made her even more aware, suddenly, of her own appearance. She was in faded jeans, the lumberjack-style shirt she favored for days with no clients and sneakers with bright pink laces! She didn't have on a speck of makeup and her hair not only wasn't up, but now it was windblown to boot.

She had planned an outfit suited to greeting royalty: a pale blue suit with a tailored jacket and pencil-thin pants, paired with a white silk blouse. She had planned to have her hair up and her makeup done.

"It's a magnificent place," Prince Luca said, glancing at the Lodge.

The two-story building was timber framed and stone fronted, and had a beautifully complicated roofline that made it fit in perfectly with the landscape of towering peaks around it. It *was* magnificent, and coming from someone who was no doubt surrounded with magnificence all the time, it was indeed a compliment.

And yet, even as he said it, she sensed, not insincerity, but a fine tension in him, as if the Prince was preoccupied with matters of significance. Again, his reaction to his surroundings made it seem as if he were not here for a relaxing holiday in the mountains.

When his eyes left the Lodge and returned to her, she glimpsed something in them that took her aback. He didn't just look preoccupied. There was a shadow of something there. Distress?

Which begged the question again: *Why was the Prince*

here? To heal some wound? The thought made him seem all too human. Insanely, it made her want to step toward him, look into the astonishing familiarity of his brown eyes more deeply and assure him everything would be all right.

How silly would that be, especially from her, from someone who had ample evidence everything was not always all right?

"I'm sorry, Your Highness," Imogen said, avoiding a name altogether. "We weren't expecting you today."

"I believe a message was sent," Cristiano said, a bit stiffly, as if she had insulted his competence, "to your cell phone."

Since it felt as if her own competence might be in question, she felt compelled to defend herself. "Our satellite reception here is beyond spotty, so cell phone service can't really be relied on here. It's because of the forests and the mountains. I'm very clear about that when people book." She realized she sounded as if she was justifying herself, so added, "I see it as part of our charm."

The Prince tilted his head at her, considering this. "Is our early arrival a problem, then?"

"No, of course not."

Yes, it was a problem! It was very nearly dinnertime and the chef had done all the meal planning, not Imogen. What was she going to offer them? A peanut butter sandwich? "It's just, um, we aren't quite ready," Imogen said. "The chef won't be arriving until morning. And the cleaning staff isn't quite finished up."

"I trust you'll overcome these difficulties," the Prince said.

His voice was so beautiful it sounded as if he had said something outrageously sexy instead of something extremely mundane.

Of course she would overcome these difficulties. Even though she wasn't the greatest in the kitchen and cooking department, the Lodge was well stocked.

But before she could figure out the specifics of how she was going to *overcome these difficulties*, the crisp mountain air was split with a scream from inside the Lodge. It sounded as if someone was being murdered.

The scream snaked along Imogen's spine. She turned to the Lodge, frozen with shock. Neither of the men experienced that same paralysis.

They both bolted toward the front door, and she snapped out of it and ran after them, even as she registered surprise that the bodyguard would be running, with his Prince, *toward* an unknown situation.

The men, with their long legs, quickly outstripped her. Though neither man had ever been in the Lodge before, they must have followed the sound of wailing, and when she found them, they were squeezed into an upstairs bathroom with Rachel.

"Cristiano?" the Prince asked.

The bodyguard, on the floor with Rachel, looked up. His expression was calm, but his voice when he spoke held urgency.

"She's going to have the baby," he said tersely. "And she's going to have it soon."

"But she's not due for another two weeks," Imogen stammered.

"Where's the nearest hospital?" Prince Luca asked her.

"There's a walk-in clinic in Crystal Lake, but they can handle only very minor emergencies. Rachel's been going to a specialist in the city."

"I have to have the baby at Saint Mary's Hospital," Rachel managed to sob. "They're set up for it. They know—" She couldn't finish the sentence.

"How far to Saint Mary's?" the Prince asked Imogen.

"It's in the city. At least two hours," Imogen said quietly. "If the roads are good." She thought of that storm cloud boiling up over Crystal Mountain with a sinking heart.

"Take her by helicopter," Prince Luca said to Cristiano. "Do it now."

Cristiano gave him a questioning look, and Imogen understood immediately. He was torn. His first duty was to protect his Prince.

"Go now," Prince Luca said, in a tone that brooked no argument.

"Yes, sir," Cristiano said, and scooped up Rachel as if she was a mere child. With the Prince and Imogen on his heels, he raced outside. Imogen noticed the weather had already changed. The wind had picked up and the blue skies were being herded toward the horizon by a wall of ominous gray clouds.

Cristiano made his way to the helicopter with the sobbing woman in his arms. With surprising gentleness, he had Rachel situated in no time.

He turned, saluted the Prince. "I should be back within the hour, sir."

"Miss Albright and I will try and stave off danger until your return," the Prince said drily.

Cristiano turned and got into the pilot's seat. The engines roared to life and the rotors began to move, slowly at first, and then so rapidly they were but a blur. In moments, the helicopter had lifted off the ground and was moving in the same direction as that quickly disappearing ridge of blue sky.

Imogen hugged herself against the sharpness of the wind. A single snowflake drifted down and she tilted her head to it. Knowing these mountains as she did, she was certain of one thing.

Unless he was prepared to fly through a full-blown mountain blizzard, Cristiano was not going to be back in an hour.

"I'm sorry your arrival was so eventful," Imogen said, turning to the Prince. "I can't thank you enough for offering your helicopter."

"It was my pleasure," he said.

"Do you think it was normal labor, or do you think something was wrong?" Imogen asked him.

"I'm afraid I don't know."

She could have kicked herself. How would he know? Dealing with pregnancies was hardly going to be one of his princely duties.

"You're very worried about her," he said with grave understanding.

"Terrified for her," she admitted, and then, even though it might not be allowed, according to the protocol book, she felt driven to expand on that. "While I'm sure your position requires you maintain a certain formality with your staff, it's not like that here. We are a very small hotel, and Crystal Lake is quite an isolated community. In a way, we all become family."

His eyes rested on her very intently for a moment.

"Do you know everyone in the village of Crystal Lake?" he asked.

"Residents, yes. Visitors, no."

He contemplated that for a moment. She was sure he wanted to ask her something, but then he did not. Instead, he put his hands in his trouser pockets. She realized he was very probably getting cold. His tailored suit was obviously custom-made and absolutely gorgeous, but lightweight. The shirt underneath, which had looked white at first glance, was the palest shade of pink, and silk, which was hardly known for its insulating qualities.

"I'm sorry, Prince Luca," she said. "I'm distracted. It's very cold out. I'll show you your room and you can get settled."

Then she realized there was nothing for him to get settled with—his luggage had just gone away with the helicopter.

Still, she showed him the room, chatting about the history of the Lodge as they moved up the sweeping staircase and down the wide hallway to his suite. She was glad she had done this so many times it was second nature to her. She could not get her mind off Rachel, plus there was something about the Prince's presence that could easily tie her tongue in knots.

Finally, she opened the door of the suite she had personally prepared for him. "I hope you'll find the accommodations comfortable," she said.

He barely looked around. He went to the window, and when he turned back to her, he was frowning.

"It's snowing," he said.

She could see the window beyond him, and even though she had been expecting snow, she was a little taken aback by how quickly it was thickening outside the window.

She didn't want to let her alarm show; if this kept up, the helicopter might not be able to return. The chef might not arrive. And what about a replacement for Rachel? Imogen was not certain that she was up to handling a royal visit all on her own.

Where the heck was Gabi when she needed her?

Still, Imogen told herself it was much too soon for alarm. Sometimes these autumn squalls were over almost before they began.

With a calm she was far from feeling, she said, "The weather in these mountains can be very unpredictable. We have a saying here—*if you don't like the weather, wait a minute.*"

"I am from the mountains, too," he said. "Casavalle is in a sheltered valley, but there is quite a formidable range of mountains behind it that acts as a border to the neighboring kingdom, Aguilarez. This actually reminds me of my home. I understand this unpredictable weather."

But if he was from a mountainous region, and if this reminded him of home, why come? Why not choose something less familiar for a getaway?

None of your business, she reminded herself firmly. Her business was to make sure he was comfortable and cared for, for the duration of his stay.

"I'll have dinner ready in about an hour, Prince Luca. Would you prefer I bring it to you, or will you come down?"

"I'll come down, thank you, Miss Albright."

She noticed the Prince looked exhausted. Almost before she had the door closed, he had thrown himself on the bed, and his hand moved to his tie, wrenching it loose from his throat. He looked up at the ceiling, his expression deeply troubled.

She shut the door quickly and made her way down the stairs. She stopped at her office and used the landline to call Rachel's husband, Tom. There was no answer, and so she left a message for him to contact her as soon as possible. And then she tried Gabriella's number.

That same cheerful message she'd been getting for three days came on.

"You've reached Gabi. I must be hiking mountain trails. You know the drill. After the beep."

The beep came, and Imogen said, "I certainly hope

you are not hiking the mountain trails right now, Gabriella Ross! There's a terrible storm hitting. Please let me know you are all right as soon as you can."

But of course, Gabi would be all right. She had, just as Imogen had, grown up in these mountains. She knew what to do in every situation. Tourists might sometimes be caught unaware by the fickle nature of mountain weather, but locals rarely were. Imogen suspected her urgent request for Gabi to call her had an underlying motive that served her.

She was here alone with a prince, a blizzard was setting in and she needed Gabi's help! Plus, she needed to know what the heck was going on with Gabi. What better circumstance than riding out a blizzard together to inspire confidences?

She sighed and went to the window. Night was falling, and between the growing darkness and the thick snow, she could no longer see the tree line at the edge of the lawns.

With worry for both Rachel and Gabi nipping at her mind like a small, yappy dog nipping at her heels, she went to the kitchen and once again investigated the contents of the fridge.

She sighed at all the unfamiliar items, then grabbed a package of mushrooms, some cheese and a few other ingredients. Despite her distress over Rachel's departure and the brewing storm, she had a job to do, and she would do it.

CHAPTER THREE

PRINCE LUCA VALENTI woke to pitch-blackness. He almost wished for the disorientation that came with waking in a different time zone, in a strange bed, but no, he was not so lucky.

He knew exactly where he was and what day it was. He was at the Crystal Lake Lodge in the Rocky Mountains of Canada.

And it was the worst day of his life.

Oddly, since it was the worst day of his life, his thoughts did not go immediately to the sudden onslaught of difficulties he was experiencing.

Instead, for some reason he thought of *her*, Imogen Albright. It wasn't that the wind had tangled her hair, or that she had looked adorable and completely unprofessional in her plaid shirt and faded jeans and those sneakers with the neon pink laces, that made him think of her. It wasn't that she hadn't addressed him correctly, or that she had offered her hand first. It wasn't even the look of distress on her face when they had found the maid in such anguish on the bathroom floor.

No, it wasn't those things that made her, Imogen Albright, his first waking thought.

And it was not really that the fragrance in this room was like her—fresh and light and deliciously clean—and that it had surrounded him while he slept and greeted him when he opened his eyes.

It wasn't any of that.

No, it was the way her eyes had met his and held for that endless moment after he had told her the Lodge was a magnificent building.

When he had glanced back at her, she had been looking at him, those huge blue eyes, an astonishing shade of sapphire, with a look in them that had been deep and unsettling.

He had felt—illogically, he was sure—as if she *knew*, not just how troubled he was, but something of him.

It was as if Miss Albright had easily cast aside all his defenses and seen straight to his soul. For a moment, it had almost looked as if she might step toward him, touch him again—and not his hand this time, either.

Had he actually taken a step away from her? In his mind, he had, if not with his body. It had seemed to him, in that brief encounter, Imogen Albright had seen all too clearly the things he most needed to keep secret.

That this was the worst day of his life.

And there had been something in her eyes that had made him want to lean toward her instead of stepping away.

Something that had suggested she, too, knew of bad days and plans gone awry. That she, somehow, had the power to bring calm to the sea of life that was suddenly stormy. In the endless blue sky of her eyes, in that brief moment, he had glimpsed a resting place.

Still, wasn't *awry* an understatement? His life—strategically planned from birth to death—was veering seriously off the path.

At this very moment, Luca was supposed to be a newly married man, not alone in a bed in some tiny mountain village in Canada, but in the sumptuous honeymoon suite that had been prepared within the Casavalle palace for him and his new bride, Princess Meribel.

Meribel was of the neighboring kingdom of Aguil-arez, and years of tension between the two kingdoms were supposed to have been put to rest today with the exchange of nuptials between them. Instead, here they were in chaos. In an attempt to minimize the mess, he had issued a statement this morning.

Irreconcilable differences.

Not the truth, but the truth might have plunged both kingdoms into the thing Luca was most interested in avoiding: scandal.

Meribel's tearful announcement to Luca the night before the wedding had come on the heels of other disturbing news.

His father's first marriage—the one that had ended in the kind of scandal that the Kingdom of Casavalle now avoided at all costs—might have produced a child. A child who would now be an adult. An older sibling to Luca.

Which would mean the role Luca had prepared for his whole life was in jeopardy. The eldest child of the late King Vincenzo would head the monarchy of Casavalle. Was it possible that was not him? It made the ground, which had always felt so solid under his feet, feel as if it was rocking precariously, the shudders that warned of an impending earthquake.

Luca was a man accustomed to control, raised to shoulder the responsibility to his kingdom first, above any personal interests. And yet this whole cursed year had been a horrible series of events that were entirely—maddeningly—out of his control.

Maybe today was, in fact, not the worst day of his life.

Wasn't the worst day of his life that day four months ago when his father, King Vincenzo, had died? With so many things unspoken between them, with Luca needing the gift he would now never receive?

His father's approval.

On the other hand, if one was inclined to look for blessings in terrible situations—which Luca admittedly was not—perhaps it was a good thing his father had died before everything in their carefully controlled world had begun to shift sideways.

The cancellation of his wedding to Princess Meribel meant the cementing of the relationship between Casavalle and Aguilarez was now, once again, in jeopardy.

There was a possibility that the throne—by law—would go to a person unprepared to take it. A person who had not spent their whole life knowing it was coming, every breath and every step leading to this one thing: taking the reins of his nation.

Luca's thoughts drifted to Imogen again.

His brother, Antonio, was supposed to be here at Crystal Lake Lodge. But with the news this morning, Luca had felt a need to deal with these issues himself, as they would have more effect on his life than on anyone else's. Besides, it had felt necessary to get away from Casavalle as the people discovered the wedding they had been joyously anticipating for months was now not to be.

The disappointment would be palpable. Every face he encountered would have a question on it. He would have to say it over and over again—irreconcilable differences—hiding the truth.

Luca had come here armed with a name. He had almost asked Imogen if it was familiar to her. She had said she knew everyone in this village. The village his father's first wife, Sophia, had escaped to, hiding from the world after the disastrous end of her royal marriage. But in the end, Luca had not asked Imogen. He wanted to phrase any questions he asked very carefully. A kingdom relied on how these questions were answered. There would be time to get to the bottom of this.

And speaking of time, he looked at his watch and calculated.

He had obviously missed the dinner Imogen had said she would prepare. He glanced at his cell phone. It was 3:00 a.m. but he was wide-awake. Hello, jet lag. It would be breakfast time in Casavalle, and Luca was aware of hunger, and of the deep quiet around him.

Why hadn't the sound of the helicopter returning woken him? It was unusual that Cristiano had not checked in with him on his return. Unless he had, and Luca, sleeping hard, had missed it?

Was there news of the woman? The baby?

Good *baby news would be refreshing*, Luca thought, not without a trace of bitterness. He was aware of feeling, as well as sour of mood, travel rumpled and gritty. He reached for the bedside light and snapped it on. Nothing happened. He let his eyes adjust to the murkiness and looked for the suitcase Cristiano would have dropped inside the door.

There was none.

He got up and searched the wall for the light switch. He found it and flipped it, but remained in darkness. Still, he made his way to the closet and the adjoining bathroom. No suitcase. And no lights, either. He went to the window, thinking, even in the darkness, he would be able to see the outline of the helicopter on the lawn.

Instead, what he saw was a world of white and black. Pitch-dark skies were overlaid with falling snowflakes so large they could have been feathers drifting to earth.

Mounds of fresh snow were piled halfway up the window-pane, and beyond that, the landscape wore a downy, thick quilt of snow. No wonder the quiet had an unearthly quality to it, every sound muffled by the blanket that covered it.

Even though a mountain range separated Casavalle from Aguilarez, and even though he was, as he had told Imogen, accustomed to the unpredictable weather of such a landscape, he was not sure he had ever seen such a large amount of snowfall in such a short time. It seemed to him well over a foot of snow was piled against the panes of his window.

He had not heard the helicopter return because there had been no helicopter return.

He looked at his cell phone again. No messages. Not surprisingly, as it appeared there was no signal. Miss Albright had warned them the region did not lend itself to good cell phone service.

It was apparent there was no power, no doubt knocked out by the storm, but did that also mean there would be no phone landline, either? He recalled glancing at an old-fashioned phone when he'd entered this room. It was on the desk by the fireplace, and he fumbled his way through the darkness to it and lifted the receiver.

Nothing. He set the phone back down. Luca contemplated what he was feeling.

He was still single when he should have been married.

He was outside of the shadow of protection for perhaps the first time in his entire life.

His cell phone was not working, and his computer was not here.

The snow falling so thickly outside should intensify the feeling that he was a prisoner of the circumstances of the worst day of his life.

Instead, he felt something astonishingly different, so new to him that at first he did not know what it was.

But then he recognized it, and the irony of it. The snow trapping him, his marriage failing before it had begun, the lack of communication with the world, Cristiano being far away, a possible new contender for the throne, all felt as if they were conspiring to give him the one thing he had never known and never even dared to dream of.

Freedom.

He shook off the faintly heady feeling of elation. His father would not have approved of it. The current circumstances of his life required him to be more responsible, not less.

But still, for a little while, it seemed he had been granted this opportunity to experience freedom from his duties and his responsibilities whether he wanted that freedom or not.

He did not know how long the reprieve would last.

And he realized he had no idea what to do with this time he had been granted. Though the first order should be fairly simple. He needed to find something to eat.

He opened his bedroom door and was greeted with a wall of inky darkness. He became aware of a faint chill in the air. Obviously, the heating system was reliant on power. He fished his cell phone back out of his pocket and briefly turned on the flashlight, memorizing the features of the hallway before he turned it back off to conserve the battery. Feeling his way along the wall, and using his memory, he found the sweeping staircase and inched his way down it.

He didn't use the flashlight on his phone again as his eyes began to adjust to the darkness. He saw an arched entry to a room just off the foyer at the base of the stairs. Dining hall?

He entered and paused, letting the room come into focus. Not a dining room, but some kind of office and sitting room combination. There was a large desk by the window, a couch and a fireplace, which it occurred to him they might need.

They.

He could well be stranded here with Miss Albright. He felt a purely masculine need to protect her and keep her safe against the storm, and he went over to investigate the fireplace. Of course, he was not usually the one lighting fires, but he would have to figure it out. Miss Albright protecting him and keeping him safe was embarrassingly out of the question.

He moved deeper into the room, and jostled up against the sofa. A small thump on the floor startled him.

A cell phone was on the floor, and the bump had made it click on, its light faintly illuminating the fact that Miss Albright was fast asleep on the sofa! The cell phone must have fallen from her relaxed hand.

He picked it up, and a photo filled the screen. The picture was of Miss Albright, laughing, her face radiant with joy, as she gazed up at the man she was pressed against. Her left hand was resting against his upper arm, and a ring twinkled on her engagement finger.

It was a small ring, nothing at all like the heirloom Buschetta ring he had given Princess Meribel on the occasion of their formal engagement. That ring had been carefully chosen from the famous Valenti royal collection as the one that would show not just her, but her family and her kingdom, how valued an alliance this one was. The ring, by the famous Casavallian jeweler, had been appraised at fifteen million dollars.

In retrospect, had Meribel accepted that ring with a look that suggested a certain resignation? Had she looked at the ring longer than she had looked at him? Certainly, there had been nothing on her face like what he saw in this picture of Miss Albright.

Carefully, Luca set the phone on a coffee table in front of the sofa. He could taste a strange bitterness in his mouth.

Love.

Obviously, that radiant look on Miss Albright's face came from someone who loved and was loved.

It was the very thing he had trained himself never to desire, the thing that had nearly collapsed the House of Valenti when his father's first marriage, a love match, had ended in abandonment, scandal and near disaster instead of happiness.

Luca had been taught by his father that love was a capricious thing, not to be trusted, not to be experimented with, an unpredictable sprite that beguiled and then created no end of mischief in a well-ordered life.

Meribel's admission of loving another—of carrying another man's baby—total proof that his father's lessons had been correct.

And yet that glance at the photo of Miss Albright and her betrothed had made him feel the faintest pang of weakness, of longing for something he had turned his back on. Something unfamiliar niggled at him, so unfamiliar that at first he could not identify it. But then he knew what it was. He felt jealous of what he saw in the photo of Imogen and her man.

The feeling was unfamiliar to the Prince because, really, he was the man everyone perceived as having everything. Soon to be King, Luca had wealth and power beyond what anyone dared to dream.

And yet, what was the price? A life without love?

What was it like to love as deeply as Meribel loved, so deeply that the future of a nation could be jeopardized? What was it to feel that kind of joy? That kind of abandon? What would it be like to lose control in that way? To give oneself over to a grand passion?

His family's history held the answer: to give one's self over to a grand passion was an invitation to ruin.

And it seemed his father's personal catastrophe, more than thirty years in the past, still had the power to wreak havoc. Had there been a child from the King's brief first marriage? Was the claim real, or in this world so filled with duplicity, was it just a lie, a sophisticated extortion attempt of some sort?

Luca glanced once more at Miss Albright's sleeping face.

He saw sweetness there, and vulnerability. He became aware of that feeling of protectiveness again, especially as he felt the chill deepening in the air. Still, he did not want to risk waking her by lighting the fire.

Instead, he saw a blanket tossed over the back of a wing chair, quietly made his way to it and went back and laid it over her.

Some extraordinary tenderness rose in him as the blanket floated down around her slender shoulders. He reminded himself that she was committed to another. Then he noticed her hand. The ring that had been in the photo was missing.

Not that that necessarily meant anything. Maybe she didn't wear it to do chores.

Luca forced himself to move away from her, and once again went in search of something to eat.

He found a cozy dining room, and on a large plank harvest table, perfectly in keeping with the woodsy atmosphere of the Lodge, sat a single table setting and a bowl of soup—mushrooms clustered in a thick broth and garnished with fresh herbs.

Beside the soup was a plate of cheeses, gone unfortunately dry around the edges, along with strawberries and grapes. All were artfully placed. He considered that for a moment. He wondered if Imogen had been disappointed when he did not come for dinner. He sampled her offering, taking a slice of cheese. Unfortunately, it was as dry as it looked, but it piqued his hunger. He turned his attention to the bowl of soup. It probably only needed heating. Forgetting he would need power to do that, Luca scooped up the bowl and went in search of the kitchen.

CHAPTER FOUR

IMOGEN WOKE WITH a start, struggling to think where she was. Then she remembered. She had frantically come up with a plan for the Prince's dinner, but when he had not come down for the meal she had been somewhat relieved. Her offering had hardly seemed princely!

Then she had come to her office, the place in the Lodge where the cell signal booster was located. She had tried desperately to get news of Rachel, but the thickening storm outside had made even intermittent service impossible. And then the power had gone out completely. It was the reality of life on a mountain, but sometimes nature's reminders of human smallness and powerlessness could be incredibly frustrating.

She must have fallen asleep on the couch. But she didn't recall covering herself with a blanket. She pulled it tighter around herself, until only her nose peeked out. The Lodge was already growing cold. She would have to get up soon and light some fires, but right now…

A crash pulled her from the comfort of the blanket. The unmistakable sound of shattering glass had come from the direction of the kitchen.

Here was another reality of mountain life: the odd creature got inside. On several occasions raccoons had invaded. Once a pack rat, adorable and terrifying, had resisted capture. On one particularly memorable occasion—a framed picture in the kitchen giving proof—a small black bear had crashed through a window and terrorized the cook for a full twenty minutes before they had managed to herd it out the door.

Aware of these things, Imogen stood up and looked around, her eyes adjusting to the darkness. There was a very heavy antique brass lamp on the side table beside the sofa. She picked it up and slid off the shade. She tip-toed across the floor and down the short hall, past the dining room, to the kitchen. She took a deep breath and put the lamp base to her shoulder, as if it was a bat she might swing.

She went through the door and saw a dark shape huddled by the fridge. She squinted, her heart thudding crazily. Too big to be a raccoon. Wolverine? Small bear? What had the storm chased in?

"Get out," she cried, and lunged forward.

The dark shape unfolded and stood up. It wasn't a bear! It was a man.

"Oh!" she said, screeching to a halt just before hitting the shape with her heavy brass weapon. She dropped the lamp. The weight of it smashed her toe, and she heard the bulb break. She cried out.

The shape took form in front of her in less time than it took to take a single breath. It was Prince Luca. He took her shoulders in firm hands.

"Miss Albright?"

What kind of dark enchantment was this? Where a bear turned into a prince? Where his crisp scent enveloped her and where his hands on her shoulders felt strong and masterful and like something she could lean into, rely on, surrender some of her own self-sufficiency to? The pain in her foot seemed to be erased entirely.

She bit back a desire to giggle at the absurdity of it. "Oh my gosh. I nearly hit you. I'm so sorry. Your Highness. Prince Luca. I could have caused an international incident!"

He didn't seem to see the humor in it. His handsome face was set in grim lines. His eyes were snapping.

Somebody else had eyes like that when they were annoyed. Who was it?

"What on earth?" he snapped at her. "You were going to attack what you presumed to be an intruder? Who would come through this storm to break into your kitchen?"

"I wasn't thinking a human intruder. I was thinking it might be a bear."

"A bear?" he asked, astounded. He took his hands from her shoulders, but his brow knit in consternation.

"It wouldn't be the first time."

"Seriously?" His face was gorgeous in the near darkness, and his voice was made richer by the slight irritation in it.

"It's not unheard of for them to get inside. Or other creatures. Storms, in particular, seem to disorient our wild neighbors in their search for food and shelter."

His brows lowered over those sinfully dark eyes. "I meant seriously, you were going to attack a bear with—" He bent and picked it up. "What is this?"

"A lamp base."

"It is indeed heavy."

"As I found out when I dropped it on my foot."

"It seems impossibly brave to attack a bear with a lamp. Or anything else for that matter."

"I may not have thought it through completely."

"You think?" He set the lamp base carefully aside.

"On the other hand, I've lived here all my life. I've

learned you have to deal with situations as they arise. You can't just ignore them and hope they go away."

"It was extraordinarily foolish," he said stubbornly.

"You obviously have no idea what a bear can do to a kitchen in just a few minutes."

"No. And even though Casavalle has missed the blessing of a bear population, I have some idea what it could do to a tiny person wielding a lamp as a weapon in the same amount of time."

Did he feel protective of her? Something warm and lovely—suspiciously like weakness—unfolded within her. She saw the wisdom of fighting that particular weakness at all costs.

"Let's make a deal," she said, and heard a touch of snippiness in her tone. "I won't tell you how to do your job, if you don't tell me how to do mine."

He was taken aback by that. Obviously, when he spoke, people generally deferred. Probably when he got that annoyed look on his face, they began scurrying to win back his favor. She just pushed her chin up a little higher.

The Prince shoved his hands in his trouser pockets and rocked back on his heels and regarded her with undisguised exasperation.

"Are you all right, then?" he asked, finally.

"Oh sure," she said, but when she took a step back from him, she crunched down on the broken bulb, and let out a little shriek of pain.

To her shock, with no hesitation at all, Prince Luca scooped her up in his arms. Imogen was awed by the strength of him, by the hardness of his chest, by the beat of their hearts so close together. His scent intensified around her, and it was headier than wine: clean, pure, masculine.

The weakness was back, and worse than ever!

"There's more broken shards over here," he said, in way of explanation, "and it's possibly slippery, as well. I dropped the soup bowl."

"That's the sound that made me think there was a bear in here."

"Ah. Well, let me just find a safe place for you."

As if there could be a safer place than nestled here next to his heart! An illusion—the way she was reacting to his closeness, being nestled next to his heart was not safe at all, but dangerous.

He kicked out a kitchen chair and set her in it. He slipped a cell phone from his pocket and turned on the flashlight, then knelt at her feet.

"You should try and save the battery," she suggested weakly.

He ignored her, a man not accustomed to people giving him directions. "Which foot?"

"Left."

Given the stern look of fierce concentration on his handsome face as he knelt over her foot, he peeled back her sock with exquisite gentleness. He cupped her naked heel in the palm of his hand and lifted her foot. Her heart was thudding more crazily now than when she had thought there was a bear in her kitchen!

"Miss Albright—"

"Imogen, please." Given the thudding of her heart and the melting of her bones, that invitation to more familiarity between them was just plain *dumb*.

"Imogen." His voice was a soft caress, and his tone was one that might be used to reassure a frightened child. Perhaps he could feel the too-hard beating of her heart and had mistaken it for pain and fear instead of acute awareness of him?

"There seems to be a bit of blood here." He leaned in closer, so close that his breath tickled her toes and made her feel slightly faint. "And just a tiny bit of glass. I think I can remove it with tweezers, if you can point me in the direction of some. A first aid kit, perhaps?"

"On the wall over there." Her voice, in her own ears, sounded faintly breathless, as croaky as a frog singing a night song.

He set her foot down carefully, stood and crossed the room. She took this brief respite from his touch to try and marshal herself, to slow down the beat of her heart.

She told herself it was a reaction to the circumstances, to the adrenaline rush of waking to a crash in the night and preparing to do battle with the unknown, and not a reaction to his rather unnervingly masculine touch and presence.

But as soon as he returned with the first aid kit and knelt at her feet again, she knew it had nothing to do with the circumstances. Even in the dark, his hair was shiny. There was a little rooster tail sticking up from where he had slept on it. She had to fight the urge to smooth it back down.

A nervous giggle escaped her as he picked up her foot again, his hand warm, strong, unconsciously sensual.

"Am I tickling?" His voice—deep, and with that faintly exotic accent—was as unconsciously sensual as his touch.

Her giggle deepened, and he smiled quizzically.

Oh, that smile! Though somehow it seemed familiar, she realized it was the first time she had seen it. It changed his entire countenance from faintly stern and unquestionably remote. His smile made him even more handsome. He appeared dangerously approachable, and as if he was quite capable of enchanting people with hidden boyish charm.

"No," she managed to gasp out, "not tickling. It's just this situation strikes me as being preposterous. I have a prince at my feet? Somehow when I got up this morning, I could not have predicted this event in my day."

"Yesterday morning," he corrected her, absently. "It's already a brand-new day."

She contemplated that. It was, indeed, a new day, ripe with potential, full of surprises. When was the last time she had allowed herself to be delighted by the unexpected? A long, long time ago. Since her breakup with Kevin, she realized now, she had tried desperately to keep tight control on everything in her world.

"It's true," he continued, and she detected an unexpected edge of harshness to his voice, "that sometimes we cannot predict the surprises our days will hold."

"Ouch."

"Sorry."

Tentatively, she said, "You said that as if you've had an unpleasant surprise recently." She realized she was being much too forward and was glad for the darkness in the room that hid her sudden blush of insecurity. "Your Highness."

He looked at her. "Shall we just be Luca and Imogen for a little while?"

His invitation to familiarity was quite a bit more stunning than hers had been. It was as stunning as finding a prince at her feet, giving tender loving care to her very minor wounds.

Maybe she was dreaming! If she was dreaming, would she give in to the temptation to reach out and touch the dark silk of his hair? Her fingertips tingled with wanting.

She tucked her hands under her thighs.

"Luca," she said experimentally, and then, "Ouch!"

"It's a bit of disinfectant. It'll just sting for a second."

Had he done that on purpose? To distract her from the question she had asked about his recent unpleasant surprise?

He finished with her foot, cleaning and bandaging it with exquisite sensitivity. Imogen had to steel herself over and over again from gasping, not with pain, but delight.

"That's great," she said, the second he was finished. She started to get up. "Thank you."

His hand on her shoulder stayed her. "Don't get up yet. I have shoes on. Let me find all the broken glass and clean it up."

"No, I'll just—"

"Do as you're told?" he suggested drily.

Despite herself, she giggled again.

He lifted an eyebrow at her. "What?"

"I can clearly see you are used to telling people what to do, but I was just wondering if you've ever cleaned up anything before in your whole life? It doesn't seem very...er...princely somehow."

"Ah, most monarchies have come out of the dark ages," he said, amused. "I might not be quite as pampered as the fairy tales would have you believe."

"Still, I don't think it would be appropriate for you to be mopping up, while I sit here and watch!"

"I think we are stranded here together in this storm, Imogen. Perhaps, for the duration, we could pretend to be just ordinary people?"

She stared at him. Nothing about him was ordinary, and probably never could be. Yes, he would have to *pretend* to be ordinary.

She, on the other hand, possessed that quality of being ordinary quite naturally and in great abundance.

It seemed to her it was a very dangerous game he was inviting her to play. Prince Luca was not ordinary. She was. Their positions in life were completely at odds. Their stations dictated that they could never be friends, never mind the *more* that his exquisite touch on her injured foot had triggered a weak longing for.

And yet life had dealt them a surprise, and they were going to have to get through it together. What if she let go—just a little bit—of that need to be in control?

And was there something ever so faintly wistful in the way he had said that, too? As if he was experiencing a longing of his own? Perhaps to leave his role behind him, however briefly, and try some very ordinary things?

Wasn't that what she had learned in her lifetime of work here at the Lodge? That everyone—no matter how famous, no matter how rich, no matter how successful—needed a place where they could just be themselves. The holiday they needed most, whether they recognized it at first or not, was to have a break from lives that were far from ordinary, where they could be normal, if just for a tiny space in time.

"All right," she agreed slowly. "The broom closet is over there, by the door."

It became evident in seconds that, though he might not have been pampered, his experiences with a broom and dustpan were limited! For a man who exuded grace and confidence, his efforts to clean up were clumsy.

And it was so darned endearing! Was it possible Prince Luca, as an ordinary man, was going to be even more compelling than he was in his royal role?

CHAPTER FIVE

"WHAT BROUGHT YOU to the kitchen in the first place?" Imogen asked, as Luca finished wiping up the spilled soup and used his flashlight on his phone to scan the floor for any remaining glass from the lightbulb.

"I was as hungry as a—"

"Bear!" She finished the sentence for him, and they both laughed. It was such an amazing sensation to share laughter with him. He threw back his head when he laughed, and the sound of it was deep, pure as water bubbling over rocks.

Someone else she knew laughed like that, with a kind of joyous abandon that made the laughter contagious, though she couldn't put her finger on who it was at the moment.

Still, as her laughter joined his, it almost felt as if she had not truly laughed ever before. Or at least for a very, very long time.

"I'm having a bit of jet lag. My schedule is turned around," the Prince explained to her. "I was going to try and reheat the soup you left for me. I'll also chalk it up to jet lag that I forgot I would need power to do that."

"And you're still hungry?"

"Ravenous."

"Well, we can raid the fridge for things that don't need

cooking, or we can find something to cook using the fire-place in the office."

"The latter sounds like the Canadian experience I'm looking for."

She laughed. "Would you like to try a real Canadian experience of the most ordinary kind? Have you ever had a hot dog?"

"A what? You're making me nervous. I didn't know they ate dogs in Canada."

"We don't!"

Then she saw he was teasing her. Of course he knew what a hot dog was! And just like that they were laughing again, the chilly air shimmering with a lovely warmth between them.

"Hot dogs it is. Fast and simple. And some would say delicious. Especially cooked over an open fire." She directed him to where the hot dogs and buns were in the freezer, and she hobbled over and found condiments, which she shoved into a grocery bag.

He took the bag from her and crooked his elbow, and they made their way back down the hallway and to the office with her leaning quite heavily on him. He insisted she go straight to the couch while he figured out the fireplace.

"There's a generator here," she explained to him, "but I'll only want to start it for an hour or so a day, just to keep stuff from spoiling in the fridges and freezers. I don't want to run out of fuel for the generator by running it too much. We can use the fireplaces for our main source of heat and for some cooking and heating water. We might have to chop some wood. I'm not quite sure if that was in your expectation of ordinary."

"You sound as if you're getting ready for a long haul."

The truth was she was feeling quite delirious about the

potential of a long haul, snowed in with the handsome
Prince! And she could see from the look on his face, he
was feeling anything but!

"I just want to prepare for the worst-case scenario."

"What is the worst-case scenario?" he asked quietly.

"We got snowed in here for a week once, when I was
a child."

"A week?" he asked, appalled.

"It was glorious," Imogen told him. "It was at Christ-
mas. We had guests, and we quickly all became family.
We made gifts for each other and cooked over the fire.
We popped corn and roasted wienies—"

"Wienies?" he asked, clearly trying to hide his horror.

"Another name for hot dogs."

"Go on," he said.

She cast him a glance, and it seemed, impossibly, as
if he was genuinely interested.

"We played board games and charades. We sang and
played outside in the snow. Christmas is always wonderful up here, but that is my favorite memory ever. It was
so simple. Real, somehow."

"You love Christmas," he guessed softly.

"Of course I do! Doesn't everyone?"

He was silent.

"Go on," she encouraged him softly, and then held her
breath, because surely a prince, no matter how ordinary
he was trying to be, was not going to share details of his
private life with her.

But then he began to talk, his voice low and lovely,
a voice one could listen to forever without tiring of it.

"Christmas is a huge celebration in Casavalle," Luca
said, hesitantly. "Even as we speak, preparations will
have begun."

"It's October," she pointed out to him.

"Yes, I know. But it is an absolutely huge undertaking preparing for the season. To begin, there are over six dozen very old, very large live Norway spruce trees lining the drive to the palace. They are all decorated with lights. I think I heard once that there are over a million lights on those trees. When lit, they are so brilliant, no other illumination is used on the driveway.

"The central fountain will be having blocks of ice that weigh in the tons placed in it for the ice-carving competition. We can't always count on cold weather in the valley bottom, so there is a complicated refrigeration system beneath the fountain that prevents melting. A decorated outdoor hedge maze is a favorite with children.

"The head woodsman will be searching the forest for the perfect tree for the castle's grand entrance hall. That tree will be over forty feet high, the angel atop it almost touching the ceiling of the front foyer. The foyer is so large that choirs assemble to sing there, in front of that tree, throughout the holiday."

Imogen wondered if her eyes were growing rounder and rounder.

"Have you heard of the jeweler, Buschetta?"

"I don't think so."

"He was one of my kingdom's most celebrated artisans. His inspiration was Fabergé. He started doing jeweled ornaments for the main entry Christmas tree in the late eighteen-hundreds, and his family continues the tradition. They are wondrous creations—they appear to be one thing, but just as the famous Fabergé eggs, they hold a secret. So a hidden compartment might hold a manger scene of the baby Jesus. It might hold a miniature of an entire town, or a replica of the castle. It might commemorate a special royal event, like a birth or a wedding or a coronation."

What did she hear in his voice when he spoke of special royal events? What great pain? But he moved on quickly, his voice once again even and calm, someone who had given out this particular information many, many times, like a museum tour guide.

"Each year the new ornament is unveiled—its secret revealed in a special ceremony—and it is put on display on a special table. The next year it will be hung in the tree. People come from around the world to see the Buschetta ornaments. The collection is considered priceless. That's part of the reason we start getting ready for Christmas so early in Casavalle—to accommodate the huge crowds, which are quite a boon to our economy."

It all sounded very posh, and while she felt awed by it, she became aware she didn't hear any love for it in his tone.

"Tell me more," she encouraged him.

"The entire palace has to be ready for the unveiling of the tree, so teams of house staff will be hauling decorations—some of them centuries old—from attic spaces and vaults and cellars. The kitchens will be mad with baking.

"Christmas mass is celebrated in the palace cathedral, and the day after Christmas the doors of the palace are thrown open to all the citizens of Casavalle. Huge buffets of all that baking will be set out, along with vats of mulled wines and hot chocolates. It's quite magnificent, really."

It did sound magnificent. She would be totally awed, except what did she hear in his voice?

"Magnificent, but?" she pressed.

He hesitated. "It's not as you described. It's not really warm and fuzzy, but rather magnificent and regal and very formal. The day after Christmas, my brother, Antonio, and I will stand for hours, greeting people at the palace doors. As a child, I dreaded it. My feet would get sore, and I'd be bored out of my head, and I was not allowed to squirm or go off script."

"Off script?" Imogen murmured, distressed at the picture he was painting.

"A quick formal greeting. To the inevitable question about what I had received for Christmas, I answered, 'Everything I had wished for.'"

"And it wasn't true," she guessed quietly from the tone of his voice and his expression.

He shot her a quick, pained look, then made himself busy readying the fire. Was he deliberately turning away from her so she could not read his expression?

"Of course it was true," he said, not looking at her, but crumpling paper, adding kindling and then a log. "I received magnificent gifts. Often I received gifts from other royal families and from around the world. Sometimes, children I did not know sent me things."

She could not stand having his back to her. She could not stand it that she could not see his face when she could so clearly detect something in his voice. She got up off the couch and hobbled over beside him, sank down on her knees in front of the hearth.

A good thing, too, because the fire he was laying was a disaster! Had she really thought a prince would know how to lay a fire?

"Christmas isn't really about the things you get," she said softly, glancing at him and then surreptitiously rearranging his crumpled paper and the too-large bits of kindling he had stacked in a heap.

"I suppose it isn't," he said, his tone stiff.

"It's about the way you feel."

"And how is that?"

"Loved. Surrounded by joy. Giving of your heart to others. Hopeful for the coming year. Having faith somehow, that no matter what is going on, it will all work out."

He snorted with derision. "You sound like one of those films I was enchanted by as a lad. But this is what few people understand about being a royal—it is a role you play all the time. People are looking at you and to you. Sentiment is not appreciated in leadership. In Casavalle, Christmas is about pageantry for the people. It is about giving the subjects of our small nation a memorable and beautiful Christmas."

"Even when you were a boy?" she asked, horrified. "Your own hopes and dreams were usurped by an expectation of you to play a certain role for your subjects?"

He sighed. "Maybe especially when I was a boy. Isn't that the best time to teach such things? That duty, that your responsibility to your nation will always come first? That the pursuit of personal happiness is an invitation to caprice, to calamity?"

She rocked back on her heels, ignoring the pain that caused to her injured foot. She stared at him. "Wanting to be happy is an invitation to calamity?" she sputtered.

He nodded.

"But you must have some happy Christmas memories!"

He contemplated that for way too long, then sighed. "Would you like to know what one of my strongest childhood memories of Christmas is?"

She nodded, but uncertainly. From the look on his face, Imogen was not sure she wanted to know at all.

"My parents had to go away on an official engagement. I don't recall the engagement, precisely, only that that was one of the first times I understood that duty usurped family. Antonio and I spent Christmas with staff.

We unwrapped our gifts by ourselves, ate Christmas dinner at the dining room table by ourselves. I seem to recall we debated the existence of Saint Nick, as the jolly old fellow, along with my parents, was a no-show. We got extra pudding, though."

"But what did your parents say?" she asked, appalled.

"If any explanation was offered, I'm afraid I don't recall."

She said nothing, thinking how sad it was that he could remember extra pudding, but not if he had been offered an apology or explanation. But then, to a young child, what explanation could ever take the sting of Christmas missed by parents away?

She made the mistake of glancing at him. His brows knit together in an intimidating frown.

"Please do not look at me like that," he growled.

"Like what?" she stammered.

"As if you pity me."

She turned quickly away from him. She busied herself striking a match and holding it to the paper, taking satisfaction at the first flicker of flame in her carefully laid hearth.

She could not look at him, because she knew the truth would be naked in her face. And the truth was that she *did* pity him.

And that an audacious plan was forming in her mind. She could tell by the way the snow was piled up outside the window they were going to be here together for a while. Maybe not a week, but a while. She had time.

To give the man who appeared on the surface to have everything—the finest of clothing, a personal helicopter, staff at his beck and call, wealth and power beyond his wildest dream—a sense of the one thing it seemed he had never had.

What Christmas was supposed to be all about.

She was going to give of her heart. To him. Which, if one thought of it sensibly, could turn out to be a very dangerous undertaking, indeed.

Imogen realized that she had not given of her heart for a long time. Protecting herself, nursing its brokenness, feeling fragile.

But suddenly, in the growing light of that dazzling fire, she understood her own healing lay in this direction.

Her healing did not lie in being sensible, in protecting herself from further hurt. If it did, would she not be healed already? No, somehow the key to finding her lost happiness—the happiness she remembered so clearly when she discussed that snowbound Christmas she had experienced as a child—would be found in giving of herself.

Completely, with no thought of what the repercussions of that giving might be, with no expectation of receiving anything in return.

The fire took hard, the flames licking greedily at kindling, and racing up the logs, throwing light and warmth across his face, which she could see was deliberately set into lines of remoteness.

Anyway, how dangerous could it be? Prince Luca would be here for just a short while, and then he would be gone.

On a rack beside the fireplace, with the fire tools, were several forks with long twisted metal stems and wooden handles.

"Luca, may I present to you the very ordinary pleasure of cooking a hot dog?"

She took one from the package, threaded it onto the fork stick and handed it to him, and then took another for herself.

"Not too close to the flame," she told him, demonstrating, "This is the proper open-flame cooking technique for a perfect roast."

As she had hoped, he laughed at her put-on Julia Child accent.

His laughter made her feel warmer than the fire, which would be a good thing for her to remember as she tackled the Prince as her good deed. If she got too close to his particular flame, she was going to get burned.

Doubt suddenly crowded around her.

It was way too early for Christmas.

And yet his kingdom already prepared. Why not give the Lodge over to that Christmas feeling, so that he could experience it?

To be sure, it would be a Christmas feeling that did not involve priceless pageantry, receiving lines, gifts too great to count or appreciate.

This would be Imogen's gift to the Prince for the very short time that he would be here. She would show him how very ordinary things could shine with more hidden delights than a priceless ornament with a secret compartment.

And she would start with a hot dog. She handed him another one threaded onto a stick. An hour later, feeling as full as she had ever felt, not just of hot dogs, but of laughter, they put the sticks down and packed away the remnants of the hot dogs. They sat on the floor, backs braced against the hearth, feet stretched out in front of them.

Her shoulder was touching his. He had removed his suit jacket. Beneath the exquisite, but thin, silk of his shirt, she could feel his skin, heated from being so close to the fire.

"I'm not sure I've ever eaten anything that good," Luca groaned, holding his stomach.

She turned her head to look at him and see if he was serious. He appeared to be!

"You have a little bit of mustard right—" Imogen turned, reached up. She touched his lip with her finger. After the carefree fun of cooking hot dogs together, nothing could have prepared her for the sudden intense sizzle between them. Her hand froze, his lip moved, ever so slightly, as if he might nuzzle that invading finger.

She withdrew her finger from his lip hastily. She made the mistake of licking the mustard off it.

She was aware of his dark eyes sparking on her face with something that was not quite as safe as laughter.

"I'm exhausted," she stammered. She got up hastily from where she had sat shoulder to shoulder with him beside the hearth.

She plunked herself down on the couch, pulled the blanket up to her nose and scrunched her eyelids together, hard.

She was aware he was watching her.

She thought, between the awareness of a full tummy, and the awareness of how his lip had felt beneath her fingertip, and the awareness of Luca's presence in the room with her, she would never sleep.

But her eyes felt suddenly weighted, and an almost delicious exhaustion stole the strength from her limbs and the inhibitions from her lips.

"Luca?" Her voice was husky with near sleep.

"Hmmm?"

"Have you ever built a snowman?"

CHAPTER SIX

EXCEPT FOR THE crackling of the fire, the room had grown very quiet. Luca glanced at his hostess. She was fast asleep on the couch, curled over on her side, the blanket tucked around her. She seemed to have fallen asleep with the ease and speed of a tired child. She had fallen asleep without waiting for his answer.

In the golden light of the fire, she looked extraordinarily beautiful: creamy, perfect skin; unbelievably thick, long lashes; hair a color that made him think of sunlight passing through a jar of syrup.

If he was not mistaken, there was a tiny smear of mustard by the corner of her mouth, just as there had been one at the corner of his.

He frowned. Her mouth was quite lush, that bottom lip full and plump. Since holding her delicate foot in his hand, feeling her shoulder touching his while they cooked and then her finger on his lip, he felt he was aware of Imogen in a very different way than he had been two hours ago. He considered her worst-case scenario that they might be here for a week.

Already, he could feel a dangerous awareness of her, a letting down of his guard almost from that first unfortunate moment when he had suggested they both be ordinary.

And then, one mistake leading to another, he had gone on, quite extensively, about Christmas at Casavalle and seen pity darken her eyes to a shade of navy blue that he might have quite enjoyed under other circumstances rather than her feeling sorry for him!

Imogen Albright, Lodge Manager, feeling sorry for him, Prince Luca of the House of Valenti.

Right before she had slept, she had asked him, her voice thick and unknowingly beguiling, "Have you ever built a snowman?"

"What kind of question is that?" he'd asked, a certain snap in his voice that should have shut her down completely.

Instead, she had said, drowsy and undeterred, "The snow from these early season storms is perfect for it. Heavy and wet."

And then she had been asleep, before he could tell her in no uncertain terms he was not building a snowman with her!

Her easy invitation was his own fault, of course. Jet lag was so disorienting. Luca did not generally let his guard down, and he did not share confidences with strangers. Now she thought they were going to be buddies. Which, admittedly, would have been easier if holding her foot in his hand had not made him so *aware* of her—and not in an *I want to build a snowman with you* kind of way.

Though, if he didn't generally share confidences with strangers, that did beg the question: Who did he share confidences with?

The answer made him feel lonely. And annoyed at his loneliness, and even more annoyed at what he had seen in her eyes as they lit the fire together.

Unless he was mistaken, she was going to make some misguided effort to show him happiness was not a frivolous pursuit, unworthy of any member of the Casavallian royal family. Unless he was mistaken, she was going to try and convince him to build a snowman, as if that was the key to his happiness!

He doubted he would be here a week, even if it kept snowing. Cristiano was going to be beside himself, even now, no doubt, mounting a rescue operation.

Until then, Luca would be in charge. There would be no snowman building, and he would avoid faintly playful moments, like jostling their hot dogs together in the fire! Though, the truth was nothing could have prepared him for the pleasure of a hot dog, nicely blackened over an open flame. Also, Imogen had informed him, referred to as wieners, wienies or tube steaks.

North Americans! They always seemed to want to complicate a dot.

Imogen looked like she might be a very complicated woman.

One who was engaged to another man, thank goodness! Luca had better keep that in mind when he was looking at the mustard-specked temptation of her lips, when he was remembering the slenderness of her wounded foot in his hand, when he was way too aware of the sensation caused by her shoulder touching his as they had cooked those hot dogs.

No, when dawn came, he would set out new rules. He couldn't exactly ask her to stop calling him by his name, but he could make it clear her sympathy was unwanted and overstepped a boundary.

When dawn came, he would make it clear that this was a very serious situation they were in. There would be no time for snowmen! He could use his lack of appropriate winter clothing as an excuse to avoid snow play with her.

Besides, important things needed to be done. From living in a centuries-old palace, he knew about cranky electricity. Though others were designated to look after the frequent problems, he still knew the number one concern of losing power in cold weather was with water freezing.

So firewood would have to be checked and restocked. An inventory of supplies should be made. It would probably be wise to have a plan for getting out of here if they did run out of either wood or supplies.

Fires would have to be started in other rooms or water lines would start to freeze. He would have to familiarize himself with the generator. The palace had several for exactly this situation, and though he had never personally had to run one, it felt good to have tasks to do, important things that would put the barriers, which had slipped a bit last night, firmly back in place between him and Imogen.

These were unfamiliar tasks to him, and yet there was comfort in both having a list of things that needed to be done and in taking charge of the situation.

All that would have to wait, however. Luca was suddenly aware of complete and utter exhaustion.

His sense of being in charge lasted all of two seconds.

This was, currently, the only warm room in the entire Lodge. There was one couch, and she was on it. There appeared to be one blanket and she had it.

Muttering to himself, he made his way through the darkened Lodge, back to his room. Staying in it was out of the question. He could practically see his breath already.

He stripped the blankets off the bed, went back down the steps, glanced at her still-sleeping face and made a bed for himself on the floor in front of the fire.

He thought he would sleep instantly. Instead he listened to her quiet breathing, as contented as the purr of a kitten, and he lay awake until the first light of dawn, leached of its normal brilliance because of the still heavily falling snow, finally touched the windows.

Imogen woke with a crick in her neck, and a throb in her foot. The air was chilly, and the light was weak and watery, so even before she looked to the window, she knew it was still snowing.

She sat up and swung her feet off the couch. There was a heap of blankets in front of a fire that had died to embers, and it took her a second to realize the heap was a prince!

She was almost certain the royal protocol book would not cover this specific situation, but even so she was pretty sure she was not supposed to be on the couch while His Royal Highness slept on the floor. And yet, when she remembered how protective he had been when she had hurt her foot, she doubted he would have allowed it any other way.

There was something about him that spoke, not of a man who had been pampered, but of a man who had a deeply established sense of honor.

If he was engaged to her, would he have left her when he found out she was infertile?

The question shocked her and she shook it off before she allowed herself an answer. What a ludicrous question to entertain, no matter how briefly. Men like him did not end up engaged to women like her!

She tiptoed across the room so as not to disturb him and added wood to the fire. She blew on it gently until it flared back to life. Then she turned and looked at the Prince.

His hair, so beautifully groomed when he had gotten off the helicopter yesterday, was now faintly rumpled.

The rooster tail stood up endearingly. A shadow of whisker growth darkened his cheeks and chin. It made him look faintly roguish—more like a pirate than a prince—and, unfortunately, more sexy than ever.

But then Imogen noticed, even in his sleep, there was nothing relaxed about him. In fact, he looked faintly troubled, as if he carried a huge weight he could never let go.

Except, Imogen reminded herself, she planned to help him let go of it. Had she really asked him last night if he had ever built a snowman? In the light of day, her plan to show him some normal, good old-fashioned fun seemed altogether too whimsical and faintly ludicrous.

The plan seemed even more ludicrous when his eyes opened. For a split second he looked sleepy and adorable. For a split second, he looked at her as if he felt affection for her. For a split second, she thought *I know you.*

But only for a split second. Then a veil came down quickly over his eyes, making them dark and formidable. Making him both a pirate and a prince. Making her feel as if he was entirely unknowable.

He tossed back the blanket and stood quickly. Despite very wrinkled clothing, he still carried himself with the innate confidence of a man who knew he owned the earth.

"Did you sleep well?" he asked her politely.

"Yes, you?"

He glanced at the heap of blankets and rolled his shoulders. "I'll live. How's your foot this morning?"

"It hurts a bit, but I'll live, also."

"Good. We have a great deal to accomplish this morning." He began to reel off a list. "You need to take care of your foot, so light duty for you. Will you be in charge of breakfast?"

She nodded, though it seemed the question was rhetorical. He had obviously already made the decision.

"And then I'll expect a full inventory of the kitchen supplies," he said. "I'll start putting fires in all the fireplaces, and I'll see to what we need for wood supplies. I've determined the number one priority will be to keep water from freezing."

Of course, he was right. But that tone! He owned the earth—and everything in it, including her—if his bossiness was an indicator! It made it hard to appreciate how much thought he had given this.

"I'll see to breakfast," she agreed, tilting her chin at him. "But I won't be treated like an invalid." Or as a servant to be ordered about! "I'll help you with the wood and fireplaces as soon as I'm done. I already know what we have for inventory."

He looked at her, considering her insubordination with the surprised ill humor of someone who was rarely questioned.

"I told you yesterday," she said, not backing down from the stern downward turn of his mouth, "that I will let you do your job, if you let me do mine."

"As you wish," he said, a bit tightly and as if he had no intention of letting her help him at all.

As he left the room, he seemed as if he was glad to be getting away from her.

"Well, ditto, Your Royal Mightiness," she muttered to herself. She hobbled down the hall to the nearest washroom. She had mustard on her mouth, and her hair was a rat's nest! Her clothes looked very slept in. The water she splashed on her face was jolting, it was so cold.

But it was just the jolt she needed. Luca was just trying to be helpful. He was willingly setting himself tasks that would be completely unfamiliar to him. Why was she being so prickly about it? But she knew exactly why. Last night, he had held her foot with stunning tenderness. Last night, he had confided in her. Last night, there had been warmth between them as they had cooked their hot dogs together, looking for the best position in the fire. Last night, she had decided she had a gift to give him. Now he was trying to reestablish the very barriers that she wanted to keep down, and letting her know that he didn't want any of her gifts!

And wasn't that a good thing, since she was entertaining ridiculous questions like would he have left her if he found out she was infertile?

No, a voice inside her whispered, *he wouldn't have.*

But that really just showed how ill informed she was about the realities of his life. He was a prince. Heirs would be even more important to him than an ordinary man like Kevin.

And Kevin seemed much more ordinary now than he had less than twenty-four hours ago. Imogen splashed more water on her face, needing to stop this flight of fancy right here and right now. You did not compare a prince to your ex-fiancé!

Luca was right. They needed to attend to practical matters first and foremost. Survival—not playing together in the snow, not getting to know each other better—had to be priority one.

What kind of breakfast could she make over the fire?

She settled on a kind of fireside omelet, using the heavy cast-iron skillet. She put a pot of hot chocolate off to one side to heat slowly, and on the other side, a pot of water that they could use for washing up.

"Luca." She went out into the hall and called him. "Breakfast!"

While she waited for him to come, she found her mobile phone, and under the pretense of checking for service, looked at that picture of her and Kevin. She waited for the familiar twist of loss.

How shallow did it make her that after less than twenty-four hours with a prince, it didn't come?

Speaking of the Prince, he'd come into the room. Despite rumpled clothing, there was no denying how his presence—powerful, almost electrical—filled the room.

"Service?" he asked her hopefully, pulling out his own phone.

She shook her head.

"Your boyfriend must be very worried about you."

"I don't have a boyfriend."

"But—" he stopped.

"But what?"

"Your phone dropped on the floor last night. The screen saver came on. I assumed—"

Was that why the barriers had been so firmly back in place this morning? Because Luca had assumed she was in a relationship? She scanned his features.

No, of course not, he looked every bit as remote as before she had announced she didn't have a boyfriend.

The barriers were up because he was a prince and she was a common girl. Because their lives were intertwined under unusual circumstances did not invite friendship or familiarity. She had no gifts to give him and it had been just a moment of madness that had made her think she did.

He looked back at his phone.

"We've had service at some time during the night," he said. "I have a message. From Cristiano."

As she watched, he opened it. His barriers melted. A

light came on in his face that made her want something she had no right to want.

"Look," he said softly. He turned the phone to her.

And she started to weep.

CHAPTER SEVEN

PRINCE LUCA'S RESOLVE to keep his barriers firmly in place dissolved instantly when Imogen began to cry.

"What?" he asked, distressed. He turned his phone back and stared at the picture. "It says they are both well. The baby very thoughtfully put off his arrival until they got to the hospital. Why are you crying?"

And please stop. Immediately.

"It's nothing," Imogen insisted, wiping frantically at the tears. "I'm just so happy. The baby is beautiful. Please show me again."

Luca handed his phone to her and watched her face. He would be the first to admit he was no expert on women. Good grief, he'd had absolutely no idea his own engagement was on such perilous ground. He was so oblivious to emotional language that Meribel's admission of loving another—a baby on the way that was not Luca's—had taken him completely by surprise. He could not think of a single clue that Meribel had dropped that this bombshell was about to explode in his life.

So, an expert at reading the complexities of a woman's mind, he was not.

But even so, there was something in Imogen as she looked at that picture of the maid and her baby that was not entirely happiness. There was a terrible combination of both joy and sorrow on her face.

"It's a boy," she said softly. Her tone, and her eyes— diamond tears still pooling and falling—spoke of a well of sadness that was soul deep.

And yet despite that, yesterday she had wanted to give him the gift of an ordinary experience. She had been willing to overcome whatever this was that haunted her, to give him, a complete stranger, something she had discerned he lacked.

"Let's have breakfast," he suggested. "And then should we venture outdoors? See if the snow is indeed perfect for making a snowman?"

What was he doing? Trying to make another person happy. That was a *good* thing. She was leading with her example. He never wanted to be one of those royals who was indifferent to the pain of others, above it all somehow, privileged to the point of complete insensitivity.

This offer was no different than ministering to her foot yesterday; he felt desperate to take her pain away.

And yet when he saw he had succeeded—when he saw her blue eyes sparkling with anticipation behind the tears—he felt instantly as if his decision could have catastrophic consequences. For both of them. His initial plan—distance and the very serious business of surviving the storm—had been so much better. Reasoned and reasonable.

Of course, *reasoned and reasonable* had gotten him dumped by his bride-to-be on the eve of his wedding. Maybe it was time to experiment with something new? *No!*

"Of course, I don't have the right clothing," he said hastily. "I guess it wouldn't be a good idea to get my only clothes wet. Hypothermia and all that."

She went from crying to laughing in one blink of her gorgeous blue eyes. "I'll keep you from getting hypothermia."

He had a sudden forbidden flash of sharing body warmth! "It would be better if we just didn't invite it in the first place."

There was that look in her eyes again: as if she could see right through him.

"We keep plenty of winter clothing here," she said.

"What? Why?"

"All kinds of people arrive thinking they know what a vacation in the mountains entails, but many are ill-prepared for the realities of the Canadian climate. We stock everything so that our guests can have a safe, enjoyable stay, even if they haven't prepared properly."

"Oh," he said. "Snowman making it is, then."

Luca didn't want to admit, even to himself, how he felt he was looking forward to the activity.

To chase any remaining sadness from her eyes, he told himself. But he knew that was not completely it. Maybe it was chasing some all-prevailing somberness from his own soul that he was looking forward to.

And so, after eating a breakfast that was as delicious as it was humble, she led him down the hall to a large storeroom. He noted with relief that she was barely limping.

She held open the door, and they both squeezed into a coatroom made tight with two walls hung with hooks that held winter jackets, sturdy pants, woolen shirts. The far wall was covered with cubbies stuffed with mittens, scarves and toques. Neat shelves above the hooks held rows of boots organized according to size.

"It's like the quartermaster's store," he said. She was

very close. Her scent—sweet and clean and light—tickled his nostrils.

"I know," she said. "We could make snowmen all week long without any risk of hypothermia at all."

She was teasing him. Danger!

"It's not going to be a week," he replied.

She lifted one of those shoulders. "Talk to Mother Nature. It's her plan, not ours."

He was not sure he wanted to be in this tight little closet with Imogen Albright thinking about what Mother Nature might have planned for a man and a woman alone together in the middle of a blizzard.

Without even considering his choices he grabbed things he thought he might need, and with his arms full of clothing, he brushed by her, to the washroom down the hall.

Imogen considered the Prince's departing form. Crazy, but she, a common woman with the most unromantic of jobs, managing a small hotel in the middle of nowhere, seemed to be making the Prince uncomfortable in some way she could not help but delighting in.

Oh, she could feel the discomfort, too. A faint sizzle between them, a primal kind of awareness. It was no doubt the circumstances of being stranded together in a snowstorm, and she should be careful about reading too much into it.

One of them should be putting on the brakes.

But she didn't feel like putting on the brakes. She felt like having some fun, living with spontaneity and verve, for once. She was aware he was turning the tables on her; she could tell he felt sorry for her when she'd reacted— overreacted—to the baby like that.

If she was totally honest about her reaction to the

baby, it wasn't just her own loss that had brought on the unexpected tears.

It was the look on Luca's face, the unguarded tenderness with which he had looked at that photo.

Maybe he didn't even know it, but he was a man who wanted babies of his own. Something she could never give him.

Even if she was fertile, she reasoned with herself, she would never be giving the Prince babies.

So why not just give herself over to giving him what she could?

Her motivation could be very simple: she had felt sorry for him when he revealed details of what seemed as if it might have been a cheerless childhood. Imagine having no fond memories of Christmas.

And so this experience was going to be good for both of them. She was determined about that.

She chose some winter clothes for herself, shut the door of the closet and changed in there. The door had a full-length mirror on the back of it, and she studied herself.

One might hope to be a bit glamorous for a playdate with a prince, but that was a hard look to accomplish in winter clothes. The puffy pink coat and blue pants, padded with insulation, made her seem as if she was quite plump. Her hair was rather messy from sleeping on the couch, but she quickly covered the worst of it with a toque.

With its reindeer dancing around the brim and the too-big pom-pom, the toque hardly seemed an improvement, but there was no point dwelling on it. Still, there was something in her eyes that gave her pause. Despite the fact they were slightly red rimmed from crying, they were now sparkling. There was a look about her of—what?

Excitement. She contemplated that. It was true that it had been a long time since she had felt any excitement about life.

Imogen had not noticed a sparkle in her eyes since the day she had told Kevin she would not be having their baby. Two griefs: the loss of Kevin and the loss of a dream of having children of her own, of forming a family unit so much like the loving one she had grown up in.

Over the past few months, she had not believed this would ever happen. That the light would come back on in her eyes. That she would have hope that she could have happy moments again. To have hope. Was that a good thing or a dangerous thing?

"Oh, Imogen," she whispered to herself. "You don't have to sort out the whole world and its meaning right this second. Lighten up."

With that vow fresh in her heart, she took a deep breath and exited the closet.

When she came out, she could see the Prince was standing outside the front door. She went out, too, and he looked at her, then looked away, faintly sheepish.

She smiled. He wasn't looking away because she didn't look good! Unless she missed her guess, he was entirely self-conscious in his winter getup.

He looked back at her and glowered. "Don't laugh," he warned her.

She chuckled. "Why would I laugh?"

"I look a fool."

She studied him openly. He had made a complete transformation from a prince. He looked like a Canadian lumberjack. Except that nothing quite fit him. The rough woolen pants were too short, as were the sleeves of the colorful plaid jacket. The boots were too big. The toque had a pom-pom on it even larger than the one on hers. Colorful mismatched mittens hid the elegance of his hands. He looked like a boy who had grown too quickly.

"You look quite adorable," she decided.

"Adorable?" he sputtered. "Like a new puppy?"

She cocked her head and studied him. "More like a yard elf. Dressed for Christmas."

"A yard elf?" he asked, aghast. "I don't exactly know what a yard elf is."

"It's—"

"Please." He held up a mittened hand. "Don't edify me."

She laughed.

"I warned you not to laugh."

"Or? Is there some particular punishment saved for the occasion of laughing at the Prince?"

"There is," he said with dark foreboding.

"Do tell." She raised an eyebrow at him.

He jumped from the top step to the bottom one, leaned over and scooped up a handful of snow. "Death by snowball," he said.

"Seems a little harsh." She came down the steps, trying not to wince at the pain in her foot, put her hands on her hips and looked up at him defiantly. Despite his effort at a stern expression, his eyes were glittering with suppressed mirth.

"It's a serious infraction. Laughter." He took the ball he had shaped and tossed it lightly, menacingly, from one mitten to the other.

She could tell his experience with snowballs was limited. The ball was misshapen and did not look like it would survive a flight through the air.

"Yes, Your Highness," she said with pretended meekness. "Please remember I'm injured." Then she swatted his snowball out of his hand. Before he could recover himself, ignoring the pain in her foot, she plowed through a drift of heavy, wet snow. She snatched up a handful of it, shaped a missile, turned back and let fly.

It hit him smack-dab in the middle of his face.

She chortled with glee at his stunned expression. He reached up and brushed the snow away. But her laughter only lasted a moment. His scowl was ferocious. And he was coming after her!

She tried to run, but her foot hurt, and her legs were so much shorter than his in the deep snow. He caught her with incredible swiftness, spun her around into his chest.

"Oh dear," she breathed.

"What would an ordinary guy do?" he growled.

Kiss me. She stared up at him. The tension hissed between them.

"Cat got your tongue?"

She stuck it out at him. "Apparently not." Then she wriggled free of his grasp, turned and ran again. And she suspected her heart beating so hard had very little to do with the exertion of running through the snow, but rather what felt like it was a near miss of a kiss!

With the carefree hearts of children, they soon filled the air with flying snowballs—most of which missed their targets by wide margins—and their laughter. They played until they were both breathless. Imogen finally had to stop as her foot could not take another second of this. Though with her hands on her knees, breathing heavily, she decided it was well worth a little pain.

He took advantage of her vulnerability, pelting her with snowballs, until she collapsed in the snow, laughing so hard her legs would not hold her anymore.

"I surrender," she gasped. "You win."

He collapsed in the snow beside her and a comfortable

silence drifted over them as the huge snowflakes fluttered down and landed on their upturned faces.

Finally, he found his feet and held out his hand to her. "We're both wet. We better get at that snowman."

She took his hand. "Before the dreaded hypothermia sets in."

He tugged and she found her feet and stumbled into him. His hand went around her waist to steady her, and he pulled her closer. She could feel a lovely warmth radiating through the wetness of his jacket. She could feel the strong, sure beat of his heart. His scent filled her nostrils, as heady as the mountain-sweet crispness of the air around them.

She looked up at him: the whisker-roughness of his chin and cheeks, the perfection of his features, the steadiness in the velvet-brown warmth of his eyes.

They were back at that question: What would an ordinary guy do?

But despite his clothing, he was not an ordinary guy. A prince! She was chasing through this mountain meadow with a prince.

Would kissing him enhance the sense of enchantment or destroy it?

It was something she was unwilling to find out. She pushed away from him.

"Yes," she said. "Let's see about that snowman."

CHAPTER EIGHT

THE SNOWBALL WAS so big it was taking both of them, their shoulders leaned into it and their legs braced mightily, to move it a single inch.

"I think it's big enough," Imogen gasped. Luca was aware she was favoring one foot, and so he had deliberately taken most of the weight. To be truthful, he was rather enjoying her admiration of his strength!

"Oh, what do you know about building snowmen?" Luca asked her.

She laughed. Luca loved seeing her laugh. It was exactly as he had hoped: the sadness that looking at the picture of that baby had caused her was erased from her eyes. Her cheeks were pink from exertion, her clothes were soaked, and her hair, where it poked out from under her toque, was wet, plastered against the loveliness of her face.

Luca had seen beautiful women in some of the most glamorous situations in the world. He had seen them at balls and concerts and coronations and state functions. He had seen them in the finest designer gowns, in the most priceless of jewelry, in the most exotic settings imaginable.

Princess Meribel, for example, when dressed up, was like something out of a fairy tale. With a tiara on her head, jewels dripping from her ears, wearing price-less custom-made clothing from designers who vied for her attention, she was the perfect Princess.

There was no "casual"—not in her vocabulary and not in her wardrobe. Even on the deck of a yacht, Meribel was elegant, refined, classic. Her perfectly coiffed hair and perfectly done makeup enhanced beauty that was already unearthly.

And also, Luca reminded himself, cool and untouch-able.

For him. Apparently she had been red-hot and quite touchable to someone else.

He shook off that momentarily bitter thought.

Because if he had married Meribel on schedule, he would have never had these glorious, laughter-filled mo-ments, chasing through the snow with Imogen.

Yes, it was true Prince Luca had seen some of the most beautiful women in the world, and yet he was not sure if he had ever seen a woman quite as beautiful as Imogen Albright, in her bulky snowsuit, dusted with snowflakes, happiness shimmering in the air around her.

She seemed natural and spontaneous in a way that made every other thing he had ever experienced artifi-cial and contrived. Imogen was real in a way he was not sure he had ever encountered it before. He found himself wanting to pull the hat from her head, just to watch her hair fall around her face.

He found himself wanting to bend her over his arm and ravish the plumpness of her lips, to find out if kiss-ing her would be as refreshingly wonderful and invig-oratingly novel, as awesomely real as the rest of this experience.

He wanted to kiss Imogen as much as he had ever wanted anything in his entire life. He steeled himself against that impulse, waited for it to pass, which it didn't. He took a deep breath.

Instead of kissing her, he inspected the huge snowball, the first for their snowman, with far more intensity than it required. "Okay," he finally managed to say. "This might be a suitable start."

"A suitable start? It's ridiculously large."

He shot her a look.

"What?" she asked.

"People don't generally *correct* me."

"Oh well," she said, with an impish grin and a shrug. "You're the one who wanted to be ordinary."

He had. And the truth was it was surpassing his expectations. Side by side, they began pushing the next ball. When they were done, he could clearly see why she had thought the first ball was big enough. This second one, somehow, had to be hoisted on top of the first one.

It was, again, a total team effort. Finally, grunting, panting, with Imogen giggling so hard she was barely any help at all, they managed to hoist the second ball into place.

The last snowball, the one that would make the snowman's head, was easier to make, thankfully, so that he didn't have to admit she was right—the snowman was too large.

And then they were making eyes out of rocks and arms out of sticks and buttons out of pinecones.

They stood back and eyed their handiwork.

"He's perfect," Luca decided.

"He's not," Imogen argued. She had no idea how refreshing these little disagreements were for him. In his world, when he spoke, everyone deferred to him.

"He's leaning precariously to one side. His eyes are different sizes. He has no nose."

"I think that's part of what I like about him," Luca said. "Perfection, in my world, is expected of everything."

He was not really sure he had realized how utterly exhausting that was until this minute.

Imogen's mittened hand crept into his.

It was unexpected. A gesture of compassion and sympathy.

"I've never felt what I feel right now," he said, encouraged by that small hand in his, or weakened by it, he wasn't sure which.

She held tight to his hand, amazing strength in her touch, turned her eyes away from the snowman and up to his, full of question.

"I feel free," he said slowly, searching for the words. "I feel the enormous freedom of no one watching me. Not meaning you are no one."

"No need to explain, I understand. Completely."

And astonishingly, he knew she did, and just like last night, when he had confessed the disappointment of Christmases past, this felt like another venture into the unknown, and possibly very dangerous territory. Confiding in someone was alien in his world. And yet he could not seem to stop himself from continuing.

"I've never had this freedom—to be able to just gad about, to laugh, to be goofy. You don't know what you've given me."

"You've given me something, too," she said softly.

He watched her face.

"What?" he whispered.

"The hope that I can be happy again."

"Why? What's happened?"

"Let's not spoil this moment," she said. "Our snowman is great, but—"

"But what? He's as perfect as I want him to be."

"What do you know about snowmen?" she teased him.

"Okay. What's missing?"

"A snow woman. He's lonely."

Luca stared at Imogen. Somehow he had the terrifying feeling that she was not talking about a snowman at all. That somehow, now, as from the very beginning, she saw something about him that others did not see.

She saw his soul.

And she saw things there that had been successfully hidden from the rest of the world. Prince Luca, the man with everything, was alone. And he was lonely.

He wondered if marrying Meribel would have assuaged that sense of being lonely. Looking at Imogen, he had a sense his marriage would have been like so much of his life. It would have been exactly like Christmas at his palace home: it would have *looked* perfect, and *felt* empty.

"A snow woman it is," he said, letting go of her hand with all possible haste.

Because he had seen her soul, too. And it promised him something else he had never had before: a resting place, someone to trust with who he really was.

Two hours later, Imogen stood back to admire their handiwork. She and Luca were now thoroughly soaked and exhausted. But an entire snow family of Mama, Papa, two children—a boy and a girl—inhabited the snow-covered front lawn of Crystal Lake Lodge. The snow still drifted down so steadily that the facial features of the snow daddy had already been completely covered by the time the rest of the family was done.

To her delight, Luca reached for her hand naturally as they headed back to the front door of the Lodge.

But then he seemed to realize how naturally it had happened and let go as soon as they were inside.

"Fires to tend to," he said, dropping her hand abruptly. *With relief?*

"We need to get out of these wet clothes first."

His face scrunched up in that barely detectable but funny way that let her know he just wasn't accustomed to someone else telling him what needed to happen first. It goaded her into feeling even more bossy!

"And into something dry as quickly as possible," she said. "Come with me."

"I'll just slip into the washroom and put on—"

"Your clothes from yesterday? Yucky."

His lips twitched. Undoubtedly another first in his world: to be called "yucky."

Still, he followed her, and so they found themselves back in the coat cupboard, going through bins of long johns that were kept for those unprepared guests. He took what she offered him without argument and went and changed.

She changed, too, and regarded herself in the mirror with a rueful shake of her head. If she had to have a pajama party with a prince, was it too much to hope for something a wee bit sexier than long johns that bulged and clung in all the wrong places?

When she saw him in his long johns she realized it was a reprieve. He could not maintain the persona of a prince in a bright red waffle-weave shirt and matching pants, long legs tucked into woolen socks.

He was still her ordinary guy, the one who had played side by side with her all afternoon.

He went off to tend to fires and she found some tinned fish and frozen bread and carried them down to the office. She stoked the fire and then toasted the bread over the flames and made slightly blackened sandwiches.

By the time she finished making sandwiches and setting a pot of hot chocolate in the coals, Imogen was astonished that the light was already fading from the sky. They had played outside the whole day.

When Luca returned, they munched happily on their sandwiches, and then before the light was gone completely, he went and fetched the first aid kit and insisted on looking at her foot.

"I almost totally forgot I had a sore foot," she told him.

"Nonetheless, let's have a look. I could see you favoring it at times. The bandage may have gotten wet today and probably needs to be changed."

As he knelt at her feet unwrapping the old bandage, she contemplated the fact that she had forgotten the injury.

It seemed to her a new realization—this one that bliss was capable of obliterating her pain.

And it seemed to her that applied not just to physical pain, but to emotional pain, as well.

She did what she had wanted to do yesterday.

She reached out and touched his hair. It was still damp from being outside. At first, she just touched it lightly, and then she ran her fingers through it, smoothing down his sweet rooster tail. Then, on pure impulse, she dropped her lips, and kissed the top of his head.

He froze. And then slowly he tilted his head up to her. And then he went back to bandaging her foot. "What was that for?" he asked gruffly.

"I'm not sure," she admitted. "Just this kind of heart-deep gratitude for an amazing day. I feel healed by it, somehow, and not just my foot."

He finished what he was doing, packed away the supplies with more care than might have been completely necessary. He rose, hesitated, and then, in some kind of surrender, came and sat beside her on the couch. They watched the flickering fire. His hand found hers.

"Tell me about it. You wouldn't earlier, but tell me now. What makes you cry when you look at babies?"

She could sense then the absolute command of his presence, because, even though Luca was dressed in long johns and his tone was gentle, it was not an invitation, but an order.

Imogen sighed. She told him everything. She told him about meeting Kevin here at the Lodge, Kevin an instructor at the nearby Crystal Mountain Ski Resort. She told him about a relationship that had felt steady and safe and secure. She told him about how she thought she had found the very steadiness that she had grown up with and had craved since her family had moved away. She told him about wanting nothing more than a family of her own.

Then she stopped, and her voice faltered.

"What happened?" Luca's voice encouraged trust.

She told him about the proposal, and the fortune cookie. "That's the picture you saw on my phone," she said, "of the night Kevin asked me to marry him."

"So why didn't he marry you?"

She sighed. She willed the tears not to fall. "I had a ski accident when I was a teenager. The worst of the injuries healed, but I suspected something that wasn't quite as obvious was wrong. In a way, I didn't want to know, because all my dreams were about family. So I just never followed up on it. But the fact that Kevin's proposal included the mention of babies forced me to find out if what I suspected was true.

"The news wasn't good. I can't have babies."

Luca's hand tightened on hers. "Ah," he said, and she knew he was thinking of her reaction to the photo of Rachel's new baby.

"Of course, Kevin said it didn't matter, and said all the right words. That it was me he loved, and we would figure it out, but right underneath the words, there was some crushing disappointment in his face that I could not bear. So I broke it off. I set him free.

"I'd like to say he seemed heartbroken by the breakup, but his reaction was more one of relief. Even though it had taken him three years to propose to me, he was engaged and married to someone else almost instantly. They're pregnant now."

He was silent for the longest while. When he spoke, his voice was low. She wasn't sure what she expected from him. He struck her as having such an inborn sense of honor, that maybe she expected outrage on her behalf.

She wondered why she had told him any of this. Could it change anything? Of course it could not.

And yet a burden she had carried for months now suddenly felt lighter.

"In time," Luca said, his voice strong and sure, "you will understand what a blessing this was."

"Not to have children?" she said, her voice strangled.

"I was speaking to your broken engagement. Your relationship sounds as if it was as comfortable as an old shoe. I think there are things in you that need better than that. Perhaps he found it—that spark, that passion, that recognition of two souls meeting—perhaps that is why his new life unfolded so quickly. Not as any kind of insult to you.

"As for children," a smile tickled his lips and he touched her chin and lifted it with his finger, so her eyes were forced to meet his, "you will be a beautiful mother one day. We live in an age of miracles. And you will have your miracle. Whether it is through science, or through adoption, or through an act of divinity, of this I am certain—the souls of your children will find their way to you."

Her mouth fell open and tears studded her eyes.

"What an amazing thing to say." Of all the things he could have said, how was it the Prince had said something so perfect?

Luca lifted a shoulder and dropped his finger from her chin.

"I feel it," he said. "Though I consider myself the most pragmatic of men, there are things, sometimes, that intuition knows. I have been trained, even as a child, to respect the gift of intuition as a tool in guiding my kingdom toward a future where sometimes it is hard to know the right answer, where sometimes facts are not enough to arrive at the correct decision."

Imogen felt his voice, his presence, wrapping itself around her.

It had been the most perfect of days, and this was the most perfect of endings. She did not really know how completely she had lived without peace until it was restored to her.

By a prince, sitting beside her in his bright red long johns!

Maybe it was all a dream.

It had to be. Because she drifted off with the deep weariness of one who had traveled a long, long time and had finally arrived at where they wanted—and needed—to be.

CHAPTER NINE

IMOGEN AWOKE. EVEN though she was faintly disoriented, she was aware of a glorious sensation from the bottom of her toes to the top of her head, filling every cell of her being, pumping through her bloodstream with every beat of her heart.

She felt something she had thought that she would never feel again. But then yesterday, building a snow family with the Prince, she had felt it again. Yesterday, just before falling asleep, she had felt it again.

That the feeling remained, even without the laughter ringing in the air between them, even without the quiet contentment of his voice weaving around her, was wondrous indeed.

She realized she had fallen asleep sitting up. Now she found herself nestled against Luca, the steady drum of his heart beneath her ear, his warmth seeping into her, better than a blanket, his tangy masculine scent dancing with her senses.

He had fallen asleep sitting up, too. His arm had found its way around her shoulders. She snuggled deeper against him. And let herself just feel it, that feeling that she had thought she would never have again.

Of being blissfully happy.

After a while, she shifted her position and allowed herself the luxury of studying his face in sleep. The tension she had noticed when she had awoken in the same room with him—could it really be only yesterday?—was gone from his features. How could she feel she knew him so well in such a short period of time?

His features: the whisker-roughened chin and cheeks, his full, sensual lips, his lashes as thick as a sooty chimney brush, filled her with a kind of delight.

His words from last night: spoken with such confidence and so hope-filled that the memory of them made her feel as warm as his body pressed against hers.

Hope.

She had wandered in the desert of despair for so long, unable to find her way out. And the way out had found her.

Taken her completely by surprise.

His words, his sharing his intuition with her, had been an extraordinary gift. Imogen felt a sudden intense desire to give him something in return, something he had never had, a continuation of the ordinary pleasures they had explored yesterday.

But what could she give him that held a candle to the extraordinary sense of hope that he had reawakened in her?

The answer whispered within her, so softly she dismissed it. But then it came again, louder.

Christmas.

She could give him Christmas. Not the trappings of Christmas, but the feeling of it. The delight of it. The sense of the miraculous that was inherent in that day. She could give him not a regal Christmas, where true meaning could become lost in pageantry, and in the pomp and circumstance, but the simplicity of Christmas, where one thing, and one thing alone, shone through.

Shone through as clearly as a star that had led wise men on an incredible journey of faith to a message that had survived over a thousand years, that was still celebrated around the world as intensely as if that babe had been born yesterday.

The message that the babe—and all babies—carried.

The message she had given up on, but that now beat again strongly in her heart.

Love was the true strength, the only way to heal a troubled heart.

Imogen contemplated that for a frightening moment.

Did she really want to be thinking about that—about love—when she was nestled into the safety of his strong, beautiful body? When she could feel the beat of his heart, and his breath stirred her hair?

Of course she did not love him! It was impossible. Despite the fun they had had yesterday—the adventure of survival that they were embarked on together—she could not know him that well. She could not love him.

Except maybe in the greater sense of that word.

The Christmas sense: where love was the force that made you better than you were before, and stronger, and able to give to others from a well of compassion deep within your own soul.

Was not the very spirit of Christmas, somehow, to give joy to a complete stranger, with no thought whatsoever of return, of what was in it for you?

She slipped out from under the protection of his arm, got off the sofa and quietly went and stoked the fire, then tiptoed out of the room so as not to disturb Luca. She had no idea what time it was, but she located her cell phone.

Because it had not been used at all, it still had battery. The time was three in the morning, but Imogen had never felt more awake.

The picture of her and Kevin's engagement had popped up as soon as she had opened the screen to check the time.

She was going to close the phone, but she made herself look at the picture. Then she took a deep breath, and with a new resolve, a sense of extraordinary strength, she deleted the photo. She waited for some feeling—sadness, regret. A feeling came, but it was not the one she expected.

A feeling of newness, of being open to whatever happened next, of not being stuck anymore.

Imogen moved on to see that although there was no cell service at the moment, there had been. A message from Gabi had arrived sometime yesterday. Imogen opened it eagerly.

I am safe. Did not get caught in the snowstorm, though my life is stormy in other ways. I will be in touch soon. Love you, my friend.

Imogen stared at the message. Gabriella's life was stormy? How was that even possible? How could her best friend have a stormy life without her awareness? Had she been that self-involved in her own misery that she had missed some unfolding drama in Gabi's life?

But how? Crystal Lake was too small for the details of people's lives not to be noticed. Everyone knew everything.

But people had suspected something was going on. Imogen had. Rachel had also known something was off with Gabi. But a storm?

Storms usually meant men! And there were no men in Gabi's life, no strangers in town causing tongues to wag.

The only stranger about was the one sleeping in Imogen's office, and no one knew about him.

And it was not as if Gabi ever went anywhere where

she might meet someone. While Imogen sometimes worried Gabi must be lonely, Gabi steadfastly claimed complete contentment with her life. She rarely left Crystal Lake, not even to drive two hours to the city. No, her big event seemed to be the delivery of new books to her store every week.

She loved reading. She loved book club. She loved teaching literacy.

Who was less likely to have a storm in her life than Gabi? Her friend was gorgeous, with her huge brown eyes and her thick chestnut hair that hung midway down her back. She was tall and curvy in the way that made men stop in their tracks and look at her twice, though her innate composure kept most of them from approaching her with their interest.

Gabriella was delightfully unaware of those second looks, of her own extraordinary beauty. She reminded Imogen just a little of Belle, in *Beauty and the Beast*, her nose buried in a book while men floundered at her feet. In fact, Gabi usually forgot she had her reading glasses perched on the end of her nose, making her look like one of those very sexy librarians.

Gabriella Ross was a self-proclaimed hater of excitement.

And yet excitement, of some form, seemed to have found her. But her friend's storm would have to remain a mystery until the storm that raged unabated outside the Lodge subsided.

Terrible, Imogen thought, using up some of her precious battery on her phone to find her way through the darkened Lodge, *to be hoping that the storm would not subside for a long, long time.*

She quickly went about the business of stoking the other fireplaces in the Lodge, and then went to a storage room and unearthed dusty boxes of Christmas decorations. Feeling delightfully like one of Santa's elves, she quietly reentered the office.

While Luca slept, she hung garlands and wreaths. She put out treasured figurines that had been in her family for generations. They might not be Buschetta, but they warmed her heart: reindeer and sleighs, Santa and his missus, a group of carolers. Finally, on the wide sill of the big window, she put out the manger scene. There were dozens of Christmas candles and she put them where, when lit, they would light the figurines. There were candles left over for the mantel. She drizzled shiny tinsel off the door and window frames. Finally, she hung two red socks.

She sat back and took it all in. The room had been transformed to a magic place. It only needed a tree.

And some gifts.

What could she give a man who had everything? How about a memory of a perfect day? Again, she made her way through the darkened lodge, searching out this and that: Ping-Pong balls from the games room, cotton balls from the first aid kit, colorful place mats that she could cut into squares of cloth.

Hardly feeling the cold, Imogen sat down at the kitchen table, and with her tongue caught between her teeth in fierce concentration, she made her gift.

When it was done she regarded it with grave satisfaction, wrapped it carefully in butcher paper and tied it with a piece of string. Then she plundered the cupboards for stocking stuffers: baker's chocolate, a package of pecans, a few pouches of hot chocolate powder.

Tonight, for Christmas dinner, they would have those little chickens that were in the fridge. She would wrap them in tinfoil and slow roast them on the coals of the fire all day.

She went back to the office and put her offerings in one of the socks. And then she went around the room and lit each of the candles.

Luca woke slowly. He could smell hot wax in the air. He opened his eyes to an enchantment.

Candles burned around the room. They lit small figurines and sent a golden glow into a room that had been transformed. Tinsel sparkled like new icicles. There were red-bowed wreaths on the doors. There was a manger scene of figurines in the window. Two bright red socks hung over a fire that blazed merrily.

His eyes found Imogen. She was adorable in her long johns, a red Santa hat with white trim and a huge pompom on her head. She was watching him, the smile on her face more enchanting than anything in the room.

"What is this?" he asked.

"It's a gift, for you. It's the gift of Christmas."

He looked at the light in her face and saw her absolute joy in giving this to him. He was not sure a gift—and he had experienced so many of them that were grand—had ever touched him so completely. She must have been up for hours getting this ready.

"It's beautiful," he said softly. What he wanted to say was, *You are beautiful.*

"We just need a tree," she said, suddenly shy, as if he had said those words—*you are beautiful.*

Astonishingly, he could feel the spirit of what she was doing, creeping into him. He couldn't wait to get a tree.

And so they ate a hasty breakfast, donned their now-dry outdoor clothes from yesterday and went outside.

She unearthed an ax from near a woodpile and they

set out across the lawn, past their snow family and into a grove of trees. By the time they got there, they were both breathless with the exertion of plowing through the deep snow.

Luca stopped in the silence of the trees.

He could feel something tightening in his throat as he looked at the sanctuary of beauty and stillness around him.

The moment was made complete when her hand found his. He looked at her to find her gazing into his face, that tiny smile of *knowing* tickling across her mouth.

"What?" he asked her.

"You feel it," she said, her voice low and husky and reverent, as if they were in a church.

"Feel what?" he challenged her. She couldn't really read his mind. And his soul. She couldn't.

"Wonder," she said.

Apparently she could!

He looked down at her and let himself feel it. The absolute wonder of this woman wanting so badly to give him something he had never had.

Luca did something he was pretty sure he had never done, something that was not in the experience of any member of the House of Valenti, something his father would have scorned.

He felt it unfurl inside of him.

A banner.

Of surrender.

He surrendered to what she was doing, and what she was offering. He surrendered himself to the unexpected gift of a perfect day.

Shockingly, it did not feel like a weakness to surrender. Shockingly, Luca felt stronger, and bolder, than he ever had in his entire life.

He felt alive.

He did something he had been dying to do since yesterday. It was part of that complete surrender. Before he could talk himself out of it, he gave in.

He lowered his head over hers and tasted the lushness of her lips.

The warmth of them was absolutely tantalizing in contrast to the cold air. Kissing her was as he had hoped—known—it would be. Real. Her lips told the absolute truth about who she was. And about who he was, too.

Her lips opened eagerly to his mouth, they welcomed him, celebrated him, danced with him. He felt as if he was drinking a wine that he could never get enough of, a sweet elixir from an enchanted land.

He made himself pull away from her, stunned by his own lack of discipline. He felt he should say he was sorry, but he was not in the least sorry, and after she had given him something so real, he could not be insincere with her.

Still, he backed away from her, aware of her wide eyes following his every move, of her breath, quickened, forming little puffs in the cold air. He forced his mind to turn away from her, and it sought desperately for a task to distract.

He went over to a tree with a sense of urgency. It was six feet high and its thick branches were weighed down with snow. He studied it carefully. He walked around it. He was not sure he had ever seen such symmetry in a tree, such vivid color, such headiness of fragrance. But of course, his every sense was heightened. It felt like the very air was shivering around him with newness.

He reached into the trunk and gave it a shake. The

snow cascaded around him, and he was rewarded with her laughter pealing through the stillness.

"This one," he declared. "This will be our Christmas tree."

CHAPTER TEN

IMOGEN WATCHED AS Luca took the ax and swung it powerfully into the trunk of the tree. A fresh bunch of snow fell on top of him, but he shook it off with ease, focused intently on his task.

A few minutes ago, it might have seemed absurd to think the Prince was showing off for her. But that was before he had kissed her.

She took off her mitten and touched her lips. They felt faintly bruised, tingly. Her life felt altered.

Imogen wished he hadn't stopped. But she understood perfectly. A prince could not go about bestowing kisses on commoners!

Still, even though he had backed off on that kiss, she was pretty sure Luca cutting down the tree was for her. Not just to give her a Christmas tree, but as a masculine form of preening.

After a few minutes, he removed the bulky jacket. The view made her mouth go dry—the full broadness of his shoulders revealed, the taut line of his stomach. His arm muscles, outlined by the fabric, tensing, relaxing, tensing again. Somehow, one would not expect a prince to be quite so buff!

Watching him work—easy strength set against this task—was like experiencing visual poetry. She could see the play of his muscles, feel his intensity, smell the faint tang of his exertion mingling with the sharp scent of tree sap.

She had been aware of Luca before. Now that she had tasted the exquisiteness of his lips, the awareness was almost painful, like what she imagined having a tattoo on tender skin might feel like.

The tree finally came down, falling slowly and silently into the snow that surrounded it. He turned and grinned at her, and she allowed herself the satisfaction of having succeeded at what she had originally set out to do.

Luca's face had lost all the sternness and all the tension that had been in it when he had first gotten off that helicopter.

Standing there, leaning on the ax, the fallen tree at his feet, he looked mischievous and boyish, intensely alive, sinfully sexy.

Really, could there be a more humble experience than taking an ax to a tree in the Canadian wilderness? And yet his face was alight with discovery, with an embracing of the spirit of Christmas that was almost childlike.

"It's beautiful," she said softly.

And she didn't just mean the tree. She meant all of it.

He put the ax on his shoulder and picked up the trunk of the tree with his free hand. The tree was huge and heavy, the snow was deep, but he forged ahead.

Imogen leaped to his assistance.

"We're a good team," Luca told her breathlessly as the Lodge came into sight.

"Yeah, a good team of plow horses."

At the stairs of the Lodge, they faced a new challenge. Laughing, gasping, the occasional curse word slipping from the royal lips—which made her laugh all the harder—they finally managed to wrestle the tree up the steps and through the doors.

Once in the office, they had to figure out how to get the tree to stand up. The rough, uneven cuts to the trunk made it nearly impossible, even using the tree stand she had unearthed.

"I think we should tie it to the wall in the corner," Imogen suggested.

"I find that an admission of defeat. Surely, if they can get a forty-foot tree to stand in the foyer at the palace, we can figure this out."

"Well, I hate to break it to you, but we aren't at the palace, and we don't have a team of dozens to help us."

"I find it insulting that you think I need staff to do something so simple."

"Have you ever done something so simple? Set up a Christmas tree?"

"Well, no."

"This has been the yearly challenge in my life since I was a babe, so—" she wagged the string at him "—let me know when you're ready."

An hour later the tree was stuffed in a corner, attached to the walls with nails and string so it wouldn't fall over.

The day unfolded with a delicious combination of ease and tension between them. The smallest decisions seemed tinged with both magic and danger.

"Usually, the first step would be lights," Imogen said, frowning at a box full of light strings, "but is there any point? I guess it would be nice if the power came back on."

But she realized she did not think it would be nice if the power came back on at all, not even if it did make the tree the prettiest thing in the whole Rocky Mountain Range!

They decided on popcorn garlands. Popping corn over a fire was more difficult than they imagined, and soon the room was so filled with the scent of scorched popcorn Luca had to open a window. It was also filled with the sound of their laughter. Finally, they got a batch just right, ate most of it and had to start all over.

When they had enough popcorn to make garlands, Imogen carefully prepared the tiny chickens in tinfoil packets and placed them in a nest of red-hot coals. Soon, the fragrance of the slowly roasting poultry chased even the scorched popcorn smell from the room.

They sat side by side on the sofa, feeling immense enjoyment in the tedious exercise of threading the popcorn onto strings.

"This is what it would have been like for my great-grandparents," she said. "Just taking pleasure in completing very simple, time-consuming tasks."

"Not for mine," he said, and they both laughed quietly, but she heard the wistfulness in his tone.

They chatted about things that existed in that tiny space where their worlds met: what books they had enjoyed, favorite movies, music.

She created a spontaneous game of twenty questions that made getting to know each other fun and surprising and full of discovery.

"Cats or dogs?" she asked him.

"Dogs," he said, and then shot back at her, "Elephants or parrots?"

She laughed. "That would depend on context. Definitely a parrot for a house pet!"

He sighed, "That shows you know nothing of the nature of parrots. Nasty things. My mother was given one for a pet once. Mark that down—worst gift ever. A parrot."

"I'm not sure an elephant would be any better."

"Actually, there's a story about that," he said. "It is said the King of Siam would gift a white elephant to anyone who displeased him. It would seem as if he was being nice, but in actual fact the care and keeping of a ten-ton mammal is extremely onerous."

"Remind me not to displease you!"

"Oh, I will!"

The game continued.

"Beach or ski hill?" she asked him.

It turned out Luca enjoyed skiing, and it proved to be one of the few things they had in common. They talked about that mutual love. Though her career as a ski racer had ended in the accident when she was sixteen, Imogen still loved to cross-country ski the mountain trails around the Lodge.

"Maybe we'll do that tomorrow," she suggested, feeling suddenly shy, as if she was inviting him on a date.

"I've never cross-country skied. I can't wait to try it."

It took a long time to make that garland, but every second of it felt wonderful, an easy companionship between them. Finally, it was ready. With great ceremony, with their shoulders brushing and their hands accidentally touching, they placed their fragrant garland in the tree, then stood back and admired their handiwork.

Finally, they were ready to open the boxes of ornaments. Imogen opened the first one, and smiled.

"Look." She held up her find to show Luca. "These are my two favorites."

Luca took them, one in each hand, turned them over and then passed them back, smiling at her questioningly.

They were reindeer made out of pinecones. They had button eyes and felt ears and tails ratty with age.

"My sisters made them," Imogen said, "when they were just small."

"Will you be with them for Christmas?"

"Of course. My sisters both work overseas, and my parents have settled in Arizona. They loved it here when they lived here, but my mother had a lifelong struggle with asthma. The cold seemed to trigger it and the climate is good for her there. So, we'll meet there again this year."

"For an admitted lover of all things Christmas, you don't sound excited about it."

Imogen hesitated. "Christmas in Arizona never feels quite right. Growing up here, after we opened gifts, Christmas morning, my dad would drive us to town and we'd skate on Crystal Lake. We'd sled on a big hill right beside the lake, and whoosh out onto the ice. It felt as if you were going a million miles an hour when you hit that ice! There was always a big fire going, and tons of hot chocolate and hot dogs. Every kid in town would be there. It was such a sense of community. We were usually so stuffed with hot dogs and marshmallows, we could barely eat Mom's turkey dinner.

"Now my folks have an artificial tree. My dad loves to golf on Christmas Day because there's no lineup on the tees. Last year, my mom refused to cook a turkey because she said it was too hot to get the oven going and the house heated up.

"I miss the way it used to be. I wish they would all come back here for Christmas, instead of me going there."

"Is today the way it used to be?" Luca asked softly.

"Not exactly," she said. "Except for that one year, we always had power."

Not exactly. Because of the kiss part. Not exactly, because of the awareness part. Not exactly, because of the part where Imogen felt as if she might catch on fire every time her hand brushed his.

Though usually people who were afraid of being burned didn't keep inviting it over and over again.

"I understand why you would want to be here," Luca said quietly. "It's magic here."

"What an extraordinary thing to say, given that you are the one who comes from a fairy-tale setting. Tell me about your brother, the one who was supposed to come here. Are you close?"

He contemplated that. "We're close in age. Antonio is only a year younger than I am. In our early years, we were tremendous friends, but as we got older, the expectations on me were different than they were on him. I'd say that the grooming to assume the mantle of leadership began in my early teens and intensified as I got older.

"So, Antonio had way more freedom than I did, and he was quite the rascal at times. I think I envied him his freedom, and he envied me what he saw as our father's favor. Both of us worked hard for the King's approval, and I think Antonio would be surprised to know I feel as if, in Vincenzo's eyes, I never quite measured up, either. I felt close to my father only when I was successful, and of course that drove me to excel at everything I ever did, from sports to lessons.

"We were competitive with each other, as brothers tend to be, but he was also one of the few people I could be myself with, with no worry about keeping up my image. I confided in him, I think, as in no one else, and so it was quite a blow when he announced his decision to join the army.

"I hoped it would be a temporary stop on his career path, but he seems to have found a place where he belongs. He's part of an elite squadron that is posted all over the world. I miss him dreadfully and envy him the camaraderie he enjoys, and the adventures he embraces."

He stopped, frowning.

"But what?"

"He's a brave man, and courageous, but I feel something might have happened to him on his last mission. He was changed by it in some way. And then my father's death followed quickly on the heels of that. But naturally, he's a soldier, so he doesn't talk about *feelings*, or at least not to me."

"It sounds as though you love him very much."

Luca smiled. "That's true, even though I don't think I have ever said those words to him."

"You should."

"Maybe I will."

"What would you be, if you weren't a prince?"

He smiled, a bit sadly. "I've always loved travel and exploring other cultures, but I feel, because of my title, I don't always get to see what's real about a place or about people. The way I have here. It's been a gift."

A companionable silence existed between them as they contemplated their families and the coming of Christmas and unexpected gifts.

And then Luca's eyes drifted to her lips. Her eyes drifted to his. He touched her hand. His fingers stroked the top of it in an unconsciously sensual way.

Magic. If it was really a fairy tale, wasn't this the part where the Prince showed up and saved the day? Rescued the damsel from the dreariness and challenges of her life? With a kiss?

Maybe in this fairy tale, she was also rescuing him.

From a life that seemed as if it bore almost unbearable loneliness.

Imogen leaned toward him. Luca leaned toward her.

But instead of kissing her, he cupped the side of her cheek with his hand.

"It's so complicated," he said, his tone gruff with regret.

"Of course it is," she said brightly, slipped away from his hand and went to turn the little chickens in the fire.

Despite the tension, she forced herself to relax, but from then on, Imogen avoided touching his shoulder and hands. They finished hanging ornaments, each one with a story that she shared with him. The little guitar had been a gift from a guest, a classical guitarist. The glass one with the scene painted inside it had been handed down to her family from her grandmother. The ugly handprint, so heavy it made the tree branch droop under its weight, had been made by her in kindergarten.

He studied that one for a long time, a smile on his face, before he hung it by a threadbare ribbon on a sturdy branch of the tree.

"More precious than Buschetta," he told her.

And she had to duck her head from the utter sincerity in his voice, and in his eyes as they rested on her. Only a few days ago, that ornament in particular would have filled her with sadness that she was not going to experience her own children making such things. Now, on the strength of his conviction, she was nursing hope. It made tears smart behind her eyes.

Late in the afternoon, the snow finally stopped. They ventured out into a world so bright and sparkling it almost hurt the eyes. The strength of the sun was already melting the snowmen. It made her feel sad, because the end of the snowstorm, and the melting of their little snow family felt as if it was foreshadowing that their time together, in this magical kingdom of their own making, was coming to a close.

Imogen, despite feeling the sadness of it, knew there was no way a helicopter could land in all that snow, and it would probably be at least one more day before the road to the Lodge opened, possibly two.

Despite her resolve to enjoy the time she had left, to not look to the inevitable goodbye the future held, the mood had already shifted by the time they pulled the little tinfoil-wrapped hens from the fire, and gobbled down their "turkey."

"Possibly the best Christmas dinner I've ever had," Luca declared.

"Don't be silly."

"I'm not. The best Christmas dinner and the best Christmas." His tone was pensive. He, too, was getting ready for the goodbye.

"It's not quite over yet," she said, and got up and took the stuffed sock down from the mantel.

She watched with pleasure as he opened it. He happily shared the chocolate and nuts with her and then carefully opened her package.

One by one he took out the snow family she had made out of Ping-Pong balls and cotton wool.

"They're beautiful," he breathed.

"I know they're clumsy and handmade, but I wanted you to have the memory."

"I will cherish them," he said with sincerity—a prince cherishing her little homemade gift, "but I didn't need them to have the memory. Imogen, I will never forget this time."

He looked at her handmade snow family again and then looked at her.

"I'm sorry. I never thought of a gift for you."

But really? The gift had been these few days. Still…

"There is a gift you can give me," she said slowly.

"Anything."

"When you arrived here, I saw something in you that was troubled. I want you to trust me with it. I want to know why you are here. Are you running away from something?"

She had shared everything with him, her every heartache. And that was the only gift she wanted from him in return. The same level of trust she had placed in him when she had shared her confidences.

Luca could have kicked himself for that *anything*. Of course this woman would require more of him than some bauble that cost the earth financially, but cost nothing emotionally.

He looked at the gift she had given him—that painstakingly crafted snow family—and felt some resistance in him melt away, just like that real snow family outside was melting away.

"I was supposed to be married," he confessed. "Two days ago."

Her mouth fell open. "You ran away?"

He snorted. "No, she did."

How flattering was it that the look on Imogen's face seemed to say, *Impossible, no one would run away from you*?

But then Imogen had coaxed a different side from him, a side that Meribel had never seen, that no one had ever seen. Maybe he hadn't even been aware he had it himself.

"The whole kingdom was preparing for a huge celebration. I wouldn't be surprised if the Buschetta ornament this year will commemorate a royal wedding."

"But what happened to your wedding?"

"I wish I knew. My fiancée, Princess Meribel of Aguilarez, came to me the night before the wedding. She told me she loved another and carried his baby. She confessed she had actually considered marrying me, anyway, passing the baby off as mine."

"But that's awful!"

"And yet she's not an awful person," Luca said. "Like me, she has been raised with the idea that duty came first. She is a princess from the neighboring kingdom. Our fathers signed marriage contracts for us when we were very young. It was to cement a relationship that has not been without its frictions. It was to secure the future of both kingdoms, to strengthen the alliances between them and to give the people peace of mind."

"That is no reason to get married!" Imogen sputtered.

"In my world it is. And in the one Meribel was raised in, it is. But in the end, her heart was stronger than her sense of duty."

"Thank goodness," Imogen muttered.

"Perhaps," he said wearily.

"And so you came here just to escape?"

"I announced the wedding had been called off because of irreconcilable differences, and then decided to take my brother's place on this mission."

"You protected her," Imogen breathed. "At great cost to yourself."

"A prince among men," he said with dry sarcasm.

"You are," she said stubbornly. "She must mean a great deal to you for you to take the brunt of the disappointment of two nations for something that was no fault of your own."

But wasn't it, at least in part, his fault? For not reading anything correctly? For not paying attention? For not noticing that Meribel was deeply dissatisfied with their engagement? Or maybe for not caring?

But for some reason, instead of admitting all that, he wanted to bask in Imogen's admiration.

For just a little while longer. His intuition had been humming since the sun came out. It was nearly over.

If he was honest about it, he felt more unsettled, more despairing, about his time with Imogen ending than he had about the end of his engagement with Meribel.

There, his concerns were largely pragmatic. What kind of chaos could result for the two kingdoms? His pride was wounded, not his heart.

Right now, for the first time in his life, his heart was ruling everything, not his head.

Imogen frowned suddenly. "What mission?" she asked.

"Sorry?"

"You said you were taking your brother's place on a mission. What mission? I can't imagine any kind of royal business that would bring you to Crystal Lake, Canada."

Before he could answer they heard the deep growl of a motor, still in the distance, but the high-pitched, incessant whining growing closer. It was a shocking sound against the deep and complete silence they had experienced for their entire time together.

"Snow machine," Imogen said. "Probably one of the neighbors, or someone from town coming to check on us."

But he suspected it was not. It would be Cristiano, who would have been relentless in his efforts to get back here.

"Gabi probably sent them."

Just like that, he thought, *it is over.* And wasn't that the thing he should have been remembering about an enchantment?

Just like a fairy tale, it came to an end.

But not always a happy one.

And yet, still, his heart ruled above his head. He turned to her.

"Kiss me," he whispered. And to himself he added, *one last time*.

CHAPTER ELEVEN

IMOGEN TOLD HERSELF there was no refusing a royal command, but the truth was, ever since they had kissed this afternoon, every other thing had been overlaid with the awareness of Luca, and of his lips, and of the way tasting them had made her feel.

That kiss had increased her awareness of *him* throughout the day until it was almost painful to be with him. She was intensely aware of the way he moved so gracefully, and of his easy strength, of the way he tossed back his head when he laughed and tilted it toward her when he listened to her. She was intensely aware of the rooster tail that insisted on springing up on the back of his head, inviting her fingers to press it down, and of the scent of him that made her want to bury her nose against his chest, more delicious than the scent of the Christmas tree that filled the room.

But it wasn't just his kiss that had increased her awareness, it was the fact that he had shared his confidences with her. Luca had trusted her.

It had made her see that, despite appearances that he was the man who had everything, he was deeply vulnerable and had led a life of almost unfathomable loneliness. It made her aware that there was a depth in those deep brown eyes, a compassion born of his own unspoken—maybe his totally unacknowledged—suffering.

So when he asked her to kiss him, she forgot his whispered, *it's so complicated.*

She forgot everything: who she had been before this moment and who she would be again after, who he had been before this moment and who he would be again after. She forgot her heartaches and her sorrows.

They melted away, until all that was left was this moment.

Luca leaning in to her, cupping the back of her head with his hand, drawing her to him, closer and closer. She closed her eyes and they connected. His lips were soft but firm; they tasted, incredibly, of wild strawberries, even though that had not ever been on their menu.

They tasted of promises: of winter days chasing through the snow and spring afternoons lying down in meadows of wildflowers. They gave a promise of finding sunlight on gray days and warmth against the cold. They gave a promise of a future full of unexpected adventures, and that included the best adventure of all, which was coming to know another person, deeply and truly.

No wonder when Luca claimed her lips, Imogen forgot his *it's so complicated*, because nothing had ever felt less complicated. In fact, she was not sure she had ever felt anything that had been more simple, more primal, more preordained, more meant to be.

The meeting of their lips, intensifying, breathed life back into her, as though for so long she had been going through the motions, sleepwalking. She tingled after being numb. She became supple after being wooden. Black and white became full glorious color. She was sharp instead of wrapped in cotton. The world was in focus, instead of being fuzzy.

Something softened in her, and Luca sensed instantly she had invited the kiss to deepen yet again between them. He plundered her mouth, and when she was gasping with need and with delight, he shifted his attention to her neck, trailed kisses down it, nuzzled her ears, dropped his head to her neck, explored her ears with his lips, anointed her forehead and her nose with his mouth. With almost frantic need, she put her hands on both sides of his head and guided his mouth back to hers. He moaned and drew her yet closer, his hands tangling in her hair. There was a beautiful savagery between them now, a hunger, a fire.

The background of all of this had been the whine of snowmobile engines, drawing ever closer. It was almost shocking when the engines stopped abruptly, plunging them into silence.

The fury, the urgency, the desperation of the kiss between them intensified. Somewhere in her was the wild thought that this kiss had the power to stop time, that if they focused on nothing else, the moment would never end.

"Your Royal Highness? Miss Albright?"

Neither of them had heard the front door open, but now they sprang apart as they heard footfalls, coming fast down the hall.

They stood, breathing hard, staring at each other. She had a sense of trying to memorize every single thing about this moment: the rapid rise of his chest, the look on his face, the faintly bruised look around his mouth.

Luca put out his hand to her, trying to bridge the gap between them. If she took it, Imogen felt he would run out the back door, escape back to the world that was just them. She reached for it.

"Sir?" The words echoed in the hallway outside the

door. There would be no world of just them. No, his world called for him to come back. The gap between them could not be bridged, because it was time.

And for them, time had just run out.

Luca dropped his hand before her outreached fingers connected with his touch. She stared at his hand, where it had fallen to his side, and then pulled her own away and used it to tuck a strand of hair behind her ear.

Cristiano burst into the room. His relief at seeing Luca was evident, but then his eyes swept the room, and Imogen felt something fragile and private was laid bare to him.

Cristiano took in the leaning Christmas tree, the decorations, the sock on the coffee table, the little snowmen figures she had made, the way Luca and Imogen were dressed, as if they were in their pajamas.

He looked confused. "Are you alone here? Just the two of you?"

Luca nodded, curtly, his eyes never leaving her face. Begging her? Promising her?

"It's just…it looks as if there was a family here. The snowmen out front…" Cristiano's voice drifted away. His eyes went from Luca to her and back again. She felt what had just transpired between them was an open book, puffy lips, mussed hair, heaving chests.

A smooth mask fell over his face. "You're all right, then, sir?"

Luca nodded curtly.

"Another snow machine is coming right behind me so that we can take both you and Miss Albright down to the village. There's power there—I've booked rooms for our meeting. We have to make haste, sir. You are urgently needed in Casavalle. I was able to contact Miss Ross and we can meet her—"

Imogen felt as if she was swimming up from the bottom of a pool. Cristiano's words registered with her as if she was hearing them from under water.

"Wait a minute," Imogen said. "You've contacted who?"

Cristiano went silent.

Imogen turned her attention to Luca. "Who are you meeting with?"

"Gabriella Ross," Luca said quietly.

"*My* Gabriella Ross?" Imogen said, hearing something dangerous in her tone.

"I'm sorry, I don't know what you mean," Luca said uneasily.

"She's my best friend."

Luca strode over to her and gazed down at her, his look stripping, all those promises gone from his eyes as if they had never been.

And really, had they ever been?

"Has she told you about her claim?" he asked, his voice a rasp.

"What claim?" Imogen said, refusing to be intimidated by him, even though he had become a stern stranger before her very eyes.

He searched her face, then turned back to Cristiano, dismissing her. Dismissing every single second they had spent together. He wasn't trudging sadly toward his world, instead of the one they had shared; he was leaping toward it.

"You have news from Casavalle?" Luca asked Cristiano.

Cristiano shot her a look. Was she supposed to bow out so they could have this conversation in private? She wasn't feeling accommodating!

"You can speak in front of her. I trust her completely."

Imogen steeled herself against the compliment. Did he really? Then why was it he had never once mentioned what he was really in Crystal Lake for?

"Unfortunately, there's been a leak about Princess Meribel's pregnancy," Cristiano said, his tone low and uncomfortable. "I'm afraid the mood of the people is not forgiving."

"This is grave news, indeed," Luca said, his brow furrowed with worry.

Imogen thought, again, just as she had when he had first told her about Meribel, that he must care about her very much. Quite frankly, after what he had told her about the Princess's plan to pass off a baby that was not his, Imogen was not at all sure Meribel deserved forgiveness.

"Tensions are quite high," Cristiano said. "Princess Meribel has gone into hiding."

The way he said this made it very clear Luca would be looked to for leadership in this difficult situation.

Imogen watched Luca change as he donned the mantle of his responsibility. Even though he was still dressed in long johns, his authority became very apparent. He went from being an ordinary man to the leader of a people before her very eyes. That remoteness was in him, the unmistakable sense of absolute command.

"Please tell me what Gabriella has to do with any of this?" Imogen demanded.

Luca looked at her coolly, as if he had never kissed her at all, as if the barriers their different worlds erected between them had never been melted away by the heat of their passion.

"I think that would be up to her to tell you," he said.

She felt rebuffed. She felt as if the man she had just kissed with her whole heart and soul, with all the passion she was capable of—the man she had played in the snow with and given the gift of Christmas to, the man who had trusted her with his deepest self—had become an untouchable, unknowable stranger before her very eyes.

She felt as if she wanted to weep.

But she heard the second snowmobile pulling into the yard.

"Get ready," Luca said to her. "We will leave immediately."

"I'm staying here," she said proudly.

"No, you're not."

"It's my job."

"I'll appoint someone to keep things going until the power is restored."

"No, you won't."

Cristiano was staring at her with his mouth open. Obviously, he had never heard anyone argue with the Prince before.

"You're coming with us," Luca said tersely. "I'm not leaving you here to deal with this by yourself."

"The power will be restored shortly."

"And then you can return here."

She straightened her shoulders and lifted her chin. "I am not your serf, Your Highness. You have absolutely no authority over me. I will do whatever I damn well please. I will not spend one more second with a man who deceived me."

Poor Cristiano actually moaned his distress at her tone.

"I never deceived you."

"I mentioned my friend was Gabi. You never said a word about my friend being your *mission,* your reason for being here. You never confided in me *why* you were here at all!"

"I didn't make the association between *Gabi* and Ga-briella. We would never use a diminutive in place of the name of someone who is—" he stopped himself, seemed to rethink what he was going to say. "Nicknames are not popular in Casavalle."

"But I just asked you, point blank, what was going on, and you still won't tell me."

But the truth was she wasn't really mad about Gabi, and that wasn't where she felt deceived.

She felt deceived because Prince Luca had just kissed her with what seemed to be his whole heart and soul, and yet he was going to rush back to Casavalle to protect the woman who had betrayed him. You wouldn't do that un-less you were nursing some pretty strong feelings.

And maybe even worse, she felt as if she had deceived herself by allowing herself to entertain the notion, no matter how briefly, that she, a woman damaged by both heartbreak and her own infertility, could have a fairy-tale ending with a prince.

"Gather up your things and go," Imogen said pee-vishly. "A kingdom awaits you."

"You're coming."

"I'm not."

"You're being particularly obstinate. You'd think you could show a little appreciation for your rescue from this dire situation."

Rescued by a prince. Every girl's dream. Or maybe just every stupidly naive girl's dream!

Imogen was insulted by his use of the term *dire*. In her mind, there had been nothing dire about being snowed in with him. Not. One. Thing.

"Well, I don't need rescuing. And this is not medieval times, where you can throw me over your shoulder and rescue me against my will."

His eyes smoldered with something that suggested he would like nothing better than to do just that.

"You said to remind you not to displease me," he told her.

Already the loveliness of the afternoon of sitting together playing twenty questions was fading.

"Go ahead," she snapped. "Send me a white elephant." Then she turned and left the room before he decided to act on it. What if—under his masterly need to control the situation—she melted instead of remaining defiant?

A few minutes later, she heard both snowmobiles start up and she watched from a chilly upper bedroom as they pulled away, spraying snow behind them.

Prince Luca's entrance had been James Bond worthy, and so was his exit.

She went back to the room they had shared. She had predicted power would be restored, but she was shocked when it picked that moment to flicker on. The overhead light seemed harsh and stripped the room completely of its charm.

Everything looked cheap and tawdry, like a set for a low-budget TV production. The tree was leaning drunkenly against the strings that kept it from falling over. The candles were all burned down and sputtering in deep wax pools. The Christmas decorations made by her sisters seemed old and hokey, and she wanted to smash that little plaster cast handprint that he had declared was more precious than his Buschetta ornaments. The room, and everything in it, seemed to mock her.

Angrily, she took down ornaments off the tree, ripped down garlands, blew out what remained of the candles. Christmas in October. It wasn't magical at all. It was completely ridiculous.

The last thing Imogen did was detach the tree from

the wall. She was so mad that, even though it had taken two of them, struggling mightily, to get the tree into the Lodge, she was able to drag it out and throw it off the stairs with perfect ease.

It was only when she got back inside to the now-naked room, that she realized something.

When Luca had gathered his things with him, even though he had left with haste and urgency, he had taken the little snow family with him.

"I wish he hadn't," she said out loud. "I would have burned them."

But somehow she knew, even though she was hurt, and even though she was angry, that was not true.

CHAPTER TWELVE

LUCA TIGHTENED HIS tie and shrugged on the suit jacket. He adjusted the diamond cuff links and matching tiepin and finally slipped on highly polished custom-made shoes.

He looked at himself in the mirror of the suite Cristiano had procured in a Crystal Lake hotel. The main street hostelry did not have the atmosphere of the Crystal Lake Lodge—not that Luca wanted to make comparisons, or look back at all. He needed to steel himself against what he felt when he thought of Imogen.

Angry, when he thought of her defying him by refusing to be rescued.

Hurt, when he thought of her accusing him of deception.

And something, beyond the anger and hurt, that was the most dangerous thing of all.

The reflection that gazed back at him was a man completely transformed from who he had been two hours ago. From his freshly shaved face to his crisply groomed hair, to the faintly aloof expression on his face, Luca looked every inch a prince.

But he knew himself to be a different man than he had been just a few days ago.

He ordered himself to stop looking back; he quashed the sense of longing. He had urgent responsibilities to tend to, and he had been trained since childhood to put the needs of his kingdom above the longings of his own heart.

Possibly to the point he did not even know what his heart was telling him!

"Thank goodness," he muttered to himself. He looked at his watch. In three minutes, his fate—the one he had moved toward his whole life—would be decided.

Naturally, he hoped it was some kind of trick—a masterful deception that had fooled even his mother, Queen Maria.

Luca recalled well her phone call saying she needed to see him. With the whole kingdom in a frenzied state of overdrive with both a royal wedding and Christmas on the horizon, he had been puzzled by the urgency in his mother's voice during that call, and the distress on her face when he had entered her suite.

Without preamble, she had asked him if he knew who Sophia Ross had been.

At first the name had meant nothing. But then he remembered. "Wasn't that the name of my father's first wife?"

Queen Maria nodded and passed him a letter.

He scanned it quickly, and then, shocked, read it again. It was from a woman, Gabriella Ross, in some tiny hamlet in the middle of the Canadian wilderness, who claimed to have found a letter in the belongings of her deceased mother, Sophia Ross. The contents of the letter had led her to believe King Vincenzo—Luca's father—might be her father.

"How did this get through security to you?" he asked, sorry that the letter had not found its way directly to him.

"It was marked personal and confidential to my attention."

Luca prevented himself from breathing an irritated sigh. Marking an envelope personal and confidential should be a way to gain it more attention in the screening process, not less. He was going to have to speak to Miles Montague, the palace secretary, about that.

"I don't believe it," he said fiercely.

"I didn't at first either. But the tone of it is so innocent. As if she has no idea the repercussions of such a claim."

"These con artists are damnably clever. Anyone who did the slightest bit of research could pose this possibility."

"But the scenario seems quite believable."

"I'm sure no effort would be spared in setting the scene when the stakes are so high. This plot could have been years in the making."

"I called her."

"You what?" Luca allowed himself a moment's more irritation at Montague. His mother should have been protected from this.

"I thought I would be able to tell something from speaking to her."

"And could you?" he had asked, his breathing constricted in his chest.

His mother had lifted a shoulder and looked at him with distressed eyes. "She had no idea the firstborn legitimate child of the King would legally be the ruler of Casavalle."

"She *claimed* she had no idea."

"Yes, that's what she claimed. She was extraordinarily soft-spoken. She owns a bookstore."

"She *says* she owns a bookstore."

"We'll know soon enough. I'm going to ask Antonio to leave immediately following your wedding to meet with her."

"I'll go myself."

"You have other things to attend to. Plus, Antonio has less at stake. You might appear faintly hostile to her."

Luca accepted his mother's judgment, but he wasn't happy about it.

"For now," his mother said, "it might be best if just the three of us know about this."

"Hopefully forever," Luca said firmly.

"In this day and age, no matter how clever the con, my dearest son, there is no way to conceal the facts. Antonio will collect a DNA sample. We'll have it analyzed by our own specialists. It could come to nothing. Of course it could! But I wanted you to know. I didn't want you blindsided by this on your honeymoon."

And then, because the wedding had been canceled and there would be no honeymoon, Luca had decided to come himself. He didn't care if he came across as hostile.

Except, now he did.

Now that he knew this woman, Gabriella Ross, was a friend—a very close friend—of Imogen's, he knew chances of her deliberately setting up such a complex charade were remote. Imogen simply would not have friends like that. And for Gabriella to have grown up here and have a business here was far too complicated a setup, even for the most robust of cons.

But there could still be an error.

Sophia could well have been pregnant by another man's child when she fled her new husband and the kingdom. It was a possibility Luca might not have given so much credence to a few days ago, before Meribel's confession, as he did now.

Cristiano was waiting outside the suite. He fell in, one step behind Luca's shoulder. Their eyes met, Cristiano's full of concern, just before Cristiano stepped in front of him and opened the dining room door.

Luca's first thought was surprise.

Gabriella Ross had come alone. She was sitting at a table by the window, looking out it, her hands curled tensely around a teacup.

While he looked very princely, and he knew it, for someone who was making a try for the throne, she looked extremely humble in an oversize sweater and blue jeans. Who met a prince in blue jeans?

Besides Imogen Albright—but then he had taken her by surprise by arriving early. And this was an arranged meeting.

The most remarkable thing about Miss Ross seemed to be dark chestnut hair, falling in a wave nearly to the small of her back.

And then, hearing the door open, she turned her attention from the window and looked at him.

Slowly, she stood up.

As soon as she stood, the illusion that there was anything humble about her faded. She stood, and it was in the air around her: a certain inherent dignity, a bone-deep grace, a queen-like composure that he knew she had been born with.

In that instant, Luca *knew*.

It was not just his eyes telling him the truth—she did look amazingly like a very beautiful version of his father—it was his heart.

It was that intuition that had kicked in when he had assured Imogen about her future and her future children.

He was in the presence of the next monarch of Casavalle.

What surprised him more than anything as he moved

forward to meet his sister—he did not need the proof of a DNA test—was that he did not feel a sense of loss.

The hostility he had harbored since hearing about the letter faded as her calm and somehow strangely familiar eyes rested on him. He felt, instead, as if he was meeting the future of his kingdom.

And it felt right.

He strode across the room to her. Though she was not petite by any means, he was still much taller than her, and she looked up at him. This close, he could see the nervousness in her.

He did what neither of them had expected.

He got down on one knee and bowed his head to her and covered his heart with his hand. "Your Royal Highness, Princess Gabriella," he said, his voice low with emotion.

"Get up," she said in a strangled voice.

He got up. He took both her hands in his and scanned her face. He kissed both her cheeks.

"My sister," he said, standing back from her.

Her eyes welled up, and he held back the chair for her.

She sank into it, shocked. "I—I—I thought there was to be a DNA test."

"Of course there will be. A formality. I know who you are."

She smiled tentatively. "I do, too. I feel something when I look at you. I feel as if I should be intimidated, but I'm not. I feel the oddest bond, as if I've known you forever. As a child, I wanted this so badly. A family. Of course, I could have never imagined it was going to be a royal family."

"You had no idea?"

She shook her head, her gorgeous hair waving around her lovely features.

"My mom died when I was three. My aunt and uncle raised me. I think they knew, but were sworn to secrecy. Then, I was looking for something else in the attic, and I found a box of my mother's things. Mostly it was baby pictures of me, but there were two letters in it. One was addressed to me, and the other was addressed to your father, to King Vincenzo. I had never even heard of Casavalle. Obviously, she never sent that letter, though it seemed apparent she loved your father very much."

"I wonder why she would love him and not send it?" Luca mused, thinking out loud.

A flicker of a veil dropped over Gabriella's eyes. He had a feeling she knew exactly why the letter had not been sent, but he respected the fact that she might not be willing to tell him, or at least not yet.

"I do hope, someday," he said softly, "I will get to know why a love with such optimistic beginnings had to end with two broken hearts. He never spoke of the failure of his first marriage—at least not to me—for he was not a man accustomed to failure. But there was some sorrow in him that I knew, even as a child, had something to do with the loss of her from his life."

"But didn't he and your mother have a wonderful relationship?"

"It was a good relationship," Luca said carefully, "but it's as if, after your mother, he said goodbye to love, and every decision from there on in was made out of a pragmatic sense of what would be best for our kingdom, including his marriage to my mother."

They both contemplated love gone so terribly wrong for a moment, and then Luca felt a need to correct any misperception he might have given.

"Despite it not being a love match, my mother was perfect for him—strong, pragmatic, loyal."

"I'm glad. Speaking of your mother, Queen Maria mentioned something to me—that as the King's eldest child, I would be next in line for the throne. Let me assure you, there is no need to be threatened by me! I don't want the job!"

"And yet here we are today, looking at the simple truth that despite all that has happened, all the secrets and all the obstacles, here I sit with you. Perhaps you cannot outrun your fate, Gabriella."

She gulped. "Surely I can refuse the obligation."

He tilted his head at her. She was nervous. And she was taken aback. And yet he could see the composure in her, the wisdom.

"Can you?" he challenged her softly. "Do you really think you can refuse what you were born to do?"

"I run a bookstore!"

"I can see it in you, though. I can see it in the way you carry yourself. I can see my father in your eyes. You don't have to decide today. But come. Come to Casavalle. Get to know your family and your kingdom. Give it a chance. If you decide to step into the shoes of the ruler, I will pledge my loyalty to you to my dying breath. I will stand behind you. I will share with you everything I have come to know."

"I just want you to be my brother."

He smiled. "I think that's what I just said. Will you come?"

She was silent, but when she looked at him, he saw the resolve in her eyes.

"Yes."

"Can you be ready to leave quickly? As soon as tomorrow?"

"I'm afraid if we don't leave quickly, I'll change my mind."

"I need one thing from you, before we leave. A favor."

"You need a favor from me? I can't even imagine what that might be."

"I need you to go and talk to Imogen Albright. You need to tell your best friend what is going on."

"Imogen? How do you know about Imogen's friendship with me?"

"I was snowed in with her at the Lodge."

Gabriella covered her mouth with her hand, and her eyes went wide. "When Cristiano contacted me to delay our first meeting because of the snowstorm, he never said you were there, at the Lodge. With Imogen."

"He would never let anyone know where I was, particularly as I was unprotected."

"You and Imogen…"

"Nothing happened!" he said, his tone way too defensive.

"And yet you know we are best friends."

"Well, of course, we conversed."

Gabriella studied him. Her eyebrow went up. She seemed to be hearing quite a lot that he was not saying.

Was that what it was like to have a sister? Of course, one other woman had had the same gift of seeing straight to his heart. And he did not have sisterly feelings toward her at all!

"The road to the Lodge will probably be closed for a few days," Gabriella told him. "I guess I could call her?"

How was Imogen going to feel when she found out her best friend was his sister?

"I can arrange for you to be taken there," he said. "I think the news that you and I are brother and sister will be shocking for her. Not the kind of news one might want to get when they are alone."

Again, Gabriella was watching him with interest. Her

lips twitched. She obviously was finding it quite endearing that he felt so protective of Imogen.

He gave her, his new sister, his most princely glare.

She laughed!

CHAPTER THIRTEEN

IMOGEN AND GABRIELLA sat across from each other at the kitchen table in the Lodge. Imogen had deliberately chosen not to light a fire and have tea in her office when Gabriella had shown up by complete surprise, riding in on the still-closed road by snowmobile.

Gabriella's cheeks were pink from her snowmobile ride, and her hair tumbled out from under her toque in a wild wave of gorgeous color.

Imogen was reeling from what Gabriella had just told her. Luca was Gabriella's brother!

It explained so much. No wonder he had seemed so familiar at times. No wonder she had thought she had recognized him when he had stepped off the helicopter.

And no wonder her friend had been so secretive. This was stunning news, indeed. Dear Gabi, Imogen's lifelong friend, was not just a princess, but the next in line to rule the kingdom of Casavalle!

"And then he tried to convince you to take from him what he has prepared his whole life to do?" Imogen asked softly.

Gabriella nodded. "I'm so sorry I never told you what was going on. It just seemed so unreal. I didn't want to appear the fool—thinking I was some sort of royalty—without confirming it, without knowing the truth."

"What are you going to do?"

"I'm going to go back with him. Just to see. Just to 'give it a chance,' as he suggested. It sounds as if we will be leaving fairly quickly."

"Yes," Imogen said, with faint bitterness. "He has urgent business to attend to." Quickly, she filled her friend in on the Prince's canceled wedding, his intended bride pregnant with another man's child.

"And so," she finished, "he's rushing back there to defend a woman who betrayed him."

Gabi was silent. When she spoke her voice was solemn and quiet. "It seems to me as if Princess Meribel had a very difficult choice to make. Betray him. Or betray herself."

Imogen looked closely at her friend. She had always known this about her: Gabi was unusually wise for someone so young, and almost scarily intuitive. In the new light of who she really was, it begged the question: Were some things ordained? Was it possible the qualities of leadership were genetic?

She sensed both the intuition and wisdom as Gabi met her gaze and held it.

"Tell me what happened between you and Luca," she suggested encouragingly. "There's something about you that's different. I can't quite put my finger on it."

"Oh!" Imogen could feel herself blushing. "Nothing happened!"

"Hmmm. That's what he said, too. Exact words, exact tone of voice."

"I was happy," Imogen admitted in a low voice. She *needed* to tell someone. "I was happy with him." She glanced up to see how Gabi would take that.

Gabi was smiling. "That's what's different! It's not as if you got something back that you lost when you broke up with Kevin. There's something brand-new in you. It sparkles."

"Well, I don't know why it would," Imogen said. "I'm angry right now, not happy."

"The anger is just a thin layer on top of something else."

"Quit being so wise! They will steal you from me to be their Queen, for sure."

They both laughed at that, and Imogen was glad for the laughter. She was not sure she was ready to admit it to Gabi, but she admitted it to herself.

The anger did mask something else. She was aware she would not trade her days with the Prince for any treasure available on earth. There was one thing Imogen was not going to share with Gabriella: in too short a time, she had given her heart to him.

Though it made no sense, though it seemed unreasonable and maybe even impossible, there was a little secret Imogen was nursing.

She had fallen in love with Prince Luca.

Nursing that forbidden love had seemed much easier before her talk with Gabrielle, because then Imogen had thought he was leaving and she would never see him again.

She had thought a quick, clean cut would be for the best.

But now her best friend's life was irrevocably tangled with the House of Valenti. Which meant chances were quite high that Imogen, through her relationship with Gabi, was going to see the Prince again.

And to be completely honest with herself, despite her initial belief that a clean cut would be for the best, now she could not determine if seeing him again would be a good thing or a bad thing.

Although her heart was singing its answer.

* * *

Imogen walked down the hospital corridor happily aware that she had been over-the-top in her selection of gifts for Rachel's new baby, who had been named Ben. She could barely see over the parcels she had loaded up in her arms.

But once she had started shopping, she couldn't stop herself. There were just too many adorable options. And Imogen knew that Rachel and her husband did not have much, so the pleasure of shopping for the new baby had been even more intense.

She had gorgeous sleepers with feet in them in a variety of woodsy themes, a tiny pair of hiking boots, a mobile with blue moose to hang over the crib and a fuzzy receiving blanket with the cutest little bear ears attached to it.

She entered the hospital room and froze. Cristiano was there, standing quietly beside the bed, talking to Rachel. And where Cristiano was… Sure enough, when she looked behind it, Luca was on the other side of the open door.

As if the Prince wasn't devastatingly attractive enough, he was holding the baby!

Imogen's eyes smarted from the beauty of the sight of that strong, capable man holding that vulnerable, tiny baby.

Luca was once again a prince. He was cleanly shaven, his hair was impeccably groomed; he wore a thigh-length belted black woolen jacket that most men could not have carried off. He looked exactly like what he was: a very wealthy, very powerful man, who was sure of himself in every situation.

And yet, despite the rather untouchable look of him, and despite the fact he was apparently urgently needed back in Casavalle, Prince Luca had come personally to the hospital to visit a woman he barely knew.

As she watched, the sleeping baby sighed and snuggled deeper into Luca's chest. The Prince stroked the baby's back and looked at him with such tenderness it felt as if Imogen's heart would break.

For the man she would never have. For the babies she would never have. For the ludicrousness of the dream that looking at the Prince caused in her.

Her mouth went dry as she contemplated that dream. Her. Him. Babies, just as he had promised. Adopted or through some miracle of science.

This was what hope did. It left you wide-open to pain.

Imogen would have backed out the door, but the top box on her mountain of parcels chose that moment to tilt crazily and fall to the floor with a crash. Luca looked up.

For one breathtaking moment, their gazes held. For one breathtaking moment, his eyes were entirely unguarded, soft with welcome.

She could have almost sworn the strength of what she felt for him shone in his eyes, too. But what did it matter?

He had given his heart to another, to Princess Meribel. And when that break healed—as she now knew hearts did, thanks to him—he would need a woman who could give him babies just like the one he held. Wasn't that what she had seen in his expression as he gazed so tenderly at that baby?

Longing?

Royal families, as far as Imogen knew, did not *adopt* babies.

"Imogen," Rachel said. "How lovely of you to come." Cristiano nodded at her, and looked at her a little too long, as if he was trying to puzzle something through. But then he bowed slightly and left the room.

Imogen saw Rachel was surrounded by wrapping paper and boxes. A gigantic teddy bear took up one whole corner of the hospital room. The generosity and obvious expense of the gifts brought by the Prince made her own purchases seem small and redundant.

But you wouldn't think so from Rachel's reaction. She opened each package and was thrilled. She particularly loved the little bear receiving blanket.

"Will you hold him?" Luca had come over to Imogen's side as Rachel unwrapped her parcels.

Imogen had been avoiding looking at him, and maybe avoiding the baby, too. It made her ache for a child of her own.

He carefully held out the baby to her, leaving her no choice but to take him.

She gazed into those small, perfect features and drank in the gorgeous smell of the newborn. She felt the sweet, warm weight of the baby melt into her. The feeling she had was not one of her own loss, but of a beautiful blessing the baby was giving the world with his mere presence.

"He's so beautiful," she breathed.

"Beautiful," Luca agreed, but when she looked up at him, he was not looking at the baby at all, but at her. She felt her heart stop at what she saw in his eyes. She looked back at the baby and cooed.

"Can you believe a prince has come with gifts for my baby?" Rachel giggled.

Imogen looked at Luca, again. Yes, she could believe it.

The baby's face scrunched up. His expression went from serene to furious in the blink of an eye. He stretched out, a tiny fist working free of the blanket and smacking Imogen in the cheek. His eyes opened—slate gray—and so did his mouth. He roared with indignation at finding himself in a stranger's arms.

"He's strong," Luca said with approval.

"And he's hungry," Rachel said, reaching for him. Imogen and Luca left to give her privacy to nurse her baby.

As they left the room, Cristiano gave her that searching look again and then went to the end of the hallway, where he could watch over his Prince but still give them privacy.

"I thought you would be gone already," Imogen stammered.

"I thought you would still be on the mountain."

"The road was finally plowed this morning."

"We're leaving very soon. I wanted to see the baby first, and make sure Rachel was recovering well."

"That was kind of you," Imogen said stiffly.

He cocked his head at her. "Have I done anything to make you think I am unkind?"

"No, of course not," she said hastily. But she felt as if her heart was on her sleeve. It wasn't his fault she had fallen for him when he cared for another.

"I've hurt you in some way," he said.

"No, not at all."

"But you seem angry."

"Do I?"

"Yes."

"Well, I'm not. I mean I do feel as if you tricked me, not letting me know you were here to see Gabi. My best friend is your sister! The news has kind of rocked my world."

"And mine," he said softly.

Of course, his.

"You must be in shock," she said. "Gabi told me that

she, not you, would be heir to a throne that is empty. She told me you want her to give it a chance. Why? She doesn't want the job. She's frightened and just wants to run the other way. Why not let her? Wouldn't that be so much easier?"

"The easy choice is not always the correct one," he told her. "Kingdoms are run by rules and protocol. Centuries-old traditions are the glue that holds them together in a world that changes very rapidly."

"But you've been groomed to be the King of Casavalle for your entire life."

"I will use what I have learned to help her."

She looked at him. She looked at him hard. "Remember when you told me that my fiancé, Kevin, marrying another would be a blessing for me?"

"Yes, I remember."

"This may be the same thing for you. When we had the snowball fight that day and built our snow family, you said to me you had never been as free as you were in those moments. If Gabriella takes the throne, your life will be more your own than it has ever been before."

"That may be true," he said.

"You are so like her, in so many ways. When you said that just now, your tone was exactly like Gabriella's. Your tone and the tilt of your head. If I'd known you were related to Gabi, it would have explained a lot."

He raised an eyebrow at her.

"I mean I felt as if I recognized you from the start. As if I knew you. Now I can see the family resemblance just tricked my subconscious mind. No wonder I felt as if I loved you. I recognized you were very like someone I did love. Barriers were removed that should have stayed in place. That *would* have stayed in place had you just told me the real reason you were at the Lodge in Crystal Lake."

"You felt as if you loved me?" he asked, shocked.

CHAPTER FOURTEEN

IMOGEN REALIZED INSTANTLY that she had said too much. Way too much.

"That came out wrong. I felt as if I cared about you." She was not sure that was an improvement!

"Past tense?"

She wished it was past tense, but she could not lie to him. "No, I suppose not," Imogen said, and then, eager to change the subject, rushed on. "You need to go talk to your Princess," she said.

"Gabriella?"

"Not that Princess!" It showed her what a serious turn her life had taken that she was trying to sort through princesses. "You need to talk to Meribel."

"About?"

"How you feel."

He regarded her thoughtfully. "You do something to me no one else has ever done."

Imogen could feel herself holding her breath.

"You boss me around."

Her disappointment was acute but she smiled with false brightness. She noticed he had managed to dodge the issue about how he felt about Princess Meribel.

"Nice to see you, Your Highness," she said, her tone

formal. "I wish you a safe trip back to your kingdom and a good life."

"Don't say that as though we will never see each other again."

He sounded faintly pleading. It could weaken her resolve. On the other hand, *the thing* she did to him that no one else ever did was not the same *thing* he did to her that no one else had ever done!

"Since you are now related to one of my favorite people in the whole world, it seems likely we will see each other again."

Did he look relieved?

She was entering into very dangerous waters.

Before he could read the turmoil in her face—before he could reach the embarrassing conclusion that she had indeed loved him—she leaned close to him.

"If you do anything—anything at all—to hurt *my* Gabriella you will have to deal with me. It won't be pretty and it won't be fun."

His lips twitched. Annoyance or amusement? Being threatened was probably as new to him as being bossed around.

He nodded, and she still could not read the glint in his eye. Was he humoring her? Or did he understand just how completely she meant business. She turned quickly on her heel and walked away from him.

Even though she wanted to, desperately, she forced herself not to look back.

Luca left Gabriella and Queen Maria together, and exited the room. His mother's grace was matched by his sister's and there was something about the two women together that made the future of Casavalle, despite the unexpected detours—or maybe even because of them—seem as secure as it ever had.

He passed through the front foyer of the palace. As Luca had told Imogen, Casavalle was getting ready for Christmas. The huge tree had been selected for the front foyer.

It soared upward, crowned at the very top with a lit angel. It was, as always, spectacular. Rather than filling him with a sense of the familiar, with homecoming, it made his heart ache for a lopsided tree, held up with strings and nailed to the wall.

Annoyed with himself for thinking so longingly of a much less spectacular tree, Luca shook off his sense of melancholy and headed for the palace secretary, Miles Montague's, office.

Miles looked both pleased and relieved to see him. A mountain of work needed the Prince's immediate attention.

"Prince Antonio has been doing a fine job in difficult circumstances," Miles told him. "But he's not you. We need you."

Ah, to be needed. But for how much longer? Luca could just imagine the adjustment everyone was going to have to make when it was no longer him that they turned to for every decision.

But for right now the work would be a balm—all the stacks of papers that needed to be reviewed, projects awaiting approval, engagements to attend, meetings to be held. It was the very thing he needed to give him back his sense of being grounded in the world.

The secretary looked down at the stack of papers. Off the top he pulled the pink slips that came with phone messages.

"Let's deal with this first. Have you ever heard of Tia Phillips?"

"No, I can't say I have."

"As I thought."

"Who is she?"

"She's been calling, insisting she's friends with Prince Antonio. She says he knew her brother. But my question is, of course, what does *knowing* mean? That he shook his hand once at a ball? That he sat next to him at a charity function? I rebuffed her as kindly as possible, but she doesn't seem to be taking no for an answer."

"Probably Canadian," Luca muttered.

"Sir?"

"Nothing, sorry."

"Sir, do you ever recall your brother mentioning anyone with the last name Phillips, male or female?"

Luca shook his head. "I'm fairly certain I know all Antonio's close friends by name. That one doesn't strike a chord. Have you asked her how Antonio knew her brother?"

"She's particularly unforthcoming in that department. She may have started crying when I asked her."

Luca raised an eyebrow. "Nut?"

"Possibly. Stalker, perhaps? The insistence of her calls made me wary of passing on the message to Prince Antonio, particularly since he has his plate full. We've fielded stalkers before. I'm afraid if I ever put her through to the object of her attentions, we'd have an even bigger problem."

"You didn't think to just ask Antonio?"

"I preferred to ask you. I didn't want to relegate the messages to the bin without running it past you first, sir."

So, there it was. *I preferred to ask you.*

The people of Casavalle, and the staff at the palace,

already saw Luca as King, as the one they could rely on to make decisions both large and small, the one they would turn to.

Of course, Miles not wanting to make the decision himself might also have been because Luca had expressed annoyance with him that Gabriella's letter had made it to his mother simply for being marked Personal and Confidential.

It was obviously making Miles extra vigilant about which messages got through to the royal family and which did not.

Despite having been hard on Miles over the letter to the Queen, Luca knew himself to be more approachable than his father had been. He had thought it would be his signature—what set him apart from his father—when he assumed leadership.

"Just toss them," Luca said of the raft of pink slips clutched in Miles' hand. "We have far bigger things to deal with than some woman who has seen Antonio's picture in a magazine, decided she is in love with him and made up some story to connect the two of them."

"My assessment, exactly," Miles said. He swept the papers into the bin beside his desk with a sigh of relief. "We do, indeed, have larger issues to deal with.

"Sir, since you released the statement calling off the wedding based on what you called irreconcilable differences, the people of Aguilarez seemed quite ready to renew old hostilities in defense of their Princess's honor. They rushed to the conclusion that she had been jilted. By you. On the eve of her wedding!"

"Wars have started for less," Luca said pensively.

"In a way it was a good thing that the truth was leaked, that the betrayal was hers, not yours. But now our people are furious. They feel the insult to you is an insult to

Casavalle and to them, personally. I am getting reports that talk around the kitchen tables and in the pubs is of nothing else. How you've been scorned, and it's a national disgrace that should be avenged.

"Naturally Aguilarez is reeling. I understand Princess Meribel is in hiding and the royal family will be having emergency talks. Her four siblings are en route to Aguilarez now."

"We need to be part of developing a strategy to defuse this situation before it gets out of hand."

"I was hoping you would have a suggestion, sir."

"Arrange a meeting with her family."

"Excellent."

"Both families are going to have to work together to minimize damage. Our relationship with Aguilarez has come so far. We can't risk it all on a matter of the heart."

"No," Miles said approvingly. "Matters of the heart have to be separated from functions of the state."

But when Luca looked back over the history of the two countries, it seemed as often as not, hearts would not be ignored.

Look at his own father, risking everything to follow love.

Now Meribel doing the same thing.

It gave him a headache. *Really?* Could people not put their personal feelings aside for the greater good?

But when he thought of that, he thought of Imogen, and it seemed his own resolve wavered. If he had a decision to make that involved her welfare or the welfare of his kingdom, how pragmatic could he be?

I felt as if I loved you.

For the first time, Luca became shockingly aware that a part of him was answering her.

And it said, *I felt as if I loved you, too.*

And the thing was, that thought of loving Imogen, loving the time they had had together, loving the freedom and the comfort of being with her, didn't make him feel bitter, as he had felt when Meribel had left him behind.

It made him feel better that he had had Imogen in his life even for a short while.

Stronger.

Wiser.

More able to do the right thing.

And suddenly, he knew exactly what the right thing to do was. He had to meet, not just with the royal family of Aguilarez, but with his former fiancée. Just as Imogen had suggested, he needed to talk to Meribel. And not just for the good of both their kingdoms.

He needed to do it for himself.

Piloted expertly by Cristiano, the royal helicopter had made the journey over the rugged mountains that separated the kingdoms of Casavalle and Aguilarez.

From the air, Luca looked down at the royal family's grounds. The palace of the House of Aguilarez was more formidable, and less decorative, than his own home. It was a fortress, its walls incorporating the strength of the mountain that stood directly behind it.

Prince Cesar Asturias was waiting to greet him as Cristiano held open the helicopter door after they landed on the ground. Despite Cesar's reputation as an unapologetic playboy, Luca had always liked him, probably the best of all Meribel's brothers.

"Your Royal Highness, welcome," he said formally, bowing slightly.

"My brother," Luca returned, and saw the immediate relief on Cesar's face.

"I was hoping we would be brothers," Cesar said. "I

don't know what the rest of the family will say today. A formal statement has been prepared and they may stick to it. But I want you to know how sorry I am."

Luca clapped Cesar on the shoulder. "As I am about to tell your family, there is nothing to be sorry for. I am hoping that we can find other ways to resolve some of the growing hostility between our kingdoms. We've been at peace for two hundred years."

"Two hundred and three," Cesar said. "But who's counting?"

Luca laughed. Cesar's quick dry wit was one of the things that Luca enjoyed about him so much.

He was escorted through the palace. He had been here many times, particularly since his engagement to Princess Meribel, but he still noted the differences between this palace and his own home. It wasn't just that there were no Christmas decorations here, yet, that made this palace more formidable, somehow. Even the artwork was darker and more warlike.

He and Cesar entered a conference room. The entire Asturias family had gathered, save for Meribel. But her mother, father and four brothers were all there, seated, their expressions grim.

Formal greetings were exchanged and then Luca was offered a seat. He looked around the table and felt some relief that his future did not hold Christmas dinners with this group of stern-looking warriors.

"Luca," said King Jorge solemnly. "I wish to apologize for the actions of my daughter. She has brought shame to our house."

"I want to suggest we all look at it differently," Luca said.

The men in the room watched him warily. You did not walk into another man's kingdom and disagree with him.

But this was part of Luca's legacy from Imogen: some-times the heart had to speak, and never mind the pomp and circumstance that could cloak real feelings and keep issues from being resolved satisfactorily.

"This is what I propose."

And he told them the plan.

When he was finished, the brothers looked relieved, and Queen Adriana's eyes, weighted with worry, were sparkling with tears.

Only the King seemed doubtful. "My daughter has brought shame on our family, neglected her royal obliga-tions and broken a promise. I'm not sure your proposal addresses the severity of her transgressions against you, her family and her kingdom."

"Again, Your Majesty, I respectfully disagree."

"What would you propose?" Queen Adriana asked her husband quietly. "I'm afraid the days when you could lock an errant daughter in a tower or ship her off to the convent are well over."

King Jorge mulled that over.

"All right, we will do it your way," the King con-ceded, and then, lest the concession be seen as weak-ness, he scowled and added, "In the spirit of Christmas, nothing else."

"Of course, sir," Luca said evenly. King Jorge re-minded him of his own father: old-school rulers, being dragged kicking and screaming into a more tolerant modern age.

The formality of the meeting dissolved, and he found himself surrounded by Meribel's brothers, clapping him enthusiastically on the shoulder. Prince Cesar wrapped his arms around Luca and lifted him off his feet.

"We will always be brothers!" he declared.

"I need to see her before I put the plan in place. I need to see Meribel."

"Of course," Cesar said. "I will take you."

King Jorge glared at him. "You know where she is, then?"

"I'm going to hazard a guess," Cesar said, meeting his father's gaze levelly.

"The world is going to hell in a handbasket," Jorge muttered. "There is no respect for authority anymore." His wife patted his arm sympathetically.

CHAPTER FIFTEEN

PRINCESS MERIBEL SCRAMBLED to her feet when her brother Prince Cesar and Prince Luca came through the door of the hotel suite she was in.

"How did you get in here?"

Her brother wagged the key at her. "Have you ever seen two more recognizable mugs than these?" He pointed to himself then Luca. "The innkeeper practically begged us to take the key."

"How did you know where I was?" the Princess demanded.

"Do you really think I wouldn't know where you were?" Cesar said. "I tracked you down the day you moved in here and put protection around the neighborhood and undercover throughout the hotel."

"I can look after myself," she said, proudly. And then more softly, "Dana can look after me."

"Ah, the mystery man is named," her brother said. "Where is he?"

"You mean you don't know?" she said. "You seem to know everything else."

Luca could see this was going to quickly deteriorate into a squabble between the brother and sister, so he stepped in.

"It's good to see you, Meribel," he said.

She rounded on him. "I am terribly sorry I did what I did to you," she said, her voice trembling, "but I won't go with you."

"Yes, I've been reminded fairly recently this is not medieval times," Luca said, and could hear the wryness in his own voice.

"I don't think it's Luca you have to worry about," Cesar chimed in. "It's Father."

"I suppose Father thinks I should be locked in a tower for the rest of my days."

"He does indeed," Cesar said. He wandered over to a fruit basket and chose an apple and bit into it. "Fortunately for you, Luca has come up with another solution."

Luca had told Cesar all the details of his solution on the way here, and Cesar had approved heartily.

"We're not here to make you do anything against your will," Luca assured her. She looked relieved, but wary.

"A solution?" she asked, and faint hope overlaid her wariness.

Luca took her in, this woman he had known since childhood, and saw how truly beautiful she was. Meribel was tiny, and yet delectably curved. Her long, dark hair was piled on top of her head in an elegant twist. Her lovely brown eyes were expertly made-up.

Even in these circumstances, holed up in a hotel room, hiding from the world, she was dressed quite formally, in a skirt and matching jacket, "correct" royal attire for daytime. Rings—minus the engagement ring he had given her—sparkled from every finger, and a diamond pendant hung around her neck.

Like him, Princess Meribel could not easily let go of the notion that you were always on show, always judged—someone was always watching. That made him feel sorry for her.

Other than that feeling, he was aware he felt nothing but relief that he would not have to spend the rest of his days waking up to her. He realized that a marriage to Meribel would have been his "tower," his prison.

"Are you well?" he asked her, crossing the room to her and taking both her hands.

She looked up at him, and her defensive expression crumpled and she began to weep.

He pulled her closer and wrapped his arms around her.

"It's the pregnancy," she said. "I've never been so emotional."

"Just like me," he said, "you've shut down your emotions, almost until it was too late."

She pulled back from him, but did not let go of his hands as she scanned his face. "Is there something different about you?"

"Perhaps I combed my hair differently this morning," Luca said, tired of women suddenly reading him as though he were an open book.

"No," she said tentatively. "It's not that."

"Do you love him?" he asked. "This Dana that you mentioned?"

"It's *that*," she said with a small smile. "That's what is different. I can't even picture you asking me that question a month ago. And the answer is yes, I love him so much."

"And he, you?"

"Yes. Absolutely."

"I'm glad."

"There's that difference again! But how can you be glad? I've wrecked everything. I left you in a humiliating position. I'm so sorry," she sobbed. "I've done a terrible thing to you."

"Shh, now—all this emotion isn't good for the baby, even if it is what's causing all that emotion."

"I tried to make it right. When I could see people were going to blame you, I leaked the news of the pregnancy."

"That was very brave."

"Partly," she admitted. "Partly it was selfish. I didn't want my baby to be born in a web of deceit. I didn't want that baby, someday a teenager, or a young adult, finding old press clippings and thinking I was ashamed of her or him, or that I had tried to hide her or him from the world. People would have eventually found out. I didn't want to feel as if I was harboring a secret."

"That was brave, too," Luca told her.

"Oh, Luca, if I was truly brave, I would have told you all this a long time ago, and not waited until the eve of the wedding to spring it on you. I'm sorry."

"I'm sorry, too."

"You have nothing to be sorry for."

"But I do. I want to own my part of things."

"Your part?" she whispered.

"I've been insensitive. Had I paid any attention to you at all, I would have known something was wrong. If I had *known* you, I would have known immediately when your attention turned to someone else.

"Instead, I allowed all this to happen. I relegated you to roles—my fiancée and my future wife—and then really ceased to see you as a person, appreciate you for who you were and are. We met our formal obligations. We attended functions together. We held hands on cue. We satisfied the hunger of both our kingdoms for a romance, but when I think about the emptiness of it, I'm appalled with myself.

"I don't even know what your favorite movie is. I don't know what music you listen to when you are by yourself. I don't know if you'd prefer a dog, a cat or a parrot for a pet. I don't know how you feel about babies. I've never gone for a walk with you in the snow, or sat with you in front of a fire. For that, I am here to ask your forgiveness."

"You are asking my forgiveness?" Meribel stammered.

"I am."

She mulled that over. She took in his face. A smile began to break out on her mouth. "I forgive you, then."

"Thank you. I did not just come to ask your forgiveness."

"What else, then?"

"I came to thank you," he said quietly. "You've given me the most incredible gift."

She pulled away from him and looked up, her eyes filled with doubt and hope. He took her chin in his hand and scanned her eyes.

"You have shown me what it means to be brave," he told her softly. "You have shown me the lengths one should be willing to go to, to welcome love into their lives."

"Th-then you forgive me, as well?" Meribel asked, fresh tears sliding down her face.

"Not at all," he said. "For me to do that, there would have to be an assumption there is something to forgive."

She had to stand on tiptoe to kiss both his cheeks. "You will always be a prince to me, not just because you were born to the title, but because you have grown into the honor."

"Thank you."

"Whoever she is," she whispered, "she is a very lucky woman."

"I don't know what you mean," Luca said, and heard the stiffness in his voice.

She scanned his face, and she was not put off and she

was not fooled. Princess Meribel laughed, and it was a lovely sound. She said, "Yes, you do."

The frankness of her gaze captured him. The truth of her words wrapped around him.

Yes, he did.

And suddenly nothing in the world seemed as important as what he had experienced whilst snowed in at the Crystal Lake Lodge.

Nothing. Not his obligations, not his kingdom, not all the treasures in the palace vault. With that acknowledgment, something in the heart of Prince Luca flew free and unfettered, like a bird that had been caged, flying toward the sun.

CHAPTER SIXTEEN

IMOGEN FELT EXTRAORDINARILY CROSS. And tired. It had been one of those days! It had begun this morning when she had opened her computer screen to see every single booking had been canceled.

Then, she'd had a call from her boss, demanding a lunch meeting in the city, which was two hours away. The drive there had given her far too much time to think. Her concern should have been getting fired—what had happened to those bookings?

Instead she had grouchily contemplated abject loneliness. Even though they had spoken several times in the few days since Gabriella had departed for Casavalle, Imogen missed her friend acutely.

There was something in Gabriella's voice that she envied. Excitement.

Imogen considered that. Gabriella, who could be counted on to be quiet and calm in any situation, was brimming with excitement and enthusiasm that spilled over into her voice. And her emails. Imogen had never seen this side of her friend before.

Apparently Book Club could not hold a candle to a real-life adventure.

Her thoughts drifted to her own real-life adventure, a helicopter settling on the front lawn while storm clouds brewed over the peaks of the nearby mountains—the day her life had been made new again.

Of course, like a constant hum beneath the surface, she was so aware that she missed someone else, too. Someone she had no right to miss.

On the drive home from her meeting with her boss, her job totally intact, Imogen realized the strangest thing.

Surely she hadn't wanted to get fired?

The Crystal Lake Lodge had been her home her entire life. She had never really been anywhere else; she had never really done anything else.

But the excitement Imogen was hearing in Gabriella's voice was making her wonder if she had not played it too safe her entire life, not just sticking with what was secure and familiar, but trying to re-create the life she had grown up with.

It was as if she had had blinders on, had not been able to see that life held options beyond the Crystal Lake Lodge.

Of course, the Lodge no longer seemed the sanctuary it once had seemed. There seemed to be laughter-filled ghosts there. Out on the front lawn where they had chased each other; in her office where she had introduced Prince Luca to the simple joy of a toasted hot dog. She had refused to put a fire in the hearth since he had left.

If she had gotten fired, she thought, maybe it would have been a good thing. Just as moving on from Kevin was proving to be a good thing.

Those few days with the Prince had shown her there was something else, not as safe, and not as comfortable, and yet a life without it seemed as if it would be empty.

Maybe it would be a good thing, an exciting thing, if her life was made new again.

But would she ever find what she had found with Luca

again? Could any other person, or any other experience, ever fill her the way that one had? Would she ever again feel as if every single moment was shivering with life?

But obviously, there was no sense mooning over a prince—a man so far out of her reach he might as well have been on the moon.

But was there a chance that she could find what she had experienced with him with someone else?

Doubtful, a little voice inside her whispered. *That was one in a billion. He is one in a billion.*

Just a little while ago, she might have been nursing a heartbreak over Kevin, but her life had felt ordered and there had been safety in the predictability of it. And yet, somehow, she wouldn't trade those days with the Prince to go back to that. She felt oddly uncertain if that's what she wanted at all anymore. And that was what was making her feel cranky! That and a four-hour round trip for nothing! To hear about her boss's grandchildren and their trip to Denmark! Not a single mention of Imogen's job being in jeopardy even after she had confessed she thought she had botched the bookings for this week.

It was full dark by the time she turned into the Lodge driveway. Partway up, she met a catering van coming down. Despite her waving her hand to get him to stop so she could find out what business he'd had at the Lodge, the van roared by her. In a few minutes that vehicle was followed by another utility vehicle, which also did not stop when she waved. The driver waved cheerily back at her, but kept going.

She tried to think if she had booked repairs, but nothing came to mind. Still, it felt like just more evidence of how distracted she had become, her tidy little world unraveling out of her control.

More grumpy than ever, Imogen came over the ridge

and arrived at the final curve in the long driveway that led to the Lodge. She went around it and slammed on the brakes.

"What?" she said out loud. She actually blinked to see if the vision went away. She had heard of people pinching themselves to see if they were dreaming, and she considered doing that. If there were any wrong driveways to take, she would have thought she'd taken one, but there was only one road that led to the Lodge.

And she was on it.

But the Lodge had never looked like this.

The Crystal Lake Lodge was absolutely glowing. Every inch of it—rooflines and corners, windowsills and porches—was all outlined with white fairy lights.

Her heart hammering in her throat, not able to take her eyes off her glowing home, Imogen inched up the driveway.

There were no cars in the parking lot, but against a dark sky, she could see smoke chugging out the chimney. She turned off her car and stepped out of it. The smell of wood smoke was tangy in the air.

Though she usually went in the side door, she went around to the front. The porch and front entryway were festooned in garlands.

There was a wreath on the door, a word peeking out from under the fresh, fragrant boughs. *Believe.*

It was an invitation to believe in something—dreams, miracles, fairy tales—and if she hadn't before, she certainly did now. Trembling with shock, with excitement, with anticipation and with hope, Imogen opened the front door.

The entryway had been transformed. Pine garlands wove their way up the staircase, but Imogen took it all in with barely a pause. She raced down the hallway, paused outside her closed office door and then threw it open.

The room was lit by the fire that burned merrily in the hearth, and by candles that burned softly. A huge tree, completely decorated, winking with a thousand brightly colored lights filled one entire corner of the room. Christmas music filled the room.

But she didn't care about any of that. Her eyes adjusted to the dimness, and she saw him, standing there, in the shadows on one side of the hearth, looking across the room at her.

"Luca."

Her lips whispered his name, but her heart cried it.

"Imogen." He pushed out of the shadow, came and stood in the middle of the room. She had seen him dressed as a prince, and she had seen him in long johns. She liked this look: jeans and a sweater with a shirt under it. It made him look ordinary, even as her heart sang there was nothing ordinary about him.

"I—I—I don't understand. What are you doing here?"

She had been frozen in her place; now she moved toward him, helpless, steel to a magnet. She came and stood before him and gazed up into the now so familiar lines of his so handsome face.

"Let me take your jacket."

Helplessly, she let him assist her out of it. Thank goodness, she had dressed nicely and put on a lick of makeup for her lunch engagement with her boss. Still, if she had known she was going to see him again, she might have made more effort to look, well, sexy.

Having dispensed with her jacket, he took her hand and guided her to the couch.

"How on earth did you accomplish this?" she whispered. "The tree isn't even nailed to the wall."

"It took a small army," he admitted, "to get all the reservations canceled and people's vacations rescheduled elsewhere. And it took the cooperation of strangers, like your lovely boss, Mrs. Kennedy, to spirit you away from the place for a day."

"But why?" Imogen asked. "Why have you gone to so much trouble?"

"Gabriella told me she felt bad that she was immersed in Christmas excitement at the palace and that you had been left out."

Imogen should have felt uplifted by her friend's thoughtfulness, but somehow it was not the answer she was hoping for: that Gabriella had sent him.

She tried to hide her disappointment. She would talk about Gabriella, too!

"You know, when I first learned Gabriella's news, I didn't even think she would go to Casavalle. And then when she went, I didn't think she would stay. I felt I knew her well enough to say she would never leave here, Crystal Lake. I certainly never thought she would accept the crown. But when I speak to her lately, I don't know anymore. She sounds happy and excited."

"She has embraced Casavalle like it is a missing part of herself. Which it is."

"You think she's going to accept the crown."

He lifted a shoulder, as if he didn't care about that!

Imogen registered that, happy for her friend and for Gabriella's embracing the adventure life had offered her, and yet achingly aware of her own loss.

"I've always worried about her being lonely," Imogen admitted. "I can't help but think if she accepts the crown it will make it worse."

"She and my mother are already fast friends. She has Antonio and I now. We are her family."

But I'm her family, Imogen wanted to wail. Instead she said, "I was thinking more about a husband for her, and children. I always wanted that for her, but she didn't. She seemed terrified of it, as if she had inherited her mom's sadness and wariness about love. Still, I thought the right person would come along."

"And they will," Luca said.

"Do you think so? Once you are a member of a royal family, how do you ever find someone to love you for you?"

"How indeed?" he asked softly.

Imogen's eyes flew to Luca's face. She should have never let it slip that she had thought she loved him. Because now he seemed to know some truth about her that made her feel vulnerable and faintly pathetic.

Ordinary girl falls hopelessly for Prince.

"I took your advice," he said after a moment. "I went and talked to Princess Meribel."

"And?"

"I told her the truth."

"That you loved her and she had broken your heart?" She forced herself to look at his face.

"Loved Meribel?" He looked puzzled. "What would make you think that?"

"I just felt you must have such strong feelings for her to be so protective of her after she betrayed you. It seemed like love to me."

"It's true that I felt intensely protective of her. Especially since I could see my part in the whole debacle. But love? A kind of love, I suppose, like a brother might have for a younger sister."

"What do you mean, your part?"

"What kind of self-centered jerk doesn't even understand the woman he plans to marry is unhappy? I missed all the cues, and so I felt responsible, at least in part, when the people of Casavalle—and many in Aguilarez, as well—turned on Meribel when they found out her pregnancy was the reason our wedding was canceled.

"So, strong feelings of protection, yes. Love? No. I never loved her, Imogen. I told myself I would in time. I told myself that she would love me, in time. But now I see that was wrong, to think such a marriage could have ever worked, or that any good could come from what would have basically been a charade."

Prince Luca never loved Princess Meribel.

"When I went to see her," he continued, "I thanked her for carrying the most important message of all—to be brave enough to accept the invitation of love if it is presented to you."

She gazed at him, wide-eyed.

"You see, I had my whole life mapped out. My marriage—my entire future—were all decided for me. It's all come crashing down, and you'd think I'd be devastated, but instead I feel this strange elation. And I feel free. For the first time ever, I can make decisions about what I want. I can map out my own life."

Imogen felt almost faint from the way he was looking at her: as if she was the destination on the map of his life, as if she was something he wanted.

"Come," he said. "Let's go to the dining room."

He held out his hand; she took it and allowed herself to be escorted to the dining room. How far did she want to allow herself to be pulled into this enchantment? As wonderful as it had been for Gabriella to set this in place, it was making her ache for things she could not have.

But was that completely true?

She had been mistaken that he loved Meribel. He never had.

And what did it mean for him that he would no longer be King? Did it mean an ordinary girl might be on his radar?

Perhaps, she thought sadly, *but probably not one unable to ever bear his children.* But he already knew that. Why was he here? Surely it wasn't just at the request of Gabriella?

The dining room, like her office, had been transformed into a Christmas fantasy. White and red poinsettias were grouped on the side serving table. The main dining table, laid with a Christmas cloth and beautiful china dishes that she did not recognize, was decorated with lit candles and an ice centerpiece, of snowmen!

"The caterers I passed did this," she deduced.

"I wanted you to think I did it myself!" he teased as he held out a chair for her. She sat down at the table, and he sat at right angles from her and removed the silver tops from serving platters.

Two perfectly roasted Cornish game hens were underneath.

She nibbled on the one he placed on her plate, but her stomach was in knots.

"It's not as good as the one you cooked in the fire," he told her, tasting his own.

"It is so! It has some remarkable sauce on it. No burned places."

He laughed, and some of the knots dissolved in her stomach. Yes, he was the Prince of Casavalle, but he was also *her* Luca, the one she had laughed with and played in the snow with. She had been given the gift of one more encounter with him. Why not embrace it?

"What will happen to you now?" she asked him, suddenly ashamed of herself for her every thought being on herself. Luca had just had the shock of his life: finding out he had a sister and that the job he had prepared for his entire life would not be his. He claimed he was happy, but was he worried, too?

"I can't know what Gabriella's decision will be, but if she chooses the crown, I am superbly qualified to act as an advisor to your friend and I will do that. I find myself feeling quite comfortable with that role. As I said before, I am cautiously relishing the thought of being free in ways I have not yet experienced. I can travel more freely. I can experience other cultures more deeply. Just like Meribel abandoning me for another turned out to be a gift, I am beginning to see that a gift might be hidden in this."

He didn't seem worried at all. They sampled all the exquisite offerings on the table, and when they were finished, Luca said, "Speaking of gifts, I have one other for you."

"I don't need any other gifts, Luca. Just being with you…"

She could feel the blush moving up her cheeks, as if she had said too much. *Way too much. Again!*

"This is what is amazing to me, Imogen, how you see *me*. Not a prince, but *me*. I want you to come back to Casavalle with me."

CHAPTER SEVENTEEN

FOR A MOMENT Imogen's heart stood still. Could she have heard correctly?

"You want me to come back to your kingdom with you?" she asked Luca weakly.

"Yes. You have shown me your world. Now come and see mine."

Suddenly she understood. She nearly laughed out loud at the absurdity of what she had thought! That *he* wanted her to come.

"Is this Gabriella's idea?" she asked quietly. "Is she feeling sorry for me that she is having all the fun, and I've been left behind?"

He regarded her thoughtfully. "If I tell you Gabriella needs you now, more than ever, will you come?"

Would she? It seemed a dangerous thing, indeed, to agree. How would she stop herself from being enchanted? She was already in love with him. What would happen if she accepted an invitation into his world?

Her heart could be broken.

She had to say no.

And yet she thought of the excitement in Gabi's voice, and her new enthusiasm for life. She thought of how, just this morning, she had almost wished she was going to be fired. How she had felt as if life was passing her by, how she had felt envious of life handing her friend an unexpected adventure.

What did it matter why she was being asked to go?

Life was shouting at her to do this. So, even while her head said no, loudly and firmly, her heart said yes.

And somehow it was what her heart said that tumbled off her lips.

A whisper, tentative and frightened.

And then more loudly, more sure, more bold.

"Yes."

"Can we get out? And walk?"

Luca looked at Imogen. She was wide-eyed with wonder, as she had been since the moment she had stepped onto the private jet that had whisked them from Canada and to his world in the blink of an eye.

He probably shouldn't have told her it was Gabriella's idea for her to come to Casavalle, but when he had invited her, she had suddenly looked so terrified.

And then suddenly he had felt terrified, too.

It was the same mistake his father had made with Sophia: jumping in. No, better to say it was Gabriella's idea, to see if they could maintain what he thought they had at the Lodge under these very different circumstances.

Now a royal limousine, as beautifully appointed as the jet, and chauffeur driven, was carrying them to the very gates of the castle.

Just as Luca had told Imogen, preparation for Christmas had begun. It was getting dark and they were just entering the long driveway lined with Norway spruce, the castle awash in light at the end of the tunnel of trees.

Because it was such a huge job, the trees that stood sentinel on both sides of Royal Avenue were always decorated first, and they had been completed.

This year they alternated: one tree completely in white lights, the next one in blue, all the way down the long driveway.

"How many lights do you think?" Imogen breathed. "A million? More? I have to get out. I have to be *in* it. It's a fairy tale come to life."

Luca tapped the driver on the shoulder, gave the quiet command, and the car came to a halt. He exited the car and took Cristiano's place, holding open the door for Imogen.

"Welcome to my home," he said quietly, as Imogen got out of the car, hugged herself tight and turned a slow circle.

She stopped when she was facing the castle. "How can such a place ever feel like home?"

Could it ever feel like her home? He looked at it through her eyes: the castle was constructed of pure white limestone that had been brought, centuries ago, from quarries on the Adriatic Islands. Its soaring spires, walls, wings, towers, were all lit with floodlights, so that the whole place glowed. It did look exactly like the opening illustration for a fairy tale.

It was all so grand compared to the Lodge. Luca felt the oddest thing. He explored the feeling, strangely paralyzed by it. It felt so odd.

He realized he felt something he had never felt before: he felt insecure. But then he looked at her wonder-filled face and remembered, probably for the thousandth time since she had spoken them, the words she had said.

No wonder I felt as if I loved you.

He crooked his elbow to Imogen, inviting her to loop her arm through his. They walked the tree-lined avenue together. It opened, eventually, to a huge front courtyard, a cobblestone driveway circled around a massive fountain. The workings of the fountain had been removed, and huge blocks of ice, weighing several tons each, had been placed there.

"What are these?" Imogen asked, and then her eyes widened. "That's what you told me about, isn't it? The ice that's brought in for the carving competition. It's so mild here. It's magical that you've found a way to keep the ice from melting, to make it happen."

That's what he had hoped for—that beyond the pomp and circumstance, she would see the magic of his world and the beauty.

"Is that the maze over there? The one the children love? It's gorgeous. I couldn't have ever imagined it."

"It's a hedge maze—part of the formal gardens. In the summer it has reflection pools and fountains. It hasn't had its Christmas makeover yet, but it soon will."

"How wonderful to picture children running through it laughing."

He saw her own regret about children flit briefly through her eyes.

"Can you get lost in it?" she asked.

"Oh yes. That's part of the fun. You and I will explore it together," he said. "I'll make sure you don't get lost."

And he meant that. Not just for the maze, but for his world. He would make sure she would not get lost in this strange new place he was asking her to explore.

She seemed to know exactly what he really meant, because she smiled tentatively, and then Imogen turned her attention to the wide granite staircase that led to the massive front doors just as they opened. Two staff members in the simple uniform of the castle—white blouses and black slacks or skirts—held the double doors open for them.

"Is someone going to come out and play the trumpet?"

Imogen whispered, and then, "It's all a little intimidating, isn't it?"

He looked at it through her eyes and felt his heart fall a little bit. The transition he would be asking her to make was indeed huge.

But then Gabriella burst through the open door. Her hair was tumbling around her shoulders, jodhpurs clung to her slender legs, and her shirt was untucked. It was just the moment of informality that was needed!

"Imogen," she called, as she came down the steps, two at a time. She took the smaller woman in her embrace. "Are you totally overwhelmed?"

"Of course I am!"

"Let me get you settled then. You can take tea in my quarters." She giggled. "And wait until you see them."

Just like that, Imogen was whisked away from him. He stared at the two departing women, slightly disgruntled. This wasn't exactly his plan. Luca's lips twitched. Again, these Canadian women just seemed to have a way of disrupting the best-laid plans.

Imogen woke the next morning and felt faintly disoriented. When she remembered where she was, she felt as if she needed to pinch herself.

She sat up in bed—a huge four-poster piece of furniture that centuries' worth of royal people had slept in—and gazed around the room. Not a room, really, but a suite. It was so opulent it took her breath away. The bedclothes were silk. Priceless paintings and wall hangings decorated the walls. When she swung her feet out of the bed, they landed on an ancient Turkish rug.

She padded to the bathroom, which had a huge marble freestanding tub, and she was pretty sure the fixtures were real gold.

She put aside the little voice that tried to tell her she didn't belong here and listened to the other one, which told her to embrace the adventure.

A soft knock came at the door, and she shrugged into the luxurious robe that hung on the back of the door. She wondered if breakfast was going to be delivered on a tray. How did you address the person who delivered it? Did you take it from them or did they set it down?

Imogen, she told herself, *you are in way over your head.*

Just the way Gabriella's mother would have been all those years ago, she thought with sympathy.

She went and opened the door.

Luca stood there. She wasn't sure if she was relieved, or appalled that he was seeing her with messy hair and still in her pajamas.

But of course, he had seen her with messy hair and not exactly as a fashionista before. He looked so good when he gave her a rakish smile.

"Are you going to sleep all day?"

"Have I?" she asked, appalled.

"Welcome to jet lag! Get dressed. I have so much to show you."

"I'm not even sure what I should wear."

"Dress to have fun. I'm going to show you the palace, and then show you the grounds on horseback."

"I don't know how to ride a horse. That's Gabriella's thing."

"Then I'll try not to put you on one that breathes fire, not today."

The tour of the palace began with the dining room, where a delightful breakfast of crunchy, mind-blowingly delicious handmade pastries had been put out. From there Luca took her for a tour of the palace. It was awe inspiring. It might have struck her to intimidated silence, except that Luca was so funny, irreverent and engaging as her personal tour guide.

The palace was truly like something out of a fairy tale.

Luca took her to huge ballrooms, staterooms, the throne room, dining rooms, long galleries and sweeping staircases, as well as kitchens. Amused by her wide-eyed wonder, he let her peek in sumptuous bedrooms and luxury bathrooms. The library took her breath away.

Most magical of all, though, was that Christmas in Casavalle was unfolding exactly as Luca had described it. The palace was being prepared, and it was both breathtaking and awe inspiring.

In a way, it made Imogen feel a little foolish about her humble efforts to create a Christmas for the Prince.

He came from this—beautifully decorated trees in every room, wreaths on every door, real pine and fir garlands lining mantels and staircases. Huge, exotic poinsettias had been imported and brought brightness to every forgotten corner. Priceless ornaments graced side tables and coffee tables that were hundreds of years old.

The last place he took her was the gorgeous tree in the entrance foyer. It was behind ropes, but he opened one and invited her in.

The aroma enveloped her. The Buschetta ornaments were beyond anything she had ever seen before.

"Has this year's been unveiled yet?"

"No, tomorrow. I am hoping you will enjoy the unveiling ceremony."

She really needed to ask questions. How long did he think she could be here? She wasn't going to be able to take leave from her job forever. In the real world there were little issues like needing a paycheck to survive.

But those questions died in her throat when he looked

at her with such warmth. He was truly happy to be showing her his home.

"Are you ready to try riding?" he asked.

She was. In fact, she was surprised to find, she felt
ready for just about anything.

CHAPTER EIGHTEEN

IMOGEN SAT WITH Queen Maria and Gabriella on a slightly raised dais in front of that amazing Christmas tree. The unveiling of the ornament was about to begin. She marveled, a little shell-shocked, at the surprise life had given her. A week ago, two, could she have ever imagined this for herself?

Sitting with royalty, in the lavishly decorated front foyer of a palace, waiting for the Buschetta Christmas ornament to be revealed?

The foyer—huge—had almost become an auditorium, with a hundred seats, all of them full, in a semicircle around the dais. There seemed to be a lot of press here, and Imogen tried to look confident and as though she belonged. She had brought her best dress with her and, giggling like two schoolgirls, she and Gabriella had selected hats for this event.

Luca wasn't here yet, and she could feel herself waiting for him. Despite the fact he was a prince, he was her rock, her touchstone, in this gorgeous new world he had introduced her to. His smile was the anchor that kept her from feeling as if she was floating in a dream.

But when he did come in, Imogen's mouth fell open. Could this man really be *her* Luca? The Luca who had donned long underwear and roasted hot dogs over the fire and built snowmen? The Luca who had patiently showed her how to ride yesterday, and who had gotten lost in the maze with her until they were both doubled over with laughter?

The Luca who had kissed her and held her hand? The Luca who had made her heart feel things it had never felt before?

This man was regal in a navy blue uniform, gold braid trimming one shoulder and a peaked cap pulled low over his eyes. His flair for wearing the uniform— the way he absolutely owned it—made Imogen feel suddenly self-conscious, as if her best dress had come from the thrift bin in Crystal Lake. She fought a desire to remove the hat, feeling suddenly as if she was in costume.

But Luca was not in costume in his imposing uniform. He was commanding, and the whole room seemed to ripple with acknowledgment when he walked in.

He nodded at her, his eyes lingered, and for a moment, it seemed as if he was, indeed, *her* Luca, but then his gaze moved on, as if he was preoccupied. He sat with Cristiano, his brother—whom Imogen had only met briefly—and some other very important-looking people on the opposite end of the dais from where his mother, Gabriella and Imogen were seated.

Suddenly, she felt as if she had been seated here by accident. She was probably supposed to have politely refused the invitation to sit with the Queen.

As if sensing she wanted to bolt, Gabriella quietly took her hand and gave her a tiny sideways smile that reminded her of her mantra.

Embrace the adventure.

Imogen took a deep breath and settled more deeply in her chair.

* * *

Luca saw Imogen right away. She looked positively beautiful in a jade-green dress and a showstopper of a hat. She didn't just fit in his world, she dimmed it with her radiance. But he couldn't let himself be distracted, not right now.

The future relations of two kingdoms rested on what he had to say today.

He noted that television, radio, online and print journalists from both Casavalle and Aguilarez were present, as well as a few representatives from media outlets around the world. The unveiling of the ornament was a nice "feel-good" filler piece for slow nights in international news.

Gabriella's presence on the dais was unexplained, for now. It was not unusual for them to have extra people at the opening of the ornament, and indeed, the town mayor was here, as was a member of the Buschetta family.

In front of them was a box, wrapped in plain brown paper. Today they would unveil this year's Buschetta ornament creation for the Christmas tree.

Luca dreaded it.

For one thing, it was the first time his father was not here.

But for another, what if the ornament commemorated the engagement that had ended so badly, or the wedding that had never happened? It could be embarrassing for him, but worse, painful for Imogen.

Queen Maria stood and took the box. She rolled it over in her hand and then turned and motioned Gabriella to come stand beside her.

Luca watched Gabriella and was taken again by her innate grace and her composure. But more, the woman seemed to glow a little more deeply each day, as she was welcomed into the embrace of a family she had not known she had, as she explored the wonders of her new life.

Carefully, Gabriella undid the wrapping.

The ornament was revealed: inside a globe of glass was a baby lying in a manger of straw. It was so lifelike Luca could almost hear it chortling as it reached for the muzzle of the donkey who nuzzled it.

The Buschetta representative came forward and touched a secret switch. The top half of the globe swung open, and he carefully manipulated the manger.

The baby swung away to reveal these words, in tiny perfect calligraphy: *Love makes all the world new again.*

He read them aloud to the audience. There was a collective sigh.

Luca cast a glance at Imogen. She chose that moment to look at him. A brand-new world shivered in the air between them, though she looked hastily away and so did he.

He made himself focus on the ornament, even though he wanted to look back at her and bask in the truth he had seen in her face when those words were revealed.

Luca felt the message in his heart. He waited until the photographers had satisfied their need for pictures.

Then he stood up, took a deep breath and held up his hand for silence and attention.

The silence was almost immediate, people leaning toward what he had to say.

It felt as if he was about to speak the most important words he would ever say.

"It has been suggested to me," he said, "that I forgive Princess Meribel. As all of you know, our engagement ended, not because of irreconcilable differences, but because my fiancée is pregnant with another man's child."

A murmur of outrage went up among the assembled.

"I will not forgive her."

A gasp, laced with a certain delighted sanctimoniousness, went up from the crowd.

"Because," Prince Luca continued, his voice quiet and firm, "there is truly nothing for me to forgive."

This caused muttering, and one reporter shouted, "She left you at the altar, sir."

Another called out, in a voice laced with outrage, "She was with another man behind your back."

"She's pregnant!"

Luca waited patiently for it all to die down. Then he spoke again, his voice strong and calm and sure.

"In fact, I just met with the Princess and I asked for her forgiveness."

This statement was met with stunned silence.

"It takes a great deal of insensitivity to be unable to recognize a relationship is not fulfilling for both parties, and I am guilty of that," he continued.

"In fact, in our meeting, I thanked Meribel Asturias for being the bravest woman I know. I thanked her for teaching me a lesson I desperately need to learn—love is everything.

"Not power. Not wealth. Not influence. Love. Love is the thing worth sacrificing every other thing for— including the promise of a kingdom."

There was complete silence. Luca could have heard a pin drop in that large room. He went on.

"Coming into this Christmas season, that is the message I want you each to hold in your hearts, that love is everything and the only thing. It is the message this beautiful ornament gives the world this year—*love makes the whole world new again*.

"Princess Meribel has brought that reminder to me this season, and I pass on her gift to each of you.

"Do not harbor one acrimonious thought of this woman. She was true to her heart, and it required her to be courageous and determined, and that is what each of us needs to be in pursuit of what is right and what is decent. That is what each of us needs to be in the pursuit of the greatest thing of all, which is love. When her baby is born, I encourage the world to celebrate that wondrous expression of love made manifest.

"Some of you will remember, a long time ago, before Queen Maria, my father loved another. She left my father, and left the kingdom of Casavalle. The circumstances were mysterious. I know the result of her leaving left my father suspicious of love, and maybe some of you felt that way, too.

"And yet I am here to tell you that love always brings a gift with it, even if it takes time for that blessing to be revealed. I promise that my father's long-ago love has left us a precious gift, and soon I hope to be able to share that with all of you.

"Please, I beg of you, go into this Christmas season with your hearts open. Forgive hurts, real and imagined, old and new, small and large. In that forgiveness, you will find you are open to the joy of the simple pleasures of being with your families and loved ones. Build snowmen and warm your hands over fires.

"Take pleasure in the greatest gift we, as human beings, are ever allowed to experience. Embrace love completely."

Luca finished speaking.

Had his words managed to repair anything? To save Meribel from a life of shame? Had his words brought love, as he had hoped?

The gallery was silent. And then one reporter put down her camera, rose to her feet and began to clap.

And then they were all on their feet, clapping with thunderous approval.

His intuition had served him again. He glanced at the people behind him: his brother looked like he was in a state of complete shock, but Gabriella's eyes were shining with tears. His mother looked as pleased with him as she had ever looked. And Imogen looked at him with a pride shining from her eyes that any man would give his life to see.

But didn't that reaction from those women he loved require something of him? Now wasn't there one more challenge? To practice what he had preached? To follow his intuition, his heart, back to the one place and the one person who called him? The place he had felt as free as he had ever felt and as complete as he could ever feel?

Did Prince Luca have it in himself to be as brave as he had just called on others to be?

CHAPTER NINETEEN

IMOGEN WATCHED AS Luca turned and took his seat. She looked around her at the emotion his words had inspired. She had never loved him more.

Or felt as devastated.

She had seen him now, completely. She had seen him as a man and as a prince. She had just witnessed his ability to inspire and lead.

It made her realize how hopeless her feelings for him really were. He was, quite simply, amazing. Everyone in his world knew it, and when this speech got out, the whole world would know it.

Women would be throwing themselves at his feet. Women who came from that same world and would fit easily into it. Women who understood wealth and power. Women who were sophisticated and glamorous.

Imogen understood Gabriella's mother, Sophia Ross. Completely.

As soon as she was able, she slipped away. She went to her room and began hastily putting things in her worn travel bag. Even the bag seemed to mock her; well used and a little frayed, it was exactly the type of thing that would embarrass him about her.

But to be embarrassed by her, he would have to be involved with her. Obviously, he had been kind while she was here. He had shown her the sights and made her laugh and made her love him even more. He had seemed to enjoy spending time with her. She was sure that was genuine.

And yet that man, who had just given that speech...

Imogen felt a shiver run up and down her spine. He was from a different world. In a different league, entirely.

She had to get out of here before she made a total fool of herself. She sank down on the bed. How did one get out of Casavalle? Every single thing about getting here had been organized for her.

There was a tap on the door.

It was more of the same: staff here to tell her something, that dinner was served, or it was time for tea. Or here to deliver freshly laundered items she hadn't asked to be laundered, or new lotions and potions for the bath.

She decided to ignore the knock, but it came again louder. And then, yet again.

She went to the door and opened it.

Luca stood there, resplendent in his uniform, looking tall and strong and sure of himself. Looking like exactly what he was: royalty.

He scanned her face, and she scanned his, wanting to memorize it, memorize what was there: happiness in seeing her.

His smile faded. "What's wrong?"

"Wrong?" she said with forced brightness. "Nothing. It's time for me to go home. I've outstayed my welcome. I know it was Gabriella's idea for me to come and you were a good sport—"

"It wasn't Gabriella's idea," he said softly.

"It wasn't?"

"Will you come outside with me? I have something I want to give you."

She knew she should refuse him. She knew she should pack her bag and get out of here with one shred of her heart intact. But she could not refuse him anything. And that line—*It wasn't Gabriella's idea*—was making something happen to her heart.

She should refuse any more gifts from him, but instead, she let her hand take the one he outstretched to her. One more moment with him, one more memory.

He led her through a labyrinth of passages in the castle and out a side door.

"This is my garden," he said, and his hand tightened on hers. It was a lovely walled space, with vines covering the stones and flowering shrubs giving off a perfumed aroma. The night was beautiful and dark, clear and crisp.

She looked into his face and saw it was just her beloved Luca under all these trappings: the royal uniform, the beautiful spaces. He was still the same Luca who had chased her through the snow, who had kissed her, who had showed her Casavalle with such pleasure.

He was beloved to her. She loved him.

"Look," he said, pointing.

She looked in that direction. It looked for all the world like a huge pile of dirty laundry was sitting in the middle of his pristine garden!

"What is this?" she asked cautiously.

"That's my gift," he said happily.

"Um, what is it?"

"Go down there and stand right in front of it," he instructed her.

She looked at him. He was so light, so filled with mischief, so playful.

So easy to love. So *himself*, somehow.

She did as he asked her.

"Ready?" he called.

She was. She leaped back when the pile of what looked to be fabric in front of her began to hiss and writhe and unfold.

She watched, fascinated, as air rushed into it and it began to inflate. An inflatable snow family took shape before her very eyes. A mama, a papa and two children.

It lit from within. The family's arms began to wave merrily.

Imogen began to laugh. And then he was at her side and they were both laughing until they hurt from it.

She had to lie down on the ground, and he lay down beside her.

"That is just about the cheesiest thing I've ever seen," she said.

"I know. Isn't it great? For me to be cheesy instead of classy is a wonderful feeling."

"Part of being free."

"Yes."

They lay there, side by side, silent, watching the stars dance in the inky skies above them.

Love makes all the world new again, Imogen thought, the message hidden in the ornament today.

It was such a simple message, and yet so profound. And so true. Wasn't she looking at the world in a brand-new way since her days with Luca?

Since her heart could not deny her love for him?

"I let you believe that," Luca confessed softly. "I let you believe it was Gabriella who needed you to come here.

"I was afraid you might not come if you knew the truth. I mean, Gabriella told me she felt bad that she was having all the excitement and that you had been left out. But it was me who couldn't stand the thought of you being left out. It was me who wanted you to see my home."

"You?"

"Imogen, I have missed you so much there are days when it felt as if the air was not enough to fill me anymore. As if I would be left empty and aching for the rest of my life. I missed you.

"And I missed what you can do to ordinary moments like this one. You transform them. You show me what I have been missing my entire life.

"Now that I've had it, I don't feel life would be worth living without it."

"What have you been missing your entire life?"

"Love," he whispered. "That very thing I just spoke of."

"Are you saying—" her voice was barely a whisper "—what I think you are saying?" It felt as if her heart was about to thud out of her chest.

"I don't know how this is possible. To feel so strongly about you after such a short period together. But I want to explore it. I want to see if it's real. I want to spend my life with you."

Imogen swallowed hard.

It was another "pinch me" moment.

And yet, looking at his face—the face she had fallen in love with—she knew he was speaking his truth.

She began to weep.

"You know I can't have your children."

"Oh, my darling Imogen, that causes me distress only because it causes you distress. If we are intended to have children one day, they will find their way to us. I promise you that."

It was the kind of promise you could hang on to. Her tears fell harder.

"And if it was just you and I, forever, I would spend each day with you in total joy, feeling complete, feeling as if not one other thing was necessary."

And then she was gathered up in his arms, and they sat for a long, long time with her nestled against his chest, in the light of the inflatable snow family and of the winking stars.

"It's the best gift ever," Imogen said.

"I'm actually hoping you will think this is the best gift ever."

She turned to him. He held out a box. He lifted the lid and a ring sparkled at her.

"In the last few days, I've lost my bride and lost my throne. Such a small price to pay to find true love and happiness. If you will have me, I would like you to be my wife."

Imogen stared at him, shocked. Logically, she understood they barely knew one another. Logically, she understood that their time together had been underlain with the intensity of being snowed in, and then her visit here, which had seemed about as real as a fairy tale.

But she had been logical her entire life; she had based all her decisions on what was solid and what was sensible. She had planned a safe route through the journey of life.

Not only had all her planning not brought her happiness, she could now clearly see her desire for predictability and safety might have been an obstacle to ever finding the true happiness she felt right now, as exquisitely, as blissfully as she had ever felt it.

She gazed into Luca's eyes.

From the moment he had stepped off the helicopter, she had experienced a sensation of knowing him.

Now she knew it was not because he resembled his sister, and her best friend.

It was not that at all.

Her heart had recognized him.

Her heart had not recognized the impossibility of it. Her heart had never been deterred by the fact she was a common girl and he was a prince.

Her heart had known.

And it knew now.

It knew that others might see it as too soon, or see their worlds as too different, or see them as going up against impossible cultural obstacles.

Her heart cared nothing for any of that. It cared only for the answer that whispered from her lips.

"Yes," she said.

And then stronger, an affirmation of the stunning power and mystery of love, an affirmation of its ability to find you, even when you hid from it.

"Yes!"

He stood up and held out his hand to her. She took it, and he pulled her to her feet and held her tight against him. He tilted her chin, so that her eyes met his. He scanned her face, and he saw the truth of her love there.

"Love has given me what a title never could," he said hoarsely. "Your love has crowned me King."

His lips took hers.

And they became one with it all: with the star-studded sky and the majesty of the mountains, with the life force that breathed through the trees that surrounded them and the earth that they stood on.

They became one with love.

* * * * *

SWEPT AWAY BY THE SEDUCTIVE STRANGER

AMY ANDREWS

To my dear friend and colleague Emily Forbes.

It was a blast – let's do it again some time!

CHAPTER ONE

Callum Hollingsworth would have had to be completely blind not to notice the sexy blonde in his peripheral vision. Thanks to a combination of excellent medical care, the passage of time and her being on his right, he wasn't.

Although it was her laugh he'd noticed first.

She was talking on her phone and even though her tone was hushed her occasional laughter practically boomed around the busy café. It was so damn…unrestrained, so carefree, he couldn't help but stare.

Callum hadn't had much to laugh about in recent times and a hot streak of envy tore through his chest as he ogled her from behind his sunglasses. Long honey-coloured hair with curly ends that brushed her shoulder blades. A glimpse of sun-kissed skin at her throat and on toned, tanned arms. Legs clad in denim that were shapely rather than skinny and knee-high fringed boots that looked more country girl than dominatrix.

She didn't wear any make-up or jewellery. In fact, there was a lack of anything flashy or ostentatious about her yet she shone like a jewel in the old-fashioned café in Sydney's Central Station as the sun streamed in through the high windows overhead.

Maybe it was the way she laughed—with her whole body—that held his attention. Maybe it was the jeans and the boots. Maybe it was her lack of pretension. Whatever, he was just pleased to be provided with some relief from the burden of his thoughts as he sat waiting for his train to depart.

For God's sake, he was about to embark on one of the

great train journeys of the world. He was leaving Sydney and going somewhere else for two months where nobody knew him or about the tumble his career had taken. He could reset the clock. Reinvent himself.

Come back refreshed and show them all he didn't give a damn.

The sooner he got to grips with his old life being over, the sooner he could get his act together. This was his chance to finally get his head out of his backside and work on being impressively happy once again. Because he sure as hell was sick of himself and the dark cloud that had been following him around for the last two years.

Nothing like moving fourteen hundred kilometres away to send a strong message to himself about the new direction of his life.

'All passengers for the Indian Pacific, your train is now ready for departure from platform ten.'

Callum gathered his backpack at the announcement over the loudspeaker. The woman on the phone crossed her legs and kept talking and a pang of disappointment flared momentarily. She obviously hadn't been waiting for the same train. Visions straight from a James Bond movie of a glamorous night between the sheets with a mystery woman on a train as a brilliant way to kick-start his new life fizzled into the ether.

He gave himself a mental shake, his lips twisting at the insanity as he headed towards the exit to the platforms.

A thrill of excitement shot through Felicity Mitchell's system as she stepped into the luxurious carriage and was ushered to her compartment by a man in a smart uniform who had introduced himself as Donald, her personal attendant. She passed several other compartments with their doors open and smiled at the couples who beamed back at her.

Booking a double suite in platinum class on the Indian Pacific was a hideous extravagance. She could have done the

Sydney to Adelaide leg in the sitting compartment or even the gold class and saved a lot of money, but it had been a lifelong dream of hers to watch the world chug by as she lay on her double bed, looking out the window. She'd spent the last of her inheritance on the fare but she knew her grandpa, wherever he was now, would be proud.

They passed a compartment with a shut door before Donald stopped at the next one along. 'Here you are,' he said, indicating she should precede him.

Felicity entered the wood-panelled compartment dominated by a picture window. A small plate of cheese and biscuits sat on a low central wooden table. A long lounge that would become her double bed sat snugly against the wall between the window and a narrow cupboard where her bags had already been stowed.

'This is your en suite,' he said, opening a door opposite the lounge to show her the toilet and shower. It was a reasonable size considering the space constraints.

Donald gave her a quick run-down on her compartment and other bits of information about the service before asking if she'd like a glass of wine or champagne as the journey got under way.

Would she? *Hell, yeah.*

'Thank you, Donald, I would love a glass of champagne.'

He smiled at her. 'One glass of bubbles coming up.'

Felicity waited for him to leave before she danced a crazy little jig then collapsed onto the lounge in a happy heap. Workers scurried around on the platform outside, ready for the train's departure in a few minutes. She couldn't believe she was finally sitting in this iconic train about to begin the trip of a lifetime.

Donald returned quickly and handed her a glass full of fizz. 'You're just with us until Adelaide, that's right, isn't it?'

'Yes, that's right. I'd love to go on all the way to Perth. Maybe one day.'

The Indian Pacific was so called because it travelled the

width of Australia between the Indian and Pacific oceans. The full trip from Sydney to Perth took three days. Her leg of the journey was only twenty-four hours.

'I think you'll enjoy yourself anyway,' Donald said.

'Oh, yes,' Felicity agreed. 'I have absolutely no doubt. I've been looking forward to this for most of my life.'

'So, no pressure, then?'

Donald laughed and Felicity joined him as the train nudged forward. 'And we're away,' he said.

Felicity looked out the window. The platform appeared to be moving as the train slowly and silently pulled away. 'Let me know if you need anything. Dinner's served at seven.'

Felicity nodded then turned back to the window, sighing happily.

Felicity emerged from her compartment half an hour later. She'd stared out the window, watching the inner city give way to cluttered suburbs then to the more sparse outlying areas as it headed for the Blue Mountains. And now it was time to meet her fellow travellers.

Her neighbour's door was still firmly closed as she headed out. Maybe she didn't have one yet. Maybe they'd be joining the train at a later stop? Quelling her disappointment, she headed for the place she knew people would be—the lounge.

And she hit the jackpot. Half a dozen couples smiled at her as she stepped into the carriage, her legs already adjusted to the rock and sway of the train. She stopped at the bar and ordered a glass of bubbles from a guy called Travis. It was poured for her immediately and she made her way over to the semicircular couches where everyone was getting acquainted.

'Hi,' she said.

The group greeted her as one. 'Sit down here with us, love,' said an older man with a Scottish accent. The woman with him moved over and made some room. 'If you don't

mind me saying so, you don't exactly look in the same demographic as the rest of us.'

Felicity laughed. 'I have an old soul.'

Every other person in the lounge would have to have been
in their sixties. At twenty-eight that made her the youngest by a good thirty years. Luxury train travel was clearly
more a retiree option than a hip, young, cool thing to do.

But that was okay. She'd never been particularly hip or
cool. She was a small-town nurse who genuinely liked and
was interested in older people. She had a bunch of oldies at
the practice who she clucked around like a mother hen and
she knew this lot would probably be no different despite
what would be a short acquaintance.

'What do you do, dear?' a woman with steel-grey hair
over the other side of the lounge asked.

Felicity almost told them the truth but a sudden sense
of self-preservation took over. If she told them she was a
nurse, one of two things would happen. She'd have to give
medical advice about every ache, pain or strange rash for
the next twenty-four hours because, adore them as she did,
too many people of the older generation loved to talk ob-
sessively about their ailments. Or they'd pat her hand a lot
and tell her continually that she was an angel.

If she was really unlucky, both would happen.

She might be a nurse but she was no saint and certainly
no angel. In fact, that kind of language had always made
her uncomfortable.

And she didn't want to be the nurse from a small community where everyone knew her name on this train journey of a lifetime. She didn't want to be the girl next door.
She wanted to be as sophisticated and glamorous as her
surroundings. She wanted to dress up for dinner and drink
a martini while she had worldly conversations with complete strangers.

Nursing wasn't glamorous.

'Oh, I'm just a public servant,' she said, waving her hand

dismissively as she grabbed hold of the first job that came to mind. She doubted it was very glamorous either but it was one of those jobs that was both broad and vague enough to discourage discourse. Nobody really understood what public servants did, right? They certainly didn't ask them about their jobs.

Or tell them about their personal medical issues.

'What do you do?' Felicity asked, and relaxed as the woman, called Judy, launched into a spiel about her job of forty years, which kicked off a conversation amongst them all about their former jobs, and that segued into a discussion about the economy and then morphed again into chatter about travel.

Felicity was in heaven. She was on a train surrounded by witty and enthusiastic companions on the inside and the rugged beauty of the Blue Mountains on the outside. For twenty-four hours she was determined to be a different person.

Tomorrow afternoon she'd be back home where everyone knew her name and stopped her in the street for advice about their baby's fever, their weird allergies or their shingles. Where everyone called her 'Flick' and the guys called her 'mate' and the older women of the town tried to matchmake her with any remotely available male.

Tomorrow would be here soon enough. Today nobody knew her and she was going to revel in it for as long as she could.

The first thing Callum noticed when he entered the restaurant at seven sharp was the sexy blonde from the café. He blinked once or twice just to make sure it was her—his vision wasn't the best after all. Then she laughed at something her companions were saying and it went straight to his chest and spiked through his pulse.

It was definitely her.

If he'd known she was in the platinum carriage too he

wouldn't have wasted the last few hours catching up on some essential reading his new boss had emailed and insisted he read before he started work.

'Can I find you a dining companion, sir?' Donald asked.

'No,' Callum said. The beautifully dressed tables seated four and there were several spare chairs around the elegantly appointed dining car but his gaze was glued to the empty one beside her. 'I've found one.'

The corner of Donald's mouth lifted a fraction. 'Good choice, sir.'

It took him only a few more seconds to reach the empty chair next to blondie. 'Excuse me,' he said. The conversation stopped as all three diners turned to look at him. 'Is this seat taken?'

Her eyes widened slightly. They were smoky grey and fringed by sable lashes. She stared at him for long moments and he stared right back. He liked that she seemed as confused by her reaction to him as he was to her.

She'd changed into a dress, a slinky black thing that showed off her neck and collarbones and crisscrossed at her cleavage. She was wearing lip gloss. Pink. Light pink—the colour of ballet shoes. The ends of her honey hair seemed curlier or maybe that was just a trick of the overhead light.

The old guy sitting opposite welcomed him heartily. 'Sit down, young fella. Save this pretty young thing from having her ear bent off by us old fogies.'

Callum didn't wait to be asked twice. He wasn't someone who believed in instalove but he sure as hell believed in instalust. He may be rusty but he knew sexual interest when he saw it.

She sure as hell wasn't looking at him with pity, like too many women had these past couple of years.

No more pity sex for him.

'I'm Jock, this is my wife Thelma and the odd one out is Felicity.'

Callum shook Jock and Thelma's hand and reached for

blondie's. *Felicity.* 'Nice to meet you,' he murmured, their eyes meeting again, an awareness that was almost tangible blooming between them.

'You were in the café,' she said after a beat or two, sliding her hand out of his.

He let it go reluctantly. 'Yes.' A purr of male satisfaction buzzed through his veins. She remembered him. Had she been checking him out at the same time he'd been ogling her?

'I didn't realise you were in the same carriage.'

'I had some work to do.' Callum grimaced. 'I shut myself away for a while. I'm in number eight.'

'Hey, you're in nine, right?' Jock asked Felicity jovially. 'You're neighbours.'

Callum smiled at her as he sent a quick thankyou up into the universe. Things were definitely looking up for him. She smiled back and for the first time in a long time his belly tightened in anticipation. His libido had taken a real battering since the accident, so it was a revelation to feel it rousing.

'So, what do you do?' Jock asked.

Callum dragged his gaze off Felicity and forced his attention on the couple opposite. She wasn't the only person on the train and this was the way these social situations worked. You ate a good meal, drank good wine and made polite and hopefully interesting conversation with strangers.

God knew, he needed something like this to get himself out of his head. But he promised himself that later he would do his damnedest to shamelessly monopolise the woman beside him. They might not end up in bed together but he intended to flirt like crazy and see where it went.

'I'm a technical writer,' he said.

The well-practised lie rolled smoothly off his tongue. He still wasn't used to the real answer. Becoming a GP after being an up-and-coming vascular surgeon was taking some getting used to. And he only had to look around at the age demographic of the other passengers in the carriage to know that admitting to being any kind of doctor would probably result in an avalanche of medical questions he just didn't want to answer.

He didn't want to be any kind of doctor tonight. He wanted to forget about the bitter disappointments of his career and just be a regular Joe. He wanted to be a man chatting to a woman hoping it might end up somewhere interesting.

'Oh?' Thelma asked, as she buttered the bread roll Donald had just placed on her plate. 'What does that entail?'

'Just boring things like industry articles and manuals,' he dismissed. 'Nothing exciting. What about you, Thelma? Are you still working?'

It was a good deflection and Thelma ran with it. The conversation shifted throughout the sumptuous three-course meal and it felt good to stretch his conversational muscles, which were rusty at best. Felicity, on the other hand, was a great conversationalist and Callum found himself relaxing and even laughing from time to time.

His awareness of her as a woman didn't let up but the urgency to get her alone mellowed.

Like him, she seemed reluctant to talk about herself, expertly turning the conversation back to Thelma and Jock or himself and more neutral topics, such as travel and movies and sport. Consequently, the meal flew by as Felicity charmed them all. It was hard to believe he'd sat for two hours and not thought once about the accident and its repercussions on his life.

That wasn't something *anybody* had achieved in the past two and a half years.

He went to bed thinking about it, he woke up thinking about it, and it dominated his thoughts far more than it should during the day.

He suddenly felt about a decade younger.

'A few of us are retiring to the lounge for some after-dinner drinks,' Jock said as he placed his napkin on the table. 'I hope you'll both join us.'

'Of course,' Felicity said, smiling at their companions before turning that lusciously curved mouth towards him. 'You up for that? Or do you...have more work to do?'

Callum wanted nothing more than to invite her back to his compartment for some *private* after-dinner drinks. Their gazes locked and her cheeks pinked up and he wondered if she could read his mind. She was a strange mix of eagerness and hesitancy and Callum didn't want to push or embarrass her.

But he could see in those expressive grey eyes that she didn't want him to lock himself away again either.

'I'd love to,' he said, resigning himself to sharing her for a bit longer, to go slowly, to drag out a little more whatever it was that was building between them.

Anticipation buzzed thick and heavy through his groin.

Felicity found it hard to concentrate for the next couple of hours, aware of Mr Tall-Dark-and-Handsome sitting beside her in a way she hadn't been aware of a guy in a long time. Every time he spoke or laughed it rumbled through his big thigh pressed firmly against hers and squirmed its way into her belly.

There was a sense that they were marking time and she was equal parts titillated and terrified. This being a whole other person thing wasn't as easy to pull off as she'd thought but she'd never felt so alive either. So utterly *buzzed*.

Not even with Ned. Sure, he'd been the love of her life and being dumped by him had been crushing, but their love had grown out of friendship and a slow, gentle dawning.

This...*thing* was entirely different.

Was she seriously going to do this? Pick up a stranger on a train? Or let *him* pick her up? She might have limited experience of the whole pick-up scene but she was pretty sure that's exactly where they were heading. When she'd booked her train ticket, meeting a good-looking stranger hadn't been part of her plan.

But here they were with a night full of possibilities stretching ahead of them.

One by one their companions left, withdrawing to their beds, making jokes about old bones and early nights. Felicity contemplated doing the sensible thing and following them. Retiring to her bed and the moonlit landscape flying by outside her window, tuning into the clickety-clack of the wheels as they rocked her to sleep.

But she didn't.

'Well,' Jock said, standing, helping Thelma up as well. 'This is way past our bedtime and my indigestion is playing up so we'll be off too.'

Felicity smiled at them and bade them goodnight, excruciatingly conscious of Callum's eyes on her as she watched their companions disappear from the lounge.

And then there were two.

'Whew,' he murmured, his gaze brushing over her neck and mouth, a smile tilting his lips into an irresistible shape. 'I thought they'd never go to bed.'

Felicity blushed but she didn't deny the sentiment. She'd thought exactly the same thing.

He tipped his chin at her martini glass. 'Another drink?'

She hesitated. This was it. This was the moment. Was she going to be the sophisticated woman on the train or the girl next door?

'It's only eleven,' he coaxed. 'I promise to have you back to your compartment before you turn into a pumpkin.'

Oh, God, oh, God, oh, God. The man had a PhD in flirting. 'Yeah. Okay. Sure.'

He grinned. 'Good answer.'

Felicity's mouth quirked in an answering grin. 'Good question.'

She flat-out ogled him as he walked to the bar. She'd seen him in the café and had been struck by his presence but he'd seemed so brooding and intense, so closed off she hadn't bothered to go there. He hadn't put a foot wrong tonight, however.

Sure, there was still a brooding quality to the set of his shoulders and the line of his mouth, but he'd been witty and charming and great with all the oldies and, good Lord Almighty, the way he'd looked at her had been one hundred percent high-octane flirty.

Nothing brooding about it.

Even the way the man leaned against the bar was sexy. His expensive-looking charcoal trousers pulled nicely against his butt and hugged the hard length of his thighs.

And they *were* hard. And hot. She could still feel the imprint of them along her leg.

He'd worn a jacket to dinner but had since shed it to reveal a plain long-sleeved shirt of dark purple. The top two buttons had been left undone and about an hour ago he'd rolled up the sleeves to reveal tanned forearms covered in dark hair.

Those forearms had caused a cataclysmic meltdown in her underwear.

He turned slightly and smiled at her and Felicity sucked in a breath. The man was devastating when he smiled and it went all the way to his green eyes. It did things to his face, which was already far too handsome for any one man. Square jaw covered in dark, delicious stubble, strong chin, cheekbones that women would kill for and sandy-brown hair longer on the top and shorter at the sides.

Hair made to run fingers through.

His laughter drifted towards her as Travis handed over the drinks and said something she couldn't quite hear. She liked how it sounded. How it rumbled out of him. She got the sense he didn't do a hell of a lot of it, though, which was a shame. That laugh was turning her insides to jelly.

The military should employ him as a secret weapon.

He headed in her direction, his gait compensating for the

rock of the train. She probably should be glued to the window, watching the moonlit bush whizzing by, and not be so obvious, but she figured they were beyond the point of being coy and, frankly, he was too damn hard not to look at with his long stride and knowing smile.

He placed her glass down and sat opposite her this time, a low table between them. She couldn't decide if she was relieved or disappointed. Neither, she concluded as he filled her entire field of vision and everything else became pretty much irrelevant.

'To strangers on a train,' he said, lifting his whisky glass, that smile still hovering.

She tapped hers against it. 'I'll drink to that.'

CHAPTER TWO

FELICITY WAS CONSCIOUS of his gaze as it followed the press of her lips then lowered to the bob of her throat as she swallowed. She was grateful for the cold, crisp martini cooling her suddenly parched mouth.

'So…what's a *young 'un*—' he injected Jock's Scottish brogue into the words and Felicity smiled '—like yourself doing on a train with the cast from *Cocoon*? Lots more people your age down in the cheap seats. Unless… Wait, are you some kind of heiress or something?'

'No.' Felicity laughed at the apt description of their travelling companions and at the thought of her being some little rich girl, although she had inherited enough money from her grandfather to buy a small cottage. 'I'm not. And you don't look like you're of retirement age either. You're, what? Thirty-five?'

She'd been wondering how old he was all night and this seemed like as good an opener as any.

'Close,' he murmured. 'Thirty-four. And you?'

'Twenty-eight.'

'Ah…' He gave a long and exaggerated sigh. 'To be so young and carefree again.'

Felicity laughed at his teasing but was struck by the slight tinge of wistfulness. 'Oh, no,' she teased back. 'You poor old man.'

He grinned at her and every fibre of her being thrilled at being the centre of his attention. 'Seriously, though,' he said, sobering a little, 'why the train?'

'My grandfather was a railway man through and through. Fifty years' service as a driver and he never got tired of trains. Of talking about them, photographing them and just plain loving everything about them. We'd go on the train into the city every day when I used to stay with them in the school holidays and he'd take me to the train museum every time without fail.'

He frowned. 'Didn't that get boring after a while?'

Felicity shook her head. 'Nah. He always made it so exciting. He made it all about the romance of train travel and I lapped it up.'

'Romance, huh?' He raised an eyebrow as his gaze dropped to her mouth. 'Smart man.'

Felicity's belly flopped over. 'That he was.'

If tonight was anything to go by, her grandfather was a damn genius.

She stared into the depths of her frosty glass as her fingers ran up and down the stem. 'He spent his entire life saying that one day he was going to take my grandmother on the Indian Pacific for a holiday of a lifetime. Then, after my grandmother died when I was twenty, he used to tell me one day he and I would go on it together. He died last year, having never done it, but he left me some money so…here I am.'

The backs of Felicity's eyes prickled with unexpected tears and she blinked them away.

'Hey.' His hand slid over hers. 'Are you okay?'

'God, yes,' she said, shaking her head, feeling like an idiot. *Way to put a downer on the pick-up!* 'Sorry. I didn't mean to get so maudlin. I'm stupidly sentimental. Ignore me.'

'Nothing wrong with that.' He smiled, removing his hand. 'Better than being cold and hard.'

Felicity returned his smile. She appreciated his attempt to lighten the mood. Sometimes, though, she had to wonder. If she was a little more hard-hearted she probably wouldn't fret so much about her patients or become so personally involved. It would make it much easier to leave it all behind at the end of the day.

'What about you?' she said, determined to change the subject. To get things back on track. 'Why the train?'

'I guess I'm a bit like your grandfather. Always loved trains. Doing all the great train journeys of the world is a bucket-list thing for me and when I had to travel to Adelaide I thought, Why not?'

It was stupid to feel any kind of affinity with a man— this man—because he was a train guy. Especially when up until about eight hours ago she hadn't even known him. But somehow she did. Her grandfather had always said train people were good people and, even though he'd been biased, right at this moment Felicity couldn't have agreed more.

Callum was ticking *all* her boxes.

'So…' He took a sip of his whisky. 'Felicity…'

Goose-bumps broke out on her arms and spread across her chest, beading her nipples as he rolled the word around his mouth. She'd never heard her name savoured with such carnal intensity. It sure as hell made her wonder what it would sound like as he groaned it into her ear when he came.

Lordy. Another box ticked.

'Is that a family name?'

She cleared her throat and her brain of the sudden wanton images of him and her twisted up in a set of sheets. 'Nope. My mother just liked it, I think. And I don't really get called that anyway.'

'Oh?' He frowned. 'You get Fliss?'

Felicity grimaced. 'Flick, actually.'

'Flick.'

He rolled that around too but it didn't sound quite the same as when he'd used her full name. She didn't hate the nickname, she'd never known anything else, but she didn't want to be a Flick tonight.

Tonight she wanted to be *Felicity.*

She shrugged. 'My cousin couldn't pronounce my full name when she was little and it stuck.'

He lazed back in his chair, his long legs casually splayed

out in front of him, the quads moving interestingly beneath the fabric of his trousers. 'You don't look much like a Flick to me,' he mused.

Felicity's pulse fluttered as she suppressed the urge to lean across and kiss him for his observation. The sad fact was, though, in her everyday life she did look like a Flick. Her hair in its regulation ponytail, wearing her nondescript uniform or slopping around in her jeans and T-shirt.

'Thank you,' she murmured, raising her glass to him and taking a sip.

'My brother calls me Cal.'

Felicity studied him for a moment. 'Nope. You *definitely* don't look like a Cal.'

'No?'

Felicity smiled at the faux wounded expression on his face. 'No.'

'What *do* Cals look like?'

'Cals are the life of the party,' she said, happy to play along. 'They're wise-cracking, smart-talking, laugh-a-minute guys. You're way too serious for a Cal.'

He laughed but it wasn't the kind of rumbly noise she'd come to expect. It sounded hollow and didn't quite reach his eyes. *Crap.* She'd insulted him somehow. Way to turn a guy off, Flick.

She had to fix it. *Fix it, damn it!*

'Anyway,' she said, hoping like hell she sounded casual instead of panicked. Nothing like ruining their evening before it had progressed to the good bit. 'I like Callum. It's very…noble.'

A beat or two passed before he laughed again, throwing his head back. It was full and hearty with enough rumble to fill a race track. It rained down in thick, warm droplets and Felicity wanted to take her clothes off and get soaking wet.

The laughter cut out and he fixed her with his steady gaze. 'Just so you know, I'm not feeling remotely noble right now.'

Felicity's belly clenched hard and she swallowed. *Eep!* This was really going to happen. He downed his whisky and put the glass on the table. 'Would you like to come back to my compartment?'

She cursed her sudden attack of nerves. But this wasn't her. She didn't do this kind of thing. Could she pull it off?

'Hey,' he said, leaning forward at the hips and placing his hand over hers. 'We don't have to. I just thought...'

Yeah. He'd thought she was interested because she'd practically done everything but strip her clothes off and sit in his lap. *God, she must look like some freaked-out virgin.* Or some horrible tease.

Felicity could feel it all slipping away. She didn't want to pass this up, damn it, but she hadn't expected to feel so... conflicted about it when it came to the crunch.

So she did what she always did in lineball calls. She picked up her phone.

He quirked an eyebrow at her. 'What are you doing?'

'I'm asking Mike what he thinks I should do.'

A bigger frown this time. 'Mike?'

'Yeah. You know, the guy in my phone who talks to me and tells me stuff like why the sky is blue and where the nearest hairdresser is.'

He chuckled. 'Yours is a dude?'

She shrugged. 'You can choose and Mike sounds like Richard Armitage so it was a no-brainer.'

'And do you always let your phone decide such things?'

'Sometimes. It's the modern-day coin toss, right?'

He chuckled again. 'Well, this ought to be interesting.'

Felicity grinned as she pushed a button and brought her phone up closer to her mouth. 'Mike, should I go back to Callum's?'

The phone gave an electronic beep then a stylised male voice spoke in a sexy English accent. 'Is he good enough?'

They both laughed then he grabbed her wrist and brought the phone closer to his mouth. Her pulse point fluttered madly beneath his fingers as their gazes locked. A smile played on his mouth again as he spoke into the microphone, his eyes firmly fixed on her. 'He's very good, Mike.'

Felicity's toes curled in her pumps at the sexually suggestive reply. *That wasn't what Mike had meant.*

'Does he know how to treat a woman?'

He didn't laugh this time, just eyed her intently as he replied. 'Oh, yeah. He knows *exactly* how to treat a woman.'

'Then you don't need me to decide, Felicity.'

He released her hand, slowly, still holding her gaze with a red-hot intensity. 'Looks like the ball is in your court.'

Felicity's heart tripped as he fixed her with a gaze that left her in no doubt they were both going to be naked within about ten seconds of the door shutting. Her breath hitched but she was aware of Travis, still at the bar, in her peripheral vision.

What would he think if they left together? Would he gossip about it with the rest of the crew? Would everyone know in the morning that she and Callum had spent the night together?

If she was back home in Vickers Hill, *everyone* would know.

But she wasn't. Was she? She wasn't *Flick* here. She was *Felicity* and *nobody* knew her.

Felicity picked up her glass and swallowed the last quarter in three long gulps. She stood, her body heating as his lazy gaze took its sweet time checking her out. 'Your compartment or mine?'

He smiled, downed the last of his whisky and held out his hand. She took it, smiling also, tugging on his hand, impatient now she'd taken the first step to get on with it.

Jock entered the lounge at that moment and Felicity halted, letting go of Callum's hand immediately, like a guilty teenager. The older man was in a pair of tracksuit pants and a white singlet.

'Jock,' she said, smiling as she walked towards him,

aware of Callum close on her heels. 'Thought you'd be in the land of nod by now.'

Jock gave them a tight smile. 'So did I but...' He rubbed his chest. 'My indigestion is really giving me hell tonight. I thought I'd come and ask Travis for a glass of milk. That usually does the trick.'

Felicity felt the first prickle of alarm as she neared Jock. The subdued night-time lighting in the lounge hadn't made the sweat on his brow and the pallor of his face obvious.

'Jock?' She frowned. 'Are you okay?'

Callum stepped out from behind her, also frowning. 'You don't look very well.'

'You need to sit down, I think,' Felicity said, ushering him over to the closest chair.

'Do you have any cardiac history?' Callum asked as Jock swayed a little, reaching for the arm of the couch.

'No. Never had any ticker prob—'

Jock didn't get to finish his sentence. He grabbed his chest and let out a guttural cry instead, folding to his knees.

Adrenaline surged into Felicity's veins. *'Jock!'* she said, throwing herself down next to him.

But it was too late. He collapsed the rest of the way, splayed awkwardly on the floor. Felicity gave him a shake but there was nothing.

'He's having an MI,' Callum said as he helped Felicity ease Jock on his back.

Felicity blinked at the terminology. An MI, or myocardial infarction, was not a term a layperson used. Nonmedical people said heart attack. 'He doesn't have a pulse,' she said, feeling for his carotid.

'Oh, my God, what's wrong with him?' an ashen-faced Travis asked, hovering over them.

'I'll start compressions,' Felicity said, ignoring the bartender as more adrenaline surged into her system and she kicked into nursing mode.

'He's in cardiac arrest,' Callum said as he automatically

moved around until Jock's head was at his knees. Felicity admired the steadiness of his voice and the expert way he tilted Jock's jaw and gave his airway support.

Technical writer be damned.

'Do you guys keep a defib?' Callum demanded. 'Some kind of first aid kit? We need more help. And we need to figure out how to get him to an ambulance.'

Felicity couldn't agree more. She had no idea if that was possible but she knew they couldn't keep him alive indefinitely. Jock needed more than they could give him here on a luxury train in the middle of nowhere.

Things were looking grim for the travelling companion she'd grown fond of in just a few hours.

'Yes. We have a defib,' Travis said, his voice tremulous as Felicity counted out the compressions to herself. 'But I've never actually used it on a real person before.'

'It's fine. I'm a doctor,' Callum said, his voice brisk.

Felicity glanced at Callum, not surprised at the knowledge given his use of medical terminology and his total control of the scene.

'And I'm a nurse.'

He glanced at her but didn't say anything, just nodded and said, 'Go,' to Travis as he leaned down and puffed some breaths into Jock's mouth.

It was satisfying to see Jock's chest rise and fall. CPR guidelines had changed recently, focusing more on chest compressions for those untrained in the procedure. But for medical professionals who knew what they were doing airway and breathing still formed part of the procedure.

And old habits died hard.

Callum's training took over and all his senses honed as he rode the adrenaline high, doing what he did best—saving lives. Travis was back in under a minute, bringing a portable defibrillator, a medical kit and the cavalry, who arrived in varying states of panic. He tuned them all out as he grabbed the defibrillator, turned it on, located some pads, yanked up Jock's singlet and slapped them on his chest.

Even Felicity in her dress and heels, pumping away on Jock's chest beside him, faded to black as he concentrated on Jock. Once this was over—which could be soon if they couldn't revive Jock—he'd think about her being a nurse. About how they'd both lied. For now he just had to get some cardiac output.

Felicity stopped compressions while the machine was reading the rhythm. Callum opened the medical kit, relieved to find an adult resus mask. At least he could give Jock mouth to mask now.

The machine advised a shock.

'All clear,' Callum said, raising his voice to be heard above everyone talking over everyone else.

Felicity wriggled back. So did he as the room fell silent. The machine automatically delivered a shock, Jock's chest arcing off the floor.

'Recommence CPR,' the machine advised, and they both moved back in, Felicity pounding on the chest again as he fitted the mask and held it and Jock's jaw one-handed.

'Where's the nearest medical help?' Callum demanded of a guy with a radio who appeared to be the head honcho.

'We're about twenty clicks out of Condobolin. Ambulance will meet us at the station. A rescue chopper is being scrambled from Dubbo.'

'How long will it take to get to Condobolin?'

'The driver's speeding her up. Fifteen minutes tops.'

Callum wasn't sure Jock had fifteen minutes, especially if he wasn't in a shockable rhythm. He wished he had oxygen and intubation gear. He wished he had an IV and access to fluids and drugs. He wished he had that ambulance right here right now. And a cardiac catheter lab at his disposal.

But he didn't. He had a defibrillator and Felicity.

He glanced at her. He didn't have to ask to know she was thinking the same thing. Fifteen minutes was like a lifetime in this situation, where every second meant oxygen starvation of vital tissues.

'Piece of cake,' she muttered, a small smile on her lips, before returning her attention to the task at hand.

He smiled to himself as he leaned down to blow into the mask. There was controlled panic all around him, with orders being given and radio static and the loud clatter of wheels on the track as the train sped to Condobolin. Somewhere he could vaguely hear poor Thelma sobbing. But amidst it all Felicity was calm and determined and so was he. Fifteen minutes? He'd done CPR for much longer.

'Check rhythm.'

Felicity stopped so the machine could do its thing. When it recommended another shock they followed the all-clear procedure again and once more the entire lounge fell silent, apart from Thelma's sobs.

Jock's chest arced again but this time it was successful.

'Normal rhythm,' the machine, no bigger than a couple of house bricks, pronounced.

Felicity gasped, a broad smile like the rising sun breaking over her face. 'I've got a pulse,' he confirmed, grinning back. 'Jock?' Callum pulled the mask away. 'Can you hear me, Jock?'

Jock gave a slight moan and made a feeble attempt to move a hand. 'Jock? Jock!' Thelma threw herself down beside them.

'Is he okay?' she asked, looking first at Callum then at Felicity through puffy red eyes.

'We got him back,' Callum said. Both of them knew he wasn't out of danger but it was something.

Felicity reached across and squeezed Thelma's arm. 'He's still very unstable,' she said gently. 'But it's a good sign.'

Callum was relieved when the train pulled into the station, even if the strobing of red and blue lights around the iron and tin structure of the roof created a bizarre discotheque. Very quickly a drowsy Jock was transported out of the train to the ambulance, accompanied by a paramedic, Callum, Felicity, Thelma and the rail guy with the radio.

Finally Callum had access to oxygen and a heart monitor. It was worrying to see multiple ectopic beats and runs of ventricular tachycardia, though, and Callum crossed his fingers that Jock's heart would hold out until he got the primary cardiac care he so urgently needed.

Callum and the paramedic whacked in two large-bore IVs and then Felicity was helping Thelma into the ambulance and he was getting in the back with Jock. There was no question in his mind that he'd stay with the old man and hand over to the medivac crew when they landed at the airstrip in approximately fifteen minutes' time.

He glanced out the back window as the rig pulled away, the siren a mournful wail in the deserted streets of the tiny outback town. Felicity was framed in the strobing lights, staring after the ambulance. She looked exactly the way he suspected they all probably looked. A little shell-shocked as the adrenaline that had ridden them hard started to ebb.

But also strong and calm. As she had been throughout.

This was not how he'd pictured tonight would end, and as the mantle of regret settled into his bones he knew their moment had passed.

He watched her with a heavy heart until she faded from sight.

CHAPTER THREE

FELICITY LAY AWAKE on her bed an hour later, staring out the window. The train was still stationary at Condobolin station, which was in darkness after the ghoulish flashing of emergency lights. Her compartment was also in darkness, except for the slice of light coming in from the hallway through her open door.

Callum hadn't returned and she couldn't sleep.

After the ambulance had disappeared she'd gone back to her compartment and showered, standing beneath the spray shaking like a leaf as the adrenaline that had sustained her during the emergency had released her from its grip.

She'd waited around in the lounge for a while after they'd gone, thinking Callum would be back soon. Some of her fellow passengers joined her, curious to know what was happening, but they didn't linger and eventually Donald had urged her to go back to her compartment and try and get some sleep.

But she couldn't. It was hard to shut her brain down after what had transpired.

She was about to give up, switch her light on and grab a book out of her bag when Callum strode by her door.

'Oh…hi,' he said, obviously surprised to see her awake and her door open as he pulled up short. She'd deliberately left it ajar because she didn't want to miss his return.

Felicity sat up and swung her legs over the side of the bed. 'You're back.' She stood and took a couple of paces towards him, conscious, as he took up all the space in her doorway, of how different she looked now in loose yoga pants and T with bare feet, compared to the high-heeled, little-black-dress woman he'd been flirting with earlier.

He looked exactly the same. Only sexier. His calm and control when everyone else around them had been losing their heads had kicked his good looks up to a whole other level.

Why was competence so damn attractive?

'How's Jock? Did the medivac transfer go smoothly?'

'Not really. He went into VF while we were waiting for the plane and we had to shock him twice to get him back.'

Felicity pressed her hand to her mouth, a hot spike of concern needling her. 'I was worried something was going down. You were gone so long.'

'I stuck around and helped them stabilise him for transport.'

'Of course.' They'd have wanted to have everything as controlled as possible before they loaded him on the chopper to avoid any chance of midair deterioration. 'What are his chances, do you think?' she asked, folding her arms.

'I don't know. He's not very stable at the moment. It's a forty-minute chopper flight to Dubbo hospital and by that time he'll be about ninety minutes post–cardiac tissue injury. He's inside the window, so fingers crossed, with some tertiary management he should be okay. I'll check on him when we get into Adelaide tomorrow.'

Felicity nodded. 'I guess we're going to be kind of late into Adelaide.'

'I guess we are. Although Donald reckons they'll be able to make up a lot of the time.'

'I'm in no hurry,' she said, and gave him a smile because she could stay on this train and look at him for a decade and it probably still wouldn't be long enough.

He smiled back, his gaze locking with hers. 'Neither am I.'

There was silence for a beat or two while they just stood and smiled at each other in some weird moment of shared intimacy as only two people who'd been through such a high-stakes ordeal could.

The train moved forward unexpectedly and jostled him inside the compartment, bringing him a step closer. He ducked his head down to glance out the window. 'Looks like we're off.'

'Yes,' Felicity said, as she half turned to find the darkened station platform appearing to slowly move.

When she turned back he was staring at her with heat in his eyes. They'd been flirty earlier but now they were just plain frank. His gaze dropped to her mouth as he took a step towards her. Her breath hitched. The atmosphere thickened and pulsed with promise.

She'd resigned herself to this not happening but suddenly it was on again.

'So…' She swallowed to moisten her suddenly parched throat as he loomed big and broad and close enough to reach out and touch. '*Not* a technical writer, huh?'

He cocked an eyebrow. '*Not* a public servant?'

She shrugged. 'I didn't want to be regaled with a dozen different medical stories or be canonised as some kind of saint.'

'You're forgetting about the lectures on the state of the health-care system.'

She laughed. 'Those too.'

Felicity supposed she should ask him more about his medical background but right now she didn't care. Not with her pulse fluttering madly at her temple and warmth suffusing her belly. 'You were great out there.'

'So were you.'

'Not quite what I expected would happen tonight.'

He smiled. 'Me neither.' And then, 'Are you…okay? It was kind of intense. The adrenaline was flowing.'

'Sure, steady as a rock.' Felicity held up a hand horizontally. It betrayed her completely by trembling.

'So I see.'

Felicity glanced from it to him, conscious of the sway of the train. Conscious that she was far away from Vickers Hill.

It emboldened her.

'That's not from the accident.'

Her hand was trembling for reasons that were far more *primal*.

He regarded her for long moments before turning slightly and reaching for the door behind him to shut it. He turned the lock with a resounding click, the noise slithering with wicked intent to all her secret places.

They were truly alone now.

Darkness pressed in on her, the only light entering from the strip at the bottom of the door and the moonlight pushing in through the window. It was enough to allow her eyes to adjust quickly.

Enough to see Callum.

He turned to face her, stepped closer, so close his breath warmed her forehead. He reached for her hand, which had fallen by her side. 'Maybe you just need to…' he slid her hand onto his chest, flattening it over his heart, his big hand holding hers in place '…grab hold of something solid?'

Felicity dropped her gaze to their joined hands. Each thud of his heart reverberated through her palm, scattering awareness to every cell of her body. She'd never had a one-night stand or done anything so spontaneous. But on a night when she'd been reminded how precarious life could be she needed it.

She needed this. She needed him.

The clickety-clack of the wheels on the track faded. 'Maybe I do,' she murmured, the scent from his citrusy cologne filling her senses until she was dizzy with wanting him.

Like a slice of lime after a shot of tequila.

His kiss, when it came, was gentle. So gentle it almost

made her cry. It was long and slow and sweet. It was every-thing she hadn't known she needed in this moment.

Earlier, if she'd been asked how this would go down, she would have said fast and furious. But this was infinitely bet-ter. Burning slow and bright, building in increments that piled on top of the next, making her yearn and ache and want even as it soothed and sated.

His hands slid around her waist. Her arms snaked around his neck. He drew her closer. She lifted up onto tiptoe.

Their hearts thundered together.

When he finally pulled away, they were both breathing hard. His eyes roved over her face, glittering with the kind of fever that also burned in her. What was he looking for?

Permission. *Sub*mission?

He had it.

'I knew you'd taste this good,' he muttered, the low, husky rumble stroking right between her legs.

His next kiss wasn't long and sweet and slow. It was hot and fast and dirty. Just as she'd imagined it would be. His lips were firm and insistent, his tongue seeking entry, which she gave him on a greedy moan. His hands slid under her T-shirt, tightening her belly and heating her blood to well past boiling.

She was so damn hot and horny she could barely see. She certainly couldn't think. All she could do was feel. And surrender.

Her bra snapped open and she gasped and pressed into his palm when his hand cupped a breast.

'God,' he murmured against her mouth. 'You feel good.'

Felicity moaned as his thumb taunted her erect nipple. 'Don't stop.'

He did, but only temporarily as he whisked both her T-shirt and bra off. 'Oh, yes,' he muttered, as he drank in the sight of her bare breasts, one hand sliding around her back, pulling her closer as he lowered his head to the opposite nipple and drew it deep into the warm cavern of his mouth.

Felicity sucked in a breath, her back arching, her hand sinking into the silky softness of his hair. His mouth tugged relentlessly at the nipple and it was equal parts delicious and dangerous. A tingling between her legs built with every hot swipe of his tongue as if he was licking her there instead.

Just then the train clacked loudly and jostled them apart as it got up to speed. Felicity held on to him, her hands curling around his biceps as their bodies lurched to the movement. His hard thighs bracketed hers, steadying them.

Hell. She'd forgotten she was even on a train. The noise of the wheels on the track and the sway was something she'd quickly become accustomed to.

And nothing outside the havoc of his mouth had registered.

'How about we get horizontal?' he suggested, his lips buzzing her neck, his big hands anchored to the small of her back. 'Before we injure ourselves?'

Felicity laughed at the imagery of them being found by Donald in the morning sprawled on the floor, her still half-naked.

God, this was totally insane.

She couldn't believe she was doing it. Getting down and dirty in her train compartment with a comparative stranger.

It was exciting and titillating and scandalous and there was nothing she wanted more.

She slid her hands onto his and eased them off her, keeping hold of him as she walked backwards the two paces required to reach her bed. The backs of her thighs hit her mattress and she sat down, looking up at him, their hands still joined.

She eased her legs apart slightly and was thrilled when he stepped between them. He released himself from her grip and cupped her face with both of his hands.

'You're beautiful,' he murmured.

'You're not so bad yourself.' There was a classic beauty

to the angle of his jaw, the blade of his cheek, the cut of his mouth.

Lordy, that mouth.

He smiled, his fingers burrowing into her hair. 'Lie back.'

Felicity shook her head as her gaze zeroed in on his fly, which was, most conveniently, at eye level. 'Soon,' she muttered, reaching out to walk her fingers along the thick bulge testing the strength of his zipper.

He sucked in a breath and a dizzying hit of sexual power surged through her system.

'I don't think that would be a good idea,' he said, but the subtle increase in pressure through his finger pads on her scalp betrayed his true desire.

'You don't like?' she asked, blinking up at him with as much innocence as she could muster.

'Oh, no,' he said with a shaky laugh. 'I like. Probably won't last too long, though. It's been…a bit of a dry spell.'

Felicity didn't understand why that titbit of information should make her so happy, but it did. She liked the idea of being the one to break his drought.

He was breaking hers after all.

'Just a little taste.' She smiled as she reached for his belt buckle.

He dropped his hands and let her have her way. Triumph pulsed through her system, rich and heady, quickening her heartbeat and tingling at the juncture of her thighs.

Her hands trembled as she undid his belt then popped the button. She glanced at him as her fingers toyed with the zipper tab. He was watching her, his eyes hooded, his mouth full and brooding.

She couldn't wait to feel it on her again. Her mouth. Her neck. Her breasts.

Lower.

But for now it was her turn. Her mouth.

Felicity's pulse tripped as she slid the zip down and the fabric peeled back to reveal his impressive girth stretching the limits of his briefs. She looked up at him, her pulse skipping a beat to find him still watching her intently. Locking her gaze with his, she slid a hand up his thigh, inside his underwear and grasped the steely length of his erection.

He shut his eyes and groaned as she pulled it free. The sound was low and needy, sluicing over her like warm rain. His hand slid onto her shoulder and squeezed before his eyes drifted open again.

She made sure he was focusing on her before she transferred her attention to the solid weight of him in her palm and thanked whoever was the patron saint of trains for that strip of light at the bottom of the door allowing her a visual she was never going to forget.

He was big and hard and perfect. Thick and long. And for tonight—what was left of it—*hers*.

She leaned forward, placed her lips against the rigid perfection of him, kissing him there like he had first kissed her. Slowly and gently, testing things out, discovering his contours and the heady aroma of him, teasing him a little with her light kisses.

It wasn't until his quad started to tremble beneath her palm that she realised the level of control he was exercising. She glanced at him, seeing it in the taut planes of his face, feeling it in his grip on her shoulder. So she shut her eyes and let him have it all, leaning forward, pleasuring him with her mouth, taking him in as far as she could.

'Yes-s-s,' he hissed, sliding both hands into her hair. 'Yes.'

His gratification spurred her on and she went harder, revelling in the husky timbre of his breath and the utter hedonism of giving oral pleasure to a man she barely knew while she was topless in the privacy of a luxury train compartment.

She felt wild and reckless and completely wanton.

So freaking *James Bond*.

And she was never going to forget this night as long as she lived.

'Oh, God,' he groaned. 'We have to stop.'

But Felicity barely heard him. She was swept away in the moment, her pulse roaring through her ears.

It wasn't until he said, 'Stop,' again and pulled away that Felicity tuned back in.

'Sorry,' he panted. 'I'm too close...'

His forehead was scrunched, his lips tight. He looked in pain and completely undone, looming over her almost fully dressed, still potently aroused but somehow achingly vulnerable.

He didn't look like a man who was used to that state of being. His vulnerability hit her hard in the soft spongy spot that was never too far from the surface. She'd give him just about anything right now.

'What do you need?'

'To be in you.' He ducked down and kissed her hard. 'Now.'

The compartment tilted as the dizzying effects of the kiss continued even after it had finished.

Him in her? Now? *That* she could accommodate.

She shimmied back on the bed, dragging her yoga pants and underwear off in the process, aware of him watching the jiggle of her breasts with laserlike focus.

'Well?' she said as she wriggled to the centre of the bed, her nipples responding blatantly to his unashamed gaze. 'Am I the only one getting naked?'

'Nope.' He grinned, immediately toeing off his shoes and hauling his still-buttoned shirt over his head.

Watching him strip was sexy. Him *watching her* watch him strip even more so.

Felicity salivated at the perfection of his chest. It was wide at the shoulders, narrow at the waist. The muscles of his abdomen were defined but not excessively. Tanned and smooth, there was only a fine trail of hair trekking south from his belly button.

She wanted to kiss his chest. Smell it. Lick it. Stroke her fingers over the hills and valleys of his abs, trail them between his hips and watch how it turned him on. Feel the weight of it as he pressed her into the bed.

He stripped off his trousers and underwear together, revealing long, lean legs—more athletic than meaty. Before kicking them away he quickly retrieved his wallet from his back trouser pocket and plucked out a foil packet.

'Condom,' he said, as he took the two paces to her bed.

Felicity smiled as she let her gaze roam over every inch of his body. He was six feet plus of lean male animal and he was hers. 'Just the one?'

He put a knee on her mattress, tossing the packet near a pillow. 'We'll improvise.' He smiled.

And then he was lying on his side next to her, his head propped on his hand, his other hand trailing down her neck, through the valley between her breasts, down to her stomach, swirling around her belly button before continuing south all the way down through the soft curls of her pubic hair, stopping just before he reached ground zero.

Felicity's breath hitched as his finger hovered, taunting her. She doubted she'd last long either if he were actually to touch her.

She groped for the foil packet and thrust it at his chest. *His totally freaking awesome chest.* 'In me. Now. Remember?'

He smiled, his finger circling just out of reach. 'I can play a little first.'

She shook her head. 'It's been a while for me too.'

He regarded her for a moment before taking the condom and easing onto his back to roll it on. It was a position Felicity couldn't resist, taking advantage of his momentary distraction to move on top of him, straddling his hips, his fully sheathed erection sliding deliciously through the slick heat between her legs.

'God,' he muttered, his hands drifting up her belly to her breasts. 'You look magnificent.'

Felicity smiled as she arched her back and rubbed herself up and down the length of him. 'I feel pretty damn magnificent right now.'

His thumbs brushed her nipples and she shut her eyes, revelling in the heady glow of sexual abandonment for a moment or two.

But it just wasn't enough.

Her eyelids fluttered open to find him watching her again with an intensity that practically melted her into a puddle. She held his gaze as she leaned forward, tilting her pelvis and grasping his girth. His hands fell to her hips as she guided him to where she was slick and ready.

Where she *needed* him to be.

The feel of him there, so thick and *big*, was incredible. His eyes on her as she slowly sank down and he filled her— stretched her—was a whole different level. Felicity gasped as she settled flush against him, leaning forward with outstretched arms, bracing her hands on his shoulders, steadying herself as she took a breath.

'So good,' she muttered.

'God, *yes*,' he panted.

And it was. *So good.* Too good to just sit and do nothing. Too good not to move. Not to flex up and down and back and forth and round and round. Too good not to find a rhythm that was perfect and would drive them both towards a conclusion that had been building between them all night.

Her fingernails curled into his shoulders, his fingers gripped her hips like steel bands as they did just that, staring into each other's eyes as the tempo picked up, finding a rhythm and an angle that tripped her switch. His fingers slid between her legs again, not teasing this time but going straight to the spot she needed it most and rubbing sure and hard.

Nothing fancy. Just merciless pressure.

'God, yes,' Felicity gasped, drumming her feet behind her on the bed, riding him harder, faster as the fabric of her world started to tear from the inside out. Her thighs trembled, her nails dug in a little harder, her belly pulled taut.

Her orgasm hit hard roaring from a tiny quiver to an all-consuming pleasure storm within seconds.

'Yes,' he muttered, working her harder, faster, vaulting upright to press his lips to her neck, whispering, 'Yes, yes, yes,' as she slid her arms around his shoulders and came apart in his arms.

He flipped her on her back then, his forehead pressed into her neck, driving in faster and faster, sustaining her pleasure as he reached his own, groaning long and low into her ear as he came hard, sweat slicking the valley between his shoulder blades, his biceps trembling, her name on his lips as he spent himself inside her until he had no more to give and they both lay panting to the rock and sway of the train.

CHAPTER FOUR

CALLUM WAS EATING breakfast the next morning when Felicity finally put in an appearance. He'd left her sleeping two hours ago when the train had pulled into Broken Hill and woken him. It hadn't woken her and he'd told a hovering Donald not to wake her for the tour she'd been booked on or for breakfast.

'Of course,' he'd said, nodding his head. 'It was a late one, wasn't it?'

Callum's smile had been noncommittal. Little did Donald know just how late it had been. They'd enjoyed two more rounds of 'inventive' sex due to lack of protection. He'd only managed two hours' sleep.

But, then, insomnia had been part of his life for the last two years. He'd learned that lying around in bed, willing himself back to sleep, was counterproductive. Ignoring the tour options, he'd showered and gone through some more of his reading, as well as contacting his ride to let her know to delay her pick-up.

'Good morning,' Felicity said as she sat in the empty chair opposite him. Callum had been staring out the window, watching the scenery flash by, as he sipped his third cup of coffee. He had his sunglasses on to deal with the excessive sunlight flooding in through the glass because the view was too good to pass up.

He smiled at her. She looked fresh from the shower in jeans and a T-shirt, her wet hair pulled back into a ponytail low on her nape. An image of her riding him last night, honey-blonde strands flying loose around her bare shoulders, slid into his mind unbidden.

'It is,' he agreed. 'A very good morning.'

A small smile touched her mouth before a blush stole across her cheekbones and she dropped her gaze to the tablecloth briefly before raising it again. 'You're kind of chipper for someone who didn't get a lot of sleep.'

Callum shrugged. 'Some things are worth losing sleep over.'

'Absolutely.' She looked like she was about to say more but one of the wait staff interrupted, filling Felicity's cup with coffee. 'About last night...' she said after they departed, spooning in some sugar and stirring absently.

She seemed wary and unsure suddenly, staring at the circling spoon, reluctant to meet his gaze. Alarm bells rang in his head and his hair prickled at his nape. Was she going to suggest that they make it something more? Was she going to ask for his number? Or a date? Was she going to morph into some kind of clingy, bunny-boiler who wanted some kind of relationship?

Because, as incredible as it had been—and it had been *incredible*—he just didn't have time and space in his life at the moment for a romantic entanglement. He was trying to get his life back on track and last night had purely been the inevitable end to a couple of hours of flirting and one massive adrenaline hit.

Hadn't it?

Hell. He didn't even know her last name.

'I don't...' She placed her spoon on the saucer and glanced at him. 'I don't usually do this kind of thing.'

Callum nodded. There wasn't one part of him that thought she did. 'Yeah. I got that.'

'Not that I think,' she hastened to add, 'there's anything wrong with *hooking up*. It's just not...me, you know? Well, of course you know because I'm totally screwing this up in a very unsophisticated way, *exactly* like I've never done this before, but look...I live in this small town where everybody knows everybody else and they're all in each other's business and all the guys my age there think of me as Flick so I don't often get the opportunity to...'

He waited for her to continue but she appeared to have run out of steam. Callum couldn't figure out where she was going with this. Was the reason she was telling him she was a small-town girl her way of saying her daddy had a gun and he was now part of the family whether he liked it or not?

'Oh, God, sorry.' She grimaced, covering her face with her hand before dropping it again and shaking her head. 'I'm babbling. I *swore* I wouldn't babble.'

Callum laughed, which surprised the hell out of him. She really was quite cute when she was flummoxed. 'It's fine, don't worry about it. I'm not judging you and there *were* extraordinary circumstances last night.'

'Sure.' She picked up her cup and sipped, her gaze zeroing in on his. 'But you and I both know we were heading to bed even before our adrenaline-induced recklessness.'

There was no point denying that one. In fact, he was damn certain they'd have done it more than three times had their flirting not been so catastrophically interrupted.

'You're very direct, aren't you?' He liked that.

She laughed. 'Usually yes. Although not so much right now. It's the nurse in me.' She glanced out the window for a beat or two before looking at him again. 'What I'm trying to say—*very inelegantly*—is that I hope you don't think...I mean *want* or expect even...that this is anything more than just last night. Just two strangers on a train, in a...bubble almost. Indulging in something spontaneous. I mean, I like you but...hell, I don't even know your last name or where you live or what kind of doctor you are or even if you're going on to Perth.'

Callum opened his mouth to tell her it was okay. He got it. He felt exactly the same way about what had happened between them. About spontaneity. About getting out of his head and just not being himself for a night. But she held up her hand to ward it off.

'No. Don't tell me. I don't want to know any of it either. I'd kind of like to keep this whole thing as a big, delicious secret. This…crazy thing I did once that'll make me smile whenever I think about it. Maybe…' she smiled '…scandalise my grandkids about it one day.'

Grandkids. Of course there'd be grandkids. And kids. With honey-blonde hair and grey eyes. She was young and, despite what she said about the guys in her town, he had no doubt someone would snap her up.

Whereas he couldn't even look that far ahead.

'So,' Callum said, forcing himself to lighten the mood, 'you just want to use me for my body and callously walk away? Pretend it never happened?'

She pulled her bottom lip between her teeth as she nodded and said, 'Yes.' She toyed with her spoon again. 'Does that make me a terrible person?'

Callum chuckled at the little frown knitting her brow. He'd never met a woman who was such a compelling mix of confidence and uncertainty. 'No,' he teased. 'Relax. It was one night. We barely know one another. I promise you haven't broken my heart and I'm not about to drop down on one knee and ask you to marry me. You are not a terrible person and we should absolutely go our own ways after this with a smile on our faces and *very* fond memories of our night.'

'Is that how you're going to remember it?' she asked, placing her elbow on the table and propping her chin on her fist. 'Fondly?'

She was teasing now and he liked it. '*Very* fondly.'

She grinned. 'Me too.'

'Good. Now…' he thrust the breakfast menu at her '…order your breakfast. You *must* be hungry.'

Her gaze dropped to the menu but he could still see the smile playing on her mouth as she muttered, *'Starving.'*

Felicity ate like the train was about to run out of food. She was absolutely famished from her vigorous night between the sheets. Callum laughed at how much she put away and the happy little bubble around her grew.

It continued when they moved to the lounge. Jock's heart attack was a hot topic with their fellow travellers and everyone was agog at how they'd saved Jock's life. They were so impressed they didn't seem to mind the fact that both she and Callum had lied to them about what they did.

Or at least they didn't call them on it anyway.

The day flew and before Felicity knew it the train was rolling through the outer suburbs of Adelaide, bringing her closer and closer to home. She was treating herself to a few days in the city first, though. The last week in October was a perfect time to do her Christmas shopping and also hit the beach before the full tilt of summer. There were no beaches in the Clare Valley. Vineyards and antique shops, amazing restaurants with gourmet offerings and dinky little tearooms for sure, but no beach.

It was back to work on Monday and the magical time she'd spent in Sydney with her best friend Luci and the train trip and last night would all soon be pushed to the side as she morphed back into Flick and her life revolved around work and small-town life.

So she was going to savour this for as long as she could.

Half an hour later the train had pulled up at the platform and she was saying goodbye to her fellow travellers and Donald as she disembarked. A part of her wanted to stay on for ever, stay in this bubble for ever with Callum. But it was neither real nor possible so she channelled Flick and let it go, stepping onto the platform.

'Well, I guess this is goodbye.'

Felicity took a calming breath as Callum's familiar sexy rumble washed over her. She turned to face him, struck again by how sexy he was as her gaze roamed over his face, trying to remember every detail.

She was curiously reluctant to say goodbye. What did she say to a man who'd given her a moment in time she was

never going to forget? Who had made her body sing? Who
had made her feel sexy and desired?

Thank you just didn't seem enough.

'Do you have someone picking you up or...?'

Maybe they could catch a lift together? Maybe if he was
also in the city for a few days they could...?

'We could share a taxi if you like. Where are you heading?'

'Oh, no, it's fine,' he said. 'I have someone picking me up.'

Of course. It was better this way really. A clean break.

'In fact...' he looked past her shoulder '...I think that
may be her.'

Her. A sick moment of dread punched Felicity in the gut.
She hadn't even asked him if he was involved with someone. She'd just assumed...

'Dr Hollingsworth?'

Felicity blinked at another very familiar voice as Callum waved and said, 'Over here.' She turned to find Mrs
Baker, the wife of Vickers Hill's police chief, heading in
their direction.

What the...?

'Mrs B.?'

'Oh, Flick, darling.' She smiled and pulled her into a big
bear hug. 'What a surprise! Oh, wait...did I get my wires
crossed? Julia was supposed to come but one of the recep-
tionists had to go home sick, which left them short-staffed
so she was ringing around to find someone else. I left a
message on her phone that I'd do it but maybe she didn't
check it and had already arranged for you to do the pick-up?'

Felicity had absolutely no idea what the other woman
was talking about. 'The pick-up?'

'Yes.' Mrs Baker nodded. 'For Dr Hollingsworth here.'

Dr Hollingsworth? Felicity glanced at Callum. *He* was
Dr Hollingsworth? The new locum? The one who'd done
the house swap with Luci?

'*You're* Dr Hollingsworth?'

He frowned, obviously confused now too. 'Yes.'

Oh, hell... *What had they done?*

'So you're not here to pick him up?' Mrs Baker asked, looking as perplexed as Felicity but oblivious to her inner turmoil.

'No.' She shook her head. 'We've been on the train together. I just didn't...' she glanced at Callum '...know it.'

'Oh, how delightful.' Mrs Baker beamed. 'What a co-incidence.'

Hmm. *Delightful* wasn't the way Felicity would describe it. She'd slept with the locum? A man she was going to have to face every day for two months?

How could they pretend it had never happened now?

'So...you know one another?' Callum asked, frowning at both of them, obviously trying to put the pieces together.

'Oh, yes.' Mrs Baker nodded vigorously. 'Flick's one of the practice nurses at Dr Dawson's surgery, aren't you, dear?'

Felicity watched as realisation slowly dawned on Callum's face. 'Oh. Right.'

'Isn't that an amazing coincidence?' Mrs Baker repeated.

'Yes...amazing,' he murmured through lips that were so tight Felicity worried they might spontaneously split open. *Fabulous.*

The man looked like he wanted to disappear. Or, at the very least, hightail it out of town. Felicity didn't know whether to be sad, mad, insulted or to push him back on the damn train herself.

'Right, well...' Mrs Baker said, still oblivious to the thick air of *what-the-hell* between them. 'Did you want a lift back home too, dear? Only we really do have to hit the road. It's a good two-hour drive, more with the peak-hour traffic.'

'Oh, no, thank you,' Felicity said, dragging her gaze off the incredulity in Callum's green eyes. 'I'm staying on for a few days.' *Thank God!* 'I'm not back till Sunday.'

'Oh, that's nice. Doing some Christmas shopping or seeing some bloke you're not telling any of us about?' Mrs Baker nudged her arm playfully.

Hardly. Given the last bloke she'd *seen* was now a certified disaster. She returned the older woman's good-natured teasing with a wan smile, changing the subject. 'Well, you're right, you'd better be off. Say hi to everyone and I'll see them all on Monday.'

She forced herself to look at Callum like he was just some guy she'd met on the train and not someone she'd torn up the sheets with in what had been, without a doubt, the most memorable—and now the most disastrous—time of her life.

'It was nice meeting you, Dr Hollingsworth,' she said, willing a smile to her lips. She wasn't entirely sure she'd managed it but she ploughed on. 'I look forward to working with you over the next couple of months.'

About as much as shoving a rusty fork in her eye.

He nodded, his mouth set in the grim line she'd first seen back at Central Station in Sydney. God—had it only been yesterday?

'Yes,' he said. 'Can't wait.'

He looked like he could do with a rusty fork too.

And then, because there *was* actually someone watching her, Mrs Baker was ushering him along and out of the station and she was staring at his back. His chinos encasing those long athletic legs, his T-shirt stretching over those big shoulders, his hair brushing his nape.

A back she'd seen naked. A back she was damn sure she'd scratched up a little at one stage. Felicity shut her eyes and allowed herself an internal groan. How was she going to work with him every day and not think about their night together?

Not remember the bunch of his muscles under her hands as he'd loomed over her, the smell of his cologne on his neck, the deep groan when he'd orgasmed—*three times.*

Not relive every moment in glorious Technicolor?

Not want a repeat performance?

CHAPTER FIVE

FELICITY ALWAYS ARRIVED at work at seven in the morning. The practice didn't open until eight but she liked to grab a cup of tea and set things up at a leisurely pace. She liked to go through each of the doctors' appointment books as well as her own to mentally prepare herself for the day.

This morning she was here at seven because she hadn't been able to sleep. She'd driven into town deliberately after dark yesterday so no one could just drop in for a chat. She'd spent three days in Adelaide, trying to figure out a strategy to deal with Callum, and she still wasn't any closer.

She wasn't worried that anyone would find out. She didn't think Callum would be indiscreet. He didn't look like the kiss and tell type.

But *she* knew. Her *body* knew.

She'd been okay with acting so wildly outside her usual character when it had been a one-off. And she'd been fine to walk away from it and get back to the life she knew, loved and understood. The place, the people, the work that defined her. But with him constantly reminding her of something sizzling and exciting?

Constantly derailing her contented life?

She didn't need that kind of disquiet. She'd been lucky. She'd already had her big love. She didn't need some crazy, hot thing with a guy who was here for two months making her question all she held dear.

And even if she'd been actively looking for a man—which she wasn't—Callum did not fit the bill. She was only interested in long-term prospects and she was perfectly happy to wait. For it to happen when it happened. *If* it happened.

There wasn't any rush despite what every woman of a certain age in Vickers Hill thought.

The kettle boiled and Felicity shook herself out of her reverie. She was getting way ahead of herself. Catastrophising as usual. Also being a little egotistical. *Like she was so freaking irresistible.* Just because the man had ravished her in bed all night didn't mean he wanted anything more from her or that he wanted to carry on while he was here.

She was making way too much of it. It was two months, for Pete's sake. She could do *anything* for two months. They'd talk, set some rules and then she'd be cool, calm and collected. Polite. Professional. Friendly even. Vickers Hill was a great place to live in the middle of a famous wine region—she could play tour guide.

Felicity heard the back door open and glanced at her watch. She frowned. Dr Dawson was early today, he didn't usually arrive until seven thirty sometimes. Now he was cutting back his hours a little on his countdown to retirement he left it as late as a quarter to eight.

Felicity had worked for Luci's father for four years and would be grateful to him for ever for employing her when she'd fled back to Vickers Hill, licking her wounds post-Ned.

She turned to greet him, a smile on her face, knowing he'd come straight to the staffroom for a cuppa. But it wasn't Dr Dawson. It was Callum standing in the doorway, all long legs and wide shoulders, looking devastating in a dark suit and patterned tie.

Her stomach dropped. Her fingers tightened around her mug. She swore muscles between her legs tightened in some kind of Pavlovian response as heat coursed to all the erogenous zones he'd taken his sweet time getting to know.

So much for being cool, calm and collected. If her body was any hotter she'd be smoking. 'Oh. Hi.'

He nodded, his gaze guarded, reminding her of the brooding guy in the café that day. 'Hi.'

Awkward.

But, then, she'd always known it was going to be.

'You're early,' she said, to sever the stretching silence. 'You know you don't start till one each day, right?'

She knew he'd been in a couple of times already, orientating himself to the practice, because she'd been talking to Luci, who'd rung to tell her that Callum's brother Seb had turned up on her doorstep in Sydney and he was now *living* with her, but had also mentioned Callum dropping in to see her father and introduce himself to everyone.

He shrugged. 'Thought I'd get settled in.' He walked into the room and set the small plastic crate he was holding on the dining table. 'I also wanted to go over the clinic charts for this week. You know...' he gave a half-smile but it was strained and tight '...be prepared.'

Felicity nodded stiffly. Oh, yeah, he was a regular Boy Scout.

In any other person, she would have been impressed by the diligence but she'd thought she'd have more time to get her game face on this morning so she wasn't feeling terribly charitable.

'You'll have access to the appointment calendar on your computer in your office,' she said. 'I'll send you an invite to join but I'll just grab the printout now.'

It was her chance to temporarily escape and get herself together. He didn't try to stop her and for the thirty seconds it took her to snatch the list of today's appointments off the reception desk she was grateful.

She needed a breather. To hit the reset button.

She stared down at the list, not really seeing it. The Dawson general practice was one of two in Vickers Hill. There were two GPs. Bill Dawson was the original and had founded the practice almost forty years ago. About twenty years later he'd taken on a partner—Angela Runcorn—because the work had been too much for one and he'd wanted to have a woman for his female patients to have a choice. He and Angela each owned fifty percent of the practice.

Four years ago, and this was why Felicity had been employed, he'd taken on a part-time GP—Meera Setu. Meera and Felicity ran the afternoon specialty clinics together, which freed up a lot of appointment time. Monday was ortho clinic, Tuesday was diabetic, Wednesday was babies and Friday was immunisation. There was no clinic on Thursdays as it was Felicity's day for home visits.

But, with Meera going on maternity leave last week for two months, Dr Dawson had needed a replacement and had advertised for a locum. Given that it was for such a short amount of time, Felicity hadn't paid much heed to the process other than encouraging Luci to go to Sydney to do her course and pushing her to do the house swap with Callum when the possibility had been floated.

Except she'd only heard him being referred to as Dr Hollingsworth. And she'd never bothered to find out Callum's last name when she'd been getting naked with him between her sheets.

She made a mental note to always find out a guy's full name before doing the wild thing. Because now she'd be working closely with Dr Wild Thing *every* day.

Like right-hand woman close. And it all could have been avoided had she stopped to find out the basics—like his name!

'Here it is,' she said, injecting a lightness into her tone as she re-entered the staffroom.

He was at the sink, spooning coffee into a mug. She placed the list on the table next to the crate because there was no way she was getting any closer to him when she didn't have to.

'Thanks,' he said, picking up his mug and leaning his butt against the counter, his feet casually crossed at the ankles, which pulled the fabric of his trousers tight across his thighs.

'I'll forward you the email folder with all their electronic charts in a bit.'

'Thank you.' The silence built again. 'I checked up on Jock. They transferred him to hospital in Sydney and put in several stents. He's doing okay.'

Felicity nodded. 'Yes. Thanks. I spoke with the hospital this morning.'

Thankfully a noise in the hallway outside alerted her to someone else arriving and Felicity almost kissed Dr Dawson as he sauntered into the staffroom, his usual chipper self.

'Ah, Flick.' He smiled as he embraced her in a warm hug that smelled of the starch Julia, Luci's mum, always ironed his shirts with. 'Good to have you back. We almost fell apart without you.'

Felicity laughed, ignoring Callum in her peripheral vision. 'I'm sure Courtney caught on pretty quickly.'

Dr Dawson chuckled in that way of his that made other people want to join in as he pulled out of the hug. 'Now, then, I see you've met Cal. I think you two are going to get along famously.'

Felicity smiled at her boss then nodded in Callum's general direction. 'Yes. Callum and I have met.' She couldn't bring herself to call him Cal—he'd always be Callum to her.

'Oh, call him Cal,' Dr Dawson said. 'That's right, isn't it, son?'

At almost seventy Bill called every male under forty 'son'. It was his term of endearment.

'Cal's fine,' Callum said, ambling over to the table and sitting down. 'Most people call me Cal.'

Dr Dawson nodded, looking pleased with himself. 'You're bright and early. If you're trying to impress me, it's working.'

'Thought I'd look at the clinic appointments for the week. Familiarise myself with some charts.'

'Jolly good idea.' Dr Dawson nodded. 'Must do the same myself. Better get to it. Monday morning is always a madhouse here. I'll just make myself a cuppa and do the same thing.'

'I'll make it and bring it in for you, Dr Dawson,' Felicity offered.

She loved Bill Dawson almost as much as she loved her own father but he made an unholy mess in the kitchen and, like a lot of men, seemed completely blind to it. Also, Callum was a little too close for comfort now.

'Oh, no, Flick. Julia would rouse on me if I made the nurses get me a cup of tea.'

Felicity smiled. She knew that was the truth. Julia Dawson had been a nurse for over twenty years before Luci, her change-of-life surprise package, had come along. She'd worked part time on Reception for many years at the practice once Luci had gone to school and still helped out when things got hectic.

There was no greater advocate for the practice nurses than Bill's wife.

'I'm offering,' Felicity said, shooing him away from the sink as she approached. 'It'll be our little secret, I promise.'

Dr Dawson capitulated easily. 'Thank you.' He grinned. 'I'll see you later, Cal,' he said, moving towards the door. 'Don't hesitate to ask if you have any questions. Pop your head in or ask Angela or even our girl Flick. She knows more than all of us put together.'

Felicity kept her back turned, fiddling with the mugs as she snorted self-deprecatingly, which produced more chuckles from Dr Dawson as he exited.

She was excruciatingly conscious of Callum's gaze burning into her back as she made two cups of tea. When she was done she picked them up and finally turned to face him. It was disconcerting to find him still watching her, his brow crinkled, his mouth set in a brooding line.

'I used to be a Cal,' he said. 'Felt like one too. The life

of the party. The centre of the world. The man of the moment. I used to be like that.'

Felicity wasn't sure what this was about. Was he annoyed all these days later that she'd told him he didn't look like a Cal? Because he didn't—not to her mind. *Especially not now.* Or was he trying to explain why he hadn't introduced himself as Cal right out of the blocks?

Or did he just miss that Cal guy and want to reminisce? She had to admit to being curious about him herself.

It was hard to figure out what he meant. He was so tense and shuttered, so hard to read. 'What happened?'

He shrugged, looking down into his mug. 'Life. Stuff.'

She nodded. She didn't know what he wanted her to say. Did he want her to push or leave it alone? Something had obviously happened to Callum to change him.

Was that why he was here? In the middle of freaking nowhere? Fourteen hundred kilometres from his amazing harbourside apartment that Luci had raved about?

'You're a long way from home,' she murmured.

'Yeah.'

Felicity almost gave up. It was like pulling teeth. But she'd always been stubborn. 'Because you wanted to trade water for wine? Or…because you're running away?'

He glanced up from his mug, piercing her with his eyes. Running away it was.

Best she remember that.

'Because I'm newly trained and thought some rural experience would be good.'

It was a sound reason. Most GPs who locumed in rural areas and weren't from rural areas did so for the experience. Somehow, though, she didn't think that's what was going on here.

But whatever. It wasn't any of her business.

'Right. Well…' She looked at the mugs in her hand. 'I better deliver this, we open in fifteen minutes. I'll email you those files in a bit. Have you been set up on the computer?'

'Yes.' He nodded. 'Thanks.'

Felicity gave him a weak smile as she headed towards the door. 'No worries. Just yell if you need anything.'

But she hoped like hell he didn't.

It was almost three hours later before Felicity got around to emailing the file, although she had managed to send the appointment calendar invite through to Callum before things had got too crazy.

In the mornings Felicity was a general dogsbody. From receptionist to nursing duties, she was a jack of all trades and Mondays were always busy. It was like medical conditions multiplied over the two-day break. Plus there was a new doctor starting so that always brought out the rubberneckers hoping for a glimpse.

Not that anybody had seen Callum yet, he was keeping his door firmly closed. A fact that didn't deter the Vickers Hill grapevine. They didn't need a sighting today. It was already in full swing because Mrs Mancini had spied him at the local supermarket, buying groceries at the weekend, and had declared him a bit of a catch.

She was surprised Mrs Mancini hadn't arrived with her gorgeous granddaughter who was a teacher at the local public school and who she'd been trying to marry off for the last two years. Three patients had already arrived bearing gifts of food for him.

Felicity picked up the plate of shortbread Mrs Robbins had brought with her. Her shortbread won the blue ribbon at the district fête every year and had been known to make grown men weep.

She took it with her to Callum's office. As far as she knew, he hadn't surfaced all morning and it was for him after all. She wanted to check he'd received the file and needed to get in there to set up for the orthopaedic clinic that started at one. There were three lots of plaster due to come off today and the plaster saw wasn't in the treatment room so it was probably in his office somewhere.

Also they needed to talk. Before the clinic. There were things to say. Although she wasn't sure how to start.

That's where the shortbread came in. If it all went badly, at least she could console herself with sugar.

She knocked on the door and opened it when she heard a muffled, 'Come in.'

Even dulled, his voice did wicked things to her pulse.

Damn. She was in trouble if his voice could make her legs weak through a closed door.

'Hey,' she said as she opened the door and shut it behind her then walked towards him all businesslike, concentrating on the plate of shortbread. 'I come bearing gifts.'

She glanced at him as she drew level with his desk and was pleased she was close enough to a chair should she collapse into it. *Glasses.* He was wearing glasses. Sexy glasses. The kind of trendy, designer wireless frames that hunky male models wore in advertisements for optometrists.

She wouldn't have thought he could look any sexier. *She'd seen him naked, for crying out loud.* But she'd been wrong. Callum with glasses was a whole other level.

'You wear glasses?'

It was possibly the dumbest thing she'd ever said. She might as well have said she'd carried a watermelon.

He peered at her over the top of those glasses. 'So do you.'

'Oh…yes.' She absently touched the frames she'd pushed to the top of her head. 'Just for reading and computer work.'

'Same here.' He took them off and tossed them on his desk and Felicity wished he'd put them on again.

He stared at her, obviously waiting for her to say something. 'Did you want something?' he asked, looking pointedly at the plate of shortbread.

His tone was brisk. Not unfriendly but businesslike. It

appeared she wasn't going to have to worry about any lines they'd crossed. He'd obviously retreated as far as he could.

It was just the bucket of cold water she needed.

'I came to check you'd received the file I sent you and to bring you these. Mrs Robbins made them for the new doctor. They're the best in the district. You also have a jar of Mrs Randall's rosella jam and Cindy Wetherall has made you a mulberry pie.'

He blinked. 'But...why?'

The incredulity in his voice would have been comical had it not been utterly genuine. Felicity shrugged. 'It's the country. That's how we welcome newcomers. Also there's a rumour going around town that the new doc is hot so you've gone to the top of the eligible list.'

'Eligible?'

'Yes, you know. Marriage, babies, the whole enchilada. We don't get a lot of new blood around here.'

His face morphed from mystified to horrified, which was another salient warning. He looked like two rusty forks would be welcome about now.

Obviously marriage and babies were not on his agenda. Or not in Vickers Hills anyway.

'What did you think you were going to get when you traded the city for the country?'

If her voice was a little on the tart side she didn't care. Honestly...for someone who'd come across as intelligent and articulate on the train, he was being rather obtuse.

'Not this.'

'Well...you'd better get used to it.' She plonked the plate of biscuits down. 'You're going to be well fed around here.'

He looked at them like they were a bomb that could possibly detonate at any moment. *Oh, for Pete's sake...* She had the strange urge to pelt him with one.

'Anyway... Did you get the files?'

He put his glasses back on and her pulse gave a funny little skip despite her annoyance. He looked at his computer screen. 'Thanks, yes. I've figured out the system and I've been reviewing all the charts for the week.'

He was being thorough. That was good. Being prepared and focused. Doing his homework.

But she still wanted to pelt him with shortbread.

'It looks pretty light,' he said, his eyes still glued to the screen. 'I'd see double the amount of patients in an afternoon in Sydney.'

There was no criticism in his voice. He was being matter-of-fact but it irked Felicity. She bit her tongue against the urge to tell him he could turn right around and go back to his precious Sydney.

It appeared their *talk* wasn't going to be necessary. It was obvious he didn't want to be here. She'd been worrying about nothing.

'Trust me, it'll take us all afternoon.'

'Okay. The clinic usually starts on time?'

'Yes. There are no appointments between twelve and one so we can have lunch then afternoon clinics start at one on the dot.'

'That's very civilised.'

Felicity gritted her teeth. Again, his tone wasn't critical but anger stirred in her chest anyway.

She supposed they didn't get time for lunch in Sydney.

'Well, you know what they say, the family that eats together stays together.'

He glanced at her. 'And you're all family here.'

Why did he make that sound like they were some kind of cult? 'Well…yes.' Where the hell was the charming guy from the train? The one she'd slept with?

Talk about a Jekyll and Hyde!

He nodded as if he was absorbing her answer before returning his attention to the screen. Felicity had to stop herself from rolling her eyes. 'Do me a favour? Have a look around here for the plaster saw when you're done with the charts?'

She'd planned on looking for it herself but frankly she didn't want to be around him any longer than she had to be. And she didn't need the temptation of a plaster saw in her hand when she felt like causing him physical harm.

'Sure,' he murmured, still focused on his computer.

Felicity wasn't sure if that was his way of dismissing her or not but she took her leave anyway.

She had no idea if he noticed.

CHAPTER SIX

CALLUM GLANCED UP as the door clicked shut. He hadn't realised Felicity had slipped out. He sighed and threw his glasses on the desk again, massaging the bridge of his nose with two fingers.

Damn it. He'd been too short with her. He hadn't meant to be, she'd just caught him at a bad moment. He'd been trying to concentrate on his work, to push away the powerful feelings of regret that were threatening to swamp him, but sitting here at his desk in a Vickers Hill general practice he couldn't deny them any longer and she'd arrived in the middle of his pity party.

He was a GP. A general practitioner. The last two years he'd been in training for this so it hadn't seemed quite real. But now he was here, in his first GP job, and it was as real as it got.

Goodbye, hot-shot surgeon. No more triple As, carotid endarterectomies or vascular bypasses. His life now revolved around tonsillitis, hypertension, reflux and asthma. No more international surgical conferences or pioneering new techniques or glitzy dinner parties. No more cut and thrust of the operating theatre. It was all rosella jam and mulberry pie...

So not the way he'd pictured his life turning out.

Sure, after this he was heading back to the prestigious north shore practice where he'd undergone a lot of his training. He'd never been given home-made anything by any of the patients there but it wasn't scrubs and the smell of the diathermy either.

Still, none of it was Felicity's fault and they had to work

together so he needed to get his head out of his rear end. He hadn't been prepared for the leap in his pulse when he'd seen her again this morning. He'd spent the last few days trying to compartmentalise her in his head as the woman on the train. A fantasy. A very sexy, very real fantasy that he thanked his lucky stars for but a fantasy nonetheless.

He'd thought he'd succeeded.

And then she'd been in the staffroom and his libido had growled back to life again as a rush of memories from the train had filled his head.

She hadn't looked like the woman in the fringed boots or the little black dress. She'd been in her uniform—a pair of loose-fitting blue trousers and a polo shirt with 'Dawson Family Practice' embroidered across the pocket. The shirt was also loose and her honey-coloured hair was tied back in a low ponytail at her nape.

But she *had* looked like the woman in the yoga pants and bare feet who'd shared her bed with him and damn if that hadn't made him all fired up. And messed with his head. Why else would he have babbled on about being a Cal?

Oh, God. He'd been inept…

But it had seemed vital suddenly that she know. To make her understand that he had been a different person once. That he *was* capable, even if that guy felt lost to him for ever.

To not judge him as the man she saw now.

Which hopefully she wouldn't because that guy had just acted like an insensitive jerk.

He'd come here to get away from the tentacles of his past. To begin his new career away from judging eyes. To get some clear air before he went back to a world that was used to seeing him as an entirely different person.

To be happy, goddamn it.

Or at least less miserable.

He just hadn't realised how hard it was going to be. He'd put too much expectation on this first day. That starting it would be some miracle cure. Some invisible line in the sand that held magical powers of career satisfaction by just stepping over it when clearly it was going to take time. He was going to have to get used to it. To the change in pace and clientele and his core duties. To take one day at a time and have faith that each day would be better than the last.

It was that or become a bitter old man. And he refused to let that damn cricket ball win.

The clinic started promptly but didn't go according to what Felicity, or the patients, were used to. Callum was efficient in the extreme. No wonder he had queried the appointment numbers when he seemed to have mentally allotted five minutes to each one and zipped through the list like he was trying to set a new world record.

Usually, with Meera, each appointment would last between ten and fifteen minutes. But Callum didn't believe in pleasantries. He wasn't rude. He was polite and respectful but he didn't dillydally either, didn't open himself to chitchat, preferring to cut straight to the chase. Review the problem. Make a diagnosis. Order a test, an X-ray, a pill or dish out some medical advice.

Thank you for coming. *Next!*

Some city practice was going to lap him up with his billing rate. But that's not what they were about at the Dawson Family Practice and by the time they'd worked their way through to their second-last patient—at *four o'clock*—Felicity was cranky. The clinics always ran until at least five and usually closer to six.

She had no doubt Callum looked on it as efficiency. There were more people in the cities, therefore more demand on GP services. Double- and triple-booking were common practice. But he could keep it as far as she was concerned. Her patients deserved more than a paint-by-numbers doctor.

Old Mr Dunnich came in, bearing a bunch of roses. He was a big old wizened bloke in his mid-eighties, used to stand six-four and didn't have the belly he was sporting now in his grape-growing days.

'These are for you, Doc,' he said in his slow country drawl. 'Don't usually go around giving flowers to blokes but the wife insisted.'

Callum seemed as puzzled by the gesture as Mr Dunnich. 'Oh…thanks,' he said, taking them awkwardly and putting them on his desk before ploughing on. 'Now, let's have a look at those bunions, shall we?'

Mr Dunnich shot her a perplexed look. In fact, she knew him well enough to see a fleeting flash of offence. Mr Dunnich's prize roses were a thing of beauty, and the perfume floated to Felicity from across the other side of the room within seconds. There wasn't a person alive—including clueless men—who didn't comment on how spectacular they were.

Felicity wasn't usually a person who harboured murderous intent but she had to suppress the urge to hit Callum across the head with the nearest heavy object, which just happened to be a tendon hammer.

It *probably* wouldn't kill him should she be unable to suppress the urge to use it.

Mr Dunnich took off his shoes and socks in silence. Normally he was always up for a chat. He could talk about his roses all day and what the man didn't know about growing grapes for wine wasn't worth knowing. But he did what all old men from the country did when feeling socially awkward—he clammed up.

Callum examined both big toes. The silence stretched, which was obviously making Mr Dunnich uncomfortable enough to try and initiate some conversation. 'The pain's getting worse, Doc, but I really don't want to have to go under the knife. I don't want to leave Lizzy alone.'

'I see,' Callum said, poking and prodding as he asked a few questions. 'Okay,' he said briskly a moment or two later. 'You can put your shoes back on.'

Mr Dunnich did as he was told. 'I'm going to try you on this new medication,' Callum said, turning to his computer and using the electronic prescription system to generate a script to give to the chemist. The printer spat it out and he handed it over. 'It's had good results for arthritic pain. One twice a day for a week then come back and see us at the clinic next week and we'll reassess.'

'Rightio,' Mr Dunnich said, taking the printout and glancing at her, obviously not sure if the consult was over. He hadn't been in and out in five minutes ever.

Felicity smiled at him encouragingly, her heart going out to him. 'I'll see you out, Mr Dunnich.'

Again, Callum hadn't been rude but he hadn't been welcoming either. He'd been brisk and efficient and oblivious to his patient's awkwardness.

'I need to find a vase for these anyway,' she said, ignoring Callum as she swooped up the roses. She buried her face in them as she caught up to the patient and linked her arm through his. 'They're gorgeous, aren't they? What are these ones called?'

The old man's wrinkled hand landed on hers as he gave her a couple of pats. 'I struck this one myself.'

Felicity was back with the roses in a vase in under a minute. She put them on his desk, desperately hoping he was allergic to them, but he didn't shift his attention from the computer, squinting at it instead as he clicked around different views to assess the X-ray on the screen.

'This radius looks good,' he declared, finally looking at her over the tops of his glasses, and it hit her again how they loaned him that extra dollop of sexy.

It wasn't a thought she welcomed. How could she have the hots for someone who didn't have a clue about connecting with his patients? Who she wasn't even sure she *liked* any more.

Because you've seen the other side...

Felicity hated it when the voice in her head was right. She

had seen a very different side to Callum. One who had been competent and *compassionate* as well as chatty and flirty.

She'd liked that guy. *A lot.*

And compassion was always going to trump competence and looking great in glasses.

'It's healed very nicely.' His gaze returned to the screen. 'Can you take the plaster off then send her in to me?'

Aye, aye, sir. 'Certainly, Dr Hollingsworth.'

He looked up abruptly, a frown between his brows. 'You don't have to call me that,' he said. 'Callum is fine.'

Felicity figured 'jerk' was even better but she wisely held her tongue.

'Looks like we're going to both get an early mark,' he said, glancing at his watch, clearly pleased with himself.

Felicity's blood pressure shot up a notch or two. She didn't want a damn early mark. She wanted her patients to feel like they were more than a body part or some medical problem to cure or treat.

'I'll just see to Pauline.'

Felicity hit the waiting area with a full head of steam and a bunch of uncharitable thoughts. 'Hey, Pauline, you can come through now,' she said, forcing herself to smile so she wouldn't scare any of the waiting patients.

Pauline had slipped on the wet tiles around her pool and put her arm out to break her fall, snapping her radius instead. She was a few years older than Felicity but with three little kids she was a regular at the practice.

Felicity led her into the treatment room and Pauline sat on the central table over which hung a large, adjustable operating theatre light. It could be moved higher and lower and angled any which way required when suturing or other minor procedures were performed.

'You ready for this?' Felicity asked as she applied her face mask, grateful for her glasses being a little more glamorous eye protection than the ugly, clunky plastic goggles that the practice supplied. Cutting through plaster kicked up a lot of dust and fibres.

'I am so ready for this, Flick. Those kids of mine have sensed I'm weak and have been running riot these last six weeks. I can't wait to show them Mummy's back.'

Felicity laughed. 'All righty, then. It looks scary and it's going to be loud, okay?'

She turned it on to demonstrate. The oscillating saw with its round blade whined as loudly as any handyman's saw. She turned it off. 'The blade vibrates, it doesn't cut. If it comes into contact with your skin it can't hurt you. But it won't, I promise. Once I get down to the last layer I'll switch to plaster spreaders and some kick-arse scissors.'

'Yep. Cool.' Pauline nodded vigorously. 'Let's do it.'

It took fifteen minutes to remove the cast. Using the loud saw was actually quite therapeutic. By the time she'd sent Pauline on her way to Callum, Felicity wasn't feeling anywhere near as annoyed as she had been.

She did, however, get some dust or fibre in her right eye, which became more and more irritating as she cleaned up the treatment room. She ambled over to the mirror hanging behind the door to see if there was anything obvious. Her eye was red from her rubbing it but there was nothing apparent in it.

Damn. She'd get a lecture from Bill for sure about wearing the correct safety equipment and she'd only have herself to blame. She'd always considered her own glasses as good eye protection—for plaster removal anyway—and now she was going to have to revise that opinion.

The irritation grew worse and out of desperation she grabbed a handful of plastic saline ampoules, twisted off their tops and moved to the sink. She leaned her head over and turned it on the side, her right eye down and bent her knees to bring her closer to the porcelain so she wouldn't make a mess.

It was an awkward position but at least the saline ran

straight into the sink as she gently trickled ampoule after ampoule into her eye.

'What on earth are you doing?'

Felicity's pulse leapt both at the unexpected interruption and who it belonged to. Not exactly the most elegant position to be found in, especially as she already felt like an idiot for being in this situation. Her earlier crankiness returned. 'What does it look like?'

'You got something in your eye?' His voice grew nearer and she could see him approach in her peripheral vision, coming to a halt, his hands on his hips as he watched her, her eyes about level with his fly.

She tried valiantly not to go back to that night again but failed.

'Give the man a cigar.'

'Is this from removing the plaster?'

'Yes.'

He held out his hand for the remaining ampoules. 'Let me help.'

'I'm fine. You've got your early mark, go home.'

She may have liquid in one eye and a side view from the other but she didn't need to see his glare—she felt it all the way down to her toes.

'Are you angry at me for some reason? Do you have something against efficiency? Or is this some self-loathing guilt trip of yours because of what happened on the train, which is suddenly now wrong and somehow my fault? Because if we've got a problem then I really wish you'd just come out and say it.'

Felicity glared right back, which was difficult considering what she was doing. Yes, she was angry but it had absolutely nothing to do with the train or any kind of guilt trip. Hindsight was always twenty-twenty but she could never hate herself over that night.

This was purely about today. Unfortunately it wasn't her place to chastise the new doctor about the way he practised. Or any doctor for that matter. There were protocols and formal procedures in place for those kinds of things.

Not that she'd ever had any cause.

If Dr Dawson asked her how Callum was going she'd say he was diligent and efficient. But if there were complaints from the patients, he was on his own.

'No problem,' she muttered. She could bite her tongue over this. She *would*. If it killed her. Because she'd be damned if she did a single thing to make him think she was playing some petulant game because she was embarrassed about what had happened between them.

'Good. Now let me look at your damn eye and see if there's anything obvious.'

'I already looked. Couldn't see anything.'

He folded his arms. 'So let me check now you've treated it.'

Felicity realised her recalcitrance wasn't doing her any favours. She could act like a two-year-old or take advantage of the professional help being offered like an adult. 'Fine,' she muttered, reaching for the paper towel dispenser nearby. He beat her to it, pulling off two sheets and passing them over as she righted herself.

'Thank you.' She injected a more conciliatory note into her voice as she dabbed at her wet face. He was offering to help. It wasn't his fault she was in this situation.

'Over here,' he said, moving to the centre of the room near the examination bed. He glanced at the overhead light. 'Where's the switch for this thing?'

Felicity tossed the paper towel on the bed and went up on tippy toes to reach one of the vertical handles. She pulled it down and located the switch. Light pooled around them. He squinted and moved so the back of his head blocked the light. The halo affect was disconcerting considering she'd been thinking of him as the devil incarnate most of the day.

'Okay,' he said, sliding his hands either side of her face. 'Let me look.'

The sizzle from his contact was also disconcerting. They were standing close. Too close. Her brain rejected the nearness while her body flowered beneath it. He wore the same aftershave as he had on the train and if she shut her eyes she could almost imagine them being gently rocked.

Felicity tried to pull away but he held on tight. 'It's better, much less gritty.'

He set his thumbs beneath her jaw and used them to angle her head. 'That's good,' he murmured, obviously ignoring her as he peered into her eyes. Or her *eye* anyway. Her pulse hammered madly at every pulse point, surely he could feel it beneath the pads of his thumbs?

He instructed her to look up then down then to both sides, which she did eagerly. Frankly she was pleased to look anywhere but right at his big handsome face in those beyond-sexy glasses. Being up this close and personal to Callum was a seriously crazy temptation.

It was madness and she reached for something to evoke a bit of sanity.

Think about Mr Dunnich.

But all she could think about was how good Callum smelled and she understood a little better why some women stayed with men who weren't good for them.

'Well…I can't see anything,' he announced.

The statement made her forget she was trying *not* to look at him as she did exactly that. *'Quelle surprise,'* she murmured, their gazes locking, his green one intense as his thumbs stroked along her jaw.

It was so damn good she swayed a little.

The sensible person inside her scrambled for a reason to pull away, for something, anything to break the spell he was weaving with the seductive stroke of those clever thumbs.

It was then that she noticed it.

'Your left pupil is misshapen.' There was an area where the black of the pupil appeared to have bled into the green of his iris. 'It's larger than the other one too.'

That did it. His hands slid off her face and he took a step back. Felicity reached for the table to steady herself as her body mourned his abrupt withdrawal.

'Yes.'

'Is that genetic or from an injury?'

The brooding line had returned to his mouth and for a moment she thought he wasn't going to answer her. 'An injury.'

She quirked an eyebrow. A rusty fork maybe? 'Are you going to make me guess?'

It wasn't any of her business but it didn't stop her being curious as hell. It was obvious from his reaction that it had been serious.

'A cricket ball.'

Felicity's wince was spontaneous and heartfelt. She almost grabbed her own eye in sympathy. 'Ouch.'

'Yeah...' His fingers fiddled with the sheet on the examination table. 'It was a bit of a mess.'

'Define mess.'

She expected him to dismiss her query and leave, and if she wasn't very much mistaken he looked tempted to do just that. But then he shrugged. 'Fractured zygoma. Blown globe. Hyphema. Partial retinal detachment.'

Her wince increased. 'Holy cow! Who was bowling to you? Mitchell Johnson?'

His lips twitched into the grimmest semblance of a smile she'd ever seen. 'One of my mates used to bowl for the under-nineteen Australian side. He's still got it.'

Maybe this was what Callum had been referring to this morning when he'd been going on about being a Cal once upon a time. He was just as tense and shuttered. 'Do you have a sight deficit?'

If anything, the line of his mouth grew grimmer. 'I only have seventy percent vision in my left eye, hence these.' He pointed at his glasses.

Seventy percent. This morning she'd been sure something had happened to Callum to change him—something big—and now she was absolutely convinced. Was the 'life' and 'stuff' he'd talked about the injury to his eye?

Had it turned Cal into a Callum?

Great. A wounded guy. Appealing to her soft underbelly. She was hopeless with them. *This* was the guy from the train, not the one she'd seen today, and she was finding it hard to reconcile the two.

'Is the mydriasis permanent?'

He grimaced. 'It's a work in progress. It's constricted quite a bit since the injury but the specialist thinks after all this time it's about as good as it'll get, and unfortunately I concur.'

'How long ago did it happen?'

'Two and a half years.'

Felicity did a quick calculation in her head. So the accident had happened six months before he'd commenced his GP training. It had probably taken that long for his eye to recover sufficiently to be useful.

Which begged the question, had it always been his plan to train to become a GP? Or had his injury caused him to change career path?

She had a feeling that was very much the case.

'So I take it being a GP hadn't been your grand plan?'

His lips twisted and his self-deprecating laugh was harsh, grating in the silence of the room. 'No.'

Felicity marvelled that such a little word could hold so much misery. This accident had obviously gutted him.

'What was your specialty before you did your GP training?'

He dropped his gaze to the sheet again. 'I was a surgeon.'

Ah. Well, now. His concentration on body parts and medical problems rather than the patient as an individual suddenly made sense. Felicity had spent some time in the operating theatres when she'd been training in Adelaide. She'd quickly come to realise she would never make a scrub nurse. Impersonalising patients and the lack of any real contact with them had driven her nutty.

She hadn't wanted to work in a place where patients were known by their operative site. The leg in Theatre Two, the appendix in Theatre Five or the transplant in Theatre Nine.

Patients had names and she liked to use them.

'What kind of surgeon?'

'Vascular.'

Felicity suppressed the urge to whistle. Impressive. She could see him all scrubbed up, making precise, efficient movements, working his way through his list, conscious of his next patient waiting. 'Did your sight issues interfere with that?'

'Oh, yes.' His tone was harsh with a bitter end note. 'My depth of field and visual acuity in the left eye were shot. A lot of the work I did was microsurgery and...' he glanced up, his gaze locking with hers '...I didn't trust myself.'

The emotions brimming in his eyes belied the hard set of his face and punched Felicity in the gut. 'But surely with time—'

His short, sharp laugh cut her off. 'They'll only give me a conditional driver's licence, they're not going to let me be in charge of a scalpel.' He shoved a hand through his hair, looked away, looked back again. 'It has improved, but not enough. Not to be a surgeon. I'm not prepared to take that kind of risk with somebody's life.'

And there was the compassion. Callum had obviously had the rug pulled right out from under him but he was a doctor first and foremost and doing no harm was the code they lived by.

It was honourable but obviously not easy. This was the man from the train. The one who had been great with Jock and Thelma and the other group of oldies. The one who had laughed and flirted with her. The one who had looked into her eyes in her compartment and *connected* with her.

She gazed at him, trying to convey her understanding. 'I'm sorry. That must have been very hard for you.'

And she *was* sorry. He may have annoyed her today but at least now she understood him a little better. Would maybe even cut him a little slack. He'd given up a lot. Having your hopes and dreams quashed wasn't easy. She knew that better than anyone.

He shook his head dismissively. 'It is what it is.'

She took a step towards him, put her hand on top of his. 'Yeah. Doesn't make it suck any less, does it?'

His gaze flicked to their hands before returning to her face and she caught a glimpse of a guy who was adrift before he shut it down and slid his hand away, tucking it in his pocket as he moved back a few paces.

'Anyway,' he said, his eyes not quite meeting hers, 'maybe take home some liquid tears to settle any residual irritation.'

Felicity didn't need him to tell her that but the way he was judging the distance to the door she figured it was just a segue to him leaving. The thought needled but she had no idea why.

'Yep, great, thanks for your help.' She turned and headed for the sink, flipping on the water and washing her hands because the other ninety-nine times today hadn't been enough.

But it gave her something to do and the opportunity for him to slip away, which he took with both hands.

CHAPTER SEVEN

CALLUM WAS LOOKING forward to the home visits even if Felicity had seemed less than impressed by his request to accompany her. She hadn't said no but she had queried the necessity of it. He felt it was essential to know about this important service, especially if he was ever going to be called out to one of the patients during his one weekend in three on-call days.

She hadn't had a comeback for that but her stony profile as she drove them to their first appointment spoke volumes.

He wasn't sure what was going on with her. Despite her protestations on Monday that they didn't have a problem and the obvious empathy in her eyes when he'd told her about the accident, the last couple of days had still been awkward.

Sure, she was polite and efficient. But he wouldn't exactly say she was knocking herself out to be friendly. Not like she was with her patients.

Not like she'd been that day on the train.

Was that where Felicity's awkwardness was springing from? The train? Did she regret what had happened? Did she resent that seeing him every day she couldn't put it away in some neat little box somewhere? Or was she worried that he'd kiss and tell and spoil her St Felicity reputation?

Because there was one thing he'd learned in his few short days at the practice—Felicity could do no wrong.

Everyone loved Felicity.

Their version of her anyway because she was a very different Felicity from the one he'd met on the train. Sure, she was as friendly and easygoing with the patients as she had been with their travelling companions, but here, in Vickers

Hill, she was very definitely *Flick*. The small-town girl, the friendly nurse, everyone's mate.

She knew who everyone was and who they were related to. She knew where everything was found, everything anyone had been treated for in the last four years and, it seemed, everyone's birthdays. As well as having practically every phone number in the town memorised.

She *was* a freaking saint.

And he'd gone and thoroughly debauched her.

He didn't think the town—aside from one or two busybodies—cared what their saint did in her private time but what if she thought they did? They hadn't talked about what had happened between them, not since discovering they would be working together, so maybe it was time they did.

He glanced at her profile. Her forehead was crinkled into a frown, her lips pursed. *Maybe not.* Safer to stick to work-related topics and hope she eventually relaxed when she realised he wasn't here to make her life difficult.

'So,' he said, his sunglasses in place as the harsh October sun cut through the glass of the windscreen, 'the purpose of the home visits is?'

'A federally funded initiative to keep older and less able patients in their homes and in the community and out of care.'

She parroted the facts as if he'd pushed a button on her somewhere that read *Press here for information*. She didn't shift her gaze off the road. Didn't glance at him for a second.

Callum ploughed on, bloody-minded now. 'What kind of things do you do when you're with a patient? Are there specific things or is it just a general social call?'

Her fingers wrapped, unwrapped and wrapped around the steering wheel again. 'A lot of different things. I deal with any specific medical issues of the day but mostly patients go into the practice if they have anything acute. I do blood-pressure and blood-sugar checks as well as full yearly health checks when they come due. I make sure their prescriptions and referrals are up to date. I do a lot of ordering.'

'Ordering?'

She at least nodded this time. 'Products. Medical supplies. Incontinence products, stoma bags, peritoneal dialysis supplies, test strips as well as equipment like feeding pumps, shower chairs or Zimmer frames.'

'Sounds busy.'

'It's not all tea and scones,' she said.

He could have cut the derision with a knife. He was about to call her on it when Felicity engaged her blinker and said, 'First cab off the rank is Mr Morley.'

Callum looked out the window to see an old-fashioned, low-set cottage that could do with some TLC. She undid her seat belt then looked at him for the first time since he'd sat in the car.

'These people know me. They trust me. They're often wary of strangers and prefer talking to a nurse about their issues over a doctor. They might be suspicious of you. Just try to...'

Callum thought she was going to say 'not screw it up' but she continued, 'Stay in the background, okay?'

She didn't give him time to reply, reaching for the handle and stepping out of the vehicle.

Her faith in him was heartening.

What followed was an intense five hours. Callum saw the gamut of small-town life all in one afternoon as St Felicity ministered to her flock. It wasn't the most efficient system he'd ever seen. Too much chatter and drinking of tea and eating of cake or whatever piece of home-made cooking was presented to them for his liking, but it appeared to be the ritual and with Felicity's advice ringing in his ears there was no way he was declining. He'd never eaten so well in his life.

He was going to have to do some serious working out when he got back to Sydney.

He followed Felicity's lead after earning her glare when he'd declined something at their second stop. It just wasn't done, apparently. And she was right, the patients were leery of him to start with so if eating food that was offered at all their dozen stops helped with the warming-up process then when in Rome…

That all changed when they got to their last call—Meryl's house. She didn't appear to have a last name or require any kind of formal address as Felicity's other patients had.

Just Meryl, apparently.

Her house was a small cottage with a deep bull-nosed veranda. Dreamcatchers and wind chimes of all types and sizes hung from the guttering. The pungent spice of incense prickled Callum's nose and a small shrine with a Buddha and a variety of candles and flowers was set up in one corner of the living room.

Meryl took to him right away. She was sitting in a big stuffed recliner and was possibly the most wrinkled person Callum had ever met. But there was a strength and agility to her movements that made him think she was probably younger than she appeared.

He stuck out his hand when Felicity introduced them. Her hand was soft but her grip was firm as she pulled him nearer, forcing him to lean in closer.

'Cal,' she murmured, immediately shortening his name in a husky voice that sounded like the product of a pack-a-day habit. She looked straight into his eyes, taking her time to study him. 'You have an unhappy aura,' she finally declared, releasing his hand.

Callum glanced at Felicity for an interpretation in case there was one other than the obvious—Meryl was a little nutty. She shot him the most faux innocent eyebrow-lift he'd ever seen in his life. He should have known that someone who lived in a house guarded by dream catchers was going to be a little…alternative.

'Meryl reads auras,' she said, a small smile playing on her lips.

That little knowing smile drew attention to her mouth and it was just about the sexiest damn thing he'd ever seen. All week he'd been trying not to think about that mouth and where she'd put it on his body. Her attitude towards him had helped. But now she was finally pulling the stick out of her butt it was impossible not to go there again.

Impossible not to want to familiarise himself with it again and kiss the smile right off that sexy mouth.

'Hmm, it's looking a little happier now,' Meryl mused.

Callum blinked at the running commentary on the state of his aura, pulling his gaze from Felicity's. He gave himself a mental shake. The last thing he wanted Meryl proclaiming was his aura's massive erection.

'Sit down here, Cal,' Meryl said, patting an old vinyl chair beside her.

Callum would rather sit outside in the car but there was no way he could get out of this without looking rude. The normal rules of doctoring just didn't apply in the community, certainly not in a house that could have belonged in Oz.

He glanced at Felicity, who was obviously finding the situation highly amusing.

'What colour's Felicity's aura?' he asked, turning to give all his attention to Meryl. Thankfully, Felicity was on his right so he could see her smile slowly deflating.

Although he was sure she had no cause to worry. The saintly Felicity's aura was no doubt rainbowesque and probably smelled like strawberries and candy canes.

'It'll be the same as usual,' Meryl said, flicking her gaze to Felicity. Callum was inordinately pleased when the older woman raised an eyebrow. 'Or maybe not… It's *usually* so balanced but it does look a little…ruffled today.'

Callum smiled as the tables were turned and Felicity

frowned and put a hand to her belly. Meryl's gaze cut back to him and he pressed his lips together so she couldn't see him gloating, although there was something all-seeing about Meryl that couldn't be easily dismissed.

Her eyes narrowed speculatively. 'You're staying at Luci's place, right?'

Callum nodded, feeling on solid ground with standard questioning. 'Yes. And she's staying at my place in Sydney.'

'And how long are you staying in Vickers Hill?'

'I'm here for eight weeks.'

'No.' Meryl shook her head slowly as her gaze darted all around his head before she peered into his eyes. It was more thorough than any of the dozens of specialists with their fancy high-powered microscopes had ever managed.

Frankly, it put an itch up his spine.

'You'll be here for much longer than that.'

Callum broke the eye contact with difficulty. No. *He was going back to Sydney*. To his harbourside apartment and his job that started in the New year. Vickers Hill was just a pit stop. A place for some clear air.

He glanced at Felicity, who wasn't looking so sure of herself now either. She appeared ready to deny it if he didn't.

'I can assure you,' Callum said, dredging up his most positive smile for Meryl. It wasn't one he'd used a lot these last two years and it didn't feel right on his face. 'I'm only here short term.'

Meryl just smiled and patted his hand. 'You'll see. It's okay,' she assured him. 'It'll work out. You were meant to come here. It's your destiny. It's in your aura.'

Callum didn't know what to say to that. Clearly Meryl wasn't about to change her mind and what did it matter what some crazy old lady on an incense high who read auras said?

He was in charge of his destiny.

'Right, well.' Felicity clapped her hands together. 'Let's get your blood pressure checked, Meryl.'

Callum vacated the seat, grateful to her for rescuing him

from any more talk of auras and destinies and staying in Vickers Hill.

He could have kissed her.

He *really* could have kissed her.

Callum was looking out the passenger window of Felicity's car when she rolled to a stop in front of Luci's house. He still wasn't used to living in a place that was so country kitsch. It was a turn-of-the-century stone cottage with a chimney and a wraparound porch along which grew a thick bushy passionfruit vine laden with fruit. The entire garden was beautifully manicured and a riot of colour that reflected the froufrou decor of the interior.

Lots of lace at the dinky little windows and white shabby chic furniture complemented the exposed oak ceiling beams and the oak kitchen tops. It was a far cry from his sleek, minimalist apartment dominated by huge unadorned windows from which to admire the stunning water view.

Callum glanced at Felicity, who was staring straight ahead at some point on the road. They hadn't talked at all from Meryl's to here. He figured they were both lost for words. 'So… Meryl…she's a little…colourful?'

Her head snapped around to glare at him. 'And what's wrong with that?' she demanded. 'We can't all be hip, cool Sydneysiders.'

Callum blinked at her unexpected vehemence, holding up his hands to indicate his surrender. Her chest rose and fell markedly. 'Hey,' he murmured. 'It wasn't a criticism.'

She glared at him for a beat or two before returning her attention to the road and huffing out, 'Sorry.'

Callum sighed. Okay. *Enough.* Enough of this. Something was obviously bothering her and he couldn't ignore it any longer, hoping she'd snap out of it. He was going to have to mention the elephant in the room.

Or the car, as it turned out.

'You don't have to worry about me saying anything to anyone about what happened between us.'

That earned him another short, sharp, slightly askance glance. 'I didn't for a minute think I had to.'

Callum raised both his eyebrows. Okay…so what was this all about? It couldn't be his work. He'd been his usual competent, efficient self. He may not be fully resigned to his new career but he knew he did good work. The same way he always knew he did good surgery.

He was a Hollingsworth—they always excelled at what they did.

'Okay. Well…sorry. It's just…you've been angry at me all week and I thought…I just needed to reassure you, that's all. If that's what you're worried about.' He thought maybe, deep down, she was, she just didn't want to acknowledge it so it was worth saying again. 'I don't kiss and tell and what happened that night is between us only.'

'Good.' She glanced away, fixing her gaze on the steering wheel. 'Thank you.'

It wasn't exactly the immediate easing of tensions that he'd hoped it would be. Hell, if she was strung any tighter she'd explode. 'Only we haven't really talked about how we're going to handle it. You know, now that we're working so closely together, and maybe we should because I feel like we've got off on the wrong foot.'

Considering they hadn't put a foot wrong when they'd just been two strangers on a train, their missteps since had been ridiculous.

'I was planning on ignoring it.'

Callum surprised himself with a laugh at her candour. He didn't think she'd meant it to be funny—more like a morose statement of fact—but it was. 'Yeah. So was I.' But neither of them were doing a very good job. 'And then…'

He stopped himself before the words he'd been about to say slipped out of his mouth. They clearly hadn't been through his rigorous filter. It must be the after-effects of the incense. Or maybe the very present effects of her perfume. It was the one she'd been wearing *that* night. He hadn't really noticed it at the time but right now it was achingly familiar, taking him right back.

She turned her head and their eyes met. 'And then, what?'

His gaze dropped to her mouth. He should leave it alone. Tell her it didn't matter. Walk it back. But the air in the car grew heavier as the space between them seemed to shrink and the urge to pull her ponytail loose slithered thick and dangerous through a head teeming with very bad ideas.

'And then you said Meryl reads auras and had this little half-smile on your mouth like you just knew it was going to throw me, and it was so damn sexy all I could think about was kissing you.'

'Oh. Right,' she muttered, her gaze falling to *his* mouth now. 'That doesn't really help.'

Callum shook his head and somehow, when he stopped, it had inched closer to hers. 'Not even a bit?' Her perfume filled his head and he could see the movement of her throat as she swallowed.

'I think what happened on the train should stay on the train,' she said, her voice husky.

'I agree.' And he did. Or he had, anyway.

'I mean it was…lovely but—'

'Lovely?' His gaze locked with hers as he quirked an eyebrow at the insipid description. 'Why don't you go all the way and tell me it was *nice*?'

She shrugged. 'It was that too.'

But that smile was there on her mouth again and heat flared in his belly. He gave a playful groan. 'You make it sound like we held hands and sang "Kumbayah" all night.'

She laughed, that great big sound she'd used so frequently when they'd been on the train but he hadn't heard since. 'How would you describe it?'

It was a leading question and they were playing with fire. He wondered if she understood how slim the thread was to which he was clinging. But she was looking at his mouth once more and he was pretty sure she'd angled her head closer because he hadn't moved a muscle this time.

In fact, he was barely even breathing.

'Hot,' he muttered, his voice thick in his throat, his gaze dropping to her mouth. 'Sexy. Mind-blowing.'

'Erotic,' she whispered, her pupils dilated.

Callum nodded as he lifted his hand and pushed back an escaped honey-blonde tendril. His fingers whispered across her cheek and jaw as they withdrew. '*So* erotic.'

'Oh, God,' she moaned, her voice low and needy like it'd been when he'd first slipped inside her. Her hands went to the lapels of his jacket and tugged.

Callum didn't need any more encouragement, his mouth meeting hers like they'd never been apart. Like they'd picked up where they'd left off at hot, sexy and mind-blowing, heading straight for erotic.

She smelled good and tasted better and he slid his palms onto her face, holding her steady so he could kiss her harder, deeper, wetter. He ran his tongue over her bottom lip and when she moaned and moved closer still, he thrust it fully into her mouth, his erection surging as her tongue stroked against his.

His heart pounded in his chest, his pulse whooshed like Niagara Falls through his ears and his breathing went from husky to laboured as his whole world narrowed down to just her. Her mouth. Her kisses. Her moans and sighs. The desperate grip of her hands on his lapels.

Just Felicity. In his arms. Again.

And God alone knew where it would have ended up had there not been a firm rap on Felicity's window that scared the life out of him and her also, if the way she grabbed at her chest as they broke apart was any indication.

He was expecting to see half the town with pitchforks out to save St Felicity from his clutches but it was just Mrs Smith from across the road, who'd introduced herself the day he'd moved in and had given him a friendly wave every day since.

She didn't look so friendly now.

'My God,' Felicity muttered under her breath. 'I think I just had a heart attack.'

Callum knew how she felt. What the hell was he doing? He was too old to be necking in cars, for crying out loud. They both were.

Certainly too damn old to be sprung doing it.

'Mrs Smith,' Felicity said, as she wound her window down.

Callum admired the note of cheerful innocence in her voice like nothing was going on here. Like maybe his neighbour hadn't noticed she'd had her tongue down his throat. But the delicious vibrato in her voice betrayed how very much *had* been going on.

'Flick Mitchell,' Mrs Smith said, a scandalised note raising her voice to a higher register. 'Dr Hollingsworth.' Her tone for him was rather more accusatory. 'This is hardly appropriate behaviour in broad daylight. I don't need to tell you that Vickers Hill prides itself on public decorum. Just because your parents don't live here any more doesn't mean you should let your behavioural standards slide. It's important to always act like a lady, Flick. I know your mother taught you that.'

It was on the tip of Callum's tongue to tell the old biddy he was more interested in Felicity being a *woman* than a lady but Felicity was nodding her head and saying, 'You're right, Mrs Smith, I'm terribly sorry. You have my assurance it won't happen again.'

Mrs Smith peered down her nose at him. 'And what about your assurances, young man?'

It had been a long time since anyone had called Callum *young man*. He was just getting used to Bill calling him *son*.

Anyone would think they'd been accosted by an angry father with a shotgun instead of a little old lady from across the street, and a dozen different responses flipped through his head. They all died on his lips as Felicity turned pleading eyes on him.

Hell. He was a sucker for that look. Who was he kidding? He was a sucker for any way her face looked. He gritted his teeth and put his hand on his heart. 'I promise there will be no more public displays of affection between Felicity and myself, Mrs Smith.'

Because next time he'd make damn sure he dragged her inside first. Away from prying eyes.

She nodded, satisfied, but wasn't finished with them yet. 'I guess you'll be going home now,' she said pointedly.

'Yes.' Felicity nodded. 'Callum was just leaving.'

Callum didn't want to leave. He very much wanted to finish off the kiss that had been so rudely interrupted. But it was obvious the mood was in tatters and Mrs Smith wasn't going anywhere until *he* did. He glanced at Felicity, who lifted one shoulder in a slight *it's-not-worth-the-aggro* shrug.

'Right,' he said, reaching for the handle. 'I'll…see you tomorrow.'

She nodded but refused to meet his eyes. The last thing he saw as she drove away, apart from Mrs Smith's evil eye, was Felicity's stony profile.

They were back to square one. Worse than square one. If the kiss had been one step forward, this was definitely two steps back.

'Oh, God,' Felicity groaned into her mobile phone a few hours later. 'This is *so* bad. I'm never going to live this down. Why did it have to be Mrs Smith? Now the whole town's going to know. They'll have us married off by the end of next week.'

Luci's laughter floated down the line to her. She'd rung half an hour ago ostensibly to check on the house but also to grill Felicity over a little rumour she'd heard, courtesy of her mother. Poor Luci hadn't been able to get a word in edgewise over Felicity's self-flagellation.

'I say screw the town and just go for it.'

Felicity blinked. 'Well, look at you. Only a short time in the big city and you're completely corrupted. Mrs Smith would be horrified.'

Another laugh. 'Hey, haven't you been telling me to go for it? To move, to have an adventure, to get out of my rut? The same can be said for you, missy. It's been four years since Ned. You deserve a rampant public display of affection and you're twenty-eight years old, for God's sake. Unless…he is a good kisser, right?'

Good? The man was *sublime.* He must have been standing at the top of the queue when they'd been handing out the kissing gene. Ned had been a great kisser too so her bar was set very high. 'Ooh, yeah.'

'Oh, *really*? That good, huh?'

'Well…a girl doesn't like to kiss and tell.'

Which was a good reminder that Callum had said the same thing and there wasn't a lot she could tell Luci without telling her everything and she wasn't ready to do that yet. She didn't want to make it a thing.

The man was here for eight weeks—not someone to blow her precious reputation on. Plus his bedside manner kinda sucked and she was confused as to why something that should have been a major turn-off didn't seem to matter where her body was concerned.

'Anyway, I've been gabbing on and on about me and I haven't even asked you what's going on with you. How's Sydney? Tell me about Seb.'

'Oh, I hardly ever see him,' Luci dismissed airily.

Felicity had known her friend long enough to hear the tell-tale waver in her voice, indicating she wasn't being entirely honest, but Luci ploughed on, talking about her course and Sydney and the weather and her work, and Felicity let her go on while her mind churned through bigger issues.

Like why the hell she'd let Callum kiss her in broad daylight. The fact that she'd actually initiated it by pulling on his lapels was something she chose not to focus on.

She'd been cranky that he'd invaded her space today. After three frustrating clinics on the run, every second of which she'd wanted to shake him for his efficiency over humanity approach, she'd needed some time out.

And then he'd made that comment about Meryl. Although, to be fair, Meryl had been called much worse things than colourful and Felicity's irritation had, in truth, been more about her blemished aura and Meryl's predictions.

Most of the town thought Meryl was certifiable but she'd been right too many times for Felicity to discount.

So why, if she'd been so damn cranky at him, had she kissed him? In broad daylight? Blemishing much more than her aura?

And how was Vickers Hill going to react?

CHAPTER EIGHT

BY THE TIME Monday rocked around again Felicity was on her last nerve. Between the speculation that was running rife in Vickers Hill—phone calls from her mother, whispers at the supermarket, unsolicited advice from just about everybody—and enduring another afternoon clinic with Callum's same robotic approach, she was just about done cutting him slack.

If they hadn't kissed on Thursday and tripped the Vickers Hill grapevine into overdrive, she may well have bitten her tongue for longer—it wasn't her place to comment on how he did his job. But they had and Felicity was just about out of her be-nice-to-the-locum store.

It was ironic that everyone thought they were having wild monkey sex when all she wanted to do was strangle him with his stethoscope.

Yeah, the man could kiss. But he *sucked* at connecting with his patients.

It was the last straw when Callum asked her to 'Send in the bunions when you're ready' as she was opening the office door to show a patient out. Felicity's vision went a hot, hazy red as her brain exploded and practically leaked out her ears. She slapped the door shut with the palm of her hand and turned on a dime to glare at him.

'Mr Dunnich,' she said, shoving her hand on her hip.

He glanced up at her from his screen and she hated the way her heart did a funny little leap as he peered at her through those sexy, rimless frames.

'He's the bunions?'

'No,' she said, her voice register sitting squarely in the

frosty zone. 'He's *Mr Dunnich*. That's his name. Or Alf if you're ever invited to be that familiar.' Felicity doubted he would be. 'He's the one whose wife insisted he bring you roses last week, remember?'

'Oh. Yes…'

He was eyeing her warily now. It was obvious he knew he'd done something wrong but equally obvious that he was clueless as to what.

'She had a stroke two years ago and now he's her full-time carer,' Felicity continued, her voice low from the rough edge of emotion that had welled out of nowhere in her chest. 'The roses give her so much pleasure and he knows it.' Her voice cracked and she didn't care how insane she sounded.

Mr Dunnich wasn't just bunions to her.

Callum stood, his forehead crinkling. 'Is there something wrong, Felicity?'

'The person who was just in here with the *hamstring* is called *Malcolm*. The person before that with the *carpal tunnel* is *Stefanie*.'

Pressure built in Felicity's chest as her desperation for him to understand mixed with the emotions she always felt when she was talking about her patients. She sucked in a breath and blew it noisily out of her mouth before she totally broke down and her message was lost amidst incoherent accusations and ugly snot crying.

'They all have names. We don't refer to our patients as their body parts around here. They're *people*, not medical conditions.'

'God…sorry.' He grimaced, pulling his glasses off and throwing them on the table. 'I'm still adjusting to a new mindset. It's a bad habit.'

'Well, break it,' she snapped. Felicity understood that a lot of surgeons had that mindset. But a lot didn't so it was a choice. A bad one.

His jaw clenched. If Felicity hadn't gone to the dark side

she'd have recognised it as a sign to back off. But this had been brewing for a week and she was all-in now.

'Have there been complaints?' he demanded, hands on hips.

'No. Country people don't complain, Callum. They endure. But these are *my* people. They're going to be here long after you swan off back to Sydney and I'm not going to sit around and watch you treat them so impersonally because you're too...'

A thousand adjectives came to mind, pumping through her head as quickly as her blood pumped through her chest. Some glimmer of propriety did prevail, however. 'Too... *cavalier* to take a personal interest in them.'

His green eyes turned to flinty chips of jade. 'I would defy *anybody* to say I haven't given them the very best treatment. I've been thorough and efficient and effective and I *really* don't like your tone.'

'What? Your city surgical nurses don't call you out on your behaviour?' she demanded, keeping her voice low, aware there was a waiting room full of people outside and very thin walls.

'I think they have a little more respect for their colleagues.'

'Oh, really? Well, guess what? You have to earn respect out here. It's not just given to you like some damn golden halo from on high. It takes more than a pair of scrubs and I *will* advocate for my patients whether you like it or not. I've been biting my tongue for a week now but no more.'

'This?' he said, shaking his head in obvious disbelief. '*This* is why you've been angry at me for a week?'

'What? A little too trivial for you?'

He shook his head at her, his mouth a flat line. 'Oh, well, please,' he said, his tone bitingly sarcastic, 'by all means do let me have it all. I'd hate you to pop a lung keeping it all in.'

Felicity wasn't sure about popping a lung but she sure as hell felt like she was about to blow a vessel in her brain as her blood pressure hit stroke levels. She stalked over to his desk and stabbed her finger at the woodgrain surface.

'It's not about efficiency. There's more to being a good family practice doctor than thoroughness. A GP role is about *connection* and forming long-term *relationships*. It's about *community* and earning trust so that people can and *will* tell you stuff that they'd never tell anyone else because you're their doctor and they're scared out of their brains about something. For Pete's sake.' She shook her head. 'Don't they teach you any of this in GP school? Or does the big hot-shot city surgeon not need to listen?'

'Of course,' he snapped. 'I'm just not...the touchy-feely type.'

'You don't *have* to be. But you can't be robotic about it either. You're just going through the motions at the moment, Callum. Ticking the boxes. Frankly, your bedside manner sucks.'

'Oh, no.' He shook his head vehemently. 'It damn well does not. My bedside manner is great. *All* my patients love me.'

'Well, I'm sure they do when you're talking to them post-op when they're high on drugs and whatever surgical miracle you've performed for them.'

'Oh, yeah?' he snorted. 'This from St Felicity.'

Felicity had no clue what he meant but she wasn't about to get distracted from her point.

'Seriously. Just think about it for a moment. How much *actual* time would you spend with each patient, not counting the hours you're cutting them open? An hour? Two? In general practice, if you stick around a place long enough you're going to see that person multiple times over many years for a variety of different things. You're going to be there with them through good and bad, thick and thin. You're going to tell them they're pregnant or miscarrying, or have cancer or are in remission. You're the person they're going to trust with their lives. The one they're going to break down in front of and who they're going to look at with eyes that are desperate for answers and cures you just don't have.'

Felicity's breath caught as her throat thickened. Damn it. She was getting emotional again. But this stuff meant something.

'They *have* to be more than the sum of their parts to you, Callum. *That's* what being a good GP is about. Forget what they taught you in surgical school. None of it is relevant here.'

Even as she said the words she realised that was the crux of the problem for him. This career move had been forced on him by his eye injury and clearly his heart wasn't in it. It was a fall-back position for him, not a calling. Not like it was for Bill and Angela and Meera.

All the rage and anger that had buoyed her to say what she'd been itching to say flowed out of her, leaving her curiously deflated. 'Why are you even here, Callum? Is it really what you want? You don't seem to be very invested in the job and you're a long way from home so I'm wondering if maybe you're just running away?'

'No.' He shook his head. 'I'm not running away. I just needed a…circuit-breaker. A fresh start. Some clear air for a while. But I am going back. I *will* go back.'

Felicity studied his face. It was so grim and determined it spoke volumes. 'To prove yourself?'

He didn't admit it but she could tell by the tightening of his face that she'd hit close to the bone. 'You have a problem with that?' he asked, his tone defensive.

'No.' And she didn't. But it was fair warning. The man was good-looking. A great kisser. And knew how to melt her into a puddle in bed. It would be easy to get swept away by that and forget he didn't want this job or small-town life.

'But why become a GP? You could have retrained in another surgical speciality. Something that doesn't require a lot of precision. Orthopaedics. All hammer and chisels and power tools. Lot of grunt. Very manly.'

He laughed and it helped to ease the tension. Felicity was relieved. She'd been pretty harsh on him.

'Even that involves a degree of microsurgery and I just can't trust myself.'

'So become a physician. Plenty of specialties to sink your teeth into.'

He shook his head again. His frame was erect, his head was held high, but there was defeat in his gaze. 'I can't work in a hospital. There's that smell, you know?' He looked at her earnestly and Felicity nodded. She knew that smell. Like it had been scrubbed with disinfectant only seconds before you walked into it.

'I love that smell. It's been running through my veins since I was a kid. It's addictive. And it's associated with surgery to me. Having to set foot in a hospital every day for work and not go to the operating theatres would be torture. A constant reminder of everything I've lost. That I'm living out the consolation prize instead of the dream. I can't do it.'

Part of Felicity wanted to tell him to harden up. That life wasn't fair. That it threw you curveballs. But she figured he'd learned that lesson plenty over the last couple of years.

'So you chose general practice.'

'Yes.'

And here they were.

'So *choose* it,' she said.

'Okay, fine,' he huffed, sitting in his chair, rubbing a hand over his eyes. 'What do you suggest to improve my skills? Teach me.'

She narrowed her eyes at him. 'Seriously? It's not rocket science.'

'Seriously. I mean it.' He nodded. 'Give me some pointers and I'll employ them for the remaining patients today. You can critique me at the end. Give me a score out of ten.'

Felicity suppressed an eye-roll. Just like a man to make it competitive. But she had to give him chops for taking what she'd said on board. Especially given its level of frankness.

She'd known some surgeons in Adelaide who would have had apoplexy if she'd spoken to them the way she'd spoken to Callum.

The fact he seemed keen to improve was also encouraging.

'Fine.' A stray piece of her fringe fell over her right eye and she absently blew it away as she pulled up a chair.

'How about you start by calling them by their names? And *thinking* about them that way too. As *people* first. And instead of focusing on their problem and trying to solve it as soon as possible, then calling out "Next", like you've set a mental timer, maybe you could try a little conversation. Talk to *them* when they're here, *not* your computer screen, and about something other than whatever it is they're coming in for. The weather. The weekend markets. Their kids. Their grandkids. Their mothers-in-law. Harvest season. Mulberry pies. Anything.'

'Conversation, huh?'

Felicity heard the amusement in his voice and couldn't stop the smile that curved her mouth. She had first-hand experience of how good he was at conversation. 'Yeah. It's okay, we have time. Pretend you're on a train.'

He smiled too and she breathed in sharply as his whole damn face came alive. For a moment they just sat there smiling at each other, Felicity's hopes and *heart* floating foolishly outside her body somewhere. 'Who knows, you might even discover you *like* being a GP.'

His smile faded a little, a good reminder that Callum was only temporary and not to get carried away. Not to let herself become some kind of consolation prize—his words.

'How about we start with Mr Dunnich?' she said, forcing her legs to stand and dropping her gaze to her trousers, where she brushed at invisible creases.

'The bunions?'

Her head snapped up to find him grinning big and wide. The kind of grin that made Felicity wish she was still seated.

'And the roses,' he added quickly. 'And the wife with a stroke who he cares for. And adores.'

Felicity refused to laugh but she had to fight the urge as she nodded in acknowledgement. 'Correct.'

Callum felt suitably chastised as he waited for Felicity to get Mr Dunnich. If he'd known this was what had been bugging her all week he'd have had it out with her sooner. On Friday and again today he'd figured it was the kiss.

It was almost a relief it had been about this.

The fact the entire town thought he'd besmirched St Flick was way beyond his scope of practise but the way he interacted with patients he could fix. The practical experience he'd had during his training had been very different from Vickers Hill. Most of his practical had been at the busy north shore practice he was heading to in the New Year. Scheduling was always tight and that's how he'd learned.

Get them in, get them out. *Next.*

He'd even been applauded for it.

The fact that it wasn't the way they did things here hadn't even occurred to him and he was grateful to Felicity for finally mentioning it.

Or perhaps cracking up about it was a better descriptor.

She'd asked him if a city nurse had ever called him on his behaviour and the truth was a nurse probably wouldn't have dared talk to him like that in one of his theatres. He'd been the surgeon and he'd ruled the kingdom. Not only that, he came from a long line of surgeons. The Hollingsworth name was well known in Sydney. And he'd been the heir apparent for a long time.

God. He sounded like an arrogant douche.

The door opened, pulling Callum out of his reverie. 'Ah, Mr Dunnich.' Callum half rose. 'Come and sit down.'

Mr Dunnich approached more tentatively than he had last time and Callum cringed internally. He'd been too busy at the computer to acknowledge Mr Dunnich last time until he had sat down and it was clear the man was wary of him.

Callum smiled and indicated a chair for his patient. 'How are you?' he asked as the old man sat.

Mr Dunnich shot a glance at Felicity, as if he was waiting for an interpretation. 'Fine, thank you, Doctor.'

Callum grimaced at how formal Mr Dunnich was this time. No *Doc* today. The fact that he was responsible for it didn't sit well at all. He obviously had some ground to make up and he was determined to do just that.

'How are the toes going?'

Mr Dunnich bent to take off his shoes. 'Much better,' he said. 'Those pills worked a treat.'

Callum performed the same examination on the toes as he'd done last week but this time, aware of Felicity's scrutiny, he commented on his patient's neatly pressed trousers. 'That's a perfect crease you've got going on there.'

'Oh…yes.'

'Do you get them dry-cleaned or iron them yourself?'

'Do it myself,' he said, pride strengthening his voice. 'Twenty years in the army when I was a lad. Some things you never forget.'

'Really? I might have to drop mine around too.'

Mr Dunnich glanced at him awkwardly and Callum grinned and winked. He was relieved when the old man and then Felicity laughed. 'Me too,' she added.

'Not on your life.' Mr Dunnich chortled.

'Please thank your wife for the roses last week. I took them home and they were perfect in Luci's house.'

'Oh, yes,' Mr Dunnich agreed cheekily. 'Luci's house was made for roses.'

'Does your wife have a favourite?' Callum enquired as he indicated Mr Dunnich should put his shoes back on.

'No. No one in particular but she does love the climbing roses best. Every morning without fail we have a cuppa out on the front porch so she can look out over the arbour where they all climb. Gets some Vitamin D too before the day becomes too hot. Except the last few days. Lizzy hasn't really wanted to.'

Callum frowned. 'Is she sick?'

'No, I don't think so,' he said, straightening now his shoes were back on. 'Communication has been hard since the stroke but I've got pretty good at understanding her. She says not. I think she's just kinda down, you know? I'm a little bit worried about her, to be honest. She's never been that kind of person.'

'That's no good.' Callum's medical antennae pinged. It had been such a long time since they'd done that. It was nice to have them back.

He flicked a glance at Felicity. Her brows were drawn together in a concerned V. Maybe Mrs Dunnich needed to be checked on. 'How about we add Lizzy to Felicity's home visit list on Thursday? Just to give her a once-over, put your mind at ease?'

Mr Dunnich brightened. 'Yeah?'

'Absolutely, Mr Dunnich,' Felicity confirmed. 'We're here to support you and Lizzy.'

'Okay, then, thank you. I'd really appreciate it. I'll make you some of Lizzy's rhubarb tartlets. I've got rhubarb coming out of my ears.'

'That sounds fabulous,' she agreed, and Callum wondered where the hell she put all that food if every Thursday was the same as the last one. Her figure was about as perfect as it got without a single sign of twelve different carbohydrate-laden snacks.

'Right, then, it's settled,' Callum said. 'Now, I think I'll write you up for a month's worth of the medication for your bunions and let's assess again after that. Sooner, of course, if the pain worsens. Does that sound like a plan?'

'Sure does, Doc.'

Callum couldn't deny how satisfying that *Doc* was as

he turned to the computer and ordered the medication, the script printing out quickly. He pulled it out of the printer and handed it to Mr Dunnich, standing at the same time.

'See you next month, Mr Dunnich,' Callum said. 'And Felicity will see you on Thursday.'

'Call me Alf,' he said, also rising and holding out his hand, which Callum took. 'I'll make sure to have some extra tartlets for Flick to give to you.'

Callum smiled. The people of Vickers Hill obviously prided themselves on the gourmet reputation of the town, nestled as it was in the middle of wine country. They also seemed intent on making him fat.

'Or she might just keep them for herself,' Felicity said. Mr Dunnich laughed as amusement lit Felicity's eyes and they dared him to surrender to his fate.

'Rhubarb tartlets are my favourite. I would love that.'

Callum let out a breath as he sat at his desk after Alf left with Felicity. If the shine in her eyes was anything to go by, he'd nailed it. There had certainly been no tight-lipped, jaw-clenched, silent disapproval.

The door opened and he braced himself for his next patient—a torn ACL. *Oops*. No. *Jane Richie* was his next patient. But he needn't have worried, it was just Felicity.

'Now,' she said as she walked towards him with an I-told-you-so swagger. 'That wasn't so hard, was it?'

He rolled his eyes. 'You're a gloater, aren't you?'

'I have no idea what you mean,' she said, batting her eyelashes at him in an exaggerated manner with a big grin that transformed her entire face, and in that moment he saw the same thing that everyone else around here did—Flick, who was all things to all people. Who was popular with everybody and loved by all.

Who belonged to them.

It was a sobering thought. She'd been the girl on the train

to him since the beginning but seeing her here in her natural habitat it was clear that train girl had been the aberration.

Still, he wasn't ready to let that version of her go either. There were obviously two sides to Felicity and he was privileged to have seen the side that obviously no one here had. 'Let me make it up to you for being so obtuse and… What was it you called me? Cavalier? Come to my place for dinner tonight. I'm a pretty mean cook.'

The remnants of her smile slid from her mouth as she sat on the chair Mr Dunnich had just vacated. 'No.'

'*Just* dinner.'

'No.'

'Are you worried about Mrs Smith?'

'No. I'm worried about us. Together. Alone. Somewhere near a bed.'

A thick slug of desire hit Callum low in the belly. He'd been thinking about them alone *on* a bed an inordinate amount of time ever since the kiss in the car. 'You think I can't control myself?'

'I think you know as well as I do that *neither* of us will be able to control ourselves.'

Callum liked it that she wasn't playing coy or trying to pretend there wasn't a thing simmering between them. She may have been trying to ignore it for a week but she wasn't in denial.

'And we're not going there.'

He frowned, getting his thoughts back on track. 'We're not?' It was the right thing to do given they had to work together and he was here for only a short period of time but…

'No. I'm going to be your friend.'

Callum didn't have many female friends. The ones he did have he didn't want to sleep with.

The same couldn't be said for Felicity.

'You are?'

'Yes. I'll take you touring on the weekends. We'll visit some art galleries and antique shops. There's some great lookouts and a heritage trail. We'll drink wine and eat gourmet food at a bunch of different wineries. It'll be fun.'

Not as much fun as drinking wine and eating gourmet food off her body. 'Okay...'

'Are you free on Saturday?'

'Yes.'

'Good. I'll pick you up at eleven.'

CHAPTER NINE

FELICITY WASN'T NERVOUS when she picked Callum up on Saturday. She was confident they could be friends, despite the very definite tug of her libido and crazy speculation from the entire town.

Her libido didn't rule her actions and the town could talk all they wanted. Felicity knew from old they would anyway. As long as she and Callum knew where they stood, the town could go on building castles in the air.

Of course, the second she saw him walking down Luci's flower-lined pathway her confidence nosedived. She didn't know if it was the riot of colour and prettiness all around him making him seem so damn male or the way he filled out his snug blue jeans, but her belly looped the loop.

Friends. She could do this. *They* could do it.

They had to. Vickers Hill was not the place to be reckless. To be the girl from the train. She would be here long after he'd left and she didn't want to be walking around with everyone talking about her behind her back. She didn't want to be an object of gossip or, worse, pity.

Besides, sex was easy. A friendship could be more enduring and, she suspected, less pain in the long run. Above all else, she sensed that Callum needed a friend more than anything now. He'd been through a lot and was still working things out. She had no doubt he could find lovers. But he was in Vickers Hill for a reason—for clear air.

Sex would just fog it all up.

Felicity braced herself as he opened the car door and climbed in beside her. She smiled and said, 'Hi,' trying not to notice the way his T-shirt fell against his stomach. It was difficult when she knew exactly what was beneath.

'Hey,' he said. She couldn't really see his eyes behind the dark sunglasses but she could feel them all over her. 'You look great.'

Felicity blushed, reminding her of how he'd made her blush on the train. She was wearing a dress she'd bought at Bondi with Luci. It was strappy and light in an Aztec pattern, baring her shoulders and arms. The skirt was loose and flowing, the hem fluttering around her knees.

'Thanks,' she murmured, returning her attention to the road as she engaged the clutch. She wasn't going to tell him he looked great too. She hadn't bought him here to flirt with him and if she said, 'You don't look so bad either', that's what she'd be doing.

She didn't want the time he had left here to be one long slow tease between the two of them until one, or both, of them cracked. She was genuine about forming a friendship with him. Absolutely certain that it was their destiny.

Or, if nothing else, sensible.

'Where are we off to?'

'Pretty Maids All In A Row cellar door,' Felicity said, pleased to be slipping into tour-guide mode. It was a role she often played for visitors. She loved Vickers Hill and the entire Clare Valley. It may be smaller and further away than the renowned wine-growing region of the Barossa but it was known for its foodie culture and many high-end restaurants.

'That sounds like a mouthful.'

'It is a little.' She laughed. 'But they have a Riesling to die for and my favourite menu of all the local wineries. They do this rabbit dish that will make you weep. But first I'm going to take you on a bit of a scenic drive around.'

'Sounds good to me.' He nodded. 'Lead on.'

By the time Felicity pulled into the winery car park an hour later she didn't think she'd laughed so much in her life. Cal-

lum had been an entertaining companion—very *Cal*like—
as she'd driven him all around the valley to give him a good
overview of the district that surrounded Vickers Hill.

During lunch—rabbit and a very fine Riesling—they
talked a lot of shop. Callum was keen to know all the ins
and outs of the practice and the different relationships and
Felicity was happy to impart all she knew.

It was only when they were relaxing over dessert and
she was feeling the buzz from her second glass of wine that
things turned personal.

'So how come,' he asked, supporting his chin in his palm
as he leaned his elbow on the thick slab of timber that made
up the table, 'somebody hasn't snapped you up by now, St
Felicity.'

Felicity laughed. 'St Felicity?'

'Yes. *Saint.*' He grinned. 'Vickers Hill's very own. You're
the woman who can do no wrong, don't you know? I have
a feeling that the town will apply to have you canonised
any day now.'

If he only knew how very unsaintly her thoughts had
been today he'd be shocked. 'I think I have to be dead for
that to happen.'

'A trifling detail,' he dismissed with a flick of his hand.
'Seriously, though, were you born in Vickers Hill? Because
your people do love you.'

'Born, bred and schooled. Stayed here until I left to go
to uni in Adelaide to study nursing.'

'And you came straight back and have dedicated every
waking moment of your life to the good people of the Hill?'

Felicity laughed. 'No. I've only been back for four years.
I worked in Adelaide for just over seven years.'

'Whereabouts?'

'At the general hospital, in their emergency department.'

'And you came home because you were...' He raised both
eyebrows. 'Over it?' She shook her head. 'Burned out?' She

shook it again. 'I know,' he said, smiling, drawing attention to his lips, 'St Felicity was sacked.'

'No.' She laughed.

'It was drugs, wasn't it? It's okay, you can tell. You're secret is safe with me.'

'No,' she said, laughing harder. 'Try again.'

'Hmm.' He narrowed his eyes, his gaze roaming all over her face for long moments. 'I know,' he announced. 'It was because of a man, wasn't it? He broke your heart.'

Felicity's breath hitched at his startling accuracy. She hoped her face didn't betray how badly her heart had been broken as she forced joviality into her voice. 'Bingo.'

Callum's face morphed from teasing to serious in one second flat. 'Oh, God, sorry. I didn't mean... I shouldn't have been kidding around. That was...dumb.'

'It's fine. It was four years ago. I'm over it.'

It was a startling revelation to realise she *was* over it. The hurt had lingered for such a long time. But she could put her hand on her heart right here, right now and honestly say that all the feelings she'd had for Ned were no more.

She'd always *love* him in that nostalgic we-were-good-to-gether-and-you-used-to-mean-the-world-to-me way. They'd had a lot of great times. There'd been a lot of love. But she was over the heart*ache*.

She was healed. And not crazy glued back together but actually fully knitted.

'How long were you together?'

'Four years. He—Ned—was a nurse. We went through uni together and we both worked in A and E. We were friends first and it kind of developed slowly from there. Crept up on us, I guess.'

'So how did it all go wrong? What happened?'

To this day, Felicity still didn't fully understand it. It had been so sudden. 'One day he just said he'd met somebody else. Just...' Felicity splayed her hands '...like that. We were a few weeks off taking a holiday to New Zealand. I thought he was going to propose.' She gave a half-laugh and shook her head, thinking about how damn clueless she'd been. 'On the day he dumped me I was asking him if his passport had arrived yet and he just blurted it out. "I've met somebody else and I want to be with her."'

His hand slid across the table and covered hers. 'I'm so sorry. That must have been devastating. What a total creep.'

His quick insult surprised a laugh out of Felicity. 'He said he hadn't meant it to happen, he hadn't been looking for it. For what it's worth, I believed him. He was never the kind of guy who was always looking over my shoulder, you know?'

He winced. 'We're all creeps, aren't we?' He withdrew his hand and placed both of them over his heart. 'I sincerely apologise on behalf of the entire male sex in that case.'

She laughed again. 'It's okay. I survived.'

'You did,' he murmured, his gaze locking on hers as he dropped his hands to the table. 'Kudos to you.'

'Oh, I licked my wounds for a long time, don't you worry about that. It was pretty messy for a while.'

'Did you never suspect?'

'Never.' Felicity had been completely blindsided by Ned's admission. 'Apparently he'd known her for a month.'

He blinked. 'Wow. That's a *big* call.'

'Yeah. But they got married a month later and have two kids so they must be doing something right.'

'And you came home?'

Felicity nodded. 'I did. Home to my old bedroom and my father's country music playing on the radio and my mother's home cooking.'

'Just what the doctor ordered,' he teased.

'Yes.' She'd put on six kilos in that first month. It had taken her another year to get them off. 'Then Dr Dawson gave me a job, even though I had no practice nurse qualifications. Sure, I'm Luci's friend so he knew me well and probably couldn't say no to me when I burst into tears in front of him one day, but I will be forever in his debt for that. He was a saviour. *Work* was a saviour.'

Work had got her through days when all she'd wanted to do was curl up in a ball. It had saved her from ringing Ned a hundred times a day, screaming and/or crying at him until she was hoarse.

'You were lucky, then.'

His voice was even but there was a gravity to his words and all the teasing light had dimmed from his eyes. Of course. Callum had never had that when his life had gone pear-shaped. She'd relied on work to get her through her grief but he hadn't been *able* to work. The mere fact he *couldn't* had been at the very crux of his grief.

'Yeah, I was,' she agreed.

'Well,' he said, tossing his head as if he was trying to shake off the black cloud that had descended around them, 'for what it's worth, I'm glad you weren't with that lying, cheating scumbag the day you stepped on the train.'

Felicity laughed. 'So am I.' The heaviness of the conversation suddenly lightened as good memories crowded out the bad. Sitting opposite him now, it felt like they were back in the dining carriage.

'What about you?' she asked. 'A woman ever broken your heart? No.' She shook her head. 'Let me guess. You do all the breaking, I bet.'

'I'll have you know a girl called Susie Watts smashed my heart to smithereens when I was nine years old.' He put a hand on his chest. 'She dumped me for Jimmy Jones because he had a bigger bicycle than I did.'

Felicity sucked in some air through her hollowed cheeks in an appropriately sympathetic noise. 'Ouch.' But the urge to laugh was overwhelming. 'I'm sorry. That's awful.'

He narrowed his eyes. 'You don't look very sorry.'

Laughter bubbled in her chest. 'No, I was just thinking…'

'Thinking what?'

'A guy called Jimmy Jones? He sounds like one of those

bad boys some girls are fatally attracted to. Maybe it wasn't just his bicycle that was bigger.'

'Oh, no,' Callum groaned good-naturedly, shutting his eyes before opening them again. 'Kick a guy when he's down.'

She did laugh this time. 'Sorry,' she said, trying to make herself stop.

He drank his coffee and watched her patiently—intently—a smile turning the fullness of his lips into two plush crescents. God, he was *sexy*. The way he smiled was sexy. The way his hair brushed his ears was sexy. The way he tilted his head was sexy.

The way he looked at *her* was sexy.

'So, you didn't answer my question,' Felicity said when she'd pulled herself under control. 'Ever had your heart broken? In an *adult* relationship?'

He placed his coffee cup back on its saucer. 'Not really.'

'You more a play-the-field kind of guy?' Everything about him oozed masculine confidence. She could see him at some hip Sydney bar mobbed by women.

'There's been a couple of longer-term relationships but they were never love matches and when you're working long hours and studying all the other hours left in the day they tend to take a back seat until they fizzle out. They were light and fun and mutually enjoyable while they lasted. And then…'

Felicity waited for him to continue after his abrupt cessation. When he didn't she cocked an eyebrow and prompted him. 'And then?'

He shifted in his seat, sitting more upright, pulling his arm back and propping his bent elbow on the curved back of the chair. 'After the accident…people didn't really know what to say and frankly I was pretty awful to be around sometimes. Most people in my social circle were in medicine and a lot of them dropped out of the circle—I guess because I was the elephant in the room. I was their *what if*.

A rather sad reminder of how you could be riding on top one second then on your butt the next.'

'Did they think it was contagious?' she asked drily.

He smiled. 'I think maybe they thought of me more like a bad omen. Surgeons are all about the successes. We don't like to talk about failures. We certainly don't like to be confronted by them.'

'And it was the same with women?'

'No. Ironically, my sex life had never been better.' He fiddled with his coffee cup for a moment. 'And I'm not very proud to say I kind of drowned myself in that for quite a while.' He shrugged. 'I was throwing myself a huge pity party and it wasn't like there was much else to do. Until I realised that about ninety percent of the action I was getting amounted to *pity* sex.'

'Oh.' Felicity wanted to reach out and touch him like he'd touched her, but he seemed so far away now. 'What about the other ten percent?'

'Some kind of sick sexual healing for the blind man thing.'

Felicity grimaced. 'Oh, dear.'

'Yes.' He frowned into his coffee. 'After that I kind of just stopped. It was a real downer for my libido.'

Felicity knew she shouldn't get into a conversation about his libido in case it veered into flirting territory but she was a sucker for a wounded guy and the nurse inside her urged her to try and turn that frown upside down. Soothe it right off his face.

'Your sex drive seemed in perfect working order to me,' she murmured, hoping her voice sounded light and teasing rather than coy and flirty.

'Ah, well,' he said, lifting his gaze squarely to her lips, sucking away all the oxygen between them, 'that's because you woke it up.'

Her mouth tingled under his intense scrutiny and she could barely breathe. She probably shouldn't feel so damn turned on, especially as he didn't look entirely happy about his newly roused libido.

But she did. 'I'm…sorry?'

He shook his head, his eyes lifting higher and locking with hers. 'I'm not.'

The words both pleased and petrified Felicity. Was it just a statement of fact or a subtle reminder of the thing they were trying to ignore? Luckily for her, a waiter chose that moment to clear their table, breaking their eye contact and the accompanying tension.

For now.

Felicity pulled her car up outside Luci's house at around four. She waved at Mrs Smith, who was in her front garden, watering her plants. The old biddy didn't even pretend to be minding her own business.

'Uh-oh,' Callum said. 'Bouncer at six o'clock.'

Felicity laughed at the idea of Mrs Smith in a black T-shirt with Security stamped across the front in big white letters. Not that she needed it—she'd taught at the primary school for almost thirty years. Nobody in Vickers Hill messed with her.

'Thank you for today,' Callum said as he undid his seat belt. 'I had a really great time.'

'So did I.'

And she had. They'd had their moments when teasing and banter had definitely branched into flirting but they'd pulled back and just enjoyed each other's company.

As much as two people who were trying to deny their sexual attraction could.

'We should do it again,' he said.

Felicity nodded. 'Oh, we will. By the time you get out of here I promise you'll have seen every inch worth seeing.'

She realised the potential double entendre about the same time as Callum, his eyebrows rising as he tried to suppress a grin. 'None of those inches include me.'

He laughed. 'Just checking.'

She rolled her eyes at him. 'Seriously? Mrs Smith is over there, probably trying to read our lips, so show a little decorum, please.'

'Of course.' He nodded and moulded his face into solemn lines but there was mischief in his eyes. 'So...my turn for the chauffeuring next time but I can't do next weekend because I'm on call.'

'That's okay. I'm actually going to an art exhibition on Thursday night at Drayton's Crossing. We drove through there on our way to lunch? It's a friend of mine but if you want to come along it should be fun. You can drive if you want.'

'Ah...okay.'

Felicity gave a half-laugh. 'Your enthusiasm is overwhelming. It won't be MOMA but she's really good, I promise. She has sell-out showings in Adelaide but this is a fundraiser for the local fire service and she's a Clare Valley girl.'

'No, it's not that.' He smoothed his palms up and down his jeans, which was distracting as hell. 'I can't...drive at night on my conditional licence. My visual acuity and depth of field in my left eye deteriorates badly in the dark.'

'Oh, okay, sure.' She shrugged. 'So I'll drive. I don't mind.'

But she could tell that *he* minded. *A lot.*

'It's not okay,' he growled, shoving a hand through his hair. 'I feel like a damn teenager on a curfew.'

His frustration was almost palpable. He'd obviously lost a degree of independence as well as his career and Felicity wanted nothing more than to soothe him, but it was probably the last thing *he* wanted from her. A guy like Callum who had turned his back on a steady supply of pity sex probably just needed a bit of understanding.

Being able to jump in a car and drive whenever she

wanted was something she always took for granted. Any restriction on that would be a constant irritant for her too.

'I can imagine that's a real pain in the butt.'

'Yeah,' he huffed, looking out his window for long moments. 'I've got used to taking a taxi everywhere in Sydney.' He glanced at her. 'I don't suppose they have any Ubers in Vickers Hill?'

'Ah, no.' Felicity smiled. 'But we do have an old-fashioned taxi service and I'm perfectly fine to drive us to Drayton's on Thursday, I promise. Hell, this car's been there so many times it could do it without any assistance from me.'

'Fine. But I drive on our next daytime outing.'

Felicity nodded. 'It's a date.' *Damn it.* She cringed at her flippant choice of words, her cheeks heating. Way to make it awkward, Flick. 'Well, you know, *figuratively*, of course.'

He laughed. 'Of course.'

Between that gaffe and Mrs Smith starting to pace up and down her footpath Felicity just wanted today to be over. She'd had a great time but clearly it was only going to be downhill from here.

'Well…I'm pretty sure Mrs Smith is about to turn her hose on us so I think it's time I left.'

'Sure.' He reached for the doorhandle. 'Thanks again.'

He was out of the car before she remembered she hadn't given him the gift from Mr Dunnich. 'Wait,' she called out quickly before he shut the door.

He ducked his head back in the car. 'What? Mrs Smith is giving me the evil eye.'

Felicity smiled. Mrs Smith hadn't lost that school-teacher glare—the one that could see straight through a kid and know exactly what they were guilty of. She reached over to the back seat and grabbed the plastic container with five of the most perfectly formed rhubarb tartlets she'd ever seen.

'This is from Alf. He made me promise I'd give them to you. Not keep them for myself.' She thrust the box of temptation into his hands. 'You have no idea how hard that was.'

'I appreciate your restraint,' he murmured as he took the container, looking at her with eyes that left her in no doubt he appreciated much, much more.

Unexpected heat arced between them like a solar flare. 'Don't,' she said, trying to mentally pull herself back from this different sort of temptation. 'There were six. I ate one.'

He chuckled and it oozed into the car all around her. 'I appreciate your lack of restraint too.'

Felicity's breath caught in her throat as his gaze turned copulatory. Was he thinking about her lack of restraint in bed that night? Because she sure as hell was. She swore she could almost feel the rock of the train around them again.

Then he was straightening, the car *actually* rocking slightly as the door shut. He waved at Mrs Smith, earning himself a scowl, before he swaggered down Luci's path like he was striding along a hospital corridor instead of a path lined with lavender and sweet peas.

Two weeks down. Six more to go.

CHAPTER TEN

THE DAYS FORMED a steady rhythm, which Callum was starting to appreciate. He'd thought he'd needed the pace and the unpredictability of the north shore practice to keep his mind off things. He'd thought if he slowed down, if he had too much time to be idle, he'd have too much time to dwell on the state of his life.

And probably in the city that would have been true.

But there was something surprisingly satisfying about the slower tempo in the country. It took his mind off himself more effectively than keeping a frantic pace ever had because it freed up his mind from multiple foci—a jampacked appointment book or surgical list to get through each day—and allowed him the space to think more holistically. He wasn't skimming the surface. He had time to sink down deeper into the layers.

He realised now that he hadn't needed to keep physically busy—he'd just needed to be mentally challenged. That was what he'd always loved about surgery—the mental challenge of the detail involved—and now he was finding a similar appreciation in the way general practice involved the minutiae of people's lives. That they were, as Felicity had said, the sum of *all* their parts, not just the product of one.

Even in the mornings, when he wasn't at work, he didn't feel the constant churn of loss and regret that continually threatened to swamp him back home in those rare quiet moments. Life in Sydney and the constant mix of pity and expectation from people for him to *bounce back*, to be the guy he'd been before the accident, seemed a million miles away.

Everything back home had reminded him of what he couldn't have. Everything in Vickers Hill showed him what he *could*.

He'd come here hoping to break the cycle of mental self-flagellation, hoping to shrug off the old skin and grow a new one. A better one. A *thicker* one.

Deep down he hadn't thought that possible.

But as Thursday rocked around and he was lazily appreciating Luci's garden as he sipped his coffee, he was beginning to think it was very much possible. He was even beginning to think it was possible that he and Felicity could be friends.

At work it seemed possible anyway. They were getting on well and it was easy to keep her straight in his head in a place where she was so clearly 'the nurse'. From what she wore to how people treated her to what they called her, everything existed to create that mental barrier.

Everyone called her Flick and every day she was dressed in the same navy pants and polo shirt as the other staff, her hair pulled into the same low ponytail. People spoke to her with both respect and affection. At work she *was* Flick and through tacit agreement they didn't talk about the train or that weird moment in the car on Saturday. They kept things professional, and it worked.

Even the art show tonight was kept in perspective when both Bill and Julia as well as Angela and about a dozen of his patients were also attending. Yes, *she'd* invited him and he was going *with* her but it was merely an act of kindness extended to the newbie in town.

It was the embodiment of country hospitality. An invitation that could have been issued by any one of the practice employees. But it had been issued by her. By *Flick*. And he was looking forward to it immensely.

Unfortunately it wasn't *Flick* who picked him up. It was most definitely *Felicity*. In that little black dress from the train. Or maybe it wasn't the exact one. But it was similar. Figure-hugging, a great glimpse of cleavage, a very distracting bow on the side that looked like it might be the way in—and *out*.

Okay. Not the one from the train—he'd have remembered that bow.

Did she know how tempting that damn bow was? Had she done it on purpose? He supposed there weren't a lot of places or events in Vickers Hill that required dressing up so why wouldn't she when she had the chance? It was obvious from the train that she was as partial to getting all girly as the next woman.

He just wished she'd chosen the light and summery look from the weekend when she'd taken him to lunch at the winery. The whole girl-next-door thing suited her.

There was nothing girl-next-door about this dress.

Not the figure-hugging, not the cleavage, not the sexy high heels. Not that damn bow or the sway of her hips or the swing of her long, loose hair. This was a Pavlov's dog dress.

And he was salivating like crazy.

It certainly drove out the mushrooming frustration he'd felt as he'd waited to be picked up like some teenager who'd had his keys taken off him by his parents. The black cloud that had been building all afternoon had blown right away as he'd opened the door, and by the time he'd slid into the car seat beside her, it was long gone.

Music, low and sweet, flared to life on the radio as she started the engine. Her bangles jingled. Her perfume enveloped him, filling his head with her scent and a string of bad ideas.

'You look…lovely,' he said as she smiled at him.

'Thanks.'

She reached for her seat belt but not before he saw a tiny slip in that smile, a slight dimming of the sparkle in her eyes as she buckled up.

Had she been hoping for more?

Unfortunately, lovely was about as polite as he could get right now. The next level up was *sexy*. The one after that was not for polite company.

He was okay with being friends. He understood the reasons for it and thought it was doable. But he wasn't stupid enough to deny there was the possibility of a very different relationship if they chose to go down that path.

Which they hadn't.

'I'm worried about Lizzy Dunnich,' she said, as she drove off.

Callum dragged his mind out of his—and her—pants. It was hard to concentrate on shop talk when she looked like the woman from the train, but at least it would help him to keep the division between the two very different women straight in his head.

'Is she unwell?' Felicity had obviously decided to keep her on her home-visit schedule after she'd seen her last week.

'No. Nothing specific I can pinpoint. Just a feeling. Like Alf says, she's just really withdrawn. But Bailey—that's their Labrador—has taken to not leaving her side. I'm worried he knows something we don't.'

Callum hadn't owned a dog, growing up, and they'd never come into his realm of practice when he'd been putting on a pair of scrubs every morning, but he'd read enough anecdotal evidence about the canine-human connection to understand why Felicity was worried.

'You think she might be…'

'Yeah.'

The white of her knuckles around the steering wheel drew his attention. *My* people, she'd called them that day she'd finally exploded at him for his poor connection with the patients.

And Mrs Dunnich was one of them.

'She's eighty-six,' he said gently, staring at her profile. 'And she's already had one stroke.'

'Yeah,' she said again, her eyes glued to the road.

He wasn't telling her anything she didn't already know. Lizzy Dunnich didn't have a whole lot of ticks in her column.

But this one felt close to him too.

As a surgeon he'd had patients die. The last one, not long before his accident, had been a fifty-eight-year-old woman who'd presented with a dissecting abdominal aortic aneurysm. They'd rushed her to Theatre but he hadn't been able to stem the haemorrhage.

Her death had been a professional loss—not a personal one. He hadn't known the woman. He hadn't eaten homemade rhubarb tartlets from her family recipe. He hadn't met her husband. Telling him had been as awful as it always was, but his scheduled theatre list had been severely disrupted because of the emergency and he'd still had three more patients to deal with so the death had been quickly filed under 'Impossible save', as triple As too often were.

'Why don't I drop by on Saturday and see them? I'm on call so—'

'Oh, would you?' she interrupted, her voice charged with hope.

'Of course.'

Her exhalation was noisy in the confines of the car. 'Thank you,' she said, glancing at him quickly before returning her attention to the road.

Callum's night vision might be rubbish but he could still see the shine of unshed tears in her eyes. He'd never met a woman who wore her emotions so openly. Once upon a time that would have made him want to run as far away as possible.

Tonight it made him want to pull her closer.

Felicity was still stewing over the word *lovely* when they arrived at the art show. She shouldn't be. Callum's offer to see Mrs Dunnich should be dominating her thoughts and she should still be grateful for that but somehow his *lovely* resonated the most.

Now she understood his dismay that day when she'd described their time on the train as lovely. It was such an... insipid word.

It shouldn't bother her. They were *friends* and attracting Callum wasn't her aim.

Absolutely not.

She'd worn the dress for *herself.* Because she didn't get the opportunity to dress up very often and everyone else would be making the effort. Because she was single and one day she hoped not to be—Mr Right *could* be in Drayton's Crossing. Because rocking a little black dress was a marvellous thing and putting one on one of life's great joys. Like sexy lingerie and expensive chocolate.

She'd worn the dress for herself, damn it.

But then Callum had said 'lovely' and she'd realised she might have possibly, somewhere deep in her subconscious, worn it for him...

'There's Bill and Angela,' Callum said, his hand at her elbow.

Felicity looked around the transformed space. It had Veronica's artistic signature all over. Gone was the quaint hundred-year-old farmers' hall and in its place was a high-class bordello. Hundreds of metres of rich burgundy velvet were draped artfully overhead and lined the walls to form a dramatic backdrop to the paintings. There was a heavy reliance on gold brocade, plush velvet chaises and art deco standing lamps covered with red chiffon shawls to create a seductive pink glow.

Curvy women dressed in corsets and fishnet circulated with trays of champagne and canapés amongst the crowd milling around the paintings.

It was hard to believe this was little old Drayton's Crossing. It could be in any posh city gallery anywhere in the world, and while she knew about three-quarters of the peo-

ple in the room, there were certainly some she didn't rec-
ognise. Probably from Adelaide. Veronica's art was highly
sought after and her exhibitions, regardless of location, were
always well attended.

'You want champagne?'

The fine hairs on Felicity's nape prickled as Callum's
voice, low and close to her ear to be heard over the noise,
did funny things to her equilibrium. She was conscious of
his presence behind her. His bulk, his heat, the waft of his
citrusy aftershave. The warmth of his breath on her temple.

Her eyelids fluttered closed, she swayed a little as she
fought the urge to lean back. Let herself drape against him.

And wouldn't *that* just give everybody something more
to gossip about?

They weren't in a city gallery somewhere. They were in
Drayton's Crossing, for Pete's sake.

Felicity locked her quads and cleared her throat. 'Yes,
please.' Anything to remove the temptation of him from her
orbit long enough to get back some control.

'Be right back,' he murmured. 'Don't go away.'

Not much chance of that with legs as useless as two wet
noodles.

She watched him go. Somehow he seemed more hip,
cool, stylish and sexy than any other guy in the room—even
the arty types who clearly weren't from these parts. He was
wearing a suit the colour of roasted Arabica beans that he'd
teamed with a purple shirt, left open at the neck. No tie.

He looked the ultimate in casual, urban chic. And the
way those trousers pulled across his butt as he walked away
should be utterly illegal.

There was nothing *lovely* about it.

By the time he came back, Felicity was talking to an old
friend from Vickers Hill and she was on much more steady
ground. In fact, for the rest of the night, as they went from
painting to painting, there was always someone she knew,

someone to introduce Callum to and mingle with to prevent them from being alone.

Because they needed to avoid that at all costs. She wasn't stupid, she could tell people were openly curious, watching them and their every move. It was why she tried extra hard to project a friendly, collegial discourse between them.

She was careful about her stance and other nonverbal cues, she kept the conversation about the paintings and suppressed the urge to touch him, which was surprisingly difficult. She'd never realised how tactile she was in conversation until she had to physically stop herself a dozen times from touching Callum's arm.

She seriously deserved an award for her portrayal of *just-friends-nothing-to-see-here-move-along-please.*

Finally, she got to introduce him to Veronica. Felicity had been trying to get to her all night but her friend had been swamped with both buyers and well-wishers.

'V.,' Felicity said with a smile as her friend enveloped her in an enthusiastic, champagne-slopping hug. 'This is fabulous. You must be so pleased.'

'Absolutely thrilled, darl.' Big hoop earrings matched wild brown curls and the whole kaftan-alternative vibe Veronica had going on. Not for the first time, Felicity wished she oozed the same brash sexiness that was like a second skin for Veronica.

'I've sold just about every painting. Reckon the Clare Valley fire service will get about fifty k out of their cut by the end of the night.'

'That's amazing. They'll be giving you the keys to the valley next time you're home,' Felicity teased.

One of the things she most loved about Veronica was that she hadn't lost her connection with her roots. Her artwork may be hung in galleries around the world but at heart she was a small-town girl.

'As long as they're able to open every cellar door in the district then I'm fine with that.' Veronica laughed in her disarmingly self-deprecating way before turning her attention to Callum. 'Well, hello, there,' she said, as Felicity took a nervous sip of her remaining champers. 'So *you're* the guy she's doing.'

Felicity almost inhaled her drink at the outrageous statement. 'V.,' Felicity warned, coughing and spluttering on the bubbles that had almost gone down the wrong way as Callum threw back his head and laughed, seemingly unconcerned.

'What?' Veronica asked with a faux aura of innocence. 'All I was going to say is I approve, darling.' She eyed Callum up and down. 'If you've got to be in trouble with the town, might as well make it worth your while.' She held her hand out to Callum. 'Hi, I'm V.'

'Callum.'

'Callum, huh?' Veronica shook her head. 'You look like a Cal to me.'

Callum grinned and Felicity wanted to stomp on his foot. 'I get that as well.'

'I *bet* you do, darl.' Veronica laughed, tapping his shoulder lightly. She switched her attention to Felicity. 'He's good in bed, right? I can just tell.'

Felicity glanced around, hoping nobody was eavesdropping. She'd forgotten how outrageous Veronica could be. She had no filter and lived to scandalise.

'I am not doing him.' Felicity hissed, while Callum—Cal—chuckled some more. Which *was* true. *Currently*, she wasn't. 'The gossips have got it wrong as usual.'

'Well, you should make it right,' Veronica murmured, her gaze eating Callum up again. 'If you can't beat them, darling, you might as well join them.'

Felicity was beginning to regret introducing them. Veronica's attention was a little too lascivious for her liking as a spike of something that felt very much like jealousy prodded Felicity in the chest.

Thankfully she noticed a couple heading their way with an artistic fever in their eyes, clearly intent on monopolising the *artiste* for as long as Veronica was willing to put up with them. 'Oh, look,' Felicity said, tipping her chin at the approaching zealots, 'Buyers incoming. Don't let us keep you.'

She shot her insanely vibrant and attractive friend a sweet smile as she seized Callum's arm and pulled him away. Veronica laughed, clearly neither fooled nor insulted, blowing a couple of quick air kisses before turning her attention on her fans.

They ended up in a corner, near a standing lamp emanating a very distracting pink glow. The crowd had thinned slightly, which enabled them to have a little more privacy.

Not that that had been the objective.

She had no idea what to say to Callum after Veronica's directness. At least everyone else had been discreet about their curiosity. She slugged back the dregs of her champers and immediately wished she could swig another. But as she was driving she grabbed a soda water off a passing tray instead. Callum snagged a beer.

Felicity sipped and wondered whether she should mention Veronica at all—apologise for her maybe. Explain she lived to scandalise. But frankly she was still too embarrassed to head down that track.

'V. seems like a hoot.'

Well. That was settled, then. Looked like they were going to talk about her whether she wanted to or not. 'She is. Sorry about that. She loves to shock people.'

He shook his head, tracking Veronica's movements. 'I think she's fabulous.'

Felicity nodded. Yes. He would. Veronica was probably much more his type than she was. She could imagine him back before his injury with someone delightfully brash and flirty like Veronica. Someone who was socially outgoing, confident in herself and her sexuality.

'She's gorgeous, isn't she? So out there and…' Felicity cleared her throat of the sudden husky stricture threatening to close it right off '…sexy.'

His head swivelled in Felicity's direction, one eyebrow cocked. 'Sexy, huh?'

Heat suffused her face as he studied her like he was seeing her through new eyes, his gaze drawing her in as if they were the only two people in the room. 'A woman can appreciate sexiness in another woman,' she said, a defensive streak in her voice a mile wide.

He held up his hands in mock surrender. 'I totally agree. It's a kinda sexy thing to admit, actually.'

So she was sexy now instead of lovely?

Heat flared between them. She suddenly wished they *were* the only two people in the room. The thought was nine parts thrilling, one part panic inducing. She couldn't afford to lose her head in front of all these people and lose all the 'just mates' groundwork she'd laid over the last hour or so.

'Who, me?' she murmured, keeping her voice low and silky. 'Impossible. I'm *lovely*, remember?'

'Ah.' He chuckled, his lips twitching on the rim of his glass before he took a mouthful of beer. 'Sorry about that. It was a bad word choice.'

'Oh, I don't know,' she said, the irritation from earlier returning with a vengeance as she mimicked what he'd said that day they'd visited Meryl. 'You could have said *nice*.'

He glanced around before his gaze drifted to her mouth. 'Trust me, it was cleaner than what I was really thinking.'

The low admission rumbled from his lips and stroked her in all the good places. She should just leave that alone. But some devil inside her wanted to know what he thought of her black dress.

'Oh?' She hoped the vibrato in her voice didn't betray how very badly she *needed* to know.

'It's not really for…' he looked around again before returning his gaze to hers, lowering his head and leaning in slightly as his voice went down a register '...polite company.'

Felicity was beyond caring about polite as his warm breath stirred the wisps of hair at her temple. A wave of goose-bumps swept down the side of her face and fanned out across her neck. She swayed closer, as if he was pulling her with an invisible thread, locking them in a private little bubble amidst all the colour and movement around them.

'Maybe you should whisper it?' she suggested, turning her lips towards his ear, her voice almost as low and rough as his. She was thankful for her heels bringing their heights closer.

She swore she could *feel* his smile as he leaned in to do just that, his lips brushing her hair.

Felicity's breath hitched and something deep and low clenched down hard as he whispered a very dirty word. It wasn't Shakespeare. It was bald and base and primal.

Such a freaking turn-on.

'And for what it's worth,' he muttered, pulling back so he could stare into her eyes, '*you* are the sexiest woman in the room tonight.'

Felicity swallowed as her legs threatened to melt to jelly again and land her on her butt.

'*Ah*. Here you are!' Angela said, sliding an arm around Felicity's waist, seemingly oblivious to the mood. 'Cal, I need to borrow Flick for a moment. Someone has to come with me while I pay for my painting and stop me from buying another one. She's disciplined like that.'

Felicity didn't get a chance to refuse as Angela dragged her away, but she did glance over her shoulder to find Callum had her firmly in his sights, carnal intent blazing from his eyes.

How they were going to get home without pulling over and jumping each other's bones she had no idea.

CHAPTER ELEVEN

THEY LEFT AN hour later. An hour during which Felicity spent as much time *away* from Callum as possible, mingling with other people as she fought to get her body back under control. Because, while it was clear now that their sexual attraction was never going to allow them to be the friends she'd hoped they could be, it didn't mean succumbing to their attraction was the right thing either.

There was no point getting close to him when it would be *her* heart bruised in the end. Sure, she could have a fling with him but the truth was she'd never been good at casual sex.

Feelings always came in to it for her. Not necessarily love but a very definite connection. That's just the way she was.

It was like a reverse superpower. Her kryptonite. It made her weak.

Before Ned she'd had three serious relationships. Two had lasted six months. One had lasted nine. She was an emotional person—she liked to be invested and committed to the men she dated.

She liked being attached to another person.

But Callum was a different prospect. He'd already admitted to not forming attachments. To having a string of affairs with women during his darkest hours. And he was still coming to terms with a lot of baggage.

It didn't take a brain surgeon to figure out she'd be the more invested of the two of them if she let this thing become more than what had happened on the train. And in her car. And here tonight. She already liked him way more than was wise, especially now he'd proved to be a halfway decent doctor as well.

And then where would she be? Vickers Hill had always felt safe to her. It was her home, the place she'd run to after Ned. The place where she'd come into her own and found her feet. She didn't want to have to run from it as well because it was too painful to stay.

So she wasn't going to go there. But…she was Callum's lift home so she had to find some way to reboot the direction of the night. Maybe her overwhelming desire to have sex with him *was* going to get in the way of a friendship but that didn't mean she couldn't be friendly.

And for that she had to steer the conversation. Because she had no doubt if she steered it the wrong way, Callum would merrily follow.

'Tell me about your brother,' she blurted out as she pulled out of the car park, hyper-aware of the intimacy created by the glow of the dashboard lights and the slow ballad playing on the radio. 'Sebastian, right?'

Callum frowned, obviously not expecting that after the tension that had been building between them. 'Seb,' he corrected. '*That's* what you want to talk about?'

Felicity did not take her eyes off the road. 'That's what I want to talk about.'

He didn't answer for long moments and Felicity held her breath. Was he going to call her on it? Was he going to slip his hand on her leg and turn her into putty?

Everything seemed to hang in the balance as the seconds stretched. Then he sighed and said, 'What do you want to know?'

She shrugged, gripping the steering wheel hard as relief coursed through her system. 'Everything, I guess. He is living with our Luci after all. I'm pretty sure she hasn't told her parents yet so I feel like someone should at least know something about him.'

'In case he's a serial killer?'

Felicity ignored the derision. 'Exactly.'

'Anything specifically? "Everything" is kind of broad.'

'Is he older or younger than you?'

'Three years younger.'

'And he lives with you?'

'No. He doesn't live anywhere in particular, he just crashes at my place when he's in Sydney.'

Felicity frowned at the section of road lit up by her headlights, conscious of dry bushland flying by in her peripheral vision. Seb Hollingsworth—who was living with Luci—was some kind of…drifter?

'So he's…homeless?'

Callum's low chuckle enveloped her, wrapping her up, reminding her how alone they were. Not that being surrounded by people had seemed to matter back at the art show either.

'No. He has a boat that he's doing up with plans to live on it, eventually.'

'Does he have a job to support that plan?' A thirty-one-year-old guy with no fixed abode wasn't exactly inspiring confidence.

'Yes.' Callum chuckled again. 'He's a community health physician, employed by the government. He travels around a lot, mainly in rural areas.'

'Which is why he doesn't have his own place?'

'Yes. That and the fact he's allergic to putting down roots ever since his pregnant girlfriend was killed in a hit-and-run accident a few years back.'

Felicity blanched at the casual imparting of such a tragic tale, flicking a quick glance at him before returning it to the road. The awful news socked her right in the centre of her chest and tears pricked her eyes. 'Oh, God.' She absently patted her chest. 'How *awful* for him.'

'Yes. It was a terrible time. He kind of changed after that. Moved in a completely different direction. Sold their house, bought a motorbike and a run-down boat and started working away a lot.'

Felicity had no doubt something like that could irrevocably change a person. It seemed like both the Hollingsworth men were good at running away. 'Sounds like he's a bit of a wherever-I-lay-my-hat kinda guy.'

'Yeah,' he agreed. 'I think that sums him up perfectly.'

'Are you close?'

Right from the beginning, Callum had come across as utterly self-contained. It was hard to reconcile him having a sibling. If she'd been forced to guess she would have said he was an only child.

He shrugged. 'We're not bosom buddies. But we have a solid relationship built on mutual respect for us both needing our own space.'

Well…that was suitably vague… And sad. It seemed to her that the Hollingsworth brothers could have been a great support to each other during their respective tragedies if they'd come together instead of running away.

But, then, what did she know about sibling relationships? She *was* an only child.

'So,' he said, interrupting her thoughts, 'does Seb pass muster now he has a tragic backstory?'

He was teasing but Felicity didn't see the funny side. 'I don't think it's something you should be making light of,' she chided, aware that she probably sounded like some puritan but unable to easily shake off the lingering sadness of Seb's tragedy.

'Its fine.' He laughed. 'Every year for Christmas Seb sends me a brochure from the guide dogs society. We're blokes, we talk smack and joke about our problems, that's how we bond.'

Felicity rolled her eyes. *Men.* She'd always wanted a brother. Now she wasn't so sure. She wondered what Luci, fellow single child, nurse and sucker for a wounded man, was making of Seb.

'Well, does he or doesn't he?' Callum prompted.

Knowing more about Seb was comforting. She just hoped Luci's vagueness when she talked about him wasn't because she was falling for him. Luci was getting over a painful divorce and Seb Hollingsworth didn't sound like he was ready for a relationship.

Kind of like his brother.

'I'm not about to ring Luci and tell her to get out of the house.'

'Good.' He nodded. 'From what I can gather, she's fine with him being there anyway. And if she wasn't he'd have probably just crashed in the boat. Or, if he'd been absolutely desperate, at my parents' place.'

So Callum had parents in Sydney. 'They don't get on?'

He shrugged. 'Their relationship is a little...fraught.'

'They don't approve of his lifestyle?'

'They don't approve of his *career* choice. They're surgeons. In fact, *all* the Hollingsworths are surgeons,' he said, a core of something that sounded like bitterness infecting his voice. 'Seb chose something outside the field so he's always been a disappointment to them.'

Felicity couldn't begin to imagine her parents being disappointed in *anything* she'd chosen, let alone medicine. The son of a train driver and the daughter of a dairy farmer had only ever wanted happiness for their child. They'd retired to the coast now but were thrilled that Felicity had found her niche in life.

'They must be very proud of you, carrying on the family tradition?' she observed.

'They *were*.'

'Were?' She sneaked a peek at his face, his profile contorting into a grimace, before she looked back at the road.

Surely they'd supported him during and after his injury?

'They think I've given up a little too easily.'

Felicity touched his arm without thinking, just as she would have done to anyone to express her empathy. 'I'm sorry.' No wonder Callum and Seb ran away from their stuff when there was no one for them to run *to*.

'It's fine,' he dismissed, with a shrug, dislodging her

hand. 'I'm used to their indifference. We both are. They're just not cut out to be parents. Some people aren't.'

'But still…' She couldn't wrap her head around it.

'It's fine,' he repeated. 'Don't feel sorry for me. Seb and I grew up with a lot of privilege that many of the kids around us didn't. We didn't want for anything.'

Materialistically, maybe not, but Felicity didn't have to be a psychologist to know what kids needed most were engaged, interested, supportive parents.

'And I think we turned out kinda okay despite them. Well…' he shot her a lopsided grin '…*I* did at least. The jury's still out on Seb.'

Her mouth twitched. Callum Hollingsworth in full charm mode was a force to be reckoned with and she didn't have it in her after such serious subject matter to deny him a little lightness. 'Yeah,' she murmured, sneaking him another look. 'You're kinda okay.'

He grinned at her for a beat or two. Felicity's pulse fluttered and her breath hitched as the moment stretched. She broke it by looking back at the road and the far reach of the headlights illuminating the ghostly white trunks of gum trees.

He didn't say anything for a while and the music filled the space between them. 'About before…' he said eventually.

'No.' Felicity shook her head. 'Let's not do this. Let's mark it up to champagne and vanity and never talk about it again. Okay?'

She held her breath, waiting for his agreement. What she'd do if he didn't, she had no idea. If he looked at her and said *Screw that*, what *would* she do? Probably pull the car over and do him on the side of the road.

'We seem to do that a lot,' he said after a silence that was loud enough to obliterate the music. 'Avoid talking about this thing between us. I'm not sure it's very healthy.'

'No.' Felicity shook her head again vigorously. 'Unhealthy would be flat-out denial. I'm not denying it. I'm ignoring it.'

'And by *it* you mean our red-hot sexual attraction?'

Felicity's fingers tightened around the wheel at Callum's unnecessary summation. 'Yes,' she muttered.

As if she needed any reminding.

'That. But you and I are *not* going there. So there's no point talking about what happened before because nothing happened.'

The fact he'd turned her on in a crowded room with just one, dirty, whispered word didn't count.

He gave a short, sharp laugh. 'Now, *that's* denial.'

Yeah. He had her there. But she only had two options and pulling the car over and having him prove that word to her wasn't a viable one. So she had to forge ahead.

With conversation.

Or turn the music up really loud and not talk at all.

She chose the latter.

Callum was still thinking about that trip home on Thursday night and their awkward goodbye when he dialled Felicity's number on Saturday morning from the Dunnich garden. It was a walk in the park compared to what he was about to tell her. He'd put up with a dozen awkward goodbyes in exchange for this one sad hello.

'Hey,' she said, her voice perky.

She'd used that tone of voice with him all day yesterday. *Perky.* So damn cheerful. It had been amusing then but it grated this morning.

He'd never met a woman so determined to keep him at arm's length.

'What's up?'

For a moment he didn't want to tell her. He just wanted to soak up the November sun beating down on his neck and get lost in the heady aroma of roses and the lazy drone of bees, knowing she was in his ear, breathing and perky.

'Callum?' she prompted, some of the perkiness dissolving.

His heart punched the centre of his chest with slow, precise jabs as he took a steadying breath. 'I'm at Alf's.'

There was a pause on the end of the line, a pause that was so damn loud he could practically hear every thought careening through her head. 'What's happened?'

Her voice was low, serious, resigned. All the perkiness was gone. It was matter-of-fact now. Professional. But he could also hear the slight huskiness. Could picture her big grey eyes growing bright.

'It's Lizzy.' Callum looked over his shoulder to the open back door. He could see Alf's silhouette as he talked on the phone in the central hallway. 'She's had a massive stroke.'

No pause this time, no grilling him for the details. Just, 'I'll be right there', and the phone going dead.

Callum put his phone in his back pocket and went inside, the cool and relative darkness a stark contrast to the bright morning outside. He pushed his sunnies on top of his head and headed for Alf, who hung up the landline as he neared.

'That was our daughter in Adelaide,' he said, his usually strong, slow drawl weak and tremulous as he stared at the device. 'She's going to let everyone know and then head up to us.' He glanced at Callum. 'Do you think she'll h...?' His voice wobbled and cracked. 'Hold on till then, Doc?'

Callum was surprised Lizzy had even lasted this long. Her breathing was affected by the stroke. It had improved since he'd placed some nasal prongs on and run in a trickle of oxygen but Callum didn't think she'd see out too many more hours.

He slid his hand on Alf's shoulder and gave a squeeze. 'I reckon she will, Alf.' Because he needed hope now more than anything.

He nodded, his lips trembling, suddenly looking every one of his eighty-plus years. 'Did you get hold of Flick?' he asked gruffly.

'Yes. She should be here shortly.'

'Rightio,' Alf said, staring at the door to his bedroom and straightening his shoulders as if he was going into battle. How did a husband say goodbye to a wife he'd been with for almost seventy years? 'I'm going back in.'

Callum nodded and wished he didn't feel so out of his depth. He hadn't done this in a long time—stood by and done nothing while a patient slowly slipped away.

He was used to action. To *saving* people.

But Alf had been adamant after Callum had diagnosed the stroke that Lizzy not go to hospital and produced an advance care directive that stated Lizzy didn't want any extraordinary measures taken to save or prolong her life in the event of another major stroke.

'She wants to be here with her family and Bailey by her side,' he'd said.

And Callum understood that, he just didn't know what Alf needed of him right now. It felt wrong to be witnessing something so intimate when he barely knew them. It felt like an intrusion. But he knew he couldn't leave Alf either.

It was why he'd suggested Felicity come and sit with Alf until his family arrived and the old man had jumped at the idea.

'Can I bring you in a cup of tea or something?'

'No, thanks, Doc,' Alf said, and quietly slipped into the room.

A well of uselessness swamped him, familiar and overwhelming. He'd felt like this after the accident when the extent of his injury had sunk in. He'd hated it then and he hated it now.

He had to be able to do something, surely?

He wandered aimlessly to the open front door, pulling his sunglasses down as the brightness jabbed into his permanently dilated left pupil like a knife. He looked up and down the street, willing Felicity's car to arrive, for her to walk through the front gate.

She'd know what to do.

A mix of floral aromas tickled his senses as he waited and his gaze was drawn to the beauty of Alf's garden. It drifted to the arbour that arched over the gate and was covered in climbing roses, and he wondered if these were the ones that Lizzy liked so much. They were pretty, a champagne colour and smaller than the ones growing on individual bushes. Dainty and feminine. Very much like her.

An idea hit him then and he smiled as he strode back into the house and searched the kitchen for a pair of scissors. Maybe filling her room with the aroma of her beloved roses could be his contribution?

Who knew what she could still hear, see and smell?

Locating some scissors in a drawer, he headed back out, stopping at the first bush near the front porch and snipping one of the blooms. The front path was lined with bushes and as he had no real idea what he was doing, apart from avoiding the thorns, he figured he might as well snip one from each. Clearly arranging flowers wasn't his forte but they didn't need to be pretty—they just needed to provide some joy and, hopefully, some peace.

For Alf as well as Lizzy.

He was halfway through when Felicity pulled up. The surge of relief that flooded his chest flowed cool and electric through his veins.

'Hi,' she said as she pushed open the gate and walked under the arbour.

'Hi.' She was in strappy sandals, denim shorts that came to just above her knee and a tank top. She was Flick and she was exactly who he needed. 'I'm sorry for calling you for this—'

She shook her head, interrupting his apology, her loose ponytail brushing back and forth between her shoulder blades. 'You did the right thing. Is she…?'

'No,' he assured her quickly, and her shoulders visibly relaxed. 'She's unconscious but hanging on. Alf's family are driving up from Adelaide. I thought he needed a familiar face to wait with him until they got here.'

'Of course.' She gave him a sad smile, her expression full of empathy. 'What happened?'

'We were all chatting out in the back garden. Alf and I left Lizzy and Bailey there, watching a couple of the magpies they feed frolicking in the sprinkler, so he could take me in and show me some of his wines. We'd been gone a couple of minutes when Bailey started to bark.' Callum wiped the sweat off his brow with the back of his hand. 'Alf knew straight away. When we got to her she was slumped in the wheelchair, unconscious.'

'Oh, no,' she murmured. 'Poor Mr Dunnich.'

'He's been really good. Stoic, you know?' Callum had no idea how long it would last.

'Yes, he's country down to his bootstraps. And what about you?' she asked, peering at him hard as if she was trying to see behind his dark shades. 'Are *you* okay?'

The question surprised him. No colleague had ever asked him if he was okay over a work situation. Sometimes things went wrong and you just got on with it.

But, as he'd learned over the last three weeks, that wasn't the way they did things in Vickers Hill.

'Yes. Thanks.' It felt surprisingly good to have been asked. He may not have known the Dunniches for long but he'd been incredibly moved by Alf's gentleness as he'd laid Lizzy on the bed and stroked her hair. 'Better now you're here.'

Maybe that was one of the things he wasn't allowed to say but it was true. And not in a *hey, baby* way. In a *human* way. She knew Alf and Lizzy and she knew him.

They were all connected.

She glanced at the scissors in his hands and the stems he'd already picked. 'I didn't know what else to do,' he said. 'All I really know about her is how much she loves roses so I figured...'

Overly bright eyes smiled at him. 'I think that's a really beautiful thing to do. Lizzy would love that.'

Callum's chest swelled. He'd felt like a clumsy fool with his black thumb cutting pretty roses in someone else's garden—completely conspicuous. But Felicity's compliment validated his instincts.

'You can leave them in the kitchen if you want. I'll find a vase for them in a bit.'

'I can do it,' Callum dismissed.

A tiny frown caused a little V between her brows. 'Oh… okay, sure. Thanks.'

It was Callum's turn to frown. She didn't sound so sure and he certainly didn't know the etiquette here. 'Is it? Okay?'

'Of course. I just…didn't think you'd want to stick around. You don't have to, you know. I've got this.'

She was letting him off the hook. Three weeks ago Callum would have taken that offer and run with it. Left the nurse to deal with relatives and the patient comfort stuff.

But he wasn't that person any more. *Thanks to her.*

'I'd like to stay…if you don't think it's intruding.'

'That would be great,' she said, her smile gentle, her hand sliding onto his arm and giving it a pat.

Callum glanced at it, surprised at how comforting it was. 'Is she in the bedroom?' He nodded and she edged around him, her hand dropping away. 'I'll see you in there,' she murmured.

He watched her disappear inside the house, the imprint of her hand still marking his skin. Kind of like the way she'd marked his life. In just a few short weeks the girl from the train had taught him more about himself than he'd learned in thirty-plus years. More about being a doctor. More about the things that actually mattered.

Whatever did or didn't happen between them he knew one thing for sure—he was *never* going to forget Felicity Mitchell.

* * *

Callum stepped into the room fifteen minutes later. He'd found a vase under the sink and arranged the blooms. It was never going to win a floral arrangement competition but it wasn't bad for his first time.

He placed them on an old-fashioned dressing table.

'Thanks, Doc,' Alf said. He was sitting on a chair beside the bed, holding his wife's hand. Felicity was sitting next to Alf, holding his hand. 'Lizzy loves her roses, don't you, darlin'?' he asked, patting her hand a couple of times.

'Do you remember that time Bailey dug up those new bushes she'd planted when he was a puppy?' Felicity asked. 'And how hard Bailey worked to get back into her good graces.'

Alf chuckled. Bailey, who was lying on the bed with Lizzy, whined and thumped his tail at the mention of his name but he didn't move his head from Lizzy's thigh.

Callum listened for the next couple of hours as Alf regaled them with stories about Lizzy and their life together. There was so much humour and love in every one but Alf's voice often cracked and Callum could only guess how hard it was for him to watch his beloved wife slipping away.

Her respirations changed as they chatted in the bedroom and by the time the first family members arrived Lizzy's breathing had slowed right down. There were more due to arrive over the course of the afternoon and Alf was praying that everyone could get here before the end, but deep down Callum didn't hold out much hope.

Callum and Felicity moved out to the kitchen to give the family time together. They didn't really talk much, just kept busy, making cups of tea and coffee and refilling them as often as required. At lunchtime Callum went out and bought some loaves of bread and sandwich fillers, which they turned into a couple of crammed platters, and later, for afternoon tea, they were able to rustle up enough home cooking to satisfy everyone.

By the time Lizzy took her last breath at four o'clock, all the family that could be there were by her side. Callum marvelled at her staying power. He had clearly underestimated Alf's wife. It was as if she'd been hanging on for all her family before passing away.

They were washing up when Bailey howled. All the hairs on Callum's nape stood on end. Felicity's hands in the hot, sudsy water stilled. He waited for her to say something but she didn't, she just stood in silence for long moments. He wasn't sure what he should do but he wanted to do *something*. To give her some comfort. He knew how close she was to Alf and Lizzy but she'd held herself together today. He'd seen how hard it had been, seen her rapid blinking on more than one occasion as she'd comforted an upset Alf.

Tentatively, he slid an arm around her shoulders. She was stiff, like she might shatter into a thousand pieces, and for a moment he thought she was going to stay like that until he murmured, 'I'm sorry.' Then her shoulders suddenly slumped and her body leaned against his, her head resting on his biceps.

He dropped a kiss on her honey-blonde hair and they stayed there for a long time as he gently rubbed his hand up and down her arm.

A part of him wished he could do more but this, doing nothing, was somehow so much more intimate.

It felt right.

CHAPTER TWELVE

FELICITY STARED OUT of the window of Callum's car as he pulled up in front of her place and cut the engine. She'd offered to leave her car at Alf's so the large extended family had an extra car to get around in the next few days, which had left Callum to drive her home.

It was seven in the evening and the shadows of the gum trees in her front yard were just starting to lengthen. She and Callum had stuck around and notified all the right people and made the arrangements for Lizzy to be taken away. She'd wanted to free Alf and his family from the burden of it all so they could just grieve and hold each other.

Alf's 'I don't know what I'm going to do without her, Flick' ran on a continuous loop through her head. His devastation had reached inside her and squeezed her gut and still weighed heavily against her chest.

'We need to keep an eye on Alf the next little while,' she said. Felicity hadn't even registered the silence in the car until she broke it.

'You don't think he'd try to…'

Felicity shook her head, her gaze fixed on the shadows outside the car. 'No. But they've been together a lot of years. It wouldn't be the first time a spouse had died close on the heels of a long-term partner.'

'Good point.'

'I'll organise some community health services,' she said, her brain flipping through the options. 'And I'll mobilise the Country Women's Association.'

Felicity knew the CWA would rally around Alf. Lizzy

had been the local president for about twenty years—Alf would never have to cook again.

'His daughter said quite a few of them were sticking around until after the funeral and she was going to stay on until Christmas. Apparently they're all going to spend it here with Alf.'

Christmas. It was hard to believe it was only five weeks away. 'That's good.'

They lapsed into silence again. Felicity looked at her house. It seemed so quiet and empty after the fullness of Alf's house today. She had never minded the quietness. It had been one of the joys of moving back to Vickers Hill after living in an apartment on a busy main road in Adelaide. But she didn't want to face the quietness now. She didn't want to be alone.

She turned her head to look at him. 'You want to come in for a drink?'

To say he looked taken aback by the offer was an understatement. 'There…seem to be a lot of reasons why I shouldn't.'

Felicity nodded. There were. But.

'I need a drink. A big one. And I don't want to be alone right now.'

His eyes searched hers for a beat or two. She wasn't sure what he was looking for but he must have been satisfied because he reached for the release button on his seat belt. 'I could definitely go a drink.'

Felicity was thankful as she unlocked her front door and Callum followed her into the house that she had no Mrs Smiths to worry about. Sure, people gossiped in her street too—where didn't they?—but her neighbours were mostly families, young mums too busy just getting through the day to worry about what Felicity was doing in the privacy of her own home.

'You were so good with Alf's family today,' he said from behind her as he followed her into her formal lounge room.

'Well, I've had plenty of practice,' she said as she poured them both a slug of her favourite whisky.

'Sure. I just figured you'd be...'

Felicity smiled to herself as she screwed the lid back on the bottle then turned, handing him his whisky. 'An emotional wreck? A blubbering mess?'

'I was thinking more along the lines of not quite so contained.'

She smiled again. Callum was treading carefully. 'Lizzy's death isn't about me and my feelings. It's about them. Her family. Me bursting into tears because *I'm* sad doesn't prioritise their grief and also puts the onus on them to comfort *me* during a time when they should only be thinking of themselves. It's selfish. Not helpful.'

'So you just...don't?'

'That's right.' She nodded. 'You just suck it up. Come home, have a drink and a long cry in the shower.'

Felicity looked into the depths of the amber fluid. The tears that had been threatening since she'd got the phone call this morning pushed closer to the surface. She blinked hard, swirled the whisky around the glass a few times before raising it towards him.

'To Lizzy.'

He tapped his glass against hers. 'To Lizzy.'

Felicity slugged back half of hers, sucking in a breath as the whisky burned all the way down. '*You* were pretty great too today,' she mused as she watched him over the rim of her glass.

He smiled. 'I had a good teacher.'

Felicity laughed. A short, sharp sound that was more wounded than joyous. It hurt. Deep inside her chest where it had been hurting all day.

He frowned and took a step towards her. 'Are you okay?'

'Nope.' Her voice wobbled, her smile wobbled. Everything wobbled inside as the soft concern in his voice undid her. 'But I will be tomorrow.'

A tear escaped. And then another.

'Felicity,' he whispered, placing his drink down on a nearby table and taking the step that separated them, his hands on her hips. 'Don't cry.'

She didn't want to, not in front of him, but crying came as naturally to Felicity as laughing. She'd thought the tears would hold off until she was alone. She was wrong.

'Sorry,' she said, embarrassed, dashing them away with her hands.

'Don't,' he said. 'Don't ever apologise for being who you are.'

It didn't help. The tears came faster.

'Hey,' he murmured, taking her glass and discarding it too before sliding his hands up her back, urging her against him.

Felicity went, shutting her eyes and bunching her fingers in his T-shirt, letting the tears fall. It was beyond her power to stop them.

'I'm sorry,' she repeated, the even thud of his heart comforting beneath her ear.

'Shh,' he said, his chin resting on top of her head. 'It's okay.'

It certainly felt okay, standing in the circle of his arms, weeping quietly. Losing Lizzy had taken a little chink out of her soul, as had every patient she'd ever lost. It was inevitable for someone like her whose emotions were barely skin deep, but having Callum here with her helped.

She glanced up at him. She was close enough to his neck to see every individual whisker, to press her nose to his throat and inhale the citrus essence of him. Fill herself up with that instead of the echoes of Alf finally breaking down and whispering, 'My darling, my darling, my darling', like his heart was shattering.

She angled her head back until she was looking into his eyes, eyes that told their own story of loss right there for the whole world to see.

'Thank you,' she said, rising up on tiptoe and kissing him.

For being here. For being *there*. For being better. For being what she needed exactly when she needed it.

Like right now.

He eyed her warily as he pulled back, his hands moving to her hips and pushing her away gently. But Felicity held firm. The night stretched ahead of her and she didn't want to be alone for any of it.

'Felicity?' His hands branded her hips as his confused eyes searched hers. Was he trying to find some kind of meaning as to why she'd kissed him? 'I'm not sure we should be doing this.'

Felicity was very sure they *shouldn't* be but she wanted it anyway. And the accelerated thud of his heart beneath her palm told her maybe he did too.

'I didn't mean this to be—' He stopped abruptly, obviously finding the right words difficult. 'I was just…trying to comfort you.'

'I know.' She did. And she appreciated it.

But…

She raised her hand, tracing her fingers along his jaw and up the side of his face. 'I just need a different kind of comfort tonight.'

He stared at her for long moments before covering her hand with his and bringing it to his mouth, dropping a kiss on her palm. It was such a gentle gesture Felicity's eyes welled with tears again.

His mouth lowered and he kissed her, soft and slow, like their very first kiss on the train before it had turned hot and heavy. The tears spilled over, trekking south, his thumbs wiping them away as he cupped her cheeks either side of her jaw, his gentleness so sweet she sighed his name against his mouth.

He eased away slightly. 'Take me to the nearest bed.'

The low, gravelly request slid right between her legs and,

without a word, Felicity took him by the hand and led him to her bedroom.

She turned as they crossed the threshold, seeing her bed in its usual unmade disarray. 'It's a little messy, I'm afraid I don't see the point in making my bed when—'

His mouth cut her off as his hands slid to her waist, bringing their bodies flush against each other. 'I don't care about mess,' he muttered, coming up for air, feathering kisses along her jaw to her ear. 'I just want to be inside you.'

Felicity's eyes fluttered closed. 'Oh, God,' she breathed, her hands on his shoulders. 'I want you inside me too.'

And then he was kissing her mouth again as he pulled at her tank top, peeling it off, and she was rucking up his T-shirt and hauling it over his head then reaching for the snaps on his shorts as he reached for hers, pushing them down his legs, kicking out of her own, their kissing stop-start as they shimmied out of their clothes.

Then they were naked and breathless and falling on the bed together in a tangle of limbs and impatience, and he was rolling her on her back, kissing down her neck to her breasts, sucking each nipple in turn, making her cry out and arch her back and forget everything about the day except this moment.

Nothing mattered right now but how they could make each other's bodies sing. Nothing mattered but him.

Her fingers tangled hard in his hair, holding him at her breasts, begging him for more. And he gave her more. More and more, his tongue taunting her until she saw stars. Until she was so damn wet and tingly and restless she was begging him to stop, begging him to finish it, to thrust himself inside her and take them both where they wanted to go.

Her nails dug into his back and she dragged his mouth off her nipple. 'I want you inside me.'

He kissed her hard before mumbling, 'Condom,' then heading back to torture her nipples some more.

Condom. *Right*. Bedside drawer.

Desperately she reached for it, crying out and arching her back when he resumed what he'd been doing, only the other side this time, his hard tongue circling and circling and circling until her eyes were rolling back in her head and her nipple was slippery and elongated, then sucking it deep into his mouth, his teeth scraping against the tip.

Her hand found a loose foil packet and she snatched it up, tearing it open as she pushed on his shoulder. 'Condom,' she panted.

He lifted his head and Felicity almost whimpered at the relief, the cool air stiffening her wet nipples into tight, hard cones. He grabbed the condom from her and shifted slightly to his side, sheathing himself in one deft move. Then she was reaching for him, grasping his shoulders, pulling him over her, spreading her legs wide so he could settle deep, reaching for his erection, exulting in his guttural groan as she squeezed all his glorious length, guiding him to where she was slick and needy.

'There,' she gasped as he nudged, thick and hard against her, tormenting her with the promise of his girth. 'Right there.'

'Oh, yeah,' he murmured, his voice a low growl. 'Right there.'

And then he was sliding home and she was calling out his name, wrapping her legs around his waist, asking him for more, feeling every hot, hard glide, shivering and shaking with each thrust, tilting her pelvis to meet each one, digging her fingers into his buttocks, revelling in the tremble through his thighs and biceps and the harsh suck of his breath as the friction built and the tension mounted, his arms hard bands of muscle bracketing her shoulders.

It wasn't long before the whole world started to unravel. A tiny ripple that started deep and low became two, then three. Then became stronger.

A contraction. Two. Three.

Then a shudder undulating along her pelvic floor.

Felicity gasped as the shudders escalated, increasing in intensity until she could barely stand it, her eyes flying open to find him watching her, their gazes locking in an intensely intimate moment.

The moment of mutual release.

'Yes,' he muttered, his brow crinkled in concentration, his biceps like granite in her peripheral vision, as his hips pumped faster and harder. 'I can feel you. I can feel you.'

Felicity cried out, fighting the urge to shut her eyes as she came, showing him all that she was as she flew apart. He joined her in the maelstrom moments later, his eyes wide open too, gifting her every second of his orgasm as it slammed through his body, the wonder and intensity of it reflected in his gaze until they were churned out the other end, sweaty, spent and utterly exhausted.

It was dark in her room but the red luminous figures on Felicity's bedside clock told her it was ten past one. She should be tired from the emotion of the day and the expended energy of the night. But she wasn't.

Callum was in her bed and while that was something she was going to have to deal with—*tomorrow*—she was going to enjoy it for the night. Like she had on the train.

She was tracing patterns on his chest as he stroked lazy fingers up and down her back. 'What do you see when you look at me?'

'Fishing for compliments?' Even rumbling through his chest wall straight into her ear, his voice didn't lose any of its amusement.

She smiled, her finger circling one flat, brown nipple. 'No. I'm being serious.'

His hand paused for a moment, missing a beat or two before continuing its steady pace. 'Okay. I see an incredible woman, a great lover and amazing nurse. I see—'

'No.' Felicity pushed off his chest, propping her head on her hand as she looked down at him, stroking a finger along his chin, under his bottom lip. 'I mean, what do you physically see? With your eye the way it is.'

He went very still. 'Oh. Right.'

Her finger paused on his chin. *Damn*. Way to kill the mood, Flick. 'I'm sorry. It's okay. I shouldn't have asked.'

Except lying here with him she'd realised she didn't know anything about the nitty-gritty of his eyesight. Mostly because he'd seemed so closed off about it but it seemed uncaring not to enquire.

Sure, it was easy to forget when looking at him that he had any kind of sight deficit. His misshapen, slightly dilated pupil and the fact he couldn't drive at night were the only indications. But it was hardly something *he* could forget. It wasn't like it was out of sight.

It *was* his sight.

'No. It's fine,' he assured her. 'You just took me by surprise, that's all. Nobody other than my specialists and the medical board have ever really asked.'

Felicity stroked her finger along his bottom lip. It was full and tempting. 'Didn't any of those women you shamelessly slept with after the accident ever ask?'

He smiled and she traced the curve of his mouth all the way to the corner and back again. 'They seemed more interested in bagging the blind surgeon than the details of my injury,' he said, his voice heavy with derision.

'Well, I'm interested,' she said, tapping his chin lightly.

'In the details or...' his hand slid onto her hip and lightly stroked '...bagging the blind dude?'

Felicity laughed, his tone light and more self-deprecating now. 'Huh. Been there, done that. Three times already tonight.'

His hand swept to her butt, scattering goose-bumps down the backs of her thighs and arrowing heat right between her legs. 'Fourth time's a charm.'

'Patience,' she teased, dropping a quick kiss on his mouth. 'Now, tell me how you see me.'

He sighed dramatically but kept up the drugging sweep of his hand from hip to buttocks and back again. 'At the moment, in the dark, not much with the left eye, you're kind of a dim blur.'

He was becoming a bit of a blur too as heat streaked to her pelvis. 'What about during the day? In normal light?'

'If I cover up my good eye, you'd be pretty blurred. The acuity in my left eye is shocking but my right eye compensates and if I'm wearing my glasses then the blurriness improves even further. But if you're standing on my left I probably wouldn't see you at all because my peripheral vision in that eye is pretty much nonexistent.'

The bitterness that had tinged his voice when he'd first told her about it was missing now. She wasn't sure if that was significant or just the result of three really good orgasms.

God knew, if she was any mellower at the moment from those orgasms and the very distracting stroke of his hand, she'd be floating away like a dandelion puff.

'They can't operate to help in any way?'

'They did what they could in the beginning. I've had quite a few surgical interventions, including laser work on my retina, but…frankly I don't think any of the specialists thought I'd have any kind of worthwhile vision so they're seeing it as a win.'

'And they think it's as good as it'll get?'

'It may improve marginally, in time but it's taken over two years to get where it is and most of that progress was made in the first year.'

'Are you still friends with the guy who bowled the ball?'

'Sure.' He shrugged. 'It's not his fault. It was a freak accident and I should have been wearing a helmet. I had one in my car but…'

Yeah. But…

Felicity was sure he'd done the should-haves and if-onlys over and over. It had been an expensive error in judgement and her heart went out to him. There was just something about this man that made her want to make it all better for him.

Enough bringing them down.

They had tonight and she was up for a little sexual healing.

'So, to recap,' she said, sliding her leg over and rolling up to straddle him, settling her slick heat over his semihardness, 'what you're saying is you see things right in front of you reasonably well in reasonable light, especially if you have glasses on.'

He chuckled, his hands moving to her hips. 'Yes.'

'So...' she arched her back, lifting the hair off her nape and piling it high on her head, two-handed '...it's not so good at the moment.'

'I can see enough,' he murmured, the heat from his gaze like an infra-red beam fanning over her breasts, prickling her nipples to tight, hard buds. 'And I have a pretty good imagination.'

'Would this help?' she asked, letting her hair go, leaning forward at the hips, reaching for the switch that was looped through the wrought-iron lattice of her bedhead.

She flicked it on and sat back to admire the effect of a dozen tiny fairy lights, embedded in plastic hearts woven through the metal, glowing soft and pink.

It was kind of how she felt now. Her heart on a string, all happy and glowy inside her.

'Oh, yes,' he muttered, his gaze zeroing in with laserlike intensity, his hands sliding up her sides.

His singular focus was an instant turn-on. 'Light not too harsh?' she teased.

He shook his head as his fingers stroked the undersides of her breasts. 'It's perfect.' He cupped them fully. 'You're perfect.' He brushed his thumbs across her aching nipples. 'So beautiful.'

Felicity moaned as his rapidly swelling erection pushed

hard against the knot of tingling nerves between her legs and she rubbed herself against him for maximum effect.

'God,' he groaned, vaulting upright, curling an arm around her waist and hauling her close. Felicity arched her back, offering her nipple to his questing mouth. She buried her hand in his hair, her eyes fluttering closed as his hot, wet mouth closed around her and she let herself get lost in the pleasure.

CHAPTER THIRTEEN

FELICITY WAS SITTING at the central island bench in her kitchen the next morning, reading the Sunday paper she had delivered to her door. A steaming-hot cup of coffee sat at her elbow as she tried to concentrate on some political scandal instead of the speech she had to give.

She'd heard the shower being turned on about fifteen minutes ago so it wouldn't be long now.

She'd been awake for a couple of hours, just watching him sleep, admiring the play of early morning shadows across his face and body. He looked so damn sexy in her bed.

When he was asleep. When he was awake. When he was thrusting into her, silhouetted by a fuzzy pink glow.

They would be memories she would treasure for ever.

But it couldn't be any more than another one-night stand. It would be too easy to spend the next five weeks in his arms and too hard to say goodbye. He wasn't ready. There were issues he still had to work out. And she didn't want to invest in someone who'd probably break her heart. It had taken her a long time to feel whole after Ned and she'd learned to be more guarded since then.

She just couldn't be the girl from the train here in Vickers Hill. She wasn't that reckless. Not in real life. Not with her reputation and not with her emotions.

'Good morning.'

The gravelly male voice coming from behind her ruffled all the tiny hairs on Felicity's nape. But there was wariness in his tone too. Was he feeling unsure after waking to an empty bed?

'Morning,' she said, not bothering to turn and acknowledge him, just slipping off her stool and heading for the percolator. 'Want a coffee?'

'Sure.' His tone was all wariness now.

She picked up a mug and poured him one, steeling herself to face him.

'Here you go,' she said, turning, mug in hand and a smile on her face. He was standing near the bench in his clothes from yesterday, except for his bare feet.

His hair was damp and he smelled like her shampoo.

Coconut had never smelled so damn good.

She slid his coffee across the bench, keen to keep something solid between them. 'Sit,' she said, leaning across to shift the newspaper out of the way.

Felicity didn't wait to see if he followed her command. She turned back to the percolator and poured herself another coffee. Her third for the morning. When she was done she made a beeline for the stool that was on her side of the bench and sat down, taking a sip of her drink.

He took one too and said, 'I feel like I'm about to get a "Dear John" speech.'

She shot him a nervous smile. 'Am I that obvious?'

He placed his mug on the countertop. 'Just say what you have to say, Felicity.'

She nodded. The direct approach was good. Rip that sticking plaster off and get on with it. 'Last night was…'

God, where did she even start with last night? The train had been good but last night had been better. It'd been emotional, not just sexual. A deeper connection born not just from what they'd shared yesterday but from three weeks of spending practically every day together.

And that scared the hell out of her.

'It's okay,' he said, his lips curling in a derisive smile. 'I think we can skip the compliments.'

'Okay.' She placed her mug down on the granite benchtop too. 'Last night was inevitable. It's been building for the last few weeks and after the train…well, I think we both know the train was never going to be enough when we've had to work together so closely.'

'*I* think if the next words that come out of your mouth are that you regret it or that *I* should regret it or that it was wrong or dumb or any other ridiculous statement then you should stop right there.'

Felicity gave a half-smile at his pre-emptive statement. His mouth was set in a hard line, his green eyes steely. He was even sexy when he was cranky. 'Nope.' She shook her head. 'No regrets.'

Never.

His mouth relaxed and his shoulders lost some of their tension. *Sexy, sexy, sexy.*

'But this can't become a regular thing,' she continued. 'I can't keep having sex with you and fooling myself that it's just some crazy interlude. Some mutual fun while you're here…that it'll all be okay. I'm just not built that way. I'm not the girl from the train. I was never really her. I'm just Flick from Vickers Hill.'

He didn't say anything for long moments, just stared at her as if he was trying to figure her out. 'Are you telling me…' he placed his bent elbow on the bench and supported his chin in his palm '…you don't even want to be friends?'

If only. Friends would make everything so much easier but that line was somewhere behind her now. 'I think I'm probably always going to want more than that from you.'

'Like…friends with benefits?'

She shook her head sadly. 'Like friends with *emotions*.'

Her admission sat him back, his arm dropping to the countertop. 'I see.'

She wondered if he did. Really did. 'You know what I thought last night when I turned those lights on? That that was me. That was my heart. Glowing all pink and beautiful inside my chest.'

He swallowed then, a light dawning in his eyes as the information slowly settled in. 'Are you trying to tell me that you're…?'

'No. I'm not,' she assured him. Quickly. Definitively. *She couldn't be*. It had taken her almost a year to realise she'd loved Ned. It would be preposterous to be in love with Callum after a few weeks. 'But…I *am* that kind of girl. Absence *doesn't* make my heart grow fonder. *Presence* makes it grow fonder and we can't keep doing this…' she waved her finger back and forth between them '…without…consequences. I *like* you, Callum.'

He was scheduled to leave on Christmas Eve and she was already sad about that day five weeks from now.

'I like you too.'

Felicity suppressed a snort. She didn't need to hear some quick-fire, city-slicker patronising response. He knew *exactly* what she meant. She folded her arms. 'A little *too* much.'

He dropped his gaze to his coffee as her point hit home and he fiddled with the handle. 'So we just…what?' he asked, glancing at her. 'See each other at work and that's it?'

'Yep.' Felicity nodded. 'Just colleagues…just two professionals. That's all.'

His gaze searched hers for what felt like an age, as if he was trying to assess just how serious she was. She didn't blink. Not once. Even though her hands were shaking around her mug and her pulse whooshed like a raging river through her ears.

'Okay. Sure. If that's what you want.'

Felicity nodded, amazed at her outer calm. 'It is.' Even though what she really wanted was for him to say, 'To hell with that,' pick her up and throw her down on her bed. The temptation to spend every night like last night almost overwhelmed her now she'd done herself out of the chance.

But he was going back to Sydney. He *had* to go back to Sydney. He had to work out what he wanted.

And living in a state of denial was preferable to living in a state of hope.

Two weeks later, in early December, Callum strode into the Parson's Nose—one of the many excellent gourmet pubs in town—searching the crowded room for his brother. If he'd been surprised to get a phone call from Seb—they had more of a texting relationship these days—he'd been utterly gobsmacked when Seb announced he was in Vickers Hill.

Today was Thursday, which was normally his day off, but Bill's brother had died a few days ago and the funeral was this morning so Callum had been covering for the old man. He hadn't minded and there had been the added bonus of seeing Felicity. But Bill had insisted he'd return for the afternoon appointments despite Callum encouraging him to take the whole day off.

Callum kept hearing from Julia about Bill retiring and all her grand plans for them but, as far as Callum could see, Bill wasn't ready to go yet. He certainly didn't seem to be in any hurry about finding a replacement.

'*Cal!*' Callum's head swivelled towards the voice and he squinted, trying to locate Seb. Finally he clocked his brother, waving and grinning, near the bar.

Callum made his way through several groups of people as Seb slid off his stool. When he finally reached the bar he pulled his brother in for a bear hug as they slapped each other on the back. The circumstances of their lives the last few years had meant a lot of separation but it was always good to see him again.

'Missing me, dude?' Callum said as they pulled apart.

'Always.' Seb laughed.

They settled on their bar stools and Seb waved the bartender over, ordering Callum a local beer. They watched as he poured then they clinked their glasses together and toasted brotherly love.

'What on earth brings you to sleepy little Vickers Hill?' Callum asked, swiping froth from his top lip.

'Well, it's not the surf.' Seb grinned.

Callum laughed. 'No. Definitely not.' He sighed. 'I *do* miss the surf.'

'Maybe I should be asking what on earth brings *you* to Vickers Hill?'

His brother may be younger but, being the black sheep of the family, he was never one for taking things at face value and always the one to ask probing questions. Even as a kid he'd wanted to know the whys, whats and wherefores of everything.

'I needed some...clear air.'

Seb regarded him over the rim of his beer glass for a beat or two. 'Have you found it?'

That was a much harder question to answer. Trust Seb to be the one asking it.

'Yes. And no.'

Seb lifted an eyebrow. 'Now, that requires further explanation so spill it, big brother.'

Callum didn't even know where to begin. In five weeks he *had* managed to find clear air regarding his career. He'd arrived here conflicted, hoping like crazy that a change in pace and scenery would enthuse him for his new path.

And it had.

He'd seen a different side to what had felt like the yoke of general practice and he'd been a better doctor out here then he'd been the last two years in any of his placements.

Thanks to Felicity.

Felicity...

Yeah. The air there was *far* from clear. Pretty damn murky, actually. She'd been strict about their interactions and things between the two of them had been exactly as she'd wanted. They saw each other at work from one p.m.

four days a week and rarely outside any more, apart from bumping into her at the shops or petrol station.

But that hadn't stopped the trip in his pulse whenever he heard her laughter or checking her out *every single time* she walked into the room. She'd been stringing tinsel up around the office all this week and she'd started wearing very distracting Christmas T-shirts and a red Santa hat with a cute white pom-pom on the end.

She seemed pretty damn cheerful, her easiness with him so effortless considering he had to check himself constantly. The urge to flirt, to slip into banter, to yank on that distracting white pom-pom was harder to suppress than he'd thought.

He had to keep reminding himself of what she'd said and who she was. She was a sensitive, empathic woman who'd taken him on to advocate for her patients and wasn't ashamed of how close her emotions bubbled to the surface. She'd got teary talking about her grandfather the first day he'd met her. Not to mention her reaction over Seb's fiancé and, of course, her tears for Lizzy Dunnich.

I'm that kind of girl.

That's what she'd said. And he was aware of it every day, watching her with the people she worked with and her patients. The way she cooed over the babies and clucked over the oldies, cheered over the wins and bossed the noncompliant with such a loving hand.

She *wasn't* like other women he'd met. She wasn't the kind he could play with and leave. Just walk away from and know she'd be okay. She'd told him she liked him. A woman had never told him she liked him. They'd confessed their love, their desire, their admiration. Their wildest sexual fantasies. But, looking back, he wasn't sure any of them had *liked* him.

And he'd never really told a woman he liked her either. In fact, he'd taken himself by complete surprise when he'd said it back. But it had felt right and he found himself not wanting to screw it up. To leave with her still liking him, even if it meant having to ignore his libido.

Because he *was* going back to Sydney.

He had to go back. He had a lot to prove.

'Uh-oh,' Seb said, waiting with a cocked eyebrow, clearly amused at Callum's prolonged contemplation. 'That bad?'

He glanced at his brother. 'There's this woman...'

'It's always a woman.' Seb chuckled.

Callum shook his head. 'Felicity isn't just any woman.'

'Felicity?' Seb frowned. 'Do you mean Flick? Luci's friend?'

'Yep.' And he told his brother everything.

'Well?' Callum asked after he'd run out of steam and his beer glass was empty.

'Well, what?'

'What do you think? Am I crazy?'

'Hell, Cal,' Seb groaned. 'Don't ask me. Luci has me so tied up in knots I don't know what to do any more either.'

'Luci?' It was Callum's turn to frown. '*My* Luci?'

'*Your* Luci?'

'I mean the one in my apartment?'

'Yes. She's the reason I'm here today. Her uncle died—'

'I know,' Callum interrupted. 'I've been covering the morning appointments for her father.'

With Felicity.

'Right. Well, she came back for the funeral and I know coming back and facing the town again was hard so...I thought I'd be here for her.'

'You *know*?'

Seb shrugged and, if Callum wasn't very much mistaken that was a smile breaking across his brother's face. 'We... talk. We've got close.'

Callum blinked. Could Seb actually be taking an interest in another woman after all this time? He hoped so. His brother had been to hell and back. 'Good for you. You've been through a lot, man. You deserve to be happy.'

Seb looked him straight in the eye. 'So do you, Cal. So do you.'

Callum appreciated the sentiment but his loss had been nothing compared to Seb's. 'Well,' he said, changing the subject, 'I'm sure Luci is very pleased to have you here.'

'Oh, she doesn't know yet. I only made up my mind this morning and jumped an early flight.' Seb checked his watch and quickly downed the dregs of his beer. 'So I'd better get going. The funeral should be over by now.'

He stood and Callum followed suit. They shook hands and shared another bear hug. Seb mumbled something about spending Christmas together and then he was striding out of the pub, his 'So do you, Cal,' lingering in his wake.

Felicity pulled up outside Luci's the day before Christmas Eve, a bunch of nerves knotting so tight in her stomach she feared it was going to burst open under the tension. Or she was going to throw up.

One or the other.

Callum was leaving tomorrow. In the morning. He'd be back in Sydney by lunchtime.

Out of sight, out of mind, right?

Fourteen hundred kilometres out of sight. Although she doubted even the North Pole would be far enough to keep him out of mind...

She glanced at the lavender growing along Luci's front path. She didn't know why she was here.

No. That was a lie. She knew.

The little farewell party they'd thrown Callum at lunch today just hadn't cut it. Giving him a polite hug goodbye in front of all their colleagues had seemed too impersonal considering what had transpired between them. She wanted to say things to him—personal things. Things she couldn't say in front of everyone at work. But still needed to be said.

Private things.

That she wished him well, that he was going to be all

right. And a brilliant GP. That she was pleased their paths had crossed and there were no hard feelings.

That she'd *never ever* forget their night on the train.

After weeks of keeping every thought and feeling strictly under wraps, she couldn't let him leave without telling him that. She had to *know* he knew.

The last few weeks had been an exercise in self-control and, somehow, she'd managed. *Just.* But with him leaving tomorrow she couldn't deny the strong pull to *see* him one last time.

To just…*look* at him.

So she'd jumped in her car and driven straight here. Hell, she hadn't even bothered getting out of her uniform.

This last time felt ridiculously momentous and Felicity took a deep breath. It caught in the thickening of her throat as her trembling fingers reached for the doorhandle. She fumbled it then stumbled out as if it was her first ever step.

She was hyper-aware of everything around her as her pulse throbbed through her temples. The sun warm on her shoulders, even at almost seven in the evening after a record run of high temperatures and concerns about bush fires. The trill of insects. The laughter of kids somewhere up the street.

The smell of lavender and meat roasting from one of the nearby houses.

'Good evening, Flick.'

Felicity startled at the imperious greeting from behind her, her heart pounding in her chest at being sprung again by Mrs Smith.

Did the woman have some kind of sixth sense? She was only coming to talk, for crying out loud.

'Evening, Mrs Smith,' she said, plastering on a smile as she turned to face the woman who she was quickly coming to think of as her nemesis. Even standing on her footpath in a baggy house dress and hair rollers she somehow still managed to look like the stern teacher who had taught Felicity in grade four.

'You here to see Dr Hollingsworth?'

'Er...' Felicity tried to figure out a response that would cause the least amount of ire from Vickers Hill's self-appointed defender of virtue.

But Mrs Smith didn't wait for any further elaboration. 'He's leaving in the morning.'

'Yes.'

'Back to Sydney.'

'Yes.'

She made a tutting sound. 'You left your run too late, my girl.'

Felicity blinked. 'My...run?'

'He's been here for two months. And you're not getting any younger.'

What the ever-loving hell...? Had Mrs Smith just implied she'd been left on the shelf at the grand age of twenty-eight?

'I'd been married for almost ten years and had three little kiddies by your age. You should be settling down with a nice local boy. What about Ed Dempsey? He's had his eye on you for a while.'

Ed Dempsey? He had his eye on every woman with a pulse. Plus she'd never quite forgiven him for putting a green frog down the back of her shirt when she'd been four.

'There's nothing between Dr Hollingsworth and I.'

'So why are you here on his doorstep at the last minute?' A sudden light dawned over her wrinkly face and Felicity felt nine years old again under her eagle-eyed gaze. 'Ah, I see,' she sniffed. 'You know...' she glanced around her as she made her way towards Felicity '...you can't expect him to buy the cow if he's getting the milk for free.'

Felicity gaped at her old primary school teacher as she contemplated hacking off her ears to unhear what had just been said. *'Mrs Smith.'*

'Oh, you don't think I know what you young people get up to these days?' She stepped off the footpath and Felicity resigned herself to a lecture about the perils of premarital sex from her ex-teacher. 'Why, I...'

She didn't get to finish her sentence and for a brief moment, as Mrs Smith stumbled, relief flowed like coolant through Felicity's system. Unfortunately, she didn't regain her footing and despite Felicity lurching for her as Mrs Smith looked around wild-eyed, desperately trying to grab hold of something, she fell hard on the road on her left side.

She cried out in pain. 'Mrs Smith!' Felicity threw herself down beside her, her annoyance forgotten. 'Are you okay?'

'No,' she managed through clenched teeth, rolling onto her back, groaning in pain as she grabbed her hip. 'I'm not.'

Out of habit, Felicity placed her fingers on the pulse at Mrs Smith's wrist. 'Where are you hurt?'

'It's my damn hip,' she snapped, raising her head as if she'd be able to see a bone sticking out or something before giving up and dropping her head back onto the road on an annoyed hiss.

Felicity was relieved to feel a strong, regular pulse, and slid her hand into Mrs Smith's to give it a squeeze, whether the older woman wanted the comfort or not. She glanced down to find Mrs Smith's left leg was markedly shorter than the right and badly externally rotated. *Damn.* Felicity would bet her life the older woman had sustained a fractured neck of femur.

'Anywhere else?'

'Isn't that enough?' Mrs Smith grouched.

Felicity pressed her lips together to stop herself smiling. 'Okay, hang on a sec.' She pulled her phone out of her back pocket and dialled Callum.

'Felicity?'

She ignored the husky query in his voice. And the tug down deep and low inside her. 'I'm outside. Opposite. At Mrs Smith's. She's had a fall on the road and I'm pretty sure she's fractured her left NOF. Can you give some help, please?'

She could have handled it herself if she'd had to but it made sense to have as much medical support as possible.

'On my way.'

The call was hung up in her ear and she quickly dialled the ambulance station, which, thanks to her home visit schedule, was on speed dial in her contacts. She was ending the call as Callum crossed the road. He was wearing shorts that came to his knees and an ab-hugging T-shirt and was carrying a couple of pillows.

Her heart missed a beat or two.

'You've called an ambulance?' he asked as he knelt on the road, his knees pressing into the bitumen. He didn't look at Felicity as he smiled at the older woman, who was noisily sucking air in and out of her lungs.

'They're ten minutes away.'

He nodded. 'How are you going, Mrs Smith?'

'I've been better,' she said, although the cantankerous edge had obviously been weakened from the pain. 'Think I might have broken my hip.'

'I think you're right,' he murmured, slipping a pillow under her head.

'What's your pain level if one is the mildest and ten is the worst pain you've ever felt?' Felicity asked.

'A hundred,' Mrs Smith panted.

Felicity believed her. Her brow was deeply furrowed and there was a ring of white around her tight mouth. Mrs Smith might be a bit of an old busybody but they bred them tough out here and she was one of the toughest characters in Vickers Hill.

'The ambulance will be here soon,' Callum soothed. 'We'll get you some pain relief and have you on the way to hospital in a jiffy. You think you can hold on for a bit longer?'

'I'll be fine,' she dismissed, her voice gruff, but she squeezed Felicity's hand harder.

Finally he looked at Felicity, their gazes meshing, a question in his eyes she was too afraid to answer.

'We'll support her pelvis in a sling when they get here,' he said, breaking their eye contact. 'I brought out a sheet to fashion one but we'd better wait for the magic green whistle to arrive before we attempt anything.'

'Agreed.' Pain relief was their priority before they attempted any kind of handling. She just wished she could have a magic green whistle for their situation. One that took them back to that night on the train and turned them into two normal people with no baggage and open hearts.

'Did you hit your head, Mrs Smith?' he asked, and Felicity was grateful that Callum's medical training had taken over. Grateful for any distraction from the question she'd seen in his eyes and from the answer she could no longer deny.

Why are you here?
Because I love you.

CHAPTER FOURTEEN

BY THE TIME the ambulance had departed it was well and truly dark. Then it was just the two of them standing in the middle of the road bathed in the silent strobing of red and blue lights as they faded down the street. The neighbours who had milled around had since melted away to their homes.

'You want a drink?'

Felicity shook her head. She needed to go now that she knew the answer to the question. She certainly didn't need to drink alcohol around him, lose her inhibitions and blurt it out.

She loved him.

It was insane and the timing sucked. It was too soon and he was leaving—he *had* to leave—but it was there nonetheless. Like a light blinking inside her, sure and steady. She was in deep.

Too deep. Too soon.

And losing him was going to hurt about a thousand times more than losing Ned ever had. No amount of crazy glue was going to put her heart back together after this.

Damn.

'Okay. But I'm assuming there's a reason you came over?'

She nodded. Not that it mattered now. 'No…I just wanted to…say goodbye.'

He shoved his hands on his hips. 'You said goodbye at the party.'

'I know. But…'

'But what?'

Yeah, Flick. But what?

Stupid tears pricked the backs of her eyes and Felicity was grateful for the night. 'I don't know…it felt too public.'

'So come inside.'

She shook her head, standing her ground. 'Here's fine.'

He looked around him pointedly. 'This isn't public? We're in the middle of the street. And…' he smiled suddenly and Felicity's breath hitched '…I'm reasonably certain Mrs Smith has the entire neighbourhood bugged.'

Felicity gave a weak half-smile despite the raging torment kicking up a storm in her gut.

A smile had never hurt so damn much.

She glanced at her car. It was three paces away but her legs were shaking so much it may as well have been on the moon. There just didn't seem to be enough oxygen between them. 'Mrs Smith ruined the mood.'

'She has a habit of doing that.' He regarded her for long moments before holding out his hand. 'Give me your phone.'

She frowned. 'What?'

'You look kind of undecided so let's ask Mike.' He waggled his fingers at her. 'Modern-day coin toss, remember?'

Felicity knew she should just walk away. But he was so damn sexy, smiling down her like that in the dark, being all flirty and charming and reminding her of that night on the train.

Playing dirty, no matter how obvious. And she was weak. No. More than that. Where he was concerned she was *feeble*.

She reached into her back pocket, tapped in her code and handed it over, her fingers trembling almost as much as her legs. He took it, navigating quickly to where he needed to be.

The light from the screen bathed his face in a sexy glow, highlighting his mouth, the dark outline of his whiskers and casting shadows under his chiselled cheekbones.

His gaze met hers as he brought the phone up to his

mouth. 'Mike, should Felicity go to Callum's house for a drink?'

'Are his intentions honourable?'

The stylised British accent seemed loud in the hush that had fallen over the neighbourhood. Felicity's lungs burned as she held her breath and he held her gaze.

'They are, Mike.'

'One drink should be okay.'

He grinned at the quick-fire response as he passed the phone back, his face fading into the night again. 'Mike has spoken.'

Felicity let her breath out in a slow, husky exhalation. 'I think it's time I stopped letting Mike make these kinds of decisions.'

'Oh, I don't know. I think he's been on the money so far.'

Felicity sighed. 'Callum—'

'Oh, come on. Besides, I have a gift for you that I was going to drop off in your mailbox in the morning and now I can give it to you personally.' He put his hand over his heart and added, 'Please...' for good measure.

And not just any old *please*. There was a vibrato to it that floated gossamer fingers around her good sense, wrapping it up in an iron web.

'Okay. Fine. But I'm *not* having a drink. You give me the gift then I'm going.'

He smiled and nodded, clearly pleased with himself. 'Absolutely.'

He led the way up the path lit by subtle solar lamps, the scent of lavender infusing Felicity's senses. It was hard to believe that Luci would be back tomorrow.

God, she had so much to tell her!

Felicity's nerves tangled into a knot as the door clicked shut behind her. 'Come in. Take a seat on the couch. I'll be right back.'

Oh, no. No way was she going to sit on Luci's cosy couch

in her homey living room. She needed to be where she could make a quick escape.

She needed to be *vertical*.

'I'll wait here,' she said, grinding the soles of her sensible work shoes into the parquet floor of the entranceway.

He shrugged. 'Suit yourself.'

Thankfully he was back quickly, placing a package no bigger and sightly bulkier than a business card in the palm of her hand. It was wrapped in pretty flowery tissue paper. 'I couldn't resist it when I saw it in town the other day.' He grinned.

His smile would have been infectious had Felicity not been hyper-aware of the confines of the small alcove in which they stood and the fact the only light in the house was coming from behind them somewhere, which only seemed to enhance his nearness, his broadness, his sexy citrus essence.

She made a concerted effort to concentrate on the wrapping as her fingers fumbled it uselessly. When finally she conquered it she pulled it back to reveal a cheap-looking plastic badge boasting the word *Saint* in tacky diamantés.

'Now it's official,' he teased.

Felicity surprised herself by laughing. She'd been hoping it wasn't something sentimental lest she cry. She needn't have worried. The badge struck just the right note. Light and funny but still sweet and thoughtful.

'You think I should wear it to work?'

'Sure. Here.' He grabbed it from her. 'Let's see if it goes with the uniform.'

'Everything goes with diamantés,' she protested as his plan became clear, but it was too late, he'd stepped right in, opening the back clasp of the badge and fingering the open collar of her polo shirt.

It brought him a hell of a lot closer and she realised she was being hemmed in. The solid door behind her, his solid chest in front of her. Her pulse skipped madly. Goose-bumps swept up and down her neck where his fingers accidentally brushed, rippling out in a hot wave to her breasts, beading her nipples into tight, hard peaks.

'There.' He stepped back but not all the way. He was still closer than he had been.

Closer than was good for her sanity.

'I think it looks perfect.'

Felicity breathed in deep, her oxygen depleted again. 'I doubt Bill would agree.'

'I think Bill would think it was amusing. Angela would think it's hysterical.'

'Yeah.' Knowing both of them, Felicity had to concede the point. 'I guess they would.'

They lapsed into silence, the lightness that had swirled around them moments ago quickly dissipating as awareness of the low light and their closeness set in again.

'So,' he prompted after long moments, 'you came to say goodbye? Before Mrs Smith so inconveniently broke her NOF?'

Felicity fixed her gaze on his shoulder. 'Yes.'

He nodded slowly. 'It's hard to believe it's been two months. It went quickly.'

'Yes.' It had and it hadn't. These last ten minutes, with her chest bursting and her heart breaking and him within touching distance, had felt like an age.

'I guess Meryl was wrong,' he murmured, shoving his hands in his pockets. The action pulled his T-shirt flat against his belly.

Felicity shrugged. Their visit with Meryl seemed a million years ago right now. 'First time for everything.'

More silence. 'I've never really said thank you,' he said, after the silence had stretched about as far as it could without snapping in two. 'The way you took me to task that day. You made me a better doctor.'

Felicity glanced at him, surprised by the statement. But the huskiness in his voice and the earnestness reflected in his gaze showed his sincerity. 'Its fine,' she dismissed. 'You'd been through a lot and you were grieving for your lost career. You'd have figured it out, I'm sure.'

He shook his head. 'No. I don't know that I would have.' He shuffled a little closer, his gaze dropping to her mouth. 'Thank you, Felicity.'

Oh, God. He was going to kiss her. Look away. *Look away.*

He was *thankful* and *grateful*. While she was *in love*. It was all so screwed up.

Look away.

But she couldn't drag her eyes off him. Thankfully, though, she still had some use of her legs and she took a step back. Or tried at least. Her shoulder blades met the door with practically no distance put between them at all.

'I'm going to miss you,' he said, his hand reaching for her, pushing back a chunk of hair that had come loose from her ponytail as they'd treated Mrs Smith, his palm lingering to cup her face. Her eyes fluttered closed. 'Are you going to miss me?'

She was going to miss him with a hunger that would gnaw away at her insides. She just knew it. Breaking up with Ned had been hard—she'd lost a friend as well as a lover. But Callum was an entirely different beast. There'd been no slow build-up to their relationship. No dawning re-alisation. It had been a headlong rush and she'd fallen hard and fast. And that was going to smash through her life like a wrecking ball.

'Yes.'

She didn't trust herself to elaborate as her eyes opened. And then she couldn't, even if she wanted to, because his head was lowering. Slowly. Inexorably.

God…why did she want his lips on hers so *freaking bad*?

'You said your intentions were honourable.'

It was supposed to sound strong, assertive, but came out

all weak and breathy. More a plea than a last-ditch attempt to derail the inevitable.

'They were,' he muttered, his lips almost brushing hers. 'I swear they were.'

And then they were on her and opening over hers, hot and hard and sure, his ragged breath loud in her ears as he demanded entrance to her mouth, his tongue sweeping inside, stroking along hers as his hands went to her waist and his body aligned with hers—hot and hard and sure.

Her pulse hammered and her breath tangled with his as she tried frantically to drag in air. His thigh slid between her legs, pressing in hard, and she moaned as heat flooded her pelvis.

'God…you taste so good,' he murmured against her mouth, and his voice was so deep and dark and needy it filled her head with heat and need and sex. She knew if they didn't stop right now they'd be on the floor in seconds and it wouldn't be sex this time, it would be making *love*, and she couldn't bear for that to be one-sided.

Rallying reserves she hadn't known she had, she tore her mouth from his. 'Callum,' she panted, pushing on his chest, desperate for some distance. 'Stop. Please, stop.'

His mouth was wet and his eyes were a little glazed as he backed up and she breathed more easily. 'Why?' he asked, his hands slipping off her waist, one shoving through his hair.

Because I love you, you idiot. 'Because I can't think, I can't be…rational when you do that. And you're leaving in the morning.'

He gazed at her for long beats before scrubbing a hand over his face. 'Maybe I could stay? I know Meera's back from maternity leave in the New Year but maybe she'd like some more time to be with her baby?'

Felicity blinked. *'What?'* Blind hope surged in her heart even as her head rejected it.

Maybe I could stay?

No. He needed to go. And it was just plain cruel to taunt her with empty possibilities.

He shrugged. 'I like it here. I like working here. I like that *you're* here.'

'No.' She shook her head, hardening her heart, refusing to let herself be carried away by his lust-induced sentiment. 'You can't hide here, Callum. It's bad enough you ran away here.'

He took a step back, clearly surprised by her frankness, although surely he was used to her speaking her mind by now? He shoved a hand on a hip. 'I was after clear air.'

She shrugged. 'You say potato…'

'You ran away too, Felicity, when you came here after Ned.'

'I wasn't running *away*. I was running *to* something.' She shook her head. 'Look…you had this brilliant life and career and you knew what you wanted, then it got blown all to hell. I knew what I wanted too and it also got blown all to hell, but I'm out the other side of it now. You're still in the middle. You said when you first came here that you had something to prove. So go home and prove it,' she said, goading him.

Goading him to leave her.

It hurt, damn it. So *freaking* much.

'Prove that being a GP is what you want.'

'It is what I want,' he snapped.

He turned away from her then, striding into the kitchen behind, placing his fists on the edge of the bench as he reached it. Felicity followed him at a slower pace. His shoulders were hunched, his head hung low between them.

'It's what you want *here*, while you're hiding away in Vickers Hill,' she said, gentler this time, speaking to his back. 'Wanting it *here* is easy. But you have to face the real world, Callum. The people that matter. The only way you're going to know if it's what you *really* want is by going back home. To your *surgeon* parents and your *surgeon* friends and their dinner parties full of shop talk about their latest surgical feats. Because it's only by going back to your old life that you'll know for sure.'

He didn't say anything for a long time. Finally he raised his head and slowly turned to face her. He leaned his butt against the bench and crossed his ankles in a casually deceptive pose but every inch of him was tense. 'Come with me.'

Felicity blinked, her heart beating hard in her chest, as hard as it was bleeding. A part of her wanted to snatch his offer up, throw caution to the wind, just as she'd urged Luci to do.

But this was *love*. And hers was too big to risk on a man still sorting his life out.

She wanted to be with him but she needed to know she wasn't another consolation prize. The consolation woman that came part and parcel with the consolation job.

'No.'

'I like you. I think there's something between us. I think it could be more.'

Felicity sucked in a breath as his rumbled admissions played havoc with her sensibilities. The man obviously knew how to push all her damn buttons. She wondered if he had any idea how much his vague, noncommittal words hurt.

She swallowed. 'No.'

God, how could such a little word be so hard to say?

He cocked an eyebrow. 'You don't want to live in Sydney? I have an apartment on the harbour. And if you're worried about a job—don't be. With your qualifications and experience you could walk into about a dozen jobs straight away.'

'No.' She said it more firmly this time as he didn't seem to be getting the message.

'Why?' he demanded.

'Because you have a lot of things to confront and you don't need me hanging around muddying the waters. You need clear air back in Sydney too. I'm not going to be your distraction. A way for you to avoid facing up to the issues.'

'So you don't think there could be more between us?'

Felicity had told herself she wasn't going to cry when she came here tonight but she was just about at the end of her emotional tether. She wanted nothing more than to take up his offer. If only he knew how much it was killing her to keep denying him.

She cleared her throat of the sudden thickening. 'Of course I do.'

'So come with me,' he repeated. 'Or are you too married to this place to contemplate leaving?'

'No. I don't have a problem with leaving Vickers Hill. I'm just not doing it for someone who's in the middle of figuring out his life.'

'Well, I'm *really* sorry I'm not together enough for you,' he said, sarcasm dripping from every word.

'I don't expect you to be, Callum. I understand you've been through a lot. I'm just saying I'm not getting involved while you're in the middle of it all.'

Felicity rubbed her hands up and down her arms. How could she feel cold when it was still so damn hot?

'There's enough pressure on relationships these days as it is,' she continued, 'and we're not going to survive if some-where down the track, when you come out the other end of this, you decide that I'm not what you want. That I was just a symptom of your deep unhappiness at the time. One that you're stuck with. I don't want to become collateral dam-age or be your consolation prize, like becoming a GP was.'

'You would never be that,' he denied quickly, taking a step towards her. *'Never.'*

Felicity took a step back, hardening her heart to the flicker of hurt she saw scurrying across his face. She didn't doubt his sincerity but he still needed time and space, whether he knew it or not.

'Please, just come to Sydney and let's see how things go?'

His words were a cruel blow. *See how things go?* She was in love with him and he wanted to test the waters.

'No.'

'*Damn it*, Felicity. You want to. I can *see* it in your eyes. Why are you being so stubborn?'

Felicity didn't have the emotional energy to go round and round the houses with him. She needed to end it—sever it. Here and now. And she knew just how to do it.

'Because I'm in love with you.' The words came out on a rush of pent-up emotions and clanged into a heap between them. It felt good to get it out even if Callum was staring at her like she'd lost her mind. 'And I want more than "Let's see how things go". You can't give that to me and I'm not settling for less. I'm sure as hell not moving halfway across the country for it.'

He took a step back, looking more and more horrified as his butt met the bench again. 'But…it's only been two months. That's…*crazy.*'

Felicity nodded. 'I know. Trust me, *I know.* But it's there anyway. You want to know something crazier? I think I fell in love with you on the train.'

He took a deep breath and let it escape as he shoved a hand through his hair. 'I…don't know what to say. I really like you, Felicity, I—'

'It's fine,' she interrupted, shaking her head. His horror would be comical if it wasn't currently tearing her heart into tiny little pieces.

She didn't need him trying to stumble through a quantification of how much he *liked* her.

'I know. I understand. Really, I do. But that's why I can't do this. Why I can't move to Sydney with you. And why I'm leaving now.'

He didn't say anything. Just stood there, his face a mix of confusion, shock and disbelief, and all the broken pieces of her heart splintered.

She blinked hard as her emotions threatened to take over.

She needed to get through this without breaking down. 'Thank you for everything,' she said. 'I will *always* remember and cherish our night on the train. And I *will* miss you.' She stopped, cleared the quaver in her voice. 'Have a good life, Callum. Be happy. You deserve it.'

And then, because she really was about to lose it, she turned on her heel and slipped out of the house.

He didn't try and stop her.

CHAPTER FIFTEEN

Two months later...

CALLUM STOOD ON a balcony overlooking Sydney Harbour.
Not his. A friend's. Taking a breather from another excru-
ciating dinner party. A murmur of conversation, an occasional laugh and bluesy notes from a top-of-the-range
system oozed out into the night air. A light breeze ruffled
his hair as the lights on the harbour blurred on the surface
of the water courtesy of his compromised night vision.

'Cal?' He turned to find Erica—or maybe it was Angelica?—standing in the doorway, smiling at him. 'Entrées
are being served.'

He nodded. 'Okay, thanks. I'll be right in,' he assured,
then turned back to the view. He could sense her lingering
in the doorway but refused to be hurried. It was rude but
he wasn't good company tonight.

He'd told Kim, a thirty-three-year-old mother of four, she
had breast cancer today. She'd sat deathly still in the chair
as if he'd gutted her while Josh, her husband, had yelled at
him then openly wept.

Try as he may, he couldn't get it out of his head. And
being here wasn't helping.

Go to dinner parties, Felicity had said. Except tonight
he just wanted to be with her. Not at this banal event where
everyone was trying to out-surgeon each other. Where they
always tried to out-surgeon each other.

It had been hard to start with—reconnecting with the
old crowd. And their stories had stirred the old fires, but
not like before. He'd spent two years during his GP train-

ing burning with envy and resentment that he wasn't in the *club* any more.

And then he'd gone to Vickers Hill...

Why did they keep inviting him back? *Because you keep saying yes, doofus.*

Maybe he needed to say no every now and then. Maybe he needed to start socialising with other GPs. Except not those at his current practice because that wasn't really working out. His billable hours had halved and he'd already had a couple of 'friendly chats' with the head of the practice about picking up the pace.

But how could he have only spent five minutes with Kim and Josh today? Felicity would never have forgiven him.

He'd never have forgiven himself.

God, he missed her. Dreamed about her. Woke up at night aching for her. Had almost called her a dozen times. Had wanted to call her today. To tell her about Kim. To share his utter helplessness and hear the soft note of empathy in her voice.

To hear her say he could do this.

A ferry horn wafted towards him from somewhere on the water and he shook himself out of his funk, throwing back the rest of his whisky and making his way inside.

He took the indicated seat next to another woman whose name he didn't remember. A sumptuous feast was served courtesy of some up-and-coming catering firm in high demand amongst the urban professional set. Absently he wondered what Kim and Josh were eating tonight.

Was it possible to stomach anything after such news?

The talk turned to shop, as it inevitably did, and Callum let it whirl around him. It took a strong stomach to dine with a bunch of surgeons as the nitty-gritty of all kinds of blood, guts and gore was openly discussed.

'What about you, Cal?'

Callum glanced in the direction of the query. It was from

Allan, one of the guys he'd gone to med school with. Allan was a transplant surgeon.

'You save any lives today in the eczema, allergies and asthma trenches?'

There was general laughter. Allan's attitude was typical and one that had dogged and bugged him during his training, but it flowed off him now.

'No. I told a woman she had an aggressive form of breast cancer.'

As a party killer it worked a treat. Callum could almost hear the loud scratching of a needle across a vinyl record as everyone fell silent.

It was bliss for about two point five seconds before Roger, a facio-maxillary surgeon, said, 'You should refer her to Charlie Maddison. He's an excellent breast surgeon.'

'Or Abigail,' Allan added, which garnered a lot of murmured support.

The conversation moved on to breast surgery. No one asked her name, her age or her prognosis. Whether she was married or had kids. Not even the name of the oncologist he'd rung and personally spoken to, arranging for Kim and Josh to go straight there and see her immediately. Nope. They'd moved on to the biggest tumours they'd ever removed.

His phone vibrated in his pocket and he pulled it out, grateful for the interruption, concealing it under the table a little as he glanced at it. He smiled when he saw it was a text from Felicity.

They had been texting back and forth a few times a week for a while now, after some initial radio silence. But with Luci and Seb all loved up and talking wedding bells they'd been included in group texts and it had gone from there.

It wasn't the kind of communication he craved but she seemed to want to keep it light and he was happy for any kind of contact. She usually sent him a picture with Meryl or Alf or any of his other regulars and he'd taken to sending her pictures of the beach and the view from his balcony because a crazy part of him hoped it might just convince her to rock up one day.

Not even her unexpected *I love you* doused that particular fantasy. Not when he missed her so damn much. Okay, it had shocked him at the time but she *had* prewarned him she was that kind of girl.

Callum smiled as he read the text—Mrs Smith says hi—and tapped on the attachment. The image opened up to reveal a selfie of Felicity and Mrs Smith, their faces smooshed together. Felicity was cross-eyed and making a fishy mouth with her lips—so very *Flick*—while the older woman glared suspiciously at the camera.

A niggle took up residence in his chest as he devoured every detail. Felicity had her saint badge on her collar and Mrs Smith was sporting one on her collar too. Her diamantés spelled out *Security*.

He laughed out loud. He couldn't help himself. It was the first time since talking to Kim and Josh he'd been taken out of himself and his lungs suddenly felt too big for his chest.

'You okay, man?' Allan asked.

Callum looked up to find everyone at the table staring at him as if he'd lost his mind.

Maybe he had.

Was he okay? *Hell, no.* If he wasn't very much mistaken, he was heads over heels in love with a chick who'd just sent him a fishy-lipped selfie. The realisation hit him like a tonne of bricks as he glanced at the woman beside him. She was gorgeous and a renal surgeon to boot. But he couldn't imagine her crossing her eyes and scrunching up her face while posing with a cantankerous old woman.

Wow. He was in love with Felicity. He'd been fooling himself that his feelings had been milder, that he'd merely been *missing* her, ignoring the emptiness inside, going through the motions because he'd been determined to prove that he could come back from his injury as if nothing had ever happened.

But it hadn't worked. Because his entire focus was screwed up. Literally and figuratively. He'd been blind to what was important.

Felicity.

The niggle grew to the size of a fist, pushing on his sternum. Who knew love could feel this *bad*? Like a freaking heart attack!

He stood up, pushing his chair back abruptly. What was he doing *here* when she was *there*? Why had he ever left?

Because she'd made him. She'd sent him away. To sort his life out. To work out what he truly wanted.

If you love something, set it free.

Well…mission accomplished. And he didn't want to feel this empty ever again. Felicity filled him up and he didn't want to spend a second longer away from her than he had to.

'Cal? Are you okay?' Allan repeated, his forehead creased.

Callum dumped his napkin on the table. 'I am now, Allan. I'm sorry but I've got to go.'

'Hey, where's the fire?' Erica—Angelica?—joked.

'In Vickers Hill.' He grinned.

Everyone looked a little mystified as he walked away but Callum didn't give a damn as he strode out of the apartment. For the first time in two months—hell, in almost three years—everything felt right.

Felicity had set him free. Because she loved him. Now it was time to go back. Because *he* loved *her*.

It was almost seven when Callum finally caught up with Felicity the next evening. He'd been travelling all day but he felt completely energised. He'd gone straight to her house in his hire car, the speech he'd been rehearsing all day bursting on his tongue, only to be told by a neighbour she was at Luci's, watering the garden.

Callum knew from Seb that Felicity was taking care of Luci's garden while they waited for a buyer in a market that wasn't exactly thriving. Undeterred by the setback, he'd driven straight to Luci's and pulled up outside her house ten minutes later.

He experienced a strange sense of déjà vu as he cut the engine. The street was quiet and the cottage looked as pretty as a picture, the waning sun glowing a lovely honey hue on the brickwork. He half expected Mrs Smith to tap on his window, narrow her eyes at him and call him 'young man.'

He spied Felicity watering the lavender further up the path, her back to him, buds from her phone firmly plugged into her ears. He climbed out of the car and headed towards her, content to stand on the footpath near the front gate and just watch her. Her ponytail swung as she moved her head to whatever beat was being piped into her ears.

A stream of dying sunlight caught the hose spray at the right angle, causing rainbows to dance in the fine mist. She'd told him once that her heart was a pink light glowing inside her and now he knew how she felt as rainbows filled up his chest.

It was a fanciful notion. Utter romantic nonsense. But he didn't care.

She turned then and his breath hitched as she spied him and went very still. 'Callum?'

It wasn't quite the rapturous welcome he'd been dreaming about but it was *Felicity* and he was here with her and that's all that mattered right now. 'Hi.'

She didn't do or say anything for long moments, just stared at him. 'What are you…doing here?'

'I rang Bill last night.'

She eyed him warily as she twisted the nozzle to cut off the spray. 'Why?'

'I asked him for a job.'

'You…did?'

Callum nodded, pleased to hear the first sign of a squeak

in her voice. A good sign, he hoped. 'He offered me his. I'm taking over his share of the practice. He's finally retiring.'

She walked towards him, frowning and nonplussed. 'But…he didn't say anything today.'

'I asked him not to.'

An even bigger frown. 'Why?'

'Because I wanted it to be a surprise.'

She'd reached the gate but kept firmly on her side. 'You did?'

He smiled as her frown lines smoothed out and her tone lightened.

'Yes. I wanted to tell you myself.'

'You did?'

He laughed then. The entire time they'd been acquainted he'd never known her to be monosyllabic. Quite the contrary.

'Yes. Because I love you.' The words came much easier than he'd thought they would. He'd thought saying it for the first time would be terrifying but it was easy.

Things always were when they were right.

'You set me free and you were right to do so. I needed that. I needed to go home to know what I wanted. To be sure. But now I know and I'm back. Because I'm yours. If—' his heart thundered in his chest, suddenly unsure of himself '—you'll have me.'

She stared at him, reaching for the gate and wrapping her fingers around the curved metal. She looked lost for words but the glassiness of her eyes said more than words ever could.

'Felicity?'

'Is it what you want?' she asked, fierce suddenly. *'Really?'*

He nodded. 'It is.' He slid his hand over the top of hers. 'You and me. Here. In Vickers Hill.'

She glanced at their joined hands before returning her gaze to his face. 'What about your job? Your apartment?'

'I resigned today. It wasn't working out there anyway since a bossy nurse taught me patients needed more than five minutes with their doctor. I have to go back for a month and work out my notice but then I'm moving here. And we'll keep my apartment as a holiday home. We can rent it out or leave it empty. I'm sure Seb and Luci wouldn't say no to bunking there while they figure out where they want to be. I know Luci's not keen to have the baby on the boat.'

She smiled then. It was only small but it was progress. 'Seems like you have it all worked out.'

He shook his head. 'No. I don't. Not really. None of it means anything without you and I'm completely terrified now you haven't thrown yourself at me that you've found a six-foot-nine, rugby-playing boyfriend, so can you please just put me out of my misery already?'

Their gazes locked and in that moment he could see love shining in her eyes. Love for him. *Only him.* He hadn't seen anything more beautiful in his life.

She pushed gently on the gate. He stepped back as she stepped through and joined him on the footpath, their bodies almost touching.

'You're the only one for me,' she murmured.

Relief flooded Callum's system. It coursed fast and cool through his chest and flowed hot to his groin. He smiled, slid a hand on her waist, drew her closer, their bodies aligning in perfect synchronicity.

His gaze dropped to her mouth as anticipation tightened his belly.

'Good evening, Dr Hollingsworth,' a familiar authoritative voice said from across the road. 'Flick didn't tell me you were back in town.'

He groaned under his breath and Felicity laughed as he plastered a smile on his face. 'Mrs Smith,' he said. 'I see you've recovered fully.'

'I see you're not back in town for more than five seconds and you're already taking liberties.'

Her disapproving gaze fell to where his body was pressed against Felicity's. *Too damn bad.* There was no way he was stepping away like some guilty schoolboy. Not now he had Felicity exactly where he wanted her.

'Indeed,' he agreed cheerfully. 'And I intend taking liberties as long as Felicity will let me, Mrs Smith, because I love her and she loves me. Consider yourself warned.'

He dipped her then, ignoring both Felicity's surprised squeak and Mrs Smith's scandalised gasp.

'Callum,' Felicity whispered, clutching at his arm while trying not to laugh. 'You're going to give her a heart attack.'

'Lucky for her we know how to do CPR.' He grinned.

Then he kissed her—long and dirty—claiming her mouth with deliberate indecency, giving Mrs Smith something really juicy to gossip about.

Because he didn't care who said what—this was right. This was for ever.

EPILOGUE

One year later...

THEY HELD THE WEDDING in Luci's back garden. Although it wasn't Luci's any more—Callum had bought it the day after he'd dipped Felicity in the street and kissed her, and they'd been happily living in sin together ever since.

Much to Mrs Smith's chagrin.

Seb and Luci and little Eve travelled to Vickers Hill for the wedding. As did Felicity's parents and Bill and Julia, who interrupted their RV trip around Australia.

Felicity wore a pink dress and, thanks to Alf Dunnich, a garland of glorious pink rosebuds in her hair. And, in a few days, they'd be heading to Sydney for two blissful sun-drenched weeks at Callum's apartment where, with any luck, they'd make a honeymoon baby.

The first of many.

Felicity couldn't have been happier as she said, 'I do', and she kissed her new husband in front of all their family and friends.

And somewhere from on high Meryl, who had passed away while Callum had been working out his notice in Sydney, was nodding her head and saying, *I told you so...*

* * * * *

OUT NOW!

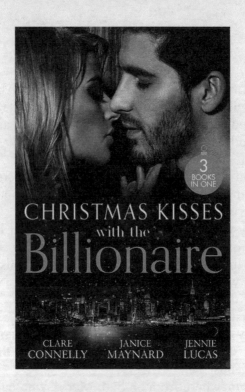

CHRISTMAS KISSES
with the
Billionaire

3 BOOKS IN ONE

CLARE
CONNELLY

JANICE
MAYNARD

JENNIE
LUCAS

Available at
millsandboon.co.uk

MILLS & BOON

OUT NOW!

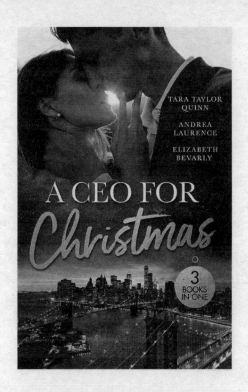

TARA TAYLOR QUINN

ANDREA LAURENCE

ELIZABETH BEVARLY

A CEO FOR Christmas

3 BOOKS IN ONE

Available at
millsandboon.co.uk

MILLS & BOON

OUT NOW!

**Available at
millsandboon.co.uk**

MILLS & BOON

OUT NOW!

3 BOOKS IN ONE

Ami WEAVER

Janice MAYNARD

Yvonne LINDSAY

CHRISTMAS NIGHTS with the Ex

Available at
millsandboon.co.uk

MILLS & BOON

OUT NOW!

Available at
millsandboon.co.uk

MILLS & BOON